Bended Love

Kat Caldwell

Ladwell Publishing

Also by Kat

Historical Romance:
Aurora's Dilemma
Stepping Across the Desert
Across the English Channel

Contemporary New Adult Romance:
Coffee Stains

Mythological Christian Fiction:
An Audience with the King

Contemporary Fiction:
Bended Dream
Bended Loyalty
Bended Love

To all the women who think they aren't enough,
know that you are.

BENDED
LOVE

One

AT THE DING OF the kitchen timer, Scarlett pulled the oven door open and whisked out her second-to-last batch of scones. Pretending she was on a reality cooking show, she hurried to place the last batch inside the scorching oven, then ran to set the timer again. Imagining that someone like Gordon Ramsey was ready to pounce on any little thing she did wrong helped to keep her entertained as she prepped for the farmer's market.

The initial burned-alive feeling from the oven heat disappeared, leaving her to the most satisfying, or the most disappointing, part of her job: evaluating the product. This time it was satisfying. Another fifty seconds was exactly what the scones had needed. Baking was such a precise art that even such a short time could make a huge difference, depending on the day's humidity. Scarlett congratulated herself with a sip of flavored tonic water.

Having baked for six months in this kitchen, a pool house her only private customer let her use, Scarlett was beginning to perfect her system. Once the scones were in, she usually kneaded the sourdough once more before letting it rest. When the last batch of scones were done, she would up the oven temperature to heat the pizza stones, then quickly dump the sourdough on the hot stones, swipe them with a clean razor to allow them to blossom in the oven, and slip them in to bake. Then she cleaned the kitchen.

Through the kitchen window the pool's cool, sparkling water taunted her. It was only June, but Kentucky heat was already bearing down on them. And though the pool house had air conditioning, the electrical bill was the one thing Scarlett had to pay for in order to use the space, so she rarely turned it on lower than seventy-eight. Carole Barten, the property owner and the top realtor in the county, had given her permission to use the pool anytime, but Scarlett got the feeling she hadn't really meant it. After all, jumping into the pool while she was technically renting the space to create her business would look odd, to say the least. She and Carole weren't friends; they conducted business together, so Scarlett wanted to look professional. And splashing around during working hours was anything but.

Another timer beeped, reminding her she didn't have time to daydream about the pool. There was a farmer's market in the morning, and she had already been paid for the four dozen cookies Carole had ordered. Trying to keep up with her checklist, Scarlett grabbed the bread dough that had doubled in size and dumped it onto the counter. Just as she sprinkled the counter with flour to knead it one last time, her phone rang. Had it been anyone other than Carole, she wouldn't have answered.

"Scarlett, doll, how're you doing? Baking the cookies for me? That's wonderful." Carole spoke in the cadence Scarlett expected from east-coasters. When they'd first met, Scarlett assumed she had studied at Harvard or Brown. Carole had actually never been to college, but she'd been married to a man for two years from the Boston area. "Do remember I need a sheet of perfectly round cookies to place into the oven. Don't forget, like you did last weekend. I want the house I'm showing to smell like I'm baking. If there's no smell I might as well buy them from the store."

Scarlett pulled each sourdough boule across the smooth counter one last time before letting them rest. She glanced at her watch. "I have everything here for you and ready." It wasn't ready, though. She had forgotten to leave six cookies raw from

Carole's order. Again. This was the third week in a row, so she'd have to make up a new batch before leaving.

"No broken cookies, right? I don't want any broken ones like last week."

The cookies had broken because Carole had dropped the box. Even admitted as much.

"There won't be any broken ones. I've made them very sturdy."

"Alright. Please leave them at the house on the counter. The cleaners should leave the sliding door open for you," Carole said.

"Okay." Scarlett left the boules and went to check her supplies, crossing her fingers she had brought enough vanilla, sugar, and chocolate chips. "I'll leave them there. Is there anything else you need?"

"One more thing."

Scarlett bit back an expletive. In all her planning, she had forgotten to make up the brownie batter. Now she didn't have enough chocolate chips to make the brownies and leave Carole her raw cookie dough. She'd have to bake the brownies at home in her small apartment. With the crappy oven that sometimes over-heated.

"Have you seen Don around? My husband?"

The question made Scarlett pause. It sounded friendly, but also out of place.

"He hasn't come around the pool house," she said cautiously. "I haven't been up to the house yet. When I go up there, I can ask him to call you. If I see him."

"No, don't worry," Carole said quickly.

"Okay."

Carole started speaking to someone else, hanging up on Scarlett without bothering to say goodbye.

"You're the one who called me," Scarlett muttered. She dumped two cups of flour into a bowl she had recently washed and reached for the baking soda as a giant splash sounded in the pool outside.

Scarlett froze. Carole didn't have children, and she couldn't imagine her letting local kids use her property out of the kindness of her heart. The local smalltown kids had started daring each other to break into properties where the owners worked all day and never used the pool. Scarlett had heard about it on the radio news as she drove her nephew, Ben, to school. He was just finishing sixth grade, but even he knew all about it. It was becoming the thing to do when they got bored, apparently.

Fear froze her in place. Most likely they'd be teenagers. Perhaps bigger than her five feet five inches. She wondered if they would run scared at the sight of her or if they would confront her. Maybe she should ignore it, since this wasn't her place. But they might try to enter the pool house. And she needed to leave here in less than two hours.

Slowly, she moved around the small table to peek out through the window.

In the pool, a woman was wrapped around a rather hairy-shouldered man who was definitely not a high-schooler. Scarlett peered closer, trying to stay hidden behind the curtain. The man's hands pulled at the strings of the woman's bikini until the woman shrieked and laughed. She threw herself backwards into the water, her giant, perfectly round breasts exposed.

And also exposing Carole's husband. His salt-and-pepper hair, usually perfectly combed, was dripping water droplets and in full disarray. Once the woman came out of the water, Don yanked the dangling pieces of her bikini off, before gripping her breasts in his hands and kissing her hard on the mouth.

Scarlett couldn't believe her bad luck. This was not something she wanted to get involved in. Carole didn't seem like the type who would appreciate another woman knowing her husband was cheating. And there was no way to sneak past the lusty couple without being noticed. Plus, ever since she had refused Don's suggestion of exchanging the electrical bill for a romp each week, he had made it a point to complain about Scarlett's use of the pool house to Carole loud enough for Scarlett to hear. And if Carole wasn't around to complain to, Don would stand with his arms crossed and glare at her until she looked away.

Everything about this was awkward.

Suddenly Don's eyes moved towards the pool house, as though he could feel her watching. Scarlett stepped further into the shadows, but Don was already wrapping a towel around his waist and marching towards the pool house. He sauntered in as she started beating the butter and sugar.

"Hey there, Scarlett," he drawled. "Didn't know you were coming in today."

"I come in every Friday afternoon." Scarlett kept her eyes on her recipe and baking supplies.

"Yeah," he said, smacking his lips. Scarlett hated the sound. One of her mom's ex-boyfriends used to make the same sound while he was thinking. "I wasn't sure Carole was still renting this place out to you. I tell her all the time what a mess you make of it. Isn't worth it to us to have you hanging around just so she can have some cookies."

Scarlett leveled her gaze at him as she beat the eggs. "Carole called before. She was looking for you."

"And what did you tell her?" Don asked. He prowled towards her, his dark eyes never blinking as they glared straight into hers.

Scarlett had to look away to measure the brown sugar, but tried to keep her voice firm and strong. "I told her I hadn't seen you. Because I hadn't."

"That's a girl," Don said, close enough to pat her butt. "Well now, part of your contract for using the pool house, Scarlett, is that you're not in our way. Isn't it?"

He picked up an unwrapped cookie and popped it into his mouth.

"I'm almost done. I'll start loading the car now." Scarlett tried to move past him, but he grabbed her wrist and pulled hard until her body slammed against his.

"There's another way to apologize," he murmured, grabbing her breast and squeezing hard. Men like Don seemed to think every breast was made just for him to touch. Scarlett knew just what to do: stay impassive. Don reacted just as she'd suspected, pushing her away with a look of disgust at the sound of the door squeaking open again.

The young woman must have been barely twenty. She stood in the doorway, her bikini bottom barely covering her private areas, like one of those influencers on social media. Her skin was smooth and tan, without a stretch mark or ounce of fat visible, and there was a mile gap between her thighs.

"Who's this?" she asked, narrowing her eyes at Scarlett.

"No one," Don said, pulling the woman into his arms. She giggled, kissing him loudly on the mouth. Scarlett kept her gaze down, wrapping cookies in plastic as quickly as she could.

"Good," the woman said. "'Cause I don't do threesomes with fat girls. Geez, have enough carbs here? Is all this your snack?"

Scarlett ignored her laughter, hoping the two of them would leave the house so she could clean up and leave. But it was clearly her very unlucky day. Don pulled the woman into the small bedroom instead of leaving. Within minutes, the pool house was filled with noises—noises no one made unless they were filming a professional video.

Maybe the woman did that for a living. Scarlett smirked at the silent putdown, trying to breathe to calm her shaking hands. She started the mixer, watching the dough come together and using the sound to drown out what was happening in the bedroom. Unfortunately, she miscalculated, turning off the mixer just as the young woman screamed out her final pleasure.

Scarlett rolled her eyes. Then came Don's yell. Scarlett thought she might vomit.

Quickly, she placed the gooey dough onto parchment paper in a long strip and rolled it up tightly. It would need an hour in the fridge, but instead of leaving the cookies already on the pan, she could leave instructions for Carole. She wouldn't like it, but she had no intention of hanging around in case Carole showed up.

With the straight metal edge of a spatula, she scraped the extra flour from the counter into a trash bag, then generously sprayed everything down with vinegar cleaner as sounds from the bedroom started again. She moved faster, circling the kitchen putting away her things, testing the scones for their temperature and grabbing the baked sourdoughs from the oven.

Then she started throwing the rest of her ingredients into two large plastic tubs. Snapping each container shut, Scarlett stacked them into towers of two. Usually she carried one at a time, but today she took the chance to grab more. Back and forth she hurried, sweat first beading and then pooling at her waistband.

When she tiptoed in for the last time to pack the sourdough, the young woman was standing stark naked in the kitchen, gulping down a large glass of water. Her nipples stood at attention, and her ass and thighs were shiny and hairless.

"You gonna clean this up?" she demanded, sighing as she finished her water. Probably the only nourishment she'd had that day.

Scarlett looked around. The kitchen was clean except for the pan prepped for Carole, the log of cookie dough, and her cooling boules. She bit back a retort and answered as simply as possible. "Yes."

She carefully placed her sourdough boules into the last boxes. When she stood up, the woman poked her in the breast through her sweaty T-shirt.

"You're not my type at all, though I guess you got nice tits. You want to join us?"

"No," Scarlett snorted.

The woman's eyes narrowed. "Prude," she said, before snapping a selfie next to Scarlett.

"What the hell are you doing?" Scarlett snapped, trying to swipe at the phone. The woman held it above her head, out of reach. Scarlett inhaled slowly. "Whatever. Keep the damn photo. I'm outta here."

She deadlifted the stacked boxes in silence and waddled out the door. With the last two containers slipped into place on the truck, she took a deep breath and headed towards the main house with Carole's order for a weekend of open houses.

Two minutes later, she pulled onto the interstate able to breathe again, praying Don would find another place to have his affair by next Friday.

Two

It took half an hour to drive from the side of town where people had pools to the squat apartment buildings where Scarlett lived with Ben. It wasn't a cute apartment that she would show off on social media—in fact the lighting was too terrible to take pictures of her baked goods, and the air conditioning worked only half the time—but its eight hundred square feet were home for her and Ben.

The apartment complex was made of two squat, two-story buildings. Scarlett had moved into her ground-floor apartment five years ago. One year later, Nasreen had moved into the other building with her son, Zander. He and Ben were the same age and had ended up becoming close friends, just as Nasreen and Scarlett did. Camila had moved in above Nasreen two years later and joined their friendship circle. Nasreen and Camila were the first friends she'd had in a long time.

Scarlett parked her second-hand truck right next to her apartment. The nice thing about such a small complex was the availability of parking spots almost all the time.

"Ben?" she called towards the small cement patio that connected to the apartment. "Come help me, would you?"

Silence.

Usually, Ben would jump the low fence around the patio like a banshee out of hell. Scarlett waited another second, but he clearly was not home. She unpacked the truck alone, hauling the plastic boxes out of the pickup bed and trudging them to her door. Each time, she noticed the peeling gray paint at the base of it. Not that she would bother telling Johnny, the owner of the complex. He didn't take kindly to complaints.

Stretching her back, she sighed. Someday she'd have her own place and she'd paint the door blue. The kind of blue at the deep end of the pool she used to go to when she was little—

"Oh, gross." She tried to push away the vivid image of Don and the young woman's naked body from her mind, but they hung on like leeches.

She unlocked her door, trying to think of something else. Once a cement block was in place to hold it open, she started pushing the boxes into her humid apartment.

"Hey, Scar!" Ben skipped towards her from the direction of Nasreen's apartment, dressed in his basketball clothes, as she returned to the truck to lock it up. Zander wasn't far behind him.

"Hey, bud. How was basketball?" Seeing them, Scarlett remembered Nasreen had signed Zander and Ben up for an afterschool basketball activity. Ben claimed it was helping him gain muscles because they lifted weights, which might help him survive the upcoming middle school years—much to Scarlett's relief. He'd been a skinny kid all his life. The doctor had told her once that it was because Rhonda, her sister, hadn't known she was pregnant at first and hadn't stopped drinking until the sixth month.

Like Scarlett, Ben was a survivor.

"I was starting to worry," she said as Ben and Zander whizzed past her into the apartment. There were remnants of ketchup on their mouths. "Did you eat dinner already? Nasreen, you don't have to buy him dinner every week."

Nasreen laughed as she came through Scarlett's door. Always ready with a smile, she was the woman who saved Scarlett from herself most of the time. "Boys were hungry. Besides, it was a snack at the rate they eat."

"We still want your pizza, Ms. Scarlett," Zander shouted from the bathroom.

"We know all that—you wash those hands good." Nasreen turned to Scarlett, who was carefully pulling the sourdough from the box. "Why you unpacking the market stuff?"

Scarlett half-groaned, half-laughed. She waited until the boys started throwing the mini basketball into Ben's door basket. "I had to hightail it outta there today, so it isn't packed right. You'll never believe what happened."

"What?" Nasreen handed her a glass of wine poured from the box in the fridge. "You're blushing, Scarlett. What happened?"

Scarlett breathed a sigh of relief that only one sourdough loaf had collapsed. She threw it on the cutting board along with a half-finished roll of hard salami and took a gulp of her wine.

"That bad?" Nasreen asked, handing her a thick slice of bread topped with salami.

"So much worse than you can imagine. Don showed up at the pool with another woman. One younger than me, I'm pretty sure. As skinny as a porn star with no problem asking me to join them in a threesome."

"Oh, nuh-uh."

"I swear she did."

Nasreen's lacquered nails flurried in the air as she spoke. "That man can't get away with this. That is sexual harassment and intimidation. What a nasty man. How does he get women to sleep with him? And why is that realtor woman still married to him?"

"You're starting to sound like a divorce lawyer. Maybe she could be your first client," Scarlett teased, feeling her heart skip a beat at the thought. Nasreen and Zander were moving away in three weeks for Nasreen to settle before starting law school. Shaking away the gloom that threatened to sneak in, Scarlett focused on the conversation at hand. "I don't know what Carole is thinking. I don't know her that well."

"Well, her husband is disgusting," Nasreen said.

"Yes, he is." Scarlett grabbed the pizza dough she had prepped that morning from the fridge as her phone buzzed from somewhere on the couch. "Would you get my phone?"

"You can't go back there without this guy being put in his place. This is what women have to put up with all the time."

"And from other women," Scarlett said, frustration at the memory growing in her chest. "Can you believe she called me fat and then asked me to join them? What is that? Who is this woman?"

"She called you fat?" Nasreen shook her head in disgust, her fingers tapping against Scarlett's phone. "Oh, the queen herself messaged you."

Scarlett leaned over, her hands busy stretching the dough. "What'd she say? Do you think she knows?"

"That her husband cheated? I dunno. Give me your face to open it up."

The phone glared, then brightened at Scarlett's face. She spread sauce over the pizza base, then reached for cheese.

"Scar, hon, you better look at this," Nasreen said after a moment. The softening of her voice sent a chill through Scarlett. "I'll fight her for you, if you want. I mean, I know I'm not a lawyer yet, but we could file a sexual harassment suit or something. Maybe get a video of him and spread the word through town."

"What do you mean?" Scarlett asked, nestling up against Nasreen.

You bitch! How dare you come onto my husband! I let you use that house cause I'm a good person and want to help you and this is how you repay me? I know who my husband is, but I didn't expect this from you! You can take these cookies out of my house! Don't come near my pool house again. Don't come near me again!

"He told her I came on to him?" Scarlett could barely breathe. She read the text again to make sure she wasn't seeing things. "I can't use her kitchen any more!"

"Like I said, we can go after her," Nasreen said, starting to get riled up. She paced the floor, her forehead wrinkled. Camila called it her 'lawyer face.'

"I don't have a contract with her. She lets me use the pool house and I bake her cookies. It's a friendly agreement."

Nasreen's wrinkles deepened. "Scarlett."

"I know."

Getting the pizzas into the oven, she broke chocolate into the melted butter in a saucepan and slowly stirred, watching the chocolate melt in a whirling design. The effect calmed her; the smell of chocolate brought her peace, allowing her to ignore the anxiety threatening to bubble up.

"Scar, hey, it's gonna be okay. We'll figure something out." Nasreen pulled Scarlett's head onto her shoulder.

Scarlett snorted. "That was the best, and cheapest, space for me to bake, Nasreen. I could expand to the markets because I had that space. And now it's just gone. Besides, Carole was going to get me more private clients." She sniffed away the tears threatening to come up. "I mean, she was a terrible client, but she had that beautiful oven. Now I'll have to go back to baking here with this crappy oven and my one counter. I should just quit the markets."

"No, honey, no," Nasreen murmured, pulling her in for a hug. "We'll figure something out. It's not perfect, but you keep baking here and use my apartment, too, if you need it. And I can help you find another place. You can't stop baking."

Scarlett grabbed her phone and read the text again. "Or I could beg Carole."

"She was driving you crazy—and he hit on you in the nastiest and sleeziest way, Scarlett." Nasreen yanked it back. "You can deny it. Politely. And maybe someday she'll admit she was wrong. But you will not beg her. You don't need to accept this treatment from her."

"Fine." Scarlett paused to refill her wine glass. With her head in the fridge, she took a short moment to blink away the tears, then straightened up. "Enough about my life. What about you? Did you pass the L-things?"

A wide grin spread across Nasreen's face. "I did!"

Scarlett shrieked with her as they both did a dance with their wine in the air. "You did it?!"

"I did it!"

"I can't believe you did it," Scarlett sang as Camila walked through the door, clearly amused at what she found.

"What're you two screaming about?" She held a beer in one hand and an unopened can in the other. Two little boys followed her into the living room. "Go play, boys. And don't let Ben say no."

"Nasreen passed her test," Scarlett said, running to check on the pizzas. The heat blasted her face as Camila shook Nasreen's shoulders in a burst of joy.

Scarlett breathed in the heat. She was so happy for Nasreen. It was her dream to be a lawyer, a dream that had gotten sidetracked when she got pregnant and Zander's dad left town. At the same time, it meant Scarlett would lose a friend. While she and Camila were close, it was Nasreen who kept them all together. Chicago was almost five hours away by car, which meant they would talk about seeing each other but probably never would.

And once she was a lawyer, she'd never return to Brax, Kentucky. While Scarlett had no means of ever leaving.

"Why're you guys screaming?" Ben called out, his head poking out from his room.

"Nothing," Scarlett shouted. "Pizza'll be done in fifteen minutes."

"Got it," Ben mumbled, and shut the door again. Scarlett breathed out.

"Tell me," Camila demanded, grabbing Nasreen's hand. "How does it feel knowing you are going to be the next amazing lawyer? Because I will tell you that being friends with the person who will be the most amazing lawyer feels great, actually. Wait, we need some champagne."

"We got broke champagne," Scarlett said, waving her glass of box wine.

Camila tapped her can against the box and winked. "Just as good. Now, what else is going on in here? Scarlett's face is all stressed out."

"What?" Scarlett asked, doing her best to relax her muscles.

"You got that big wrinkle in the middle of your forehead again. Like you had when you lost the job at the bank."

"The one I have 'cause Nasreen is leaving us?"

"We're gonna miss Nasreen, but we'll cry then, not now," Camila said, making herself comfortable on one of the three stools Scarlett owned.

"Tell her what happened, Scar," Nasreen said.

Scarlett's phone vibrated again. This time Camila grabbed it and tapped out the PIN, and her lips instantly turned down in disgust.

"That's nasty," she said, pushing the phone away as though it was germ-infested. "Who is this? And why would she send that photo?"

Nasreen took a peek and blanched as well. "That's from Carole, the lady who was buying cookies from Scarlett for her real estate business. Scar, she sent you a picture of a used condom."

"She did what?" Scarlett shrieked, grabbing the phone. "Ew! This woman is insane. Now I'm glad she fired me."

Camila swallowed a large gulp of beer, her lips still turned down. "She fired you? Were you working for her? I thought you were selling her cookies."

"I was using her pool house kitchen."

Camila snorted. "That's right. Forgot. She fired you from the kitchen? Why?"

"She thinks I slept with her husband." The injustice of the situation should have made her fighting mad, but at the moment she was just exhausted. At least she had her friends over. If she were alone she'd probably just go to bed and cry.

"That Don guy? That *naco*?" Camila shook her head. "You told me he creeped you out."

"He does," Scarlett said. "I didn't sleep with him. Some young, hot, skinny girl did. Practically right in front of me. They barged into the pool house while I was working and got naked as though I wasn't there."

Camila mock-gagged, then laughed. "Ew. That doesn't sound sexy at all."

"Not at all," Scarlett agreed. "They invited me to join them, too."

"Ew. *Qué asco*. Not even slightly okay. *Qué chafe*. That guy has a goatee."

Scarlett and Camila laughed while Nasreen saved the pizzas from burning.

"Alright, alright. You gotta send a message to her. Like what if you said, 'Your man is nasty. Don't know why you think I'd go near him.' What about that?" Camila asked. She grinned and wiggled her eyebrows.

"Absolutely not," Nasreen said. "That Carole lady has clout around this county. You need to be short and to the point, without throwing in insults." She looked firmly at Camila, who shrugged it off.

"Fine, let's write it and then you can read it, okay?"

"No sending it before I read it," Nasreen warned.

"Okay, okay. Let's tell her to check the cameras, but we'll leave off the whole part of her being a *perra*."

Scarlett laughed, but was impressed by Camila's idea. "I forgot she has cameras everywhere on the property. Why wouldn't she look at them before insulting me?"

Nasreen shook her head as she rolled the pizza cutter through the pizza. "I forgot, too. Good thinking, Camila. You should come with me to law school."

"No way. I just know this 'cause I watch too much trash television. It's how Candella, of *Tu Eres Mi Amor*, proved her fiancée was cheating."

Scarlett snorted. "Okay, let's work it out. We only need a few lines."

"We're hungry," Israel, Camila's seven-year-old, announced, appearing in the doorway. "We smell pizza."

"It's ready, but hot. You boys get your glasses of milk and sit at the coffee table," Nasreen said. The boys never pushed back to Nasreen.

"Listen to this," Scarlett said. "'Carole, I understand your anger, but I wasn't the one who was in that pool house bedroom. I left as soon as Don showed up. You can check the cameras you have around the house and see that I wasn't part of seducing your husband.'"

"It's fine," Nasreen said, after reading it again. "Send it."

Scarlett did.

"Okay, put the phone away now and let's have some pizza," Camila ordered, grabbing all the phones to place into the basket by the door. It was their Friday night rule, created by Nasreen.

For the next two hours Scarlett lost herself in being with her friends and listening to the boys talk about their day. It wasn't until she went to bed that she dared to look at her phone again.

Keep the money for the batch you made this weekend. But after this I'll be finding a new baker.

Scarlett swallowed her frustration. Right when she finally got into the Wednesday market, she lost the kitchen space to bake in.

She turned off her light, listening to the still night and trying not to plummet down a tunnel of worry. One step forward and two steps backward. It was how it always seemed to be with her.

Three

Tristen Levisay entered Camp Soul through a large ranch-style welcome arch. His footsteps crunched on the gravel road, the noise contrasting with the silence of the camp. The only other sound was birds singing. He'd expected his childhood friend, Rob, to meet him at the entrance, or at least somewhere close by, since he had no idea where to go—Rob was the owner of this place, after all. But there was no sign of him anywhere.

To the left stood a large building marked with a cross at the top, which he supposed was the chapel or church or whatever they called it. Jared's last words that morning, "Be careful with the zealots," pulsed through Tristen's head. He knew Rob wasn't a zealot, but the silence was conjuring up images of some crazy Hollywood horror movie.

He shook off the thoughts and looked around again.

Most people in Kentucky, probably including Jared, believed at minimum in a hovering-ghost-type God of the universe, mostly one who could thrash them if they deserved it. Like a superstition. The way he'd been brought up, though, was to stay clear of the churches. They were full of busy-bodies and holier-than-thous, his mother, Ivy, always used to say. They lived the same way in regard to the 'Big Guy in the Sky': stay away from his scope of wrath, and hope He stayed away from them.

That was, until Ivy had started attending a drug recovery group in the basement of a local church in January. She wasn't yet willing to go to Sunday School, but she'd started softening her views of the life after a few weeks. And when she asked if Tristen would check out the meeting for the kids of parents recovering from addiction, he'd found out Rob ran it. He had attended ever since.

Which brought him to the eerily quiet campgrounds today.

"Rob?"

Nothing. Tristen steered towards the other side of the packed dirt road and kept heading into the heart of the camp. On the left, across from the chapel-thing, was a building marked 'cafeteria'. In the same building just feet away from the cafeteria entrance was a small wooden door that claimed to be the 'Soul Marketplace'. Tristen snorted at the poor wordplay and kept walking.

He tried calling Rob on the phone, but the call went straight to voicemail. *Fine way of getting help with the sound equipment.*

For a second Tristen considered turning around and heading to Top Gym, but Jared's laughter in his head kept him going. It was one thing to make fun of thinking God was around the corner about to hit you with the switch, but it was another to run because he'd gotten spooked.

An alarm on his phone went off. He tapped it, his spirits lifting a little. Tomorrow was Thursday, the evening he got to play live music during happy hour at O'Donnell's. He'd played four times in the spring before they shut down for renovations, but live music was coming back. He couldn't be more excited.

The song he'd written the other night trickled through his head as he kept walking slowly down the road, keeping an eye out for another living soul.

Lollipops and acid drops, and babies that ruined your life. Hang the blame on me. Just the kid who was trying to give some relief, trying to find a belief. Figure out if he should be there or not. Kill himself and rot.

The words had poured out of him after a night with Rob's group. He'd listened to Tracy tell her story about growing up with a drug-addicted dad who ended up overdosing and leaving her with an invalid grandmother. While the song wasn't necessarily about Ivy, his mother, he hesitated to perform it. If Ivy heard it, she would get upset, right when she was doing better and trying to make up for the past.

At the end of the road, his phone pinged with a message from Jared, not Rob, reminding him about all the last-minute activities they needed to finish before the boxing day clinics started the next day. Tristen stuffed his phone into his pocket and went over his schedule in his head. He'd have to swing by the gym later that afternoon to get everything done. Even though he had no intention of staying at the gym full-time, he tried to take his responsibilities there seriously, especially for his mother's sake.

She was thriving at the gym. After working at the plexiglass factory for twenty years and never getting promoted, Ivy seemed to relish her new freedom in overseeing Top Gym. He never would have thought she'd take so well to running a business. She worked harder than Tristen had ever seen her work before in her life.

Since Top Gym had been strictly a boxing gym under Owen, Tristen's biological father and Ivy's once-again love interest, it had taken a lot of work to change it to her vision. In the past six months they had painted the entire place, deep-cleaned it, renovated the locker rooms, and added things like yoga and Pilates that would appeal to women to the list of classes. Tristen had to admit his mother wasn't too bad a businesswoman. It had also turned out that her dating Owen, whose shady business dealings had earned him some crazy rumors in town over the years, was good for business. Everyone wanted to see who had made Owen give up the gym, and subsequently illegal boxing and gambling.

While some had probably expected to witness a train-wreck, they'd ended up staying because the place was nicer than ever before. Memberships were picking up, and the gym was now one of the most popular businesses in the area.

Not for the first time, Tristen wondered if his mother could have saved herself—and him and his siblings—some grief in life if she had owned a business before. Throwing herself into working was much better than falling into opioids.

But that was water under the bridge, or at least in the past. No amount of wondering could change what had happened. Truth was, he was happy that she was happy. As she was only forty-five, he needed her occupied for a long while.

He stopped walking and looked around. He was going to be late for their meeting about the summer boxing camp if he didn't find Rob soon.

A faint tapping sound was echoing through the camp now. He moved towards one of the large buildings, hoping to follow the noise. The pounding sound grew louder. Tristen walked a little faster, his T-shirt already sticking to him with sweat, passing the rest of the cabins and coming to what looked like the end of the main part of camp.

A few yards away, a young man with black hair pulled into a ponytail was pounding a wood fencepost into the ground, his bare back gleaming with sweat. A young woman stood next to him, a trail of sweat running down her shirt. She held a plank of wood in her gloved hands; two long red braids cascaded over her shoulders from under a brimmed straw hat. She turned her head, then said something to the man that made him stop the pounding.

"Hey!" she called. "Do you need help?"

"Tristen Levisay," he said, sticking out his hand, his tattoo-sleeved arm a contrast against her flawlessly tanned skin. Her hand was warm, and her smile was cute. It pulled up the middle of her full top lip to show off four perfect teeth. "I came in to talk with Rob."

The man in the ponytail turned around and grinned, but it took another second before Tristen could peel his eyes away from the red-head to see that the man was the same one he was looking for.

"I thought we were going over the sound equipment today," Tristen said.

Rob wiped the sweat from his forehead, looking only slightly apologetic. "Sorry, I forgot about that. Maybe you could help me finish this first? Then we can go inside. Grab a board and hold it up for me, will ya?" He grinned.

"I have a feeling you duped me," Tristen said as he grabbed the board, and the red-head giggled.

Rob left the answer ambiguous. "Hold it up there for me. My wife is getting tired, as you can see from the past plank."

The woman swatted at Rob's shoulder but kept smiling. The left end of the plank Rob had nodded towards was significantly lower than the right.

"She's your wife?" The woman looked like she was eighteen. If that.

Rob laughed. "Yep."

Tristen leaned back and eyed the couple, recovering from his shock enough to play against his friend. "She's too pretty to be your wife."

"I like him," the red-head told Rob. "Here," she added to Tristen, "I'll give you the hammer for that pretty remark while I go fetch us all some lemonade."

Rob stood up and watched her walk off. "Five years, man, and I still can't get enough of her," he said, picking up another board.

"You been together five years?" Tristen followed Rob's fingers, indicating where he should place the nail, then started hitting at it.

"Been together almost seven. Married five," Rob said. "What about you? Want to get married?"

Tristen choked on his own saliva. He thought of Lamia and Meegan and the mess that was his love-life. "You know my situation now. I'm finally making enough money to live on."

They moved on to the next board and then the next before Rob spoke again. "You know, it isn't so much about money. We don't have a lot right now. Revamping this camp is taking most of our time and money. I think marriage is more about not letting the right one get away."

Tristen pounded the last nail in. "Guess I haven't found the right one, then. There hasn't been one I wasn't willing to let get away."

Rob saluted him with a laugh as his wife returned with lemonade.

"I didn't get your name before," Tristen said, taking the tall, sweating glass.

"It's Dariana," she said, giving that same cute smile as before. Tristen could see why Rob would want to hold on to a woman like her. Though his ex-girlfriend, Meegan, had been a looker as well—and not one to hold on to. "So, are you our new producer and soundboard teacher or not?"

"I'm here to set up the soundboard for Rob," Tristen said, polishing off his lemonade. It would have been more refreshing with less sugar and a touch of rum.

"Oh, I thought Rob asked if you could help us record and maybe teach the kids about recording."

Rob coughed on his lemonade. "What I said was that I would try to convince him."

Dariana grinned, winking at Tristen. "And I started the conversation. So, Tristen, we need some help this summer. Would you like to teach underprivileged kids?"

Tristen shifted his feet, the question catching him off guard. "I work at Top Gym."

"It's only part-time. Well, we could make it part-time," Rob said. "We're kinda in a jam. The guy we tried to hire dropped out this morning."

"I learned the sound board and recording by myself. It's not like I have formal training or anything."

"That should work," Dariana said, her perfect teeth gleaming at him. "Plus, you're a professional musician."

Tristen waited for her to laugh. She didn't.

"You're thinking of my twin brother, Talon. He's the one that sings and plays for *Art of Rendering*."

Rob clapped him on his shoulder. "We know you're Tristen, man, I can tell the difference between the two of you. And we want you if you're willing. Dariana was talking about *The Seethers*."

"Rob played some songs for me the other day." Dariana hesitated, narrowing her beautiful eyes. "Wait, are you guys not together anymore?"

Tristen shook his head, setting the glass on the tray she was still holding. "We broke up when Talon left the band for AOR. But that was months ago already," he said, glancing at Rob, who gave him a nod. Talon leaving in the fall had been the focus of Tristen's conversations at the beginning of joining Rob's men's group.

"Well, that's a shame. But at any rate, like Rob said, we know we're asking you, not Talon. So, will come to Camp Soul? We could use a sound guy. We want to send some of the more advanced kids home with their own recordings."

She was going to wear him down; Tristen already knew it. He swallowed, trying to find the words that might work, but gave up almost immediately. Dariana and Rob were looking at him with such earnest faces that he could feel any resolve he might have to say no disappearing.

"How many hours a week are you needing?"

Dariana shrieked, almost tilting the glasses off the tray. "Camp starts next week, so we could use your help by then. We probably won't record next week's kids, but we could use some help with the sound for the last day's concert. We live-stream it so their parents can watch. It would be a short volunteering position and we would really, really appreciate it."

Volunteering. "How long?"

"About three weeks," Dariana said. "But I know you'll want to stay longer. The kids are gonna love you."

"I can do it for a few weeks, but not beyond that. I have a client coming mid-July to finish his album."

Rob broke into a smile as he and Dariana high-fived each other. "We got ourselves a sound guy!" They turned to him, Rob patting him hard on the shoulders before digging his phone out of his pocket. "You're awesome, man. We were in such a bind. Get ready for the kids and heat." Rob chuckled, though Tristen was already starting to have second thoughts. "Wait, disregard that statement. Dariana, get him to sign the paperwork first before he finds out how hot it gets out here."

Tristen forced himself to laugh.

"Tristen, hold up my phone, we gotta tell everyone. Yep, aim it right at us."

Tristen did as he was told. Large numbers counted down, beeping each time they changed until the last beep held longer. On cue, Rob let out a loud whistle that almost made Tristen drop the phone.

"We got our sound guy, everybody! We're ready here at Camp Soul!" Music started playing from the phone as Rob and Dariana danced to the beat. "Get signed up for camp, everyone. We're ready for you."

Rob ended by pointing his index straight into the camera, then took the phone and slipped it into his jeans pocket.

"Don't you feel too old to be doing that stuff on social media?" Tristen asked.

Dariana giggled. "Wait, are you serious? You're a musician and you're not on social media?"

"I'm on it, sporadically, but I hate it. I never feel like I have anything to say."

"It gets your name out there. We have a whole group of teens coming in from Alabama 'cause they found our videos," Rob said, picking up his tools.

"You should put your music on there," Dariana said. "Maybe someone will use a clip for a viral video."

Everyone, mostly women, told him that. But he felt stupid recording himself. Maybe now that he was in his own place, he could try it. That way he wouldn't constantly be scared Jared was going to walk in any second and make fun of him.

"Let's go. I'll show you around. I mean, you could watch our channel and get an idea of it, but since you're here, I might as well show you myself."

They walked up the same gravel path Tristen had used, Rob pointing out the cabins, cafeteria, music room cabins, and finally the chapel.

"This is where I need some of your expertise," he said.

They entered the cool air of the dark chapel, which looked how Tristen envisioned most churches: a stage with a semi-circle of chairs around it. The sound board was at the back, as with any event center facing the stage.

"We bought a used one, but apparently it works. At least that's what I understood."

Tristen bent over it to get a better look. "It doesn't have all the latest digital stuff, but it'll do. I can teach you, but you'll probably want to eventually hire a real sound guy. It could be a lot of work for you to run sound with everything else you're doing."

"Maybe we should set up a class for the kids. You could teach them sound, right?"

Tristen snorted, sliding knobs and buttons around on the sound board. "Yeah, I guess I could. But there are certain days and hours I can't work."

"Sure." Rob fell silent as Tristen concentrated on connecting the tablet to the soundboard. "Who's this client of yours? Have I heard his music?"

"His name is Lin," Tristen said. He started checking the speakers, Rob following him. "He's from Singapore, and I doubt you've heard his album yet. It dropped in Asia and is doing pretty well, but it's had a quieter reception here, from what I can see. He's a bit crazy, but he has the voice of an angel. Like Josh Groban, although he hates the comparison."

"That good, huh?"

"Yeah." Tristen adjusted the cables. Some weren't even plugged in correctly. "Not my vibe, but that music sells. He's coming here to record his next album with me, so I have to find a studio to work in and make sure Ivy's fine at the gym before I move to Cincinnati to do all that."

"You could use our studio," Rob said as feedback pierced the air.

Tristen corrected another speaker so it wasn't pointed directly at the wall. "Sorry. What did you say?"

"You could use our studio. It's the next place on our tour. I wanted the kids to be able to record themselves and put it up on the internet if they wanted. That's what I wanted you to teach them. Not here. I mean, I need this set-up for the times we used the chapel, but it's the studio that you'll be in most."

Tristen had assumed he'd be recording in the chapel. "That's cool, man. This place is interesting."

"What do you mean?" Rob asked, looking around with him.

Tristen waved his hand around the area and shrugged. "I would have killed to go to a place like this when I was a kid."

Rob laughed. "Well, it was here, but it wasn't a music camp. When I was young, I used to hate this place. It was so embarrassing to have a grandpa who ran a summer camp, for some reason. But now I wake up excited to come into work. I wish I had been excited to come back then and spend time with my grandpa, but anyway, I think we're doing a noble thing, you know? The kids around here need it, and that excites me." He threw his arm around Tristen's shoulders and pulled him forward. "It's gonna be a great summer. We're glad to have you with us. Come on, I'll show you the studio. And since we can't pay you in cash for teaching for three weeks, what about me letting you use the studio for your client?"

"That—that would be really nice of you, Rob. Thanks." It was a good back-up plan if Tristen couldn't find something in Cincinnati before Lin came.

Rob grinned like Tristen had patted his head and told him to sit. "Gotta be outside of camp hours, though."

Tristen thought about Lin, his colorful personality and inability to filter his words. "I think that would be best."

Four

WORKING THE WEDNESDAY MARKET was completely different than working the Sunday or Saturday markets. It was smaller, which made the waitlist more competitive. Scarlett had waited for her spot for almost a year. She had hoped to make a nice bit of cash; Patty, her bread-stand competition at the weekend markets, always bragged about how much she made at them.

So far it wasn't going well. What Patty hadn't told her was that the Wednesday crowd was full of young professionals who came trickling from their offices to stroll through the stalls as a way of rejuvenating themselves for another day of work. All looking for lunch.

"Have any sandwiches or sausage rolls?" a man asked her, barely glancing at her other breads and scones when she shook her head with a stiff smile. "Man, wish you did."

From across the way Patty waved, her gray hair gleaming in the sunlight. She caught the man's attention, and within seconds he was heading over to her stall.

"Gluten-free muffins? Are these any good or do they taste like cardboard?"

Scarlett turned to find two women near her stand, one looking disinterested, the other very eagerly awaiting Scarlett's answer.

"I make sure my treats taste good," Scarlett said, gritting her teeth against the insulting question. "It's not worth eating the calories if it doesn't taste like anything, right? Let me cut one up and you can try it."

She hated cutting into her products, but if she didn't sell these, she'd end up giving them to Nasreen to take to the office.

The slim woman popped a piece into her mouth, her eyes lighting up as she chewed. "These are amazing. What flavor is it?"

Reactions like that were why Scarlett loved to bake. It was the little bit that kept her going from now until the weekend market.

She waited until the now interested woman took a bite to answer. "It's pear and pecan."

"I never would have thought that would taste good. Are you sure these are gluten-free?"

"And egg *and* dairy-free," Scarlett said, proudly. The recipe had been accidentally created one day after she'd dropped the grocery bag with the eggs and milk in it, resulting in a slimy mess in her apartment. She had scrambled to figure out how to make her stock for the next day's market and come up with her signature vegan muffin. Or rather, one day it would be signature.

"I'll take the rest of what you have here. I haven't seen you before on Wednesdays."

"No," Scarlett said, packing up her ten gluten-free muffins while her heart skipped and leapt. A sale was a sale, though it probably wasn't enough to cover the stall fee. "This is my first day here."

"Do you do individual orders? I'm always looking for better gluten-free foods for our office meetings. And if they taste like the others, then I wouldn't have to do two orders."

Scarlett eagerly pulled out the little cards Ben had made for her on a whim one day with her name and email. She had never thought of trying to pitch herself to businesses, but perhaps it was a new avenue she could pursue. "This is my card here. I can write my telephone number. It would be easier to call me and let me know what you're thinking in terms of flavors and then I can quote you the price."

The woman smiled and tucked the card away. "And would the price be lower if I order several dozen?"

"Lower than today?" Scarlett asked, fear gripping her. She didn't know how to say that three dozen muffins, or however many the woman ordered, couldn't possibly have a price lower than the ten she'd just bought.

"No, I mean lower per muffin. These were three-fifty, right? So would the price be lower per muffin if I order more?"

"Oh, right. Of course. I'll have to work it out, but I'm sure we can come to an agreement," Scarlett said, trying to swallow. Her mouth was dry after drinking a matcha tea earlier.

"I better get going. I'll talk to you soon, Scarlett. Thank you for the muffins," the woman said. She and her mute friend sashayed away. Scarlett checked her watch to see if it was too early to start taking down.

"Hey there, Scarlett," said a familiar voice.

Scarlett turned to find a smile she'd recognize anywhere. "Cory." She hadn't seen her friend in weeks. Maybe months. "What're you doing here?"

"I work near here. Did that woman buy something from you?"

"A couple muffins. She said she might order more for her office."

Cory looked impressed. "That's my boss, you know. Her name's Rebecca."

"That woman is your boss?" Scarlett asked, speaking too quickly to hide her surprise.

"Women are bosses these days, Scarlett," Cory said, chuckling.

"Shut up, you idiot," Scarlett said, throwing part of the cut-up muffin at him. It was true she was uneducated compared to him, since he had gone to college for two years, but she wasn't a moron. "I didn't mean it like that. I meant, she seems so young."

Cory shrugged. Always unimpressed by everyone and everything. "It's her father's business, so she moved up faster than everyone else. What're you doing here? Isn't this far away for you?"

"What do you think I'm doing?" Scarlett retorted, before turning to a new customer who wanted to try the sage sourdough.

While the customer debated whether to buy anything, Scarlett glanced at her childhood friend. He grinned broadly at her.

She and Cory had been friends throughout elementary and middle school. They'd become each other's firsts at fifteen to help Cory move up in the cool ranks of the lacrosse team—being a virgin on the team meant hazing. They'd never dated, but they found themselves in bed a few times a year, usually when Cory needed to lick his wounds after a breakup and Scarlett needed some physical touch.

Their relationship was that they had no relationship, but Scarlett liked Cory. He treated her nicely in bed and never made her feel badly about her body. In fact, he seemed to enjoy her breasts and round hips in ways no one had ever done before. She'd fallen in and out of love with him through the years, though he never fell in love with her.

She looked at him again after taking money from the elderly woman. He was looking very fit. Very successful.

"You work around here?" she asked, adjusting her cap as the sun's rays hit her eyes.

"Right over there." Copy pointed to a tall building with hundreds of windows. "I'm on lunch break. I always come down and get a sausage roll from Patty on Wednesdays." He scanned her tables, eating one of Patty's rolls. "You're gonna need lunch stuff to succeed in this crowd. Most of us pop in and go back to work."

"I noticed. For some reason I thought it would be more like the Saturday morning market, with stay-at-home moms or something. I didn't think it would be full of professional people," Scarlett said, giving a little laugh to ward off any impulse to blame Patty for not warning her. Of course, she could have checked out the market while she was on the waiting list, but the thought had never occurred to her. Today she would pay for that mistake. "I haven't seen you for a while."

"Been working," Cory said, polishing off the sausage roll. "Crunching numbers at Edan Enterprises. Not super glamorous, but the pay is good. They didn't care that I hadn't finished my degree."

"That's awesome." Scarlett couldn't help being a tiny bit jealous. "I'm happy for you."

"Thanks, Scar." He leveled his eyes at her, his tone turning soft. "Why you signing up for more markets? Last time we talked, you wanted to do more private catering stuff. Wasn't that realtor lady helping you start out?"

"Right. Yeah. Well, she did for a few months, but she dropped me. I never got any further than her on the private end, so here I am. I don't wanna clean houses or work in retail."

"Rhoda not paying for the kid?"

"She pays when she pays. It's not always systematic." Scarlett didn't like talking about her sister or their arrangement. Especially since Cory knew almost everything already. "At least I know Johnny wouldn't ever dare kick me out."

She paused to see if the older man slowing down might buy something from her, but he moved on quickly when he caught her watching him.

"What happened with Carole?"

"She thought I was sleeping with her husband."

Cory's eyebrows shot up. "Were you?"

Scarlett thought of Don and gagged. "Hell, no. But I did catch him with someone half his age."

"Hot?"

"Shut up, Cory," Scarlett said, swatting his arm. "But I guess she was if you like skinny girls. Anyway, Carole found out and freaked out on me 'cause she thought I was the other woman. I showed her evidence it wasn't me, but she didn't change her mind. Cut me off from baking for her and from using her oven."

"Carole sounds like a wreck," Cory said. He leaned closer to her from the other side of the table. "But let's go back to you finding her husband with the skinny woman. Give me details."

With no customers around, Scarlett got into the story, having fun with the description of the naked woman and how she'd ended up all but running away once she'd packed up her bread. Cory laughed so hard Scarlett handed him her bottle of water. She tried to be annoyed, but couldn't. He'd loved any story related to sex ever since he was about fourteen.

"What I want to know is how an old guy nailed someone you claim is so hot," he said, recovering. He paused, his lips curling into a smile. "And why you didn't join in on the fun."

Scarlett swatted at him again.

Cory caught her hand, stroking her fingers lightly as he held her gaze. "I'm not surprised he wanted something from you, Scarlett. You don't give yourself enough credit."

A couple slowed down behind him, pointing at her bread. Scarlett moved to be in their line of sight, ignoring Cory's last comment. She knew what he wanted to gain from it. Not that she was opposed, but at the moment she was working.

"This bread is delicious," Cory commented, loudly enough to pull the couple in. Within minutes, Scarlett was five loaves lighter.

"Thanks," she said, allowing herself to gaze into his eyes before looking away again. "Maybe I should hire you."

"You made the bread. I just told the truth." Cory checked his watch, but stayed where he was. "What're you doing with Ben over the summer? He have any activities this summer?"

Scarlett's body flushed with heat. Two summers before, to soothe Cory from a bad break-up, they had gone camping while Ben was at a summer camp. Cory had spoiled her with champagne and steaks and his full attention for seven days. It had been a week of sex and naked swims that ended with them not seeing each other for six months: usual behavior for Cory. After that week, Scarlett had learned her lesson and gone back to keeping things casual with him, though she couldn't help dreaming about a day he might stick around for her.

Not that she told that to anyone, especially Nasreen. She claimed Cory wasn't worthy of licking Scarlett's boots if he wasn't proud enough to be her lover in the open, but Scarlett didn't mind. During their unhappy childhoods, she and Cory had kept each other from going off the deep end several times. And if they sought casual comfort in each other's arms, so be it.

Besides, the more he came back, the more likely he would stick around permanently someday. And when that day came, if Scarlett was single, she'd happily accept him. He was a good-looking guy with a stable job. Plus, he knew everything about her. They had no secrets, and yet he was still attracted to her.

"I'm not sure yet," she finally answered. "Probably a camp or two. If I can find enough houses to clean and get extra money here at this market."

Cory wiggled his eyebrows at her.

"Aren't you seeing someone?" Scarlett asked.

He shrugged. "I'm always seeing someone. But we aren't exclusive yet."

"Yet? Wow, that sounds serious for you."

"We'll see. She's cool and hot—"

"Very important things," Scarlett teased.

Cory chuckled. "Anyway, what're you gonna do? You're good at this baking thing. You gonna cater or what? You should really grow the business so you can be more financially stable."

"Lots of people can bake," Scarlett said. "Maybe I should give it up and look for a job. Is your company hiring?"

It was meant as a joke, but Cory seemed instantly uncomfortable. He pulled his shoulders back and stood up straight. "Mine? No. Nothing you'd be interested in," he said quickly, shaking his head.

Scarlett wished she hadn't said anything.

"Sorry, Scarlett. I didn't mean you couldn't work at an office. You could. I mean, this is you." He spread his hands out towards her tables. "You gotta go for this, you know? It's now or never."

"Sounds like a Bon Jovi song," Scarlett said, pulling loaves off her table and into a plastic box. The market was over, and she'd sold only half her inventory.

"I'm serious, Scar. It's now or never. When else will you have the time to make all the stuff and really give it a go?"

"There's one great big issue."

"What's that?" Cory asked.

"I ain't got the money to expand, or whatever."

"Scarlett, what do you want from life?" he asked.

Scarlett raised an eyebrow, her lips slowing creasing into a smile. "A pony. With a rainbow tail."

Cory chuckled. When they were eleven, they'd snuck into a backyard of one of the giant houses on the other side of town one Saturday. The first thing they saw, in the middle of the yard, was a white pony with its tail dyed like a rainbow. The birthday girl didn't look old enough to talk, and yet she had a pony to ride at her birthday. She and Cory couldn't believe it. They'd talked about it for months, the idea that there were parents out there who spent that kind of money on birthday parties for toddlers.

The episode had made a deep impression on Cory. From that day forward he'd sought out kids who had rich parents and done whatever it took to become their friend. Over the following years, he'd attended birthday parties that boasted live bands, taking trips to water parks, and even going on a Disney Star Wars cruise. Scarlett barely got invited to the normal pool parties with pizza and cake.

Cory laughed. "No, like what would you like to do for a living? You know, you could expand online. Scarlett's Online Bakery." He ran his hand through the air as though caressing a rainbow. "How does that sound?"

"Sounds nice, Cory," she acquiesced. "That sounds very nice. But I lost the kitchen where I make everything."

She waited for Cory to laugh or scoff, but he just smiled.

"Okay, Scar. That boss of mine will probably forget to call, so I'll take this packet of cookies here," he said, tossing her cash. "I'll give them to HR and see what they think about buying them on Fridays or something."

"That's nice of you, Cory. I would appreciate it. But it probably won't be enough to get me on the internet."

"Well, you need a business plan. And maybe a loan. You know, to rent out a kitchen somewhere. And a website. You know what licenses you need to sell food online?"

Scarlett shook her head, starting to feel like the ground was shifting under her feet. It had taken her two months to get her permit for the Farmer's Market. She wouldn't know where to start for the internet.

"I can see you panicking," Cory said, chuckling softly. "Don't worry. I'll help you."

"When?"

"Soon." Scarlett tried to keep a straight face, but when Cory said 'soon' he rarely followed through. He must have seen her doubt, because he quickly went on. "And I'll talk to my office today and get back to you. That should bring you a sizable order."

"How big?" Scarlett asked hopefully.

"Pretty big. What were you doing for the realtor lady?"

"Carole bought four-and-a-half-dozen every weekend in exchange for me using the kitchen. Sometimes she would double that if she had multiple showings, and then she'd pay me."

"How much?"

"She'd pay a dollar a cookie."

Cory narrowed his eyes as another pair of women stepped closer, then quickly turned away. "That's so small-time, Scarlett. Why you still so small-time? You gotta triple that price. I'll call you later." He gave her a two-finger salute and winked. "I gotta get going."

She smiled tightly, trying to hide how insulted she felt.

"Sure, see you," she said, but Cory was already gone, leaving her talking to the air.

Five

Ten days later, Scarlett sat on her large cooler at the Saturday market. The morning was slow, with half the amount of customers as on opening week. That was how farmer's markets worked, though. Some weeks were great, while others were excruciatingly slow. Above her tent the sky was a hazy gray-blue, but there seemed to be no threat of rain. Whatever the reason, if people didn't show up soon, she'd be left with more than her extra freezer could hold.

"That looks good. What d'ya call it again?"

"Sausage roll," Scarlett told the tall man who had passed by her tent three times already. He seemed finally ready to buy something. "It's a kielbasa sausage wrapped in homemade croissant dough and baked together."

"They're delicious," a voice behind the man piped up. Cory.

Scarlett checked her watch. He wasn't usually one for being out and about early on a Saturday, but here he was. In the flesh.

The man bought five rolls and a dozen cookies. Scarlett packed the goodies, avoiding Cory's hungry look from the corner of her tent. She knew he wasn't hungry for food.

"Hey, Ben. How are you?"

"Bored." Ben stood up from his hiding place behind the coolers and stretched. "I'm gonna go wander. Maybe go to the library."

Cory raised his eyebrows at Scarlett as Ben sauntered away. "Library? He definitely didn't get that from you."

Scarlett would have swatted him if a family hadn't been gazing at her table. She settled for glaring at him.

"Thank you," she called after the family. They ignored her.

"Things look like they're going well today," Cory said, leaning against her table.

"It's okay," Scarlett lied, glancing at her half-full table. The market closed in an hour. "Better than the Wednesday last week."

Cory dropped her a ten-dollar bill before ripping into an empanada. "Any chance I can take you to dinner next Friday night?"

A small shiver ran down her spine. "Course. I can ask Nasreen to watch Ben."

"That's what I was hoping," Cory said, his eyes never leaving her.

"Wait here, okay? I want to ask you something," Scarlett told him as a group of women approached. They took five minutes to choose which scone they wanted, before deciding to buy one to share.

"They don't know what they're missing," Cory assured her as they walked away. Scarlett tried to smile away her disappointment.

"I was gonna ask," she said, changing the subject. "Your boss hasn't answered my voicemail or email. Do you think you could nudge her a bit?"

Cory crumpled up the plastic wrap from his now-eaten empanada and swallowed the last bit in his mouth. His eyes were difficult to read, but she knew he was either annoyed or thinking.

"Yeah," he finally said. "About that. I talked to HR, and they put your card into the pile of people they order from. They do this rotating thing to make it fair. I guess a lot of employees know bakers. They said they'll call you, but I don't know how long it'll take."

"Okay," Scarlett said, trying not to be too disappointed. "I get it. I'm happy to be in the mix. And did you talk to Rebecca about what she wanted?"

Cory shook his head. "I haven't seen her much and every time I do, it's about the project we're working on. There's never a time to say, 'Oh, and by the way, my friend is waiting for you to order muffins,' you know?"

"It's fine," Scarlett assured him. "I'll keep looking."

"I have an idea. Why don't you bring your stuff to Top Gym? It would be a great place to sell your stuff."

"That's kinda weird. I left my card the last time I came in, when I brought you that delivery, and they never called me back."

"You gotta be more proactive, Scarlett. Just go in. Jared, my brother's friend, works there, remember?"

"I know," Scarlett said. She also remembered the other man who worked there: Tristen. He was tall and built like a Viking. They had run into each other back in May at O'Donnell's, when a drunk Jared had announced Tristen thought Scarlett was pretty. The memory shot a shiver down her spine.

Cory tapped on his phone screen, waving aside her hesitancy. "There. It's done. I texted Jared. He'll expect you, so now you have to go. Anyway, feeding guys working out will be a better avenue than Rebecca."

Scarlett sighed. A couple walked past, eyeing her stand before the wife reminded the man they were on a low-carb diet.

"I don't understand low-carb diets," Scarlett muttered.

"Hey, Scarlett, Zander is at the park. Can I go?" Ben asked, running up to the tent. He eyed Cory, then looked at Scarlett for an answer. He'd told Scarlett that Rhoda said Cory was 'no good', and what Rhoda told him was gold for Ben, didn't matter what Scarlett said. Rhoda was his mother.

Scarlett never felt that way about her own mother. Maybe it was the distance that had grown loyalty between Ben and Rhoda, who hadn't raised him since he was five. Scarlett had been doing that job.

"Yeah, sure. But come back in an hour."

"Right," Ben shouted, before zigzagging through the market towards the park.

Another couple, clearly not on a low-carb diet, approached.

"We'll take a babka and a couple of those muffins," the lady said.

"My babkas freeze really well," Scarlett said as she packed the items into a bag. "If you buy another, I'll give it to you for half off."

She ignored Cory shaking his head. The lady eagerly agreed, and Scarlett was happy to collect almost forty dollars from her.

"Your babkas are worth full price," Cory said, giving her a quick kiss on the cheek. "Next Friday, yeah?"

"Of course. Will I see you at the market on Wednesday before that?"

"Maybe," he said, already dialing someone on his phone. Scarlett watched him go, impressed as always by how well he'd kept himself in shape.

"Hello, Scarlett."

Scarlett turned to find her mother's neighbor, Tammy, standing near her tent. She was a busybody that didn't know how to filter her thoughts. As if on cue, Tammy eyed Cory's receding figure and laughed. "Honey, don't waste your time on a boy who don't fit you. Find someone in your league."

She laughed harder. Scarlett forced a smile. "Hello, Tammy."

Tammy waved the comment away. "You're a hard one to get a hold of. A letter got delivered to your mother's place. Candi asked me to watch over her house while she's gone, you know? Pick up the mail and such. I didn't know she was going to be gone such a long time. Not that I mind at all, though."

Candi, Scarlett's mother, had a way of inducing fear in people.

"Thank you, Tammy. Sorry for the trouble. I'm not sure why a letter for me would go to Candi's house, but I appreciate you bringing it to me." Scarlett began to carefully stack leftover loaves into her plastic bins. "You can leave it over there."

Tammy shook her head, her frazzled hair so glued in place by hairspray that it moved as one unit with her head. "It's for Ben."

Scarlett grabbed the letter. It was addressed to Ben Terrinsworth.

"Thank you, Tammy," she repeated.

"Looks official," Tammy said, her fingers jabbing themselves nervously into her hair. "I had to deal with CPS on occasion with my grandbaby. You think something's wrong? I wouldn't want nothing to happen to that cute little boy of Rhoda's."

That cute little boy was now eleven and could appear at any time. Scarlett didn't want him hearing anything about this letter.

"I'm sure it's fine," she managed to say.

"When you see Rhoda again, you tell her I brought you the letter, yeah? She's always decent about taking care of people who take care of her people, if you know what I mean."

Scarlett had no idea what she meant. "I'll let her know," she said, hoping the woman would clear out.

"You can see the date here," Tammy pressed, signaling the post office stamp with her neon-pink nails. "See that? It took me about a day to figure out where you'd be, but I got it to you as fast as I could."

"Of course," Scarlett said slowly. "She won't be mad, Tammy. She doesn't even live here anymore."

Tammy glanced over her shoulder. Scarlett wished she would leave.

"She'll be back someday, Scarlett. And I ain't scared of her being mad at me. I wanna make sure she knows in case she wants to thank me."

"Right," Scarlett drawled.

"Back just in time," Ben declared, skidding to a halt in front of the stall and cutting the conversation short.

"Well, haven't you grown into a handsome young man," Tammy said quietly, smiling at Ben. "See ya later, Scarlett. Remember me to Rhoda."

With that, she finally walked away.

"Shouldn't we pack up, Scarlett?" Ben asked.

"Sorry. Tammy interrupted me, and now…" Her voice trailed off. "Anyway, put the rest of the savory things into that box over there. We're heading over to a boxing gym to see if we can sell the rest of this stuff."

"Seriously?" Ben whined.

"What's wrong with that?" Scarlett asked, struggling to keep her focus on the conversation.

"It's embarrassing."

She hated that she couldn't deny that truth. It did feel a bit like begging. "I'm sorry, Ben, but if I can sell this, we can pay all the bills and maybe have some left over."

"Left over for what?" he demanded, crossing his arms over his chest. "For camp? Or to buy more flour?"

She'd waited too long for Rhoda's check, which had never come. By the time Scarlett had decided to enroll Ben using her credit card, all the good camps, or at least the ones Zander was going to, were full.

"Listen, you can stay in the truck while I try to sell this stuff. Maybe it'll be enough to get you into that camping thing the church down the street is doing."

Ben snorted. "That thing costs three hundred dollars."

Scarlett swallowed hard. She'd forgotten the price. "Well, you never know. Those guys eat a lot."

Six

"You hungry?" Scarlett asked quietly. Ben hadn't spoken since they got in the truck.

"I wanna see my dad. He said he'd be back by now."

Scarlett gripped the steering wheel. She was suddenly exhausted. If she wasn't careful, she would say something she didn't mean.

"Eric thought his job ended this week and that he'd be here in time for you to spend time with him next weekend."

"He said he'd be in town this summer and that we'd hang out. He said he'd take me camping," Ben said.

That was true. But Eric had also said he wasn't sure when his job was going to be finished. Scarlett took a moment to breathe in some patience. But Ben didn't let up.

"This is so stupid. Everyone else gets to do something cool this summer except me." He huffed and threw himself against the seat. "Can I call him?"

"Who?"

"Dad."

"Do whatever you want, Ben," Scarlett said, too frustrated to keep it from showing. "Go ahead and call him. See where he is. See if he can get you into something cool for the summer."

Ben balled himself up against the car door, the phone pressed to his ear. Scarlett knew she should apologize, but Ben wouldn't like her interrupting his phone call. Instead, she gripped the steering wheel harder and condemned herself for not controlling her tongue.

Eric had first shown up four years earlier. At first, Scarlett hadn't believed he was Ben's dad. He didn't seem like the kind of guy Rhoda would spend two seconds with; her sister had always tended towards the tattooed bad boys. Eric worked the oil rigs and had one tattoo, but he was also soft-spoken and never looking for a fight. He'd grown up two streets down in the same trailer park as Scarlett and Rhoda. The whole neighborhood said Eric was a mama's boy because he never went against his crazy mother. Mrs. Molly Henderson had raised him with an iron grip, and Eric obeyed everything she said. When his father died of a sudden coronary embolism, rumors flew that Eric had poisoned the old man for his mother. Mr. and Mrs. Henderson hadn't liked each other and were known for knock-down drag-outs.

No arrests were ever made, but that didn't stop people from talking.

Scarlett glanced at Ben. His eyes brightened at something Eric had said on the phone.

"You're in town? Now?" he asked. "Okay, okay."

"What is it?" Scarlett asked as the truck jostled them going too fast over a speed bump.

"Dad's in town," Ben said, his face smug.

"What else?"

"He's gonna meet us at the gym. Says he wants to talk to you."

"About what?"

"Dunno," Ben said with a shrug.

Nasreen said Ben's moodiness was teenage hormones, but Scarlett wasn't sure. The kid's parental situation was a sticky subject, as were his memories. Sometimes he talked about what he could remember when he lived with Rhoda; sometimes he got memories confused. A few weeks back he'd told Scarlett he remembered refusing to eat and crying himself to sleep the first week he'd lived with her. His memories didn't include her sitting next to his bed until he fell asleep, and she didn't think it would be right to point it out, so she'd kept quiet. But those nights she, too, had cried herself to sleep—and many more since. Suddenly becoming the guardian of a five-year-old child had been overwhelming and life-changing. To the point that she almost had sympathy for her mother.

Almost.

They turned into the Top Gym parking lot, avoiding a deep pothole that sat right at the entrance. Despite the parking lot needing some love, it was two-thirds full.

"I'll go inside if you want to stay in the car. You can watch for Eric."

Ben yanked open the door before he remembered to unbuckle, which drew out a long, irritated gargle from him as an answer. Scarlett decided to let it go. Kids had the right to be irritated. And since she wasn't quite sure if he was irritated with her or not, she thought it best not to ask.

"Are you coming or not?" Ben asked. He stood tapping his right foot against the ground, hands on his hips.

"You can go on ahead," Scarlett said slowly, trying her best to stay calm as she arranged the sandwiches and sausage rolls. She was in no hurry to go inside and beg, even though the last time she'd turned up the guys had all seemed grateful.

Ben's glare didn't help her nerves, but he turned and marched away.

When she was done arranging the food, Scarlett heaved the basket off the truck and tried to smile.

"Okay, let's go," she muttered to no one but herself.

Jared stood at the entrance, holding the door open. He was still built like a truck, with wide, muscled shoulders and a full beard.

When Scarlett was growing up, he'd been at Cory's house a lot, fixing cars with Cory's brother.

Scarlett picked up her pace. "Thanks, Jared," she said as she and Ben slipped past him into the cool gym.

"No problem. How you doing, Scarlett?"

"Fine. Better in the air-conditioning," she said, chuckling nervously when she noticed the white, salty lines her dried sweat had created on her T-shirt.

"Cory told me you were coming by. I have some hungry guys waiting," Jared said. Ben's shoulders relaxed at the news. "Let's see the food. I usually grab a sandwich at the gas station, so I'm ready for your healthy homemade action."

"You shouldn't eat that processed stuff," Scarlet said, spreading out her assortment of sandwiches and sausage rolls on the registration counter. Inwardly, she sighed with relief. So far, it didn't feel like begging. "Try this."

She handed him half a sandwich of tuna, pickles, olives, carrots and apples. It was one of her favorites.

Jared grabbed the sandwich with a grin and bit into it. "That's good," he announced. "I'll take another one. How much do I owe you?"

"Let's say ten and call it a day."

"You have seven marked on each one, Scarlett," Jared said, his brown eyes boring into hers. He pulled out three fives and tucked them into her basket.

"Hey, it's Scarlett!"

Scarlett looked up and swallowed hard. Tristen was as attractive as she remembered.

"Hi." The word came out like rushing air. She could feel her face getting warm.

"I haven't seen you in a few weeks. You should come by here more often," he said with a wink. Scarlett was surprised by the ripple of pleasure that zipped through her. "I'll take some of these sausage rolls. John, you want some?"

"Am I allowed one?" the man at the weights called back.

"I'll allow it, since it's homemade," Tristen said. He tossed the roll to the man. "You been to O'Donnell's lately?"

Scarlett laughed. "Nah. Don't get out that much."

"We should remedy that." Tristen smiled at her, and Scarlett thought she might faint. She should have eaten something to calm her nerves.

"What're they doing over there?" Ben asked, pointing at the boxing ring before Tristen could tell her *how* she might remedy not going out much. Scarlett swallowed a sigh of frustration. "I didn't think you could kick in boxing."

Jared chuckled. "You're right. They aren't supposed to do that in boxing. They're practicing a type of MMA. Have you ever tried it?"

Ben shook his head.

"Come on, I'll show you some moves," Jared said, shoving the last of his sandwich in his mouth. "You'll need to know some of the same techniques for boxing camp."

Scarlett pulled back. "Boxing camp?"

"Yeah," Jared said. "Tristen and I are running it."

Scarlett looked at Tristen. "Okay, but I didn't sign Ben up."

"His dad signed him up this morning. Didn't he tell you?" Jared asked, walking away with a very excited Ben.

Scarlett looked to Tristen for an explanation, but the sound of weights crashing to the ground covered her attempt to speak.

He shook his head. "Damn. Duty calls. Nice to see you again, Scarlett."

"Bye," she said, still confused about the camp.

"Dad!" Ben called from inside the ring as Eric walked through the gym doors. He made a beeline to Ben.

Scarlett grabbed the last sandwich from the counter and marched over to intercept Ben's dad. Talking to a man with food was always easier.

"You hungry, Eric?" she asked, thrusting the chicken salad sandwich at him.

He eyed it.

"It's on the house," she said, exasperated. He was always thinking about money, which made it even weirder that he'd signed Ben up for boxing camp. Unless he thought she had the money for it. "What's this about boxing camp?"

"I heard about it from my cousin. Thought Ben would like it."

Scarlett crossed her arms and watched as Ben's scrawny arm shot out, punching air.

"Don't you think he would? Being around other boys and hitting stuff in a civilized manner?" Eric asked.

"Maybe," Scarlett said. "You'd have to come up with the cash, though. I got no money to pay for camps."

"I already paid for it, Scarlett."

She turned to look him fully in the face, but Eric kept his concentration on Ben and the sandwich. In profile, she could see their similarities. They both had strong chins and straight noses that looked like those statues in the history books. They also both had brown hair, but then so did Rhoda. Ben definitely had Rhoda's eyes, though. The slight slant at the corners. Rhoda used to imagine her father was a noble, Native American warrior. Of course, neither of the sisters knew who their father was. Candi had never told them.

"Look at him. He seems to enjoy it." Eric smiled, then muttered something Scarlet couldn't hear properly.

When he started to walk off, she grabbed him by the T-shirt sleeve. "What did you say about Rhoda?" She was almost certain he'd said her sister's name.

"Rhoda?" He raised an eyebrow. "Nothing. I'm just not surprised she missed her payment to you. It makes sense, is all."

"Why? 'Cause you don't pay either, remember?" Scarlett snapped, before she could think of what her words meant.

Eric's eyes narrowed for a second, but then his shoulders slumped and he plastered a fake smile on his lips. "I'm paying for the camp, Scarlett. And don't worry. Soon you won't have to do this at all."

"Whaddya mean, Eric? I won't have to do what?"

"Take care of Ben," he said. "I'm going to ask for custody."

Scarlett sucked in air through her teeth.

"You're never around, Eric," she said, panic scratching at her throat. She glanced at Ben; suddenly all her fatigue was wiped away, replaced by a fight-or-flight instinct. He wasn't her kid. She couldn't run away with him. "Your job requires too much of you."

"He's my son." Eric shoved his fingers through his hair and sighed. "Brandy is pregnant, so we thought maybe we'd give the family thing a go."

"A go? You're either in or out on family, Eric. Rhoda's his mom, and she put me in charge. I thought everyone agreed on that."

"We did. But that was before."

Scarlett bit back a scream. Thankfully, she'd had plenty of practice keeping calm in situations this frustrating.

Inside the ring, Ben laughed loudly at something Jared had said. He caught sight of Scarlett and Eric watching him and waved his red sparring gloves.

"I want him to come home with me tonight. Maybe stay the week."

Scarlett clenched her jaw, taking a beat before speaking. "You said you would give more notice last time."

Again, Eric's eyes narrowed, but this time his smile wobbled.

"Sorry about that." His voice was hard. "There are some things I need to get done for this whole custody thing, and I'd like to see Ben while I can. Before I have to get another job. Some of us work, you know?"

His comment stung. "Right," she murmured.

Eric sighed audibly. "Look, Scarlett. I'm sorry. I'm tired. I would like to see Ben when I'm in town. I don't think that's too much to ask."

Scarlett knew he was right. "I know he'll love to spend time with you. I think we should talk more about this custody thing."

Eric grinned, his gaze always on Ben, who was busy hitting a foam square. "Of course. Soon. We'll do whatever is right for Ben."

But Scarlett wasn't too sure. In her experience, the kid didn't always come out on top in grownup affairs.

Seven

Scarlett peeled the plastic wrap off the flat rectangular butter and carefully placed it over her rolled-out dough. She grinned at Nasreen, savoring the moment. "I sold almost everything yesterday. And what I didn't sell at the market, I sold at Top Gym. Remember that place? It's changed a lot."

"Yes, girl!" Nasreen jumped out of her seat. She grabbed Scarlett by the shoulders and squeezed lightly. Scarlett endured the hug. "I mean, I don't know any gym, but I'm happy for you for selling it all."

"But?"

Nasreen was unusually antsy, shifting constantly in her chair. "Nothing. I'm guess I'm nervous to go to work tomorrow. My boss was real mad when I told him I was leaving, but then he went on a work trip. He'll be back tomorrow and since he hasn't answered any of my emails, I'm thinking he's still pissed. Can you believe that?"

Scarlett could believe it. Sometimes rage filled her when she thought about Nasreen leaving, even though as her best friend she should only be happy for her. "I'm sorry, Nas. That sucks. Only a few more weeks, right?"

"Yeah. It's fine. He'll get over it. And even if he doesn't, I'm out of here. Finally. Moving on past this tiny armpit of Kentucky."

The closer Nasreen came to leaving Brax, the more she expressed her displeasure with living there. It was starting to wear on Scarlett's nerves. Not that she loved Brax or didn't see its flaws, but she was stuck here. Probably forever. So what did that say about her? It wasn't something she liked to think about.

"Where's your notebook? Let's see those details."

"I'm telling you, yesterday was a good day. I sold everything. Like I said, after the market I went to Top Gym. Cory talked to the guys over there. Do you know Jared? No, I don't think you do. That's what you get for going to school over in Salisbury."

Nasreen made a face at her as she grabbed the notebook. Camila joined them again from the bathroom, grabbing three more beers from the fridge before flopping onto the couch.

"It's the best when all the boys are at their dad's houses at the same time," she said.

Nasreen chuckled. "You can say that again. Don't get me wrong, I love my Zander, but a night with the girls? Now that's heaven."

"Anyway, seriously, I sold out. All I had left over were five loaves of bread, but that's not a big deal. I can freeze them." Scarlett took a moment to savor the hope that was taking hold in her. "I'm starting to feel like maybe I can do this, you know? Like maybe I could actually make a full business out of this."

"Course you can, girl," Camila said.

"I've been saying that since the beginning. You got talent," Nasreen said.

"I haven't even said the best part," Scarlett said. "Remember the guy from O'Donnell's a few months ago? He works at the gym. And he's as hot as ever."

Nasreen shook her head slowly.

"The boxer guy? Not the one Cory was taking classes from, but the guy I pointed out to you in March when we went out for Camila's birthday, remember? We saw that band that sounded like *The Cranberries*?"

"Oh, I remember him," Camila shouted. "He was hot. You saw him today?"

"Yesterday."

"Kinda like fate," Camila said, with a wink.

"Oh, please," Scarlett scoffed. She sighed, knowing she would break her own heart. A guy like that would never be interested in a girl like her. A guy who worked out for a living probably only dated women whose bones stuck out of their hips. Scarlett was all soft curves. Had been since puberty.

Her sigh wasn't lost on Camila. "Is someone in love? I don't blame you. I'm telling you, Nasreen, the man is super *guapo*."

Scarlett felt her face growing warm. "I also saw Eric. Which is why Ben isn't here tonight."

"Eric? At the gym or at the market?" Nasreen asked.

"Gym. He showed up wanting Ben. And get this, he signed Ben up for a boxing camp."

"Boxing camp?"

"Where'd he get the money?" Camila asked.

Scarlett rolled her eyes. "The hell if I know. He was so short when I pressed him for details. As though I'm not the one who will have to bring him to camp every day because he's leaving on a job again next week."

Nasreen exchanged looks with Camila, who crossed her arms.

"What's got you all fired up? I'd think it would be nice that Eric finally paid for something."

Scarlett set her rolling pin away and picked up her beer. With a steadying breath, she told her friends what Eric had said. "He wants custody of Ben."

"What?"

"Back up," Nasreen said. "That man can't get custody. He's never around long enough. What will he do with Ben while he's on a job?"

"He was acting super weird, honestly. And I didn't even tell you about Tammy yet. What a day!" Scarlett filled in all the missing details.

"So, Eric's in town for good?"

"I don't know," Scarlett said. "I was too shocked to ask the right questions. I mean, he's Ben's dad. And I guess I assumed that, at some point, Rhoda would take custody of Ben. What would the difference be if it was Eric?"

Tears threatened to well up, catching her off guard. At the beginning, her plan had been to not get too attached, knowing Ben could be taken away from her at any point. But as the years passed and Rhoda didn't take him, and Eric kept leaving for jobs outside the state, Scarlett had started thinking Ben would be with her until he at least graduated from high school.

She never should have dared to think that. It wasn't her place. He wasn't her kid.

"And what about this letter? Have you opened it?"

"No," Scarlett said slowly.

"Where is it?" Nasreen asked, looking around.

"Probably in my purse."

Nasreen jumped up and grabbed Scarlett's purse from the counter. "You gotta open stuff like this, Scarlett. You don't know what's in there. Maybe it's nothing."

"Maybe it's money," Camila said. "You know, like from the government. I get letters like that telling me about my benefits for the kids and stuff. Or it could be about Ben's healthcare." She shrugged before opening another beer.

"You're right," Scarlett said, but she was still reluctant. She'd gotten a letter or two like this one in her lifetime, and they never held good news.

Nasreen ripped open the letter and read it slowly. Scarlett sipped her beer to settle her stomach. When Nasreen put the letter down again, Scarlett couldn't help herself.

"What? What does it say?"

"They've assigned a 'guardian ad litem' for Ben."

"What's that?"

"It's someone who is supposed to represent the best interest of the child," Nasreen said slowly. "They're going to interview the people in Ben's life and write up a recommendation for the judge."

"A recommendation for what?" Camila asked, grabbing the letter.

"For what would benefit him." Nasreen was looking straight at Scarlett when she looked up.

"Rhoda isn't going to like that," she said.

"Doesn't matter much, does it?" Nasreen asked. "Rhoda barely visits him."

"She used to visit all the time. Something's happened. But I know she'll come around. It's only been a year."

"It's been almost two years, Scarlett."

Scarlett tried to find the discrepancy, but as usual, Nasreen was right. December would mark two years since they'd seen Rhoda.

"But you don't know her, Nasreen. She left enough money that time for almost the whole year's rent, and she took Ben and me to Cincinnati and bought him all new clothes. And remember, she bought me a new coat." Scarlett stopped when Nasreen lifted her eyebrows. "You don't know her," she repeated. "She's doing what she can to provide for her son. Not everyone can do everything the conventional way. Rhoda isn't conventional."

Nasreen scoffed but didn't say any more. They'd had a fight years back about Scarlett defending Rhoda. Scarlett understood her friend, but Nasreen didn't know half of what Rhoda had grown up with and what she had to do to survive. It was Rhoda who'd made sure they ate when Scarlett was little, by making a deal with the guy who worked at the grocery store. Every Thursday, he would bring things that were set to expire and set them in a box on top of the dumpster. Sometimes he snuck in some stuff that wasn't expiring as well. Scarlett never found out what Rhoda's part of the deal was.

That was the kind of person Rhoda was. And Scarlett was willing to give her the benefit of the doubt on anything.

Plus, she'd rather her sister leave Ben in her care than drag him around wherever Rhoda was, in whatever kind of situations Rhoda got herself into. She admired Rhoda for having that foresight.

"What are you going to do?" Nasreen asked, moving past their stalemate.

"Nothing. This looks like the end of the road for me."

"Why?"

Scarlett placed the croissant dough into the freezer and turned around, pushing aside her fear underneath all her other emotions. "Why would a judge give me custody of Ben? I have no money. I mean, shit, I don't even have a real job. Not real enough for a judge."

Nasreen shook her head. "You've been taking care of Ben for years. The judge will see that."

"I'm not going to go against Rhoda," Scarlett said. "I mean, it would be one thing for the courts to give me the custody, but I can't ask for it myself."

"Fine, fine. I don't agree," Nasreen said as she tapped her long, red nail against the side of her can. Her eyes squinted, then opened wide as though she'd had a brilliant idea.

Scarlett rolled her eyes towards Camila, who snorted beer through her nose.

"What is it, my almost-lawyer friend?" Scarlett asked, laughing as Camila struggled to hold herself together. "What are you thinking?"

"What if you convince Eric to work out a deal with him privately? Then get him on your side to get full custody."

"I could do that?"

Nasreen shrugged. "Why not? Judges love it when people work out their problems themselves. I don't see why it'd be any different this time. Who else would they give Ben to? Candi?"

They all groaned, and Scarlett couldn't help looking over her shoulder as though Candi might appear suddenly. The woman had a habit of showing up when Scarlett least expected it.

"Will you be my lawyer?" she asked, a channel of energy starting to buzz inside her chest.

"I'll help you all I can, but please don't tell the guardian ad litem that I'm your lawyer," Nasreen said, laughing. "I haven't even started classes yet. Besides, you don't need a lawyer. Especially since Eric can't afford one either. They haven't involved CPS, which means there's no accusation of harm being done to Ben. This should be settled civilly."

Scarlett picked up the letter and turned it over. "You think I should call Beth? Doesn't she work at CPS? She might know something about all this."

Nasreen shook her head, checking the time. "No, leave Beth out of it. I should go. I gotta finish up some homework for that statistics class I'm taking."

"I'll go, too," Camila said, waving her phone. "I might have a late-night date."

Scarlett wondered what Cory would do if she called him for a late-night date.

"Bye, girl," Nasreen and Camila called from the door.

Scarlett watched them walk down the hallway. Johnny, the landlord of the two apartment building, came in as they left.

"What're you doing here?" Nasreen asked, watching him walk through the door.

"Business, Nasreen," he said. He stopped mid-stride and crossed his arms, glaring at her, until she finally shrugged and left the building.

Scarlett started closing the door, not wanting anything to do with Johnny that night. He was the kind of guy that only brought trouble or bad news with him. It was always better not to see Johnny.

"Hold up, Scarlett."

Her heart stilled. She watched through the cracked door as Johnny sauntered towards her.

"My business is here with you. Wanna let me in?"

"We can talk out here," Scarlett said, trying to keep her voice from wobbling. "What do we have to talk about?"

Johnny smiled, his lips compressing in an unflattering way. "Would be best to talk privately, but okay. We can do it here. I wanted you to know that you owe me money."

Scarlett's breath caught. She tried not to show she was surprised, but when Johnny's smile hardened, she knew he could tell.

"How much money?" she managed to ask.

"Six months, unfortunately," Johnny said, carefully unwrapping a stick of gum and placing it in his mouth. He chomped on it before smiling at her again. "I need the money or you gotta get out. This is a business."

"Six months?" She couldn't think of anything else to respond with. Panic started taking over her chest.

Johnny nodded slowly. "That's right. I got it in the books. No payment all this year. Nothing since Rhoda paid that whole year a while ago."

"Why didn't you tell me sooner?" Scarlett rasped. "I don't have six months' payment, Johnny."

He shrugged. "It's none of my business to tell you anything. You're the one responsible."

Something was very wrong if Rhoda hadn't paid the rent in six months. She'd never missed a payment before. Or rather, Johnny had never complained about it before. Scarlett hadn't seen much of Johnny since Rhoda found out about the side payment Johnny had demanded Scarlett give him on her knees at the beginning.

She looked at him, realizing he was enjoying her panic. "I don't have all that right now, Johnny. When do you want the payment?"

"You better start within the month, kid. I need to know you're serious. Like three thousand dollars serious."

She knew Nasreen was paying a thousand a month, which meant Scarlett was in debt for six thousand. She swallowed hard, her body turning cold at the number.

"We could work out a different kind of plan," Johnny said. He looked her up and down with a grin that Scarlett understood. "If need be."

"No," she shot back, finding her voice again. She wouldn't get on her knees or back for Johnny again.

He reared his head, his smile fading completely. "Sorry to hear that, Scarlett. Then I expect three thousand in my account at the end of the month. And the rest of the money, which adds up to another six, by the end of September. Or you're out."

"In two months, you want me to pay you nine thousand dollars? That's more than six months of rent!"

"I guess that's called interest," Johnny mused. "In case you get ideas of taking me to court, this is your fourteen-day notice. And since you are technically paying month to month and not on a fixed lease, I'm not obligated to give you longer than two weeks. I looked up the law."

Rhoda had been paying for the apartment; Scarlett had never asked about the contract. Even if there had been a fixed one though, from the smile on Johnny's face, it wouldn't be found now. Scarlett certainly had no record of it.

"I appreciate the two weeks," she told him, her mind racing.

Johnny swaggered towards her. "Other people would pay good money for this nice little apartment." He knocked on the wood and nodded. "Can't be giving things away for free now, can I?"

Eight

Monday morning, nine o'clock, Tristen sat in his only suit in a Cincinnati court room ordered by Elijah, his lawyer, to stay silent.

"You're telling me that your client believes his twin brother is the father of this child?" Judge Sanchez looked down at Elijah, then at Tristen from over his glasses.

Tristen adjusted his position but kept his eyes slightly above the judge's glare. The lawyer at the next table over snickered quietly into his coffee, but Elijah stood his ground, never wavering from looking the judge in the eyes.

"Yes, your honor."

The judge sat back. "Well, I'll be damned. I haven't seen this before."

Tristen looked up at Elijah, but his lawyer kept his eyes on the judge.

He'd always seen Elijah as a mentor, a father-like figure. They had met in Cincinnati while Tristen was bartending. Elijah would come into town for his whiskey every Thursday and it didn't take long for him to start talking about his job, his cases and life in general. He even advised Tristen to go all in on the music.

The fact that Elijah had even bothered to talk to him, an uneducated kid from rural Kentucky, had won Tristen over right away. And when Tristen found out the reason Elijah had become a lawyer, he couldn't help respecting him even more. He became the epitome of the kind of man Tristen wished he could be.

The story went that when Elijah's uncle and guardian was thirty-five, he was accused of rape. Elijah swore his uncle would never hurt a flea, but he was a black man without an alibi, and the accuser pointed to him directly. The justice system didn't care what Elijah felt about his uncle or the fact that he had no other run-ins with the law. The DA needed to lock someone up for two sexual assaults on campus, so even though there was no other evidence against him, the gavel of justice came down for thirty years in prison.

"I felt like I'd died that day," Elijah had said, swirling his Johnny Walker Black in the heavy hotel glass. Tristen had waited, holding his breath. "That gavel pounded into my head and chest and soul. I don't remember getting home. I don't remember what else I did that day. I remember staring at the ceiling for a long time. And when I finally got out of bed, I asked how to become a lawyer. I was determined to get my uncle out."

Fortunately, his uncle got out before Elijah graduated. Another man was caught after a rape and confessed to the other assaults. Unfortunately, it was after eight years in prison. Elijah's aunt had moved on, and some in the community were never convinced his uncle was innocent. He'd ended up dying of an overdose only five years after being released.

"You're telling me that Mr. Levisay's brother had an affair with Miss Hofferman using the name Tristen, which is the defendant's name, instead of his own? And he is the one who impregnated her?"

"Judge, the reason this sounds ludicrous is because it is. This looks like an elaborate attempt by the defendant to get out of paying child support."

"I have a receipt right here that the defendant did in fact send some money to Miss Hofferman in February when she called asking for it."

"Yes, your honor," Elijah said, but the other lawyer cut him off from saying more.

"Which clearly indicates that Mr. Levisay felt an obligation to my client. And why would he feel an obligation to her unless he was the father of the child?"

"Your honor, my client sent money because he's an upstanding man, not as a way to admit to being the father. And he did so before he consulted me."

Judge Sanchez shook his head. "Has your client spoken to his brother?"

Tristen wanted to laugh, but he forced himself to keep his face neutral. He had talked to Talon many times about Lamia and the baby. The last time they'd spoken, Talon had threatened to change his number so Tristen couldn't call him again. The money had actually come mostly from Talon, collected in a moment of weakness when Tristen had made him feel sufficiently guilty.

But the money hadn't been enough for Lamia, even though she'd said it would be. The last time she'd called, Tristen had told her to get more from Talon. She had only laughed. "He found a way to escape the country, Tristen, but you're here. And I don't actually know which one of you I was dating, which could probably be called assault or something, so be glad I'm only taking you to court for child support."

She had served him papers to appear for a child support hearing at the beginning of the summer, which was when he'd called Elijah. No way was he going up against Lamia and her slimy lawyer alone. He'd never win. Elijah had spent the last decade handling criminal cases, but had taken the case for friendship's sake, saying his 'kindergarten lawyers'—as he called the interns—could do the research for the case so it wouldn't impact his workload too much.

Or possibly he'd taken it because he pitied Tristen and the bad luck he constantly seemed to fall into.

"My client did speak to his brother. He is not willing to come to the States to testify."

"To the States?" repeated Judge Sanchez. "Where is the brother living?"

Elijah shifted his eyes towards Tristen. It was the first sign to Tristen that this day would possibly not go in his favor. "He's in Portugal, your honor."

"Hmmm." The judge looked at Tristen over the rim of his glasses.

"Your honor, the man Lamia fell in love with told her his name was Tristen Levisay," Lamia's lawyer said. "It would be a strange thing for a twin brother to pull that kind of trick, would it not?"

Tristen looked over toward the guy. He didn't like the look of him. His blue suit was too shiny, his hair too perfectly swept back. There was an air about him that said he always had a trick up his sleeves.

"Your honor, I think we can clear this up before Elijah comes up with yet another excuse for Mr. Levisay. Miss Hofferman says that the father of her child has a small tattoo under his beltline on the left-hand side. If this man is willing to stand up and show us that he doesn't, then perhaps we can believe this strange story of the twin tricking my client."

Tristen froze. He had that tattoo.

Elijah leaned down and whispered in his ear, "Here we go." Straightening up, he announced, "Your honor, Miss Hofferman knows of that tattoo on my client because they were once involved almost four years ago. My client says they were together a total of three times. But last summer, when Miss Hofferman became pregnant, my client was living with another woman who is willing to testify."

That was a semi-lie. The truth was they weren't sure if Meegan was willing to testify.

"Are you saying that a man couldn't possibly be with two women at the same time?" mocked Lamia's lawyer.

Judge Sanchez glared down at all of them. Tristen had the feeling that if Judge Sanchez had a daughter, he'd be using Tristen as an example of who not to date from now on—the stupid guy who'd trusted his twin, probably left his wallet lying around, and who didn't even know what was going on or who was using his name.

Elijah turned on his heels to rummage through the two neat piles of paper on the desk. Tristen watched as his friend's dark fingers pulled up the corner of each document until he had the one that he wanted.

"Speaking of tattoos, your honor, we'd like to enter into evidence these pictures that were on Miss Hofferman's social media."

"Uh-huh. And what am I looking at?"

Tristen's ass was starting to fall asleep, and his shoulders were stiff from having his hands folded on the desk for so long. He pressed his shoulders back, distracting himself from rolling his eyes at the judge. It was obvious that he was looking at crude pictures of his brother, Talon, with Lamia. Both of them were naked, though conveniently no private parts were showing. The pictures were on social media, after all. The caption read: *My new love, Mr. Tristen Levisay. We fit perfectly together.*

"That is a picture of Talon Levisay and Lamia Hofferman, your honor. In a very compromising position."

"How do we know it isn't Tristen Levisay?" the sleazy lawyer demanded. His eyes boring into Tristen.

Tristen held his ground, staring back. He had nothing to be ashamed of and wasn't going to look away from a guy who didn't know when to stop adding gel to his hair.

"Because my client doesn't have a tattoo on his left shoulder like this one. It's strange that Miss Hofferman didn't offer *that* tattoo as evidence of the father of her child."

The sleazy lawyer scoffed. Judge Sanchez warned the lawyers to be civil, then flicked his fingers toward Tristen.

"Take off your jacket and show your left shoulder," Elijah told him.

They had practiced this very moment. Tristen took off his jacket and let it hang over the back of his chair. Then he unbuttoned his shirt only to the middle of his belly and pivoted slightly so Elijah could pull down the shoulder to prove he didn't have a tattoo.

He'd always thought Talon's tattoo of an exotic bird with the tail-feathers flowing down his bicep was stupid.

"You see, your honor? My client has no tattoo on his shoulder. His tattoo sleeve ends at the bicep."

"Judge, I ask for a recess," said the sleazy lawyer. "My client had to stay home with a sick baby today, and I will need to speak with her about this."

Judge Sanchez glared over the tops of his glasses at the lawyer, who didn't flinch, though a trickle of sweat ran down his temples.

"Alright. I have a heavy case load today anyway. We will reconvene at a later date to be set by the courts," Judge Sanchez declared, his gavel coming down with a thud.

Tristen looked at Elijah and tried not to smile. No verdict was still a good verdict in this case. Just a few weeks before Elijah had explained a few things about the court system and family law in America.

"She wants you to pay up and shut up," Elijah had said evenly. "For now, we can send a letter stating you are not the father and refuse to make the payment. Her lawyers will then send another letter back. The courts are on her side. It's kinda like you're guilty until proven innocent."

"Isn't that anti-American?"

"Welcome to my America, son." Elijah laughed his slow, ironic chuckle.

Tristen stayed standing as the judge stood up and grumbled his way out of court.

"That went well," Tristen commented.

Elijah shot a look towards Lamia's lawyer. Tristen got the hint: no talking until they were clear of the courtroom. Or clear of the other lawyer, at least.

"Let's go get a coffee and sandwich before I head back to work," Elijah said as they stepped into the fresh morning air. "You aren't my only client, you know. But you're one of the few I'll have breakfast with. There's a bagel shop around the corner here. I used to go all the time when I was in court more."

"I thought lawyers were always in court," Tristen said.

"Nah, the smart ones convince their clients to settle before going to court," Elijah said with a wink. His wide smile exposed his perfectly white teeth, reminding Tristen he should go to the dentist sometime soon.

Before he could ask more questions, his phone started ringing. "Sorry, I gotta take this as we walk. Do you mind?"

"Go ahead," Elijah said.

"Lin?"

"Whasssuuuup," Lin yelled into the phone. By the background noise, Tristen assumed he was at a party. Or an amusement park. "How's my producer? You like it when I call you that? Hm? Yes, baby. I'm on the phone. With my producer."

Tristen waited for Lin to return his focus to the call as he and Elijah crossed the street.

"You want a latte or plain coffee?" Elijah asked in a low tone.

"Plain," Tristen mouthed as Lin got back on the line. Tristen plopped into a plastic chair to endure the conversation and wait for his coffee.

"She loves it when I say I have a producer. Thinks it's so sexy," Lin said as the background noise diminished. "These girls are crazy, man."

"I thought you were in Singapore. Why you speaking English?"

"I'm in Bollywood, producer," Lin said. "Only language I can speak here to the ladies is English. But I'll be on my way to you very soon. Are you ready?"

"You're coming now?"

Elijah came back to the table Tristen had chosen with two paper cups of coffee and two breakfast sandwiches. Tristen could have kissed him. His stomach had been growling since before the judge took the bench.

"Soon, man. Soon. What day is today?"

Tristen had the date seared in his brain. For two weeks he'd stressed he would sleep in and not make it to the court on time. "It's June twentieth."

"Summer, baby," Lin yelled as the music in the background was turned up. "We're gonna make a summer album. I'll be there in a week. Maybe less."

"A week?" Tristen lost his appetite. Elijah squinted at him and the sandwich he'd dropped back onto the paper. One eyebrow shot up at him, but Tristen was too busy scrambling to think to explain anything. "Uh, okay, I found a studio where we can record."

"In Cincinnati?"

"No, in Kentucky."

"I love Kentucky girls," Lin yelled into the phone. "You have my song ready?"

"It'll be ready."

What sounded like several female voices called out Lin's name, and he giggled. "I'll let you know, producer. I'll let you know. See you soon."

"What's wrong?" Elijah asked around his last bite of sandwich when Tristen hung up. "Why aren't you eating?"

"I didn't want to chew on the phone," Tristen lied. His hunger was creeping back slowly as he tried to digest Lin's news.

"Doesn't sound like that's the problem," Elijah said. He leaned back in the metal chair and watched Tristen, making him feel like bacteria under a microscope. "Sounds more like someone took your celebratory mood away."

"That was Lin, my one and only client. He says he's coming into town soon."

"And you're not ready?"

Tristen took a bite before answering. He wished he had something different to say. "No. I'm not ready. I've been helping Ivy and Jared set up those boxing summer camps, and somehow I agreed to helping out my friend Rob with his camp, and there

there's this thing with Lamia. I mean, seriously, the last thing I want is to start making money that her lawyer seizes from me."

"You don't worry about her lawyer," Elijah said, shaking his head. "You worry about yourself. You've had how long now to get prepared for this guy?"

Tristen shrugged, but Elijah intensified his stare. "Like four months. But—"

"Stop before you embarrass yourself with lame excuses. You're worse than my kindergarten lawyers."

Tristen took a deep breath and looked away to give himself a break from Elijah's penetrating gaze.

"Tristen, look at me. You can't squirm away 'cause I say things you don't like. The truth is you had time to figure this out. And you look like you're gonna throw up from the stress just because of him saying he's coming. Instead of being excited to get started on this next step of your life."

Tristen groaned. "There is no next step after Lin, though. He's the only person I got, Elijah. And anyway, what the hell do I know about producing music? Lin is happy with me 'cause he doesn't know any better."

"You think someone else could have done a better job than you?"

Tristen had an immediate answer. "Of course. Yes. Someone else could easily have done what I did. The man's talented as shit and needed hardly any coaching. I did minimal editing, because he didn't need it."

"What about the music?"

"Some was live, some mixed."

"Did you do the mixing?"

"Yes," Tristen said, his mood lifting slowly. Lin was coming, so he'd have to get ready. Elijah was right, it was his only choice. He couldn't drop the ball.

Elijah pointed his paper coffee cup at Tristen, his face serious. "You're gonna get your ass ready for this guy, and you're gonna hype yourself, and you're gonna produce a killer album. Better than the first one. And when it climbs the charts and other people start asking for you to do the same for them, you're gonna be ready with a studio and a plan. Do you understand me?"

Tristen nodded.

"And you're gonna do great."

That part Tristen wasn't so sure about, but he didn't say so.

"Come on. You gotta get back before your mama thinks you've abandoned her."

"I won't make it," Tristen said, checking his watch. "But it's no big deal. It's really Jared's thing. I might stay in town and see if I can find a better studio than the one at the camp. Come on, I'll at least take you back to your office."

Elijah acquiesced, throwing his arm around Tristen as they left. Tristen basked in the few minutes he had left with his mentor, wondering if Elijah knew how much he appreciated him.

Nine

Tristen stayed in Cincinnati until Wednesday afternoon, exploring several spots he could turn into a music studio. Every night he scoured the web for abandoned buildings or warehouses or some other semi-secluded buildings that had potential for a recording studio. The dream was to buy a large building for cheap and slowly renovate it as he made a profit, but that dream was starting to fall apart.

The cheapest places were obviously in the worst shape. The more he visited real estate, the more he understood that the pictures agents and sellers posted on the internet didn't accurately portray the building. Somehow, they managed to keep most of the trash, the broken walls and ceilings, and bare pipes out of the ads—and a wide-angle lens made the rooms look huge. Worse than all that was the way the real estate agents talked on and on about what a great opportunity and deal each place was, even while they stood under dripping ceilings, on top of broken floors and looking through punched-out walls.

Every day Tristen thanked God Elijah was taking on his case pro bono.

There were plenty of times in his life when he'd paused his dream because of setbacks, but this time he was determined to keep going. Even before Elijah's pep talk he'd been looking at places, but after Elijah egged him on, he'd actually called and set up appointments. Elijah was right, after all. Tristen was going to have to work his ass off, like anyone else who wanted a dream to come true.

On Wednesday, after looking at a small house with a flooded basement, he drove back to Pelton and straight to Ivy's house. He'd done it so many times in the past few months that it was semi automatic, a straight shot from the city into the little town. Down the cute main street, Tristen turned left into his old neighborhood and wove around, coming to a stop in front of a small box house painted blue with a black door.

He hadn't understood the black door at first, but he had painted it for Ivy. Now he had to admit it looked good.

"Afternoon," his mother called out from her front porch, where she sat in a patio chair, knees propped up against the arm rest. There were certain things she could do that made her look much younger than she was, and that position was one of them. As strange as it might be to admit it about his mother, she looked like she could be an influencer with her long, blonde hair, perfect skin, skinny leggings under an oversized shirt, and her minimal makeup.

He was glad she wasn't. The last thing Ivy needed to start was the social media rollercoaster of likes. Or, God forbid, receiving comments that sent her spiraling. She was doing well between the group counseling and individual therapy.

"Afternoon, Ivy," Tristen said, trudging up the walkway and then the stairs. He stopped only three stairs up and plopped down. Ivy reached into her cooler and handed him a beer.

"I'd offer you a joint or some gummies, but I'm trying to stop those now. Haven't had any yet today."

Tristen smiled at her. "I'm proud of you, Ivy."

He had to give her credit for trying. It couldn't be easy quitting after smoking for almost thirty years.

"How'd it go on Monday?"

Tristen shrugged as he took a slug of beer. The sun was hitting him directly in the eyes at this angle. "More or less how we expected, I guess," he said, pulling out his sunglasses. "Elijah didn't seem surprised, but man, the judge is a bit of a harasser, and the other lawyer is slimy."

"He's a lawyer."

"Elijah is a lawyer. He isn't slimy."

"That's 'cause you like Elijah. But I bet if he was sitting on the other side of the court room, you'd think he looked slimy. That's how we think as humans, you know? Always judging those we think are against us."

Tristen turned to look up at her. "Are you going to therapy or studying philosophy?"

Ivy laughed, obviously pleased with herself. "You know, the more I go, the smarter I feel. It's weird. I never felt smart my whole life. I struggled in school, and I let opportunities to go up the ladder at the factory slip by because I didn't think I could handle the jobs. I always thought of myself as stupid, and there wasn't much I could do about it. Sometimes the simplest things confused me."

"Possibly a consequence of smoking joints and taking pills?"

Ivy kicked the air close to his shoulder.

He grabbed it and pretended to wince. "I'm just saying, maybe substance abuse doesn't make us very smart."

"Okay, you probably have a point, but what I'm saying is that for the first time I feel like a fog has lifted from my brain, and all of a sudden the things I've learned throughout my life are organized enough for me to understand and articulate."

"You've even expanded your vocabulary," Tristan said. He squinted at Ivy when she laughed.

"What's going on over here?" called a familiar voice from the street. It was Ivy's cousin, Bobbi. Tristen had grown up with her living just across the street his entire life. She was like a second mother to him and his brother. "Looks like a party I wasn't invited to."

"Well shoot, your chair over here is empty. No one's sitting in it. Shouldn't think I'd have to invite you after all these years," Ivy called back. No insult to Bobbi's weight, or suggestion that her limp made her too slow to get to the party, or anything. Tristen wondered if Bobbi noticed the absence of insults, but when he tried to share a knowing look with her, she only had eyes for Ivy.

Tristen stood to allow Bobbi to lumber by, then sat back in his spot. Ivy dangled a cold beer out for her cousin to take.

"We were talking about how smart I am," she told Bobbi as she sat down.

"The girl who almost flunked out of school?" Bobbi retorted.

"That's what I'm saying," Ivy said, rising up from her slumped position. "That's what I'm trying to say."

Bobbi waved her hand as though flicking the conversation page and looked at Tristen. "I wanna hear what happened in Cincinnati. What did the judge say? Did he drop the case?"

"No." Tristen sighed. "He didn't throw it out, not even after we showed that I don't have the tattoo that Talon does. Unfortunately, she remembered about my small tattoo that most people don't know about. I'm telling you, she knows I'm not the kid's father, but she doesn't care. She's gonna try to get me to pay for him."

"Guess you two could always have been with her at the same time," Ivy said.

"Gross, Ivy."

She shook her head, grinning. "Sorry, guess I watch too much daytime television. It happens, you know. People out there are kinda crazy and gross."

Tristen cringed at the thought. It was bad enough that Talon had slept with Lamia years after he had.

"Talon and Tristen aren't just any people," Bobbi said, picking up another beer. "And I sure didn't need to hear about what my nephews do in their private lives."

"On the one hand I feel a little bit bad for her. Lamia, I mean."

Bobbi and Ivy stared at him. Probably because all he had ever done was complain about her up until then.

"I don't feel bad enough to drop the case, but I think she was actually in love with Talon and is a bit heartbroken about him not being around for her. As much as I feel betrayed by him, I can see why she does as well." Tristen set his empty beer bottle aside and took another from Bobbi. "Of course, my sympathy stops at her trying to milk me for the money Talon is supposed to pay. She wants forty thousand dollars in back child support."

"Forty thousand?" Bobbi and Ivy spoke at the same time.

"Damn, I would have loved to have forty thousand when I was raising my kids. Would have really helped paying off the house, and maybe the car," Bobbi said.

"You're telling me," Ivy agreed. "That would have been something. Although, depending on the year, I might have blown the money on a long weekend."

Bobbi shook her head. "You never got that bad—except right after Aimee died."

Ivy touched Bobbi's arm; she looked like she was trying not to cry. Aimee was Tristen's sister, who had died of an overdose when she was a teen. It had taken a long time for Ivy to process Aimee's death. It had taken a long time for all of them.

"You two not fighting is so weird," Tristen teased. He stood up to stretch as the two women smiled at each other. "I'm thinking of asking for a DNA test."

"DNA?" Ivy asked. "Don't you think you should talk to Talon first?"

"Why? You think it might not be his? I guess I wouldn't put it past him or Lamia not to have been exclusive."

"There are lots of shows on television that prove hardly anyone is ever only with one person. I mean, who do you know that is monogamous their whole life?"

"I was only with Meegan when I was with her," Tristen pointed out.

"Didn't she cheat?" Bobbi asked.

"Ha, ha," he said as Bobbi and Ivy laughed. "She claims she didn't."

"You breaking up with Meegan can't be blamed on Talon," Ivy said, rolling her eyes. "By the way, I have something to tell you two, which I might as well do with you both here. Especially since this conversation is boring."

"Because it's not about you?" Bobbi asked.

Ivy swatted at her cousin, then took in a deep breath and waited, building drama. That much hadn't changed.

"I'll be moving out of this house," she finally announced.

"What?" Tristen looked at Bobbi, but she didn't look surprised at all. "I put my ass on the line to save this house."

Ivy pursed her lips together. "I knew you'd be upset."

"Well, I for one expected this," Bobbi said. "You're hardly here at all."

"Do you hear yourself?" Tristen asked. He stood up, needing to move. "Why didn't we just let everything go to default six months ago, then? I got arrested saving this house!" He tried to calm himself by taking a swig of beer and waited.

"I know," Ivy said quietly. "But things were different then. And it just makes no sense to have two houses."

She held her hand up, and for the first time Tristen noticed something shiny on her ring finger.

"Oh, shit." Now he felt like an ass. "You're getting married? To Owen?"

"Uh, to your father, yes?" Ivy said. She looked hurt. Her lip quivered slightly.

"Is he? Should we get some DNA evidence?" Tristen said, mocking his own pain, but Ivy didn't laugh. He took a breath and tried again. "Sorry. Congratulations, Ivy."

"Thank you," she said, smiling again. "That's all I wanted to hear."

"But back to the house that I saved. What're you going to do with it?"

"Look, back in January, I didn't know if Owen and I were seriously getting back together or not. You helped me not become homeless, Tristen."

"I know. I was there."

"Okay. Then can't you be happy for me now?"

"Sure, I'm happy for you. But what're your plans with the house?"

"You could rent it out," Bobbi suggested.

Ivy shook her head. "I'm going to move in with the man who loves me. The one who treated me the best of any other. He's taken me out for dinners and made sure I got to counseling and taken me to my meetings, and he's planning on taking me traveling. He gave me the opportunity to prove myself to him and to myself. And he gave me space."

"Space?"

"To figure myself out. Get rid of my hurts. Make some big decisions and learn to love myself."

"Love yourself?" Bobbi asked. "Thought you loved yourself plenty."

Ivy hummed, and once again Tristen was surprised an insult didn't slip out of her mouth. "Maybe if I had been taught to have the confidence in myself enough to know that I was worth treating well, then I wouldn't have made some certain mistakes in my life. Maybe I never would have left Owen behind."

"Like having us?" Tristen asked.

He was kidding, but Ivy contemplated the question.

"I don't regret having you," she said. "But I think I'd have been a better mom if I had, well…"

She left everyone hanging, her last word disappearing with the setting sun. The last ray slipped past the houses across the street, and Tristen finally pushed his sunglasses up.

"Can't change the past," Bobbi said, heaving herself up off the chair. "I'm proud of you, and happy for you and Owen both. Are we having family dinner some time soon?"

Ivy shrugged. "Ask your nephew."

"You'll do anything to get me to family dinner, won't you?" Tristen asked.

"You bet."

"Fine. You gonna tell me about the house then?"

"I'll have worked out the details by then," she said.

Tristen shook his head and let it go. Ivy and Bobbi continued talking about wedding dresses and flowers, but he wasn't listening. Decision made, he sent a text to Elijah's new kindergarten lawyer, Martin, letting him know he wanted a DNA test. That should move the whole thing forward quicker so he could finally be done with it. The results might affect Talon's life, but Tristen had to stop putting his brother before himself. Only then would he finally be able to move on with his own life like everyone else seemed to be doing.

Ten

By her third Wednesday market, Scarlett was a veteran. Since Ben was too tired and had complained for over an hour the night before, she'd begged Camila to help her. Camila had agreed to work for a free order of brownies. It was more than a fair exchange.

Thinking about the amount Scarlett owed Johnny made her so angry she could choke. What he was doing was unfair. For two nights she'd stayed up worrying and arguing in her head about it, until last night, when she'd finally looked up the laws on the internet to vindicate herself—only to find out she was wrong. Without a signed contract, Johnny had every right to tell her to get out.

She hoped she could pacify him with micro payments. The moment she got money, it would go straight to him.

"All this okay?" Camila asked, sipping her coffee as she stepped back to admire their work. The sun was up and shining bright, which boded well. People should be out and about and ready to eat. Problem was, a new booth had popped up with delicious-looking salads and smoothies, and another with artisan cupcakes decorated with Swiss meringue frosting in pastel colors. The competition was heating up.

"I think this is as good as it gets," Scarlett said. She straightened her T-shirt and positioned herself in the middle of her tent, ready to take orders.

"I think your stuff looks the most appealing," Camila told her as they watched the other vendor finish setting up.

"Even more than the empanadas guy?"

Camila thought about it, then nodded. "Even better than his. I mean, all he has is that micro-oven. It's a bit strange. I don't like approaching things that look strange."

Scarlett's first customers were vendors looking to feed themselves. When she'd first started at the Saturday market, she had felt obligated to give a discount to other vendors. She was over that by now; the market was enough of an investment as it was. After paying the season fees of five hundred dollars, she'd realized she needed a tent after a disastrous Saturday morning with sudden rainstorms. And then another table. And then some decorations to make her table look professional and not empty all the time. And that was before she'd spent the money on the local warehouse membership so she could stock up on the nine pounds of butter and twenty pounds of flour she used weekly.

"Things are looking good." Camila smiled, her dark eyes shiny under the black baseball cap. Even without makeup on, she was gorgeous with her full lips, dark lashes and pore-less skin. Scarlett pulled out her lipstick to try to compete.

"Things have to get better," she admitted, checking her face in the mirror. Her eyes were lined with worry. "I need the money. At least I had enough supplies this month and don't need to buy any more. Especially since your grandma gave me all that flour."

Camila laughed. When her grandmother had shut down her online tortilla business, she had given all her supplies to Scarlett. "Why you need the money so bad? Want a new cell phone?"

The joke between them was how long Scarlett could continue with her out-of-date cell phone. Camila was usually only one or two behind the latest.

"No," Scarlett said, pushing her friend playfully. "I gotta pay rent."

"I thought Rhoda paid your rent?"

"Apparently she decided not to," Scarlett said, letting the conversation go as a gorgeous young woman with curly red hair slowed down.

"Hi," the woman greeted them, a little too forcefully. "All these are homemade?"

"Yes," Scarlett answered patiently. People asked that question at least ten times every market, and each time Scarlett wished she could retort, "What would be the point if they weren't?" But she didn't. Better customer service not to.

The woman laughed. "That's probably a dumb question, isn't it? I was wondering if you were local. You are local, right?"

"I live in Brax," Scarlett said, watching the woman turn scones and muffins over.

"Rob, look at this! Should we get a loaf?"

"Get whatever you want, babe." The voice came from a man almost as beautiful as his wife. He was tall, with shockingly black hair and bronzed skin. "Morning."

"Good morning."

"Hubba, hubba," Camila breathed over Scarlett's shoulder. Scarlett swatted her away to finish the transaction. "Who is that hunk of a man? You know I love men with long hair."

Scarlett smiled sweetly as the woman tapped her credit card, hoping she couldn't hear Camila.

"Stop drooling, Camila," she said once the couple were walking away. "Why are you always attracted to men who are already taken?"

Camila sighed. "It's my bad luck. Oh, look. It's Cory."

"Hey, thought I'd find you here," Cory said. He smiled at Scarlett and winked at Camila. Scarlett reminded herself not to be jealous. Cory was a flirt, but Camila would never sleep with him. Not while he and Scarlett were on and off again. "Rob, what're you doing here?"

He gave Scarlett her own wink as he maneuvered the beautiful couple away from her stand. Scarlett rolled her eyes at him, shaking the sandwich she had set aside for him. He doubled back and grabbed it before continuing on with the couple.

"Why is that man so sexy?"

"Which one? Cory or the other one?"

Camila groaned as she stretched her slim body. "Both of them. You and Cory still knocking boots?"

"Only when convenient."

"It's that guy," Camila suddenly exclaimed, a little too loud. The customers nearby gave her a disapproving look. She either didn't notice or didn't care. "It's the guy from the bar. Didn't you say you saw him last week? Look at him. He's so gorgeous. And I don't like blond men. But he's like a dirty blond, you know? So not as bad as the bleach-blond boys who burn like lobsters in the sun. I need my man to be able to hold his own at the beach."

"Are you okay?" Scarlett asked, laughing at her friend.

"No, he's too pretty. Call him over here, Scarlett."

"No," Scarlett said, still laughing. Her body flushed with heat at the idea of calling Tristen over. A heat she hadn't felt in a long time.

"Why not? You know him."

"Barely!"

"But he said you were pretty. I heard him, remember that? How can you not be chasing after him? Wouldn't you like to be on his arm?"

"You are so boy-crazy," Scarlett said, peeling Camila's fingers off her forearm. She'd squeezed so hard she'd left marks. "Geez, Camila. You get too excited."

"I've got hot blood," Camila said, wiggling her hips. "He's coming over. Look alive. Maybe put more lipstick on."

Scarlett had to swat her friend's hand away from her face. "Camila, stop. Go take care of that couple over there."

"I will," Camila sang under her breath. "Good luck."

There wasn't time for Scarlett to tell her to shut up before Tristen was there.

"Hello," he said. His voice was so sexy Scarlett's heart fluttered.

"Good morning. Not working today at the gym?"

There were beads of sweat on his forehead. "Just about to go in," he said. She noticed he was breathing slightly harder than he should be. "Was out for a run first."

Another reason she shouldn't even bother trying to date him. He was all muscle where she was soft rolls. Not that he wanted to date her; he was probably being nice. Camila was much more his type.

"Hello." Camila, as though hearing her name in Scarlett's thoughts, threw her arms around Scarlett's shoulder and beamed up at Tristen. He smiled back. Scarlett's heart sank. "Nice to see you again. It's Tristen, right? Are you here to buy something, or did you come to flirt with my friend Scarlett?"

Camila laughed. She was even more charming when she laughed. Tristen joined her, but Scarlett could barely look at them. She didn't want to know how funny the question was to Tristen.

"I'm here with a large order. After last week, the guys kept pestering me about when you were coming back in. I realized I didn't have your phone number, so I thought I'd stop by. In case you sold everything today."

"Here's her phone number," Camila said, writing it on his hand with a pen. "But you can still buy stuff. Let me see the list. I'll get it packed while you and Scarlett get to know each other more."

Scarlett wanted to throttle her friend—once she survived this situation. Never again would she accept Camila's help with the Wednesday market. Or any market.

"Nice day, isn't it?" Tristen asked.

Scarlett agreed with a nod. Resorting to weather talk was a bad sign. Obviously, he liked her sandwiches and sausage rolls and nothing more.

Suddenly he started to chuckle. Scarlett met his eyes again.

"I'm sorry," he said. "I'm so out of practice. I mean, I came here because the guys were talking about your stuff all week and because I was looking forward to seeing you, but then I thought this morning that you might not come in. Like, what if you sold everything and didn't need us? So, in a panic I decided to take my run through here and see you in person. Which is why I'm here and now can't think of anything to say other than that the weather is nice."

Scarlett grinned, suddenly feeling elated. "A lot to unpack there."

His sweaty cheeks flushed. "Can I call you?" he asked. "Is this actually your number?"

Scarlett nodded. "You can call your order in, and I'll make sure to have it ready."

He looked left and right before leaning in. Scarlett's heart beat wildly in her chest as he finally looked at her, then cleared his throat. "What if I call you for something else? Like a date?"

"All ready," Camila announced, breaking up the moment. "Here you are. I'll take your card. Oh, did I interrupt something?"

"What would you be interrupting?" Cory demanded, appearing and squeezing his way closer to the table. Tristen backed away with his bag. "Got that sandwich for me, Scarlett? Hey, Tristen, I told you her stuff is the best."

"You did," Tristen said. Scarlett wondered if it was her imagination or if his voice had actually cooled. "I'll call you, Scarlett."

Scarlett tried not to get her hopes too high. Though even if all he wanted was some fun, she might take him up on it. Make Camila jealous for once.

"Okay. It was nice to see you," she said. She didn't dare watch him go in case Cory was in a weird mood. He might chase Tristen down and say something lewd. "How's it going, Cory?"

Camila moved on to attend other customers, leaving her and Cory alone.

"Rumor has it you're alone this week."

"Only until tomorrow," Scarlett said.

"Let's move our date up then. Eight o'clock tonight."

Scarlett nodded. She could work out her fantasies about Tristen with Cory without getting her heart splintered. A win-win.

Eleven

"WHAT'S WRONG?" CORY ASKED, looking down at Scarlett sprawled out on her bedsheets. He had shown up at eight on the dot, just as he'd promised. A few hours later, she felt calm and satiated for the first time in weeks, and yet she couldn't stop worrying about Ben and Eric and Rhoda and where she would live.

"Nothing," she said quickly. Cory quirked an eyebrow up at her, his dark eyes roaming her body as he buttoned his jeans. "Nothing you need to worry about."

"Ben?"

Scarlett nodded. "And Eric. I don't think I told you, since we seemed to have skipped the conversation part," she quipped, drawing laughter from Cory. They hadn't even eaten dinner until after a quick first round. That was how things usually went between them. For a blissful moment, Cory took away her worries. "But Rhoda hasn't sent any money in a while, and whatever. It's a whole situation."

"What are you saying?" Cory asked. Scarlett waved the question off, but he stood by, waiting for an answer.

"Ben's been assigned a guardian ad litem," she finally said, hating the words as they tumbled out. Her heart raced every time she even thought of it. "Eric says he's asking for full custody."

"Eric? The guy who's never around 'cause he's off working the oil fields, or whatever?"

"Yeah."

Cory snorted. "He won't get it. I mean, I guess Eric is his dad. Does Ben want to live with him?"

"I suppose he might. And if he does, then maybe I shouldn't get in his way. I don't know. I guess I hadn't considered it. I always thought Rhoda would come back and take Ben. That's how I saw it."

"Do you want to keep Ben?"

Scarlett sat up and thought about the question. "I never really got as far as that either. He's Rhoda's, you know?"

"And no one takes Rhoda's stuff," Cory agreed as Scarlett said it. They both burst into laughter, though it was short-lived. Rhoda always used to say that phrase to all the kids in the neighborhood. Her delivery of it had earned her fearful respect from any of the younger kids around.

"Remember when she threatened Nikki cause she'd taken her soda to test her?" Cory asked, chuckling.

Scarlett nodded, the memory of Rhoda holding the younger girl by the neck of her T-shirt up in the air popping into her head instantly. Nikki had been saved when the cheap cotton ripped, sending her to the ground in a dull thump.

Not for the first time in her adult life, she wondered what Rhoda was doing now to keep whatever reputation she had made for herself. Wherever she was.

"Anyway, Scar, maybe it's time to let Ben go and let Eric take responsibility. It would be easier for you, building a business and all."

Scarlett snapped out of her thoughts. She didn't like the sound of letting Ben go.

"I guess so. Anyway, the judge isn't gonna let me have him. Especially not when I lose this place." She looked at Cory, hoping he'd bite.

He did. "What do you mean, 'lose this place'?"

"Johnny came by and told me I owe three months of rent. Rhoda usually puts money into the account and it drafts out automatically. I've never checked on it because I've never had to. Johnny says it's been empty for six months now."

"Six? You're six months in the hole for this place?"

Scarlett hesitated. "It's fine. I almost have the three thousand Johnny wants right away." That was a lie, but she hoped Cory wouldn't see through it. She had almost two thousand.

Cory narrowed his eyes. Scarlett coughed and avoided his gaze, but she could feel it on her, wearing her down.

"I thought Rhoda would come through. I mean, that was the agreement. I watch Ben and she would pay for the rent. And she's done it for, what? Almost five years?"

Cory grabbed his jean jacket from the floor and put it on. Scarlett had stopped offering to let him stay the night years before because he always said no. She wouldn't mind having a strong, warm body next to her in bed, but she didn't want to ask again when she knew the answer.

"Maybe you should get a job, Scarlett."

"What about following my dream?" she asked, swallowing back her disappointment at his change in subject. She had hoped he would offer to help.

Cory shook his head. "I told you once already that you can't rely on Rhoda being around all the time, and look. The time is here. Something probably happened to her."

The words hit one of the constant worries she always held inside. "No way. Nothing's happened to her. Rhoda's fine. I mean, imagine the world without Rhoda. It's not possible."

Cory glanced at the door. Scarlett sat up. She wished she was his girlfriend so she could wrap her arms around him and ask him to come back to bed. Ask him to soothe away the fears he had opened up.

"Fine, fine. But you should still get a job."

"I have several jobs."

"Scarlett, you can't stay here like this forever. You're pretty and you're smart. Don't you want more from life?"

Scarlett understood why Cory wanted more, but she found it hard to believe in something better. She was twenty-four with no college education, barely remembered anything from high school, and couldn't think about what she could possibly do to 'get more from life'. Making more money would be nice, but she wasn't willing to strip for it, and she had no talent in anything useful besides making bread.

"Look, Scarlett," Cory said, rubbing his warm hands up and down her cold arms. "Having a dream is great, but maybe you should get a real job for now. At least something so you can pay back Johnny. And if Rhoda comes through with the payments, you'll have extra money. Nothing wrong with that, right?"

"At an office?" She'd always wanted to be smart enough to work at an office. Wear those cute skirts and one of those badge things to go up an elevator.

"Not an office. You lasted like two weeks at the bank, remember?" Cory said. "You need something that fits you. Something you won't get fired from."

Scarlett was glad the room was dark to hide her embarrassment. "Okay, sure. But what kind of job would I get? I don't want to work at the grocery store again. They don't pay enough, anyway. I can't work the gas station hours, and Tory is the foreman at the factory. I am not working for him."

"I know." Cory rubbed his forehead, something he'd done since he was a kid when he was trying to figure something out or get them out of trouble. "I've got something in mind that will be perfect for you. But let me make sure it's still available, okay?"

Scarlett looked at him, unashamed to show her hopefulness. "Really?"

He gave her a peck on the cheek. "Really. But let me look into it."

Scarlett nodded, then followed him to the door. The invitation for him to stay was on the tip of her tongue, but she held it back.

"Are you setting up at the market tomorrow?" he asked.

"Of course. Will you be stopping by to check me out?" Scarlett asked with a laugh.

Cory didn't laugh with her. "I want to make sure you still have money coming in. I could probably spot you a hundred or so. To get you through. If you need it."

"I'm fine," she said. Taking two hundred would change hardly anything, except to strip her of the meager pride she had left. And talking about money right after sex made her feel sick. "But tell all your coworkers to come to my stand at the market."

He tapped her nose before opening the door. "See you, then. Try to get some sleep."

Scarlett watched him go down the hall, then shut her door and went to bed alone. She had to get up early to finish the sausage rolls, anyway. Cory would have been in the way if he had stayed.

Twelve

"Welcome to Camp Soul! You must be Scarlett. I'm Dariana."

Scarlett was pulling some samples out of her truck and arranging them into a basket when the voice startled her. She turned to find the gorgeous woman who had bought from her at the market coming straight towards her, hand outstretched. She still had no wrinkles or sunspots anywhere, and her warm smile was as genuine as it had been a few days before.

She was not only pretty but gave off an unpretentious aurora Scarlett wasn't used to from pretty girls. Despite the genuine feeling, Dariana still made Scarlett feel self-conscious in her baggy boyfriend jeans and a T-shirt that read *Life is what you bake of it* curved around a loaf of sourdough bread. Skinny girls always made her feel more self-conscious, though.

Dariana's hand was small, but she had a firm shake. "I like your T-shirt."

Scarlett looked down, though she knew perfectly well what it said. "Thank you. I appreciate you interviewing me for this job."

Cory had actually come through, calling her just twelve hours after leaving her apartment with an appointment for a job interview at a place called Camp Soul. At this point, Scarlett would almost have taken anything. Thankfully, the job had to do with baking and not working a cash register or something else boring.

"I appreciate you coming in," Dariana said. "And that Cory knew you. The spot just became vacant, and camp starts next week. I've been scrambling, I have to say, so when Cory called, I think I cried with relief."

Scarlett tried to smile, though the story sounded a bit dramatic. "I brought some samples," she said, holding up the basket. "Two sourdough breads, a sweet bread, some croissants and, of course, the brownies."

"That sounds heavenly," Dariana said. She smelled the basket and sighed. "We're excited to offer good, quality food to the kids. And it's a super bonus that you can make this stuff from scratch already. I was trying to find a place where I could order it from and it was certainly starting to strain the budget, you know?"

"I bet," Scarlett said, a bit overcome by Dariana's enthusiasm. "Can you tell me about the job? The hours and what you expect?"

"Of course," Dariana said, her lively energy buzzing off her. "We have Mrs. Beatty, who is the head cook at the camp, and we have Maria, who works like a sous chef or whatever it's called, helping Mrs. Beatty with some of the cooking. Maria also serves the kids in the cafeteria with Rosalyn and Sarah and Tony. They take care of the cafeteria space as well. But Mrs. Beatty was hoping we could find someone who wanted to work more early mornings and help her with maybe some prep as well as baking the sweets and breads on site as much as possible. You would be here from early in the morning, around seven, until about two in the afternoon. Of course, with you making the bread and such, I also need to know if you would need to come back in during the evening hours, or how you wanted to handle that. You might have some time to work on the breads while you're here, or you could stay later than one, as well. We would pay you for those hours as long as they are you making bread for the camp."

"How much is the pay?" Scarlett asked. She'd been offered enough jobs for crap pay in the past that she no longer put up with not asking the question outright, but Dariana didn't flinch.

"Fifteen an hour."

Double the state's minimum wage. Scarlett couldn't help being impressed—or wanting to shout that she'd take it. But there was still the issue of hours that she had to work through in her head. "And you're thinking from seven in the morning until two in the afternoon? Is this Monday through Friday or Saturday as well?"

She wouldn't be able to go to the Wednesday market anymore unless she hired Camila. And she would be late picking up Ben.

But the bigger problem was how to get Ben to the boxing camp. He couldn't ride his bike into Pelton; it was too far, and there was no sidewalk on the country highway. The only solution Scarlett could think of was to drop him off in Pelton early, though he'd be pissed. At least it was on the way to Camp Soul.

"Yes, seven to two Monday to Friday, and then figuring out where and when you would make the bread. Cory told me how long it takes you to do it. Like I said, we will pay you for those hours. Also, I'll need you to let Mrs. Beatty know what ingredients she needs to order," Dariana said as they passed by long cabins with instruments painted on the doors. "These are where the kids take music lessons during the camp. Oh, my husband's right over there. He inherited this camp from his dad—I'm not sure if you know him?"

Dariana pointed at the man Camila had drooled over at the market a few days before. He looked like he could be a cowboy in his working jeans and T-shirt that fit snugly against his muscled chest. Scarlett tried not to stare or salivate, but she couldn't deny the pang of jealousy that Dariana had a husband, and so young, who looked like that.

"Rob, come over and meet Scarlett," Dariana called. Rob looked up from the window he was painting, his face breaking into a smile at the sight of his wife.

"Scarlett," he called out, jogging over to them. He grabbed her free hand and shook it vigorously. He was handsome, with a sharp nose that wasn't too big and a soft smile. His eyes met hers and never dipped down to her chest.

Happily married man. Scarlett hadn't seen one in a while.

"I'm so glad Cory knows you. We were nervous we wouldn't get the position filled before camp started. Did you tell her what we were thinking as far as hours and everything?"

Dariana nodded. "Oh, but I forgot to tell you, Scarlett—Cory let us know you would need Wednesday mornings off for the market."

"Which is fine," Rob jumped in. "We can work around that. And did you tell her that Ben can come to the camp, if she needs him to?"

"Cory told you about Ben?"

Dariana nodded. "He said you have Ben to take care of, which is no problem. Maria has kids as well, and so does Tony. The weeks where camp has open registration, which means a private church or diocese hasn't arranged to be here, the kids get to participate in the activities for free. You need to sign them up. Otherwise, we have an agreement with a woman near here who runs a daycare open to older kids in the summertime and gives a discount to our employees. Cory wasn't sure what you'd be interested in for Ben."

Scarlett wasn't sure either. "Right now, Ben is enrolled in a boxing camp for two weeks," she told Dariana.

"Top Gym's boxing camp? Rob's nephew is enrolled in that, too. Do you know Tristen?"

Scarlett cleared her throat. "I've met him."

"Tristen is such a nice guy," Dariana said. Scarlett glanced at Rob, who didn't seem put out at all that his wife's voice sounded a little dreamier than before. "Don't you think, Scarlett?"

"He seems nice," Scarlett said cautiously.

"Listen, I have an idea," Rob said. "Tristen could probably bring Ben back here with him each day after camp. I mean, if that would be helpful for you. He's helping me out a bit around here, so he offered to bring my nephew back to the camp every day. Want me to ask him if he can bring Ben?"

"Oh, no, thank you," Scarlett said quickly. "That isn't necessary. I'll figure it out."

"It's no big deal. He'll be bringing Adam back anyway. He's supposed to be here soon. Let me call him."

Scarlett opened her mouth to protest more, but then closed it. Rob was already dialing, and the truth was that it *would* help.

"You want to come with us to meet Mrs. Beatty?" Dariana asked Rob. "Scarlett brought us stuff to try. Her stuff."

"Seriously?" Rob asked, peeking into the basket. He glanced over at the window he had been painting. "Dang, voicemail. I'll clean this up, and then come. You know I can't resist carbs. Then I'll find Tristen and ask him about taking Ben."

He brushed a quick kiss against Dariana's lips before jogging back to his painting. Dariana turned them towards a right turn in the road, looking as though she was on cloud nine. Scarlett would be too, if she had a man who treated her like that.

"So how do you know Top Gym?" Dariana asked. "Rob says it's been there forever, but I had never heard of it. But then I'm from Lexington."

"Oh, well, Ben's dad found out about the gym. I knew Jared, who works there, back when we were kids, although he's older than me. Jared was friends with Cory's brother."

"And you and Cory are together?" Dariana asked.

Scarlett hesitated. "No," she finally said. "We're friends. We go way back."

Dariana smiled brightly. "Well, friendship can always deepen into something more. I like Cory. He seems nice. Although I have to say that I don't really know him that well. But the times I met him he was nice."

"He is," Scarlett said.

"So you know Jared. And you know Tristen. I think Rob is more friends with Tristen than Jared. Did you know he was in a band? His brother is in one called Art of Rendering, which I had never heard of before Rob told me. I guess they're pretty big, though. But before that, Tristen and his brother started a band called The Seethers. And they're pretty good. I like their music, and I'm a little sad they won't be coming out with a new album.

But I guess the music industry must be hard. I mean, if he came back to work at a gym in Pelton? Maybe music doesn't pay."

Dariana's familiarity with Tristen shot a bigger flash of jealousy through Scarlett's chest than seeing the way Rob treated her. It didn't seem fair for a young woman to know so many handsome and what seemed like upstanding men.

"I—didn't know any of that," she managed to say, reminding herself that she had no right to be jealous about a man she barely knew while hoping Cory might someday want to commit to something more with her. "I only met him in passing."

Remembering the way Rob had looked at his wife, Scarlett wondered if maybe it was to her advantage that he and Cory were friends. Scarlett had no idea what they had in common, but maybe if he hung out with Rob and Dariana, Cory would be more willing to settle down into a real relationship. And who better to settle with than her? She was the kind of girl a man would settle for, anyway.

"Here we are. This is the cafeteria, which obviously holds the kitchen in the back. Ready for a tour?"

The building was like all the other cabins, though longer and with a plain wooden door. The sigh above it read *Soul Chow.*

"We don't serve soul food, so Rob thought he'd take some liberties with the phrase," Dariana explained. "Come on inside, it's getting way too hot out here already."

They stepped into the dark cafeteria, which was a large, open space with dozens of long tables set up. Scarlett breathed a sigh of relief at the dip in temperature. She was sweating profusely down her back already and was sure her T-shirt was soaked. Not the greatest way to make a good impression to her new bosses.

"Mrs. Beatty," Dariana called out as they entered the largest cabin yet, with row upon rows of tables set up. "I found you a partner!"

Scarlett liked the sound of that.

As she followed Dariana between the tables towards the kitchen, she realized she didn't have the feeling of dread she usually got when she took a new job. Instead, there was a buzz of excitement running through her that she hadn't felt in a long time.

Thirteen

TRISTEN WAS ON THE way back to his car after helping Rob finish setting up the sound in the chapel when he heard an exasperated voice.

"I don't know."

Tristen slowed down. He was almost certain it was Scarlett's voice. Rob had said she'd been here today for a job interview. The thought made his heart skip a beat.

"No. Fine. You can't come?" She sounded like she was about to cry.

Just as he reached the truck, Scarlett came around the corner, stopping in her tracks when she saw him.

"Okay. Bye," she said to whoever was on the other line.

"Anything wrong?" Tristen asked. There were tears in her eyes, but she sniffed them away as he came closer.

"No, no. I'm fine," she said.

"Okay." Tristen hesitated, not wanting to leave her. He hadn't wanted to leave her at the market either, but then Cory had shown up. The memory irritated him. He didn't trust Cory. "You don't look fine."

"Hmm? My truck won't start. I don't know why. I mean, I know it's older than Salem, but it should start," Scarlett said hoarsely.

"Want me to take a look at it?" Tristen asked. Scarlett bit her lip but nodded.

Tristen popped the hood. He'd forgotten how many things went into a car motor.

"Is it bad?" Scarlett asked.

Tristen looked up, putting on his most serious face. "I actually have no idea what I'm looking at," he admitted.

Scarlett blinked, then burst out laughing. "Then why did you ask to look?"

Tristen shrugged with a grin. "I know most men would know, so I thought maybe I could see something. But the truth is, no one ever taught me anything about cars. And it's clearly not instinctual. I could call Jared, though. He's a car guy."

"I'd appreciate it, if he doesn't mind. But do you think he can come tonight?"

Tristen checked his watch, dialing Jared's number. "Maybe. I doubt he can get everything squared away tonight, but I'll take you home."

Scarlett was about to respond, but Tristen put his finger up to stop her as Jared answered his phone. "Jared. Any chance you can come look at a truck that won't start tonight? I'm at Camp Soul."

"With my daughter tonight, Tristen. I can look at it tomorrow. What do you think is wrong with it?"

Tristen put the phone on speaker. "What do you think is wrong with it?"

Scarlett shook her head, looking worn out. "It won't turn."

"Might be the battery," Jared said. "I'll stop by tomorrow and take a look. Leave the keys under the seat."

"That okay with you?" Tristen asked as he hung up. Scarlett nodded but didn't look pleased at all.

"I need my truck," she said. She took a deep breath and closed her eyes. Shadows from the trees danced on her face as the muscles in her jaw seemed to clench and unclench. "It's so dumb, too. Especially if it's the battery. Hank told me to get a new one and I didn't listen. I mean, I did listen, but I didn't have money for it, so I kept pushing it off and pushing it off..." She trailed off.

Tristen was transported to a time when he and Talon were seven. They were in the back of the car, watching Ivy from the rear window as she approached people for cash to fill up the tank. Going to the Walmart's in the area to ask for cash became a monthly ritual. Sometimes Ivy returned to the car giggling, and sometimes she was swearing. But they always ended up with enough gas to get home. Sometimes enough to stop at McDonald's on the way home.

As an adult, he wondered if his mother had been lying the whole time. He'd never thought to check the gas gauge as a kid. Either way wouldn't surprise him.

"I'm so stupid," Scarlett muttered.

"Hey," he said gently as a tear rolled down her cheek. "It's okay. It happens. You're busy working and taking care of a kid. I can barely keep my own head on straight. I don't know how you do it."

Scarlett smiled weakly at him, brushing the tear away with the back of her hand. She made 'damsel in distress' look vulnerable in an appealing way. He felt the urge to gather her in his arms and murmur in her ear.

He ignored that. "Listen, let me take you out for dinner, okay? Then I'll take you home." Scarlett started to protest, but he wasn't done. "You work the Saturday market too, right? Rob told me he saw you there. I can pick you up for that tomorrow. What time do you usually get there?"

"Seven in the morning," Scarlett said. "You don't have to do that."

"My mama raised a gentleman," Tristen told her. "Actually, it was her cousin Bobbi who instilled the gentleman in me, but it doesn't matter. We'll go out for dinner, and you'll forget about your stress and I'll pick you up tomorrow. I always wanted to sell bread at a market."

He realized he probably sounded stupid and closed his mouth. Or desperate. Maybe he sounded desperate.

Scarlett shook her head, but she was smiling. And grabbing her purse.

"Come on, I'm over here with this average Honda."

"This is really nice of you, but you don't have to take me to dinner."

"But I'm hungry," Tristen told her, hoping his grin was friendly and not wolfish. "Come on, Scarlett, I'm not dangerous."

Scarlett looked at his hand on her arm, then at him. "You don't look unsafe, though I guess the guys who don't look dangerous could be the most dangerous."

"But eventually it would come out in their face. Evil can only appear good for too long before taking its toll, don't you think?" he asked, removing his hand from her arm. Her warmth lingered on his palm.

Scarlett's eyes narrowed even more before she snorted. "Okay, I believe you."

"Great. Come on." Tristen jogged to his car, energy buzzing through him. He should take her home; she looked stressed and tired, but he didn't want to miss the opportunity to hang out with her. Maybe she'd be boring, and he could stop thinking about her all the time.

Maybe she wouldn't be boring, and he would think about her more.

"So, do you? Wanna grab something to eat? It's dinner time."

Scarlett looked at him over the roof of the car. When she didn't say anything, he opened his door and got in. When she followed, he couldn't help smiling to himself.

"I'm sorry," he said when they were both settled in the car. "I should have asked you if you have a husband or boyfriend or whatever. I didn't mean to make you uncomfortable."

"You didn't," Scarlett said. "I don't. Have a boyfriend, and definitely don't have a husband. You caught me off guard. I haven't been asked out by a man in a long time."

"It's not a date," Tristen said. He eyed her. Not that he would mind it being a date, but he wasn't sure if that was too much for her. "Not if you don't want it to be. We're simply two people who find themselves hungry at the same time. What do you think?"

"I think that sounds nice, Tristen."

He liked the way she said his name. Date or not a date, it didn't matter.

For now.

The car pulled out onto the country highway. He tuned the radio to the local station playing Johnny Cash. Scarlett smiled when he sang, but she still seemed sad.

"Everything all right?" he asked. "You don't like Johnny Cash?"

"It's not the music. Just life, you know?"

Tristen nodded. "I know."

"Do you?" Her voice was incredulous, as though she didn't believe that he had his own problems.

"What do you mean?"

"I mean, look at you. You're young and good-looking and have a job and you were a musician—"

"I like to think I still am," Tristen interrupted.

"Okay, you're a musician," Scarlett said. "And your car is running."

He laughed, and she joined him. She certainly wasn't boring, which was already a plus.

"But seriously," she said, turning to face him. "Do you have cares in your world?"

Tristen smiled, though it probably didn't reach his eyes. "I wouldn't normally tell everything on a first date—"

"It isn't a date."

"Exactly. It isn't a date. Which means I'm gonna give you everything, okay?"

Scarlett nodded, her mouth turned up in a half-smile. She didn't believe him.

"Here's my life right now. Last year my brother left our band that we had been building for about five years to become the lead singer for another band. After he left, everyone else found other jobs and I quickly became unemployed. At the same time, my ex started to become quite successful."

Scarlett breathed in sharply. "That sucks."

"It did. And still does."

"But you seem fine now."

"Right." Tristen skirted around the illegal boxing he'd done to make money. Maybe that was for their third date, if they had one. "I lived with my mother until a few weeks ago, because my ex and I broke up in February when I no longer met her expectations."

"Well, that certainly sounds horrible. I could never live with my mom again. But I bet you were never propositioned by your boss's husband to have a threesome with a woman who called you fat."

Tristen stopped the car at the red light and turned to look at her. "Is that true?"

Scarlett nodded. "Yep. Men are gross." She paused. "I mean, some men are gross."

"I agree with that," Tristen said. He looked her up and down on purpose. "And you're not fat."

Scarlett was beautiful when she blushed. There was something about her that drew him in, even though she was unlike the kind of woman he thought of as his 'type.' "What do you feel like eating? There's a new Thai place—or a really good Indian place."

"I've never had either," Scarlett said. "Never had the guts to go by myself. But I'd love to try either one."

Tristen pulled into the strip mall and put the car into park. "I'll make you a deal. We'll try Thai today and Indian next time."

He held out his hand, and she shook it with a smile.

"But you still have to listen to my life problems because I've barely begun."

"Oh, have you?" Scarlett asked, her entire demeanor much lighter than when he'd found her in the parking lot.

He grinned at her as he held the door open. "It's come to light that my identical twin brother probably knocked a woman up using my name, and now I'm in court with her trying to peg me with child support."

"Oh, I'm sorry." She sounded like she genuinely meant it now.

"I'll tell you more over Pad Thai. If you can stand it," Tristen said, leading her into the restaurant. He hadn't felt so alive since he'd first met Meegan.

Fourteen

"Good morning," Tristen called as he got out of his car. "Does all that have to go to the market?"

He was pointing at the Tupperware boxes, folded chairs, and large tent to cover them from the sun.

Scarlett looked at his car and understood the concern in his voice. "Will it fit?"

"We'll make it fit," Tristen said, grabbing a stack of three boxes. Scarlett watched him, transfixed at the reality that he had not only suggested he pick her up in the morning, but had actually arrived on time and was now loading his car.

The front of her apartment building opened and slammed shut, snapping her out of her disbelief.

"Hey, Ben," Tristen called from the trunk of his car. Ben was shuffling out, pulling his sweatshirt hood over his head. He'd be grumbling in about two seconds' time, as usual.

But when his eyes emerged through the neckline of his hoodie, they were bright and alert. "What're you doing here?"

Scarlett bit back her morning irritability. "I told you that last night when Eric dropped you off. The truck broke down, so Tristen said he'd pick us up."

Eric had claimed he had an emergency and needed to bring Ben back to her for the weekend. At ten at night. His call had interrupted the dinner-that-wasn't-a-date between Tristen and Scarlett that Scarlett had hoped it might end in a kiss. Instead, Eric had cut everything short.

"I wasn't listening," Ben said, waving her off. "I was too tired."

"I got us some coffee in the car," Tristen said, "and I brought you some boxing juuice. You start camp on Monday, right?"

"What's boxing juice?" Ben asked. He was bouncing instead of shuffling all of a sudden.

"Hand me that box, will you?" Tristen asked him. Ben grabbed it without complaint. "Boxing juice is something that'll keep you hydrated. It's in the back seat for you."

Ben crawled in the car, then poked his head back out. "This is a sports drink."

Tristen laughed. There was something contagious about the way he laughed with his whole chest. Like a fit Santa Claus—a thought that made Scarlett snort.

"Okay, I think we've fit everything in," Tristen said. "I gotta put that last one next to Ben, and we can be off. That coffee is yours, Scarlett."

Scarlett buckled her seatbelt and looked at Ben, who was already guzzling the sports drink. It felt like a road trip with a family. The kind she had only ever seen on television.

"This coffee is amazing," she said to change her thoughts to reality. No use fantasizing. They weren't a family. Tristen was doing her a favor because he was a nice guy. And Eric was trying his best to take Ben away from her. She would only torture herself with thinking this was what being a family felt like.

"Thanks. I kinda take my coffee seriously," Tristen said.

They pulled onto the highway, the radio rocking out to nineties grunge music. When he wasn't singing, Tristen told Ben all about what to expect on Monday morning, which Scarlett found charming. She never liked walking into things not knowing how they'd be structured. Ben wasn't quite the same—he joined clubs and sports leagues and never seemed to give it another thought—but Scarlett appreciated hearing what the camp would be like all the same.

"Are you excited to start working at Camp Soul?" Tristen asked Scarlett, changing the subject.

"Camp Soul? What kind of name is that?" Ben asked.

Scarlett had forgotten to tell Ben about the new job. Of course, by the time she'd gotten home and Eric dropped Ben off, all thoughts about the job had left her brain. She had only been thinking about what could have happened between her and Tristen.

"It's that music camp outside of town. Rob, my friend, runs it. They gave Scarlett a job in the kitchen," Tristen told Ben. His voice was without malice. Scarlett was amazed. "I was talking to Rob last night and he asked if I would bring you back to Camp Soul after boxing camp, so Scarlett doesn't have to go back and forth."

"You don't have to," Scarlett started to say, before remembering she didn't have a functional car. "Except maybe I shouldn't say no, since my truck literally isn't running. That is very nice of you. Thank you."

"Well, hopefully Jared will fix your truck soon, so you won't need me any more," Tristen said with a wink. Scarlett realized she suddenly wanted her truck to take much, much longer to repair.

They pulled into the community center parking lot that already held several vendor tents. "Where should I park?"

Ben popped up from the back seat, seat belt clearly not on, and pointed over Tristen's shoulders to Scarlett's usual spot.

"After we set up, I'll show you around the market," Scarlett said. "There's everything here. Even a woman who sells micro greens. I don't know why. It looks like grass."

"Grass?"

"Yep, and people eat it."

"Well, now, I have to see that."

The boys chatted as they set up the tent and Scarlett set up the tables. A few regulars, older residents who were always out and ready to buy before anyone was set up, came by for their weekly breads. Scarlett was ready for them. It was her favorite part of the morning and what had her still dreaming about one day having a bakery. She couldn't think of anything nicer than a small shop with a glass case full of breads and sweets, a coffee maker, and her regulars. It would be like a dream come true.

"Scarlett's not my mom."

The words pierced her daydream as she handed Frank his bag of weekly cinnamon rolls. "Eric is my dad," Ben was saying. "You'll meet him. He signed me up for camp."

Scarlett caught Tristen's eyes and wobbled a smile. She wasn't sure what he'd think about the whole convoluted situation. After listening to his family issues the night before there was hope that he wouldn't be too scared off, but other men had used Ben, or her situation with him, as an excuse not to see her for a second date before. It was one of the reasons she hadn't bothered to date in over a year.

"If Scarlett's not your mom…" Tristen started to say.

"She's my aunt," Ben said. "Rhoda is my mom."

As he got older, it seemed Ben felt the need to correct people about who Scarlett was more frequently. To spell it out in bold letters, **Not Ben's Mom.** It was stupid, but it always hurt her feelings. Nasreen said it was because Ben saw the world in black and white and wanted to help people understand it, since he was trying to himself.

"You're saying he thinks he's helping people?" Scarlett had asked her friend. Nasreen had been taking a psychology class at the time and seemed as fit as any other therapist to help Scarlett process it. Cheap wine that went down like juice also helped.

"I think he does," Nasreen said. "And he probably thinks he's helping you by not giving you the label of mom, but cool aunt."

"He never says the word cool. He only says I'm his aunt."

Nasreen had waved her glass of wine. "You know what I mean—don't take it personally. I mean, 'Mom' is a revered title. You can't go around giving it to anyone."

Nasreen probably didn't guess how much her own words hurt. But not because Scarlett didn't agree—she did. 'Mom' wasn't a title she believed everyone deserved simply for giving birth. Some of those women never acted like moms should.

Especially Candi, Scarlett's so-called mom.

Sometimes Scarlett liked to daydream about how much nicer her life might be had her mom given her and Rhoda up to someone else. A family willing to love her and Rhoda as they were. Willing to show them how to get through life without always falling. Someone who would be there for her when she stumbled.

There had been a few weeks in high school when she'd got a taste of that kind of love. Before Candi came back and ruined everything. That was what Candi had done; made sure Scarlett never got a taste of what life could have been like with someone who acted like a real mom.

Scarlett left the boys to have their serious conversation. Nasreen had warned her not to get involved when Ben was laying out his boundaries. She said he'd resent her for it. So Scarlett stayed out of it.

"Those smell heavenly. I can smell them through the plastic wrap," Tristen said. He was right behind her, like the married couple down the road in the chicken booth. They set up every Saturday together, then greeted their customers together. Always smiling. Of course, they sold a dozen eggs for ten dollars, so maybe they were smiling because they were making a killing.

"Have one," Scarlett said abruptly, trying to evaporate the dumb daydreams in her head. "On me. For picking us up today. And helping out. I really appreciate it."

When Tristen took the cinnamon roll their fingers touched for a moment, sending her traitorous head into overdrive on the daydream. Thankfully, a customer saved her from herself.

"You're popular here," Tristen commented, licking the frosting off his fingers. Scarlett eyed his hands, visions of licking those very fingers dancing in her head. "The customers seem to really like you. And you're good with them."

"I try to be kind and patient and not take it personally if they decide not to buy from me. I don't ever want people to feel pressured into buying something they don't want or can't afford."

He reached around her, filling the air with his cologne, and grabbed his water bottle. "That cinnamon roll was the best thing I've eaten in a long time."

"Better than the Pad Thai last night?" Scarlett asked. Her dinner had been delicious—something she couldn't wait to go back and try again. Once her rent was paid up.

"Even better than the Pad Thai," Tristen murmured. His eyes stayed on hers, dancing between right and left.

Scarlett looked away first. "Have you heard from Jared?"

Tristen's face changed immediately.

"What is it?"

"Well, it's good news and bad news," he told her. Her heart sank.

"What's the bad news?"

"Transmission is busted."

"Shit. Isn't that expensive?"

Tristen nodded, sending her heart even deeper. "It costs some money, but Jared said he'll take it to his friends and get you a family discount. Said he could probably get you a working one for about five hundred."

"Five hundred?" she whispered. "And the good news?"

Tristen shifted, glancing around the market. "That was the good news. That Jared's friend could give you a discount. He said he could rush it and get it back to you by Tuesday."

Scarlett didn't have the energy to answer him. A customer came and she put all her mental drive on helping him choose the right bread and sweet rolls, rather than allow herself to panic over her car. But once the order was complete, she couldn't stop thinking about her bank account. If it turned out to be a good market day, she might make two thousand dollars. But after paying for her spot the coming week in advance and then paying for the truck, the two thousand would dwindle down to almost nothing. She had held out hope that Johnny would take a partial payment, but his menacing text the night before telling her to have a full three thousand or get out had squashed that hope.

Scarlett wondered if Nasreen would lend her a thousand. But no, she wouldn't have it. Maybe she could get an advance from the camp. The best-case scenario would be Rhoda finally showing up and doing what she'd promised: paying the rent.

"I'm sorry things aren't what you thought they'd be," Tristen said, startling her out of her head.

"No, it's not your fault. I'm trying to figure something out. I'm behind on rent payment, and now I have this." Scarlett snapped her mouth shut before she went on. Tristen didn't need to know the details. He might think she was trying to get something from him. "It's fine. I'll figure it out. I have enough money to pay for the truck, so if you wouldn't mind telling Jared that."

"He said he could give a little more discount if it's paid for in cash," Tristen said, grimacing.

"Okay, that's fine. I should be able to."

"I'm back," Ben announced, holding up two smoothies. "And guess what Ms. Anne gave me? Some leftovers."

He handed one to Tristen and the other to Scarlett.

"Thanks, Ben," Scarlett said.

Ben peered closer at her. "What's wrong?"

"Truck's transmission is dead. Won't get it back until Tuesday."

"But what about camp?" Ben asked, his eyes showing his panic. "I have boxing camp on Monday. I have to start with everyone else. Eric paid for it. He'll be so mad if I don't show up."

"Hey, bud. I'll come get you if your dad can't. It'll be fine," Tristen said quietly.

"No, really, Tristen, you don't have to," Scarlett started to say, but Tristen held up his hand to stop her.

"It's what friends and neighbors do for each other. If you give me another cinnamon roll like that on Monday, we'll be even."

"But you don't even live close to us," Scarlett protested.

"I'll pick you up and take you to camp and then bring Ben to boxing camp. Then I'll bring him back to Camp Soul when I go to help Rob. It's what friends do."

Scarlett swallowed hard. He had said friend twice, which was nice enough of him. Being friends would be a good thing. Lovers would be better, but if he wanted to be friends, she could handle that. Unless he started dating Camila. She might not be able to handle *that.*

"We got a deal?" Tristen asked her, waiting for her to reply.

"Yes, deal. Thank you, Tristen."

Fifteen

"WHERE'S YOUR TRUCK?" NASREEN asked as she walked into Scarlett's apartment. She held a bottle of generic pink champagne in her hands; Zander was behind her, playing on his phone. "I told you not to play while you're walking. You look like a zombie. Give me that."

"Mom—" Zander got the one syllable out and stopped immediately. Nasreen glared at him with narrowed eyes and pursed lips. "…I'm gonna find Ben."

"That's what I thought," Nasreen said, nodding. She grinned at Scarlett as Zander sauntered off. "Sorry about that. Where's your truck?"

"In the garage," Scarlett said, pulling out stemless wine glasses. She didn't have champagne flutes.

"Like a parking garage?"

"I wish. Something happened to the transmission. It wouldn't start on Friday after my interview at that summer camp."

"Hold up, you went for a job interview? Where have I been? I swear, I'll be glad when I'm done with this job. My boss keeps running me ragged."

"Who was with Zander all week if you weren't?" Scarlett asked as Nasreen popped the wine cork.

"Mama was. I was in the office until ten every night. Mama said she saw Ben coming home late last night." Nasreen paused for effect. "And you, too."

Scarlett was glad she was already sweating, because she was sure her face was turning pink. "I went out for dinner last night with Tristen. He found me with a dead truck in the parking lot of Camp Soul. He offered to give me a ride home and we stopped for dinner on the way."

Nasreen jumped up. "What? You went on a date?"

"I went to dinner," Scarlett emphasized. "He made sure to tell me it was not a date. He called me a friend twice today, so get any of those ideas out of your head."

"What was dinner like?"

Scarlett couldn't help sighing.

"That good?"

"So good," Scarlett said, stressing each syllable. "Tristen is so easy to talk to. Plus, he's funny and handsome."

Nasreen gave her a half-smile but shook her head slowly. "He told you it wasn't a date, so don't go putting your head where it doesn't belong. Don't get your expectations up too high."

Scarlett stopped talking before she admitted that she had fantasized about him to help herself fall asleep. "He paid for dinner."

"Hmm. In my book, before I started working at this law firm, I would have said it *was* a date. But there are men out there who like paying," Nasreen said definitively. "Did he kiss you?"

"No. We were having a great conversation when Eric called, wanting to bring Ben back. The magic was kinda lost after that. But he showed up this morning to give me a ride to the market."

Nasreen let out a low whistle. "Not many men would do that. Actually, not many people would do that. It's like at the crack of dawn."

Scarlett rolled her eyes. "I leave here at six-thirty."

"Like I said, the crack of dawn." Nasreen leveled her gaze at Scarlett as though daring her to disagree. Then she grabbed Scarlett's hand and squealed. "I can't believe the gym guy is such a gentleman. And cute!"

"What're we squealing about in here?" Camila asked as she marched in. "Sorry I'm late, Nasreen. We had a girl not show up today at the job site. Seriously, people these days. She was even confused when I called her to tell her she was fired. Like she couldn't figure out why it was such a big deal to not show up. Can you believe it?"

"I can," Nasreen said. "The young lawyers are the laziest people I've ever met in my life."

"And soon you'll be one of them," Scarlett said.

Nasreen pretended she was offended by taking Scarlett's wine glass away. "Excuse me, but I wasn't as lazy as they are, even when I was their age."

"I apologize. I'm sorry. You'll be the hardest-working *old* lawyer they've ever seen in their lives and put them all to shame."

"That's better," Nasreen said, before busting out laughing. She poured out half the bottle into the three glasses and raised hers up. "To us. To new beginnings. To me getting that job in Chicago while I go to school."

"That's great," Camila squealed. "I knew you'd get it. Congratulations!"

"And to Scarlett, who got the job at the summer camp."

Scarlett would have preferred not to be mentioned. Getting a job in the kitchen of a camp was not the same as getting a paralegal job Nasreen planned on working while attending law school. But she kept her mouth shut and sipped the pink champagne with her friends, the bubbles breaking on her tongue a momentary distraction from her troubles. She would need to drink the entire bottle herself if she really wanted to forget.

"Is that what you were screaming about when I walked in? Scarlett's new job?"

Nasreen shook her finger and smiled cryptically. "Scarlett went on a date with the musician and didn't even tell us."

"I haven't had a chance to tell you," Scarlett protested.

"When was this? After the Wednesday market?" Camila demanded. "You met up with him after that, didn't you? Did you two hook up? Did he kiss you?"

"Wait, he was at the market on Wednesday?"

"As a customer," Camila said. "He went there specifically to find Scarlett."

"It's not that big of a deal," Scarlett said.

"Sounds like a big deal. He went there to find you," Nasreen repeated.

"He went to get some food for the guys at the gym."

"And said he would order from you personally next time." Camila's eyes widened. "Is that how the date happened? Did he call you wanting to taste your cinnamon buns?" She clicked her tongue and winked before bursting into laughter.

"Girl," Nasreen muttered, but she was also chuckling.

Scarlett huffed, trying hard to show annoyance. "My truck broke down on Friday at the camp. Like right after the interview. Tristen happened to be there and offered to take me home. Of course, I tried to refuse—"

"Why would you try to refuse?" Camila asked, her voice shrill. "Why would you do that? He's so hot, even if he is blond. Have you seen him, Nasreen? Well, believe me, he's hot. Like really hot."

"He wouldn't let me refuse," Scarlett interrupted before Camila could take over the entire conversation. "And he convinced me to go out for dinner."

"Tell Camila more," Nasreen prompted, pouring them all more champagne. She looked at Camila and spoke before Scarlett could. "It was boring because Tristen has no personality."

"No!" Scarlett threw a pillow at Nasreen. "Don't say that."

"Oh, I'm sorry," Nasreen said, imitating Scarlett's voice. "He was *so* funny and *so* handsome."

Scarlett laughed harder, her face steaming hot. Her friends knew her too well. "He took me to a Thai restaurant. We talked about our families. His seems as messed up as mine."

"And was there kissing?" Camila asked, leaning closer in.

"No kissing."

Camila threw her hands up. "Come on, how boring. When you gonna kiss him? I would have kissed him. I mean, *hija*, your car broke down and he saved you."

Nasreen shook her head. "You did the right thing, Scarlett. Don't move too fast. And besides," she said, pointing at Camila, who was swooning with her hand covering her heart. "You don't bring a man home where the babies are sleeping."

"Ben's no baby," Camila objected.

"Even more reason not to bring a man home."

Scarlett laughed at her friends and sipped more bubbly. It didn't help her worries go away, but it tasted good. And felt good. "What am I gonna do about the car? I gotta pay Jared's friend five hundred."

"That's a nice deal for a transmission," Nasreen said. "It cost me over a thousand last year."

"I know," Scarlett said. She knew she should be grateful for friends willing to help her, but there wasn't anyone who could help out with the apartment situation. Except from Rhoda.

"I'm gonna make us some grilled cheese," Camila announced. "I'm hungry. Who wants theirs with tomatoes?"

"I'll help you," Scarlett told her, but her phone rang before she could move.

"I bet it's Tristen," Camila teased, her high ponytail bobbing left and right as she danced into the kitchen.

"Camila, stop." Scarlett couldn't help laughing; she left the room so she wouldn't have to try to avoid looking at Camila. "Hello?"

"Well, hi there, honey. How's life? It's about time you pick up your phone. I tried to call yesterday, and you didn't even answer."

"Mom. I didn't recognize the number."

"You don't have my number in your phone?"

Scarlett closed the door to her bedroom, then quietly locked it. "I don't have this number. I have a different one."

"Sure, okay. Anyway, I didn't call to talk about your inability to have family phone numbers saved on your phone."

"Is there something you want, Mom?"

"You know where Rhoda is?"

"No." Scarlett sat down on the edge of her bed. She hadn't spoken to her mother in months. "She never tells me where she's going."

"But you been getting her payments, right? Did you get something for me in the mail? From Rhoda, I mean?"

"No, I haven't gotten anything."

Candi was quiet for so long Scarlett had to check that the line was still connected. "Does Rhoda usually tell you where she is?"

Candi snorted. "Rhoda hasn't told me nothin' since she was ten. Used to do whatever the hell she wanted to do. But she got smarts, unlike you. She knew how to keep me from calling the social workers. Problem is, she seems to have disappeared."

Scarlett's body turned cold. "What do you mean? Is something wrong? Did something happen to Rhoda?"

"Hell if I know," Candi said. "But there must be something wrong, 'cause I've been waiting for six months and she ain't sent nothin'. She always said it was money enough to keep my mouth shut. And sure it was. Course, I was smart enough not to push her too hard, but six months is a long time."

Scarlett wished she had brought her drink into the bedroom with her. Candi sounded as though she'd been hitting the bottle already. "Candi, I'll tell Rhoda you're looking for her if she calls or shows up, but she hasn't in a long time."

"I ain't waiting around no more," Candi said. "I'm gonna need you and Ben to come over later this week. I'll let you know the day."

Now Scarlett was almost certain Candi was drunk. She never wanted to see Ben, and she never asked Scarlett to come around. "You want us to come over?"

"To Brody's house. I rented out the trailer. You should see that place now, have you seen it? It's like the moment you leave a place it gets brighter, you know? Living in trailers is cool now. I've seen it on television. Everyone wants to get in on the trailer park life." Candi chuckled.

Scarlett didn't know if it was true or not, but she couldn't imagine anyone making her old trailer park cute. That was not a word she would ever use for it.

"I'll let you know the day."

"I gotta work, Mom."

"Don't make me come get you. You do as you're told. It's not like you got no authority anyway. You bring Ben over and that's that."

Candi hung up without saying goodbye, leaving Scarlett in silence.

"What happened? Did he ask you to marry him?" Camila teased from behind the griddle when she came back into the kitchen.

"That," Scarlett said, pouring herself the last of the wine. "Was my mom. She's back in town."

"I'm sorry, Scarlett," Nasreen said seriously. Scarlett was sorry, too. Life was easier when she wasn't taking phone calls from her mom.

"Not the worst part," she went on. "She wants Ben and me to come over this week. She didn't say when, of course, because why would she have details?"

"Was she drunk?"

"Sounded like it."

"She won't remember," Nasreen told her, shaking her head. "I wouldn't worry about it."

"Exactly, *mija*. What you need to worry about is getting a sandwich before the boys eat them all," Camila said as Zander, Ben and Miguel marched through the door. "Who's hungry?"

It would probably be the last time they ate grilled cheese on their laps together, so Scarlett tried to push away the strange phone call and relax with her friends, but it proved impossible. There was something up with Candi, not to mention Rhoda. She owed money for her truck and for the apartment, and then there was Eric trying to get custody of Ben—and, to top it off, Nasreen was moving.

"I know. Let's have a big, huge party the night before Nasreen moves," she said. "We'll have pizza and dessert and balloons, and we'll take lots of pictures and annoy the neighbors. And we'll do it at Nasreen's, so the noise complaint goes to an empty apartment."

Camila howled at the suggestion. "Perfect! I'll bring tequila."

"No tequila," Nasreen said over Camila's laughter. "I'll have to drive the next day. No tequila."

"A little tequila," Scarlett said, throwing her arm around Camila.

"And karaoke," Zander added. "My mom is so bad at karaoke. You have to hear her."

"Karaoke it is," Scarlett said. "We're gonna blow this place up. One last hurrah. And you, Nasreen, can't stop us."

Planning a going-away party might not be the diversion she was looking for, but it felt better than worrying about everything else happening in her life.

Sixteen

THE FIRST DAY OF boxing camp left Tristen in a haze, barely seeing straight. So many yelling kids, most of who wouldn't listen until the fourth time they were told something. By one-thirty he had to pop two painkillers and sneak away. There were only three kids left to be picked up, and Jared seemed to be having fun challenging them to a jump-rope contest. Tristen found more fun in folding the new shipment of T-shirts.

Besides the yelling and having to corral fifteen boys, he hadn't been able to stop thinking about everything else he had to prep before recording Lin. Plus all the stuff Ivy expected him to help with at the gym, on top of the boxing camp.

Not to mention the DNA test results and what would happen once they were presented.

But besides all that, images of Scarlett kept filtering into his lists, sending him down an entirely different thought path.

He'd enjoyed spending time with her the other night, but at the market she'd been quiet and distant, and she hadn't connected with him since. Scarlett... she was completely different than anyone he had ever dated. Her beauty was more subtle than Meegan's, his last long-time girlfriend, and Scarlett probably wouldn't demand to go only to restaurants where the final bill would be at least two hundred dollars.

He was sorry to admit it, but Meegan had been a beautiful, spoiled brat.

In the last few months since they'd split up, he'd wondered if she had only dated him because he was a musician who was slightly ahead of her in the game. That had all changed last fall when Meegan hired Clay Hirson. From that point on, she was off and running. Opening for the hottest pop singers, performing at Coachella, her songs rising to the top of the charts.

What money could do in the music business always amazed him.

Tristen shook the thought away. No use thinking like that. Meegan was rich, but she was also talented.

He shook his head again. Better to not think about Meegan at all. Or her social media, full of her music career wins and pictures of kissing Clay. Scarlett's face came back to him, and he smiled. There was something about her.

"What're you smiling like a dope for?"

Tristen looked up to find Ivy watching him, hands on her thin hips. She had a towel draped across her shoulders and wore Top Gym clothes from head to toe.

"You heading to a class?" Tristen asked, trying to ignore the question.

Ivy shrugged. "Soon. There's one in half an hour. I can't tell you enough how much I love this working-out-while-working thing. It's so healthy."

She coughed into her towel, gasping as she chugged her water bottle.

"You'd be healthier if you quit smoking everything," Tristen said. Teasing Ivy was more fun now that she was in therapy. She was no longer unpredictable with her humor.

"Hey, now, this is allergies. I quit cigarettes and I'm down to two joints a day."

"And gummies?" Tristen asked.

Ivy's eyes narrowed. "Those aren't smoking but I quit those, too. But maybe you should try them. You might relax a bit."

Tristen raised his eyebrows at her, but she chuckled. "Will you stay while I go to class, or do you need to head out already?"

"Put that 'be back soon' sign up on the counter and go to class. No one will care."

Ivy snorted. "Nice to know no one cares. But fine. Leave me. I can't believe you took another job."

"My real job is getting things ready for Lin coming. I'm supposed to be getting back to music, remember?"

"I thought you already were," Jared said, coming up behind them. "Isn't that why you can't work Thursday's shift?"

"You have a gig on Thursday?" Ivy asked. "Can I come?"

"If you want. The crowd is a bit younger, but—"

"What are you trying to say, young man?" she demanded, but she couldn't keep a straight face. "Fine, fine. I'll come to the next gig. I should probably be here with the new girl anyway. But speaking of Owen, when are we gonna have family dinner?"

"We weren't speaking about Owen."

Ivy didn't allow the interruption to deter her. "He's trying to make it a family tradition."

"I know. I'll try."

"Tristen."

"We'll figure it out. I promise."

And he meant it. Back in November, when he was still angry at Talon for leaving the band, he hadn't liked the idea of Ivy and Owen being together. Owen happened to be Talon's and his biological father, though not the guy they'd grown up with. When he'd moved to Pelton and seen them together, he'd stopped fighting against it. Owen was good for Ivy. Her starting therapy and lowering her weed intake was almost certainly due to his influence. She had changed so radically in the past months that Tristen was sometimes caught completely off guard. The reactions he was used to her having typically no longer came.

The change was nice, though sometimes disorienting.

"Any news about the DNA test?" Ivy asked.

The change in subject brought back the pounding in his head. "Shit, Ivy. I managed to stop thinking about that for two minutes."

"Sorry." She even looked sorry.

"I haven't checked my email, but I feel like Elijah would call if he had the results." He picked up the remaining sweatshirts and started folding. "But I've been thinking, what result is a good result? I mean, it'd be great if the kid was someone else's completely, but since I know he's not mine, he's probably Talon's. But what does proving that get me? Talon is in Portugal. He's about to have a daughter, and he doesn't seem too interested in coming back for this kid."

"Your brother will have to make some decisions."

"I don't have the money to pay Lamia, but I feel bad the kid's gonna get screwed over. Money-wise and dad-wise. But then I think, I shouldn't have to pay."

"It isn't your responsibility," Ivy said, nodding.

"Exactly. I've got to build my business, you know? Focus on that."

"I know," she said, putting the folded sweatshirts onto the shelves according to their size. "You have to live your life, Tristen. And only you know what's right for you."

Tristen closed his eyes briefly. He hated comments like that, abdicating advice-giving.

"What's this doing here?" he asked, pulling a roll of paper out from drawer under the counter.

"I put it there," Ivy exclaimed, grabbing the roll. "I was gonna show you this the other day, but then I couldn't remember where I put these drawings and forgot about the whole thing. This is the secret project I've been talking about."

Tristen shook his head slowly. "We already did quite a bit around here."

The projects were one of the reasons he was still in Pelton and hadn't left for Cincinnati sooner. Everything had taken longer to finish than originally planned, as usually happened.

Ivy gave an exasperated sigh and unrolled the papers on the counter. "I know, but this is different. And you'll like it. So, you know how we have to change up the whole air conditioning and ventilation system, right?"

"Yes." It was the last project. The last one before he could move on with a clear conscience.

"It's such a pain and it's gonna be expensive, but the gym is doing pretty well, so Owen is convinced we'll get the loan we need."

"I know, Ivy."

"Okay, grumpy butt. Geez. Anyway, I saw the coolest thing on social media the other day. Don't look at me like that, I checked it out and it's real. It was about how you can buy old shipping containers and use them to make buildings. Have you seen it?"

"I think that's been around."

"Sure, okay, way to make me feel behind the times, Tristen," Ivy said. She kept her face straight, eyebrows raised, until he apologized. "I was kidding. I'm old. Had no idea this was happening. But here's my idea: a cafe."

"A cafe?"

"Yeah," Ivy said, her excitement showing in her eyes. "All the big gyms have them. You really only need smoothies and some salads, and of course some fried food for the people who think their workout is enough to keep them slim. But I want people to come here and spend more time. More time here means more money here. Get where I'm headed with this?"

"Yeah, I get it," Tristen said. He was a little surprised at how good the idea was. Despite her weeks in therapy, though, he didn't want her to get a big head.

"Here, we have to cut into the wall, to make a short hallway to the cafe. All of this will be made with shipping containers. That way I get to say I'm recycling and stuff. Isn't that cool?"

Tristen looked at his mom. She was still gazing at the plans. "It's very cool, Ivy."

Ivy let the papers roll back into themselves. "You really think so?"

"I think it's a really great idea. People go grab a bit to eat after a workout, anyway. Why not have that here?"

"Exactly." She smacked her lips with satisfaction.

"I'm excited to come back and see this. When will you start it?"

A noise from the boxing ring brought an early end to their conversation. Two boys were still sparring in the ring. "There're still two kids who need to be picked up," Ivy said. "Parents these days are so irresponsible."

Tristen snorted but was cut off from saying anything about her own parenting by his phone ringing. "Hello?"

"You bastard," seethed a voice on the other end.

"Lamia."

"How dare you drag our child through this crap? Do you know they had to stick a needle into him?! He cried for an hour. Do you know what it's like to take care of a baby who won't stop crying? Oh, that's right. You don't! 'Cause you're a shit dad who doesn't come around. You don't want to take care of him, and you don't want to pay for him, but guess what?"

Tristen listened, breathing slowly, trying not to explode on her. He glanced at Ivy, who raised her eyebrows, but telling her anything with Lamia on the phone would only invite more yelling. He rolled his fingers to tell Ivy he would fill her in later and marched to the front doors for some quiet.

"I won't let you get away with this. I don't know where we went so wrong, but you can't let our child pay for our mistakes. I'm guessing you think somehow this DNA shit will prove you aren't the dad, but you're wrong. I thought I was in love with you, and you were the only one I was with when I got pregnant. I know you, Tristen. You're the boy who broke my heart."

He shouldn't even be taking the call. He should hang up. That was what Elijah would tell him to do. To not get sucked in. Not get involved. Let the lawyers handle it.

But then she said something like that, sounding tired and grief-ridden, and he couldn't help feeling bad for her.

"I'm not the father, Lamia. I wasn't with you last year. I was only with you those few times four years ago when you used to come by that bar in Lexington. You've got the wrong brother, and I think you know it."

There was a pause on the other side of the phone. For a second Tristen thought he had lost her, but then she snorted.

"You're one funny bastard." He could hear the slur in her voice now—slight, but present. The baby cried in the background for something, and Lamia gave a strangled moan in response. "You're fine. Melanie, I thought I was paying you to help. Get the baby."

"I'm hanging up now, Lamia. Don't call me again. Our lawyers are the ones who are supposed to be talking."

Slurred expletives assaulted his ear, but none of Lamia's threats kept him from tapping the red button. Silence ensued.

Tristen took a deep breath, filling his lungs to the very bottom before releasing the air. He thought about the crying he had heard and the way Lamia had sounded. Like with everything in the adult world, the kid in this struggle was innocent and yet in the thick of it all. And either Lamia didn't care that much or wasn't handling it well. The possibility of her taking drugs or drinking during the day added even more issues to the problem.

He glanced at Ivy, who was still folding clothes and putting them away. In a way, Lamia reminded him of her when he and Talon had been kids. They'd gone through a lot together, but he'd always known Ivy loved him in her own way.

Maybe Lamia loved Talon's kid in a way that would be enough. Tristen thought about that as he walked slowly down the gravel street. 'Enough to not make the kid's life a living hell' was all he could come up with.

His phone rang again.

"Hey, it's Rob. Is it still okay for you to bring Adam and Ben out to the camp?"

Tristen looked through the glass doors of the gym at the two kids left from camp. He had told Rob he'd bring them to Camp

Soul and then stay to help him set up the stereo system. "Damn it, sorry. I forgot. I was wondering why they were still here. I'll leave now."

Seventeen

"You never texted me back," a low voice rumbled near her ear.

Scarlett jumped, almost dropping the pan of brownies she was putting into the oven.

"Sorry about that. I didn't mean to scare you."

She turned to look straight into the blue eyes of Tristen Levisay. They were beautiful eyes, with specks of yellow in them. He stood leaning against the metal counter, watching her as he ate an apple. She wondered how long he'd been there.

"Hi," she said, all other words lost on her for a second. "You didn't scare me."

"You almost dropped the brownies," he pointed out.

The hot air from the oven blasted her face, cranking the temperature up on her necklace before she could adjust the pan and close the door. She turned to face him, hands on hips.

"And if I had, you'd be cleaning them up off the floor," she told him.

"Would I now?" His voice seemed an octave lower than a minute before, his eyes more intense. Scarlett stepped back and tried to behave as a friend would, despite her heart fluttering uncontrollably. He chuckled and tossed the apple core. Perfect pitch into the waste bin. "Doesn't change the fact that you never texted me back."

"Well, did you ever consider that I might have a fantastic reason to have not texted? Like maybe I was in the hospital or was visiting a retirement center. Or I was sick in bed."

"Were you any of those things?"

"No," Scarlett admitted, pressing her finger gently against the sandwich bread dough to see if the indent would bounce back quickly. It was time to preheat the bread oven. "I, um, forgot."

Tristen watched her, his gaze steady. If he didn't believe her, he didn't say so. She should have come up with a better lie; it made her look flakey. But the truth was worse. She hadn't texted him because she'd been scared he would show up that morning to pick her up. If he had, the chances of her falling for him would have skyrocketed. Because who does that, picks a girl up out of kindness?

"How'd you get to work?"

"Eric," Scarlett said. She peeked at him from the sink. "Ben's dad. He offered to come get us. I'm sorry I didn't reply to you."

She hadn't gotten a confirmation from Eric until late the night before. If he hadn't answered her, she had planned to order a ride-share. Anything to avoid making Tristen help her again.

"I had coffee ready and everything," he said, acting hurt. Scarlett, had she not learned with all her previous relationships, might have let his doe-eyes affect her. "Will you let me take you home? I thought we could get some ice cream with Ben. It's so hot out."

It was too early to check the brownies, but she peeked inside anyway. She needed the heat burning her eyes to keep herself aware of who she was. He was probably being nice for Ben's sake. Like that movie in the nineties with Tom Cruise when he liked the kid more than he liked the girl. Until the ending when he fell all over himself telling the girl he loved her.

But that kind of thing wouldn't happen to a girl like her. She wasn't Renee Zellweger.

"I don't know," Scarlett answered, dragging her words out. "I have to wait for this bread to finish baking."

"I can wait. Do you mind me waiting with you? I brought the coffee I had ready for us this morning."

"Isn't it cold?" she asked, gently placing the boules of sourdough bread into their box.

"They have these genius inventions," Tristen said, pulling out a thermos and wagging it at her. "They're called thermoses."

Scarlett stopped what she was doing and gave him a look she often gave Ben when he was snarky.

Tristen laughed. "Dang. Your mom glare is scary. Here, try this. It's a new coffee from Hawaii that a friend of mine sent over."

"You have friends in Hawaii?" she asked, taking the cup from him. His fingers lingered, holding the cup back; he was smiling. "Have you been there?"

"I've never been. It's on my bucket list. Have you?"

Scarlett snorted. He kept his eyes on hers as she sipped the coffee, trying to think of a response that wasn't 'Have you seen me?' or 'Do you really think I could afford something like a trip to Hawaii?', but all her words drifted away when the coffee hit her tongue.

"This is amazing. What is this called?"

"Kona coffee. I like to imagine myself sitting in a hammock, watching the ocean while I'm drinking it. It would be better than the view I have from my practically empty living room."

"You sound like a commercial," she said. "Maybe you could become an influencer and then they'd pay you to travel there."

"Right, if I ever get the hang of social media."

Scarlett held her cup out for more coffee, and he readily complied. "I can't believe you aren't comfortable on social media. There are so many people out there making stupid videos all day long. You at least have something to videotape."

"Such as?"

"Your music. All you have to do is set up a tripod and record yourself. I'm sure you'll get views. You're like the Viking god playing guitar, or whatever you play."

She moved away to put the bread into the oven. Once she started talking, it was like she had no control over herself. She had called him a Viking god, and now he was grinning. Shit! She had shown him all her cards, ruining her hope of keeping her attraction to him under wraps.

"When I used to box, they called me the Pelton Viking."

"You used to box?" Another reason he wouldn't want to hang out with her too often; he was much more interesting than her. She placed the sandwich loaves, evenly spread out, in the bread oven before pulling out the brownies out. It wouldn't take too long. She should be able to leave the camp in less than an hour.

"Yes. All through high school."

"High school? You're allowed to box in high school?"

"If you do it illegally," Tristen said. He settled on the counter to explain. "My dad, or really my stepdad, got out of jail when I was about thirteen. He came home to find me and Talon trying to work out with this makeshift sandbag we had put together. He decided to string it up on the magnolia tree and make it into a punching bag for us. There were lots of mornings that he went out and punched it himself, which was better than him hitting us."

"And he forced you to box in illegal matches?"

He shrugged. "Force is a strong word, Scarlett. It started out to keep us out of trouble. But after we'd trained for almost a year, the guy running the place thought we could win some fights. Which we did, but that was a long time ago. And the point was, I thought it was funny you called me the Viking."

He left off the god part. She wondered if it was false humility or if he preferred to forget about her thinking he was attractive.

"Was it for money?"

Tristen nodded, a harder edge to his eyes now. "There was money involved. We made some. But Luke, my dad, he made more. Took it with him, as far as I know."

"What a jerk."

"He had a lot of demons," Tristen said. "I don't know, I haven't thought about him and the money for a long time. Talon and I used to talk about it, wondering where it might be. That was when we were struggling to make it as musicians, you know?

Working odd construction and carpentry jobs or bartending and then playing on the weekends. It's like when you dream about winning the lottery. We would talk about what might happen if Luke came back and felt compelled to give us our fair share after all these years." He laughed, shaking his head. "The things you dream about."

"He never came back?" Scarlett stirred the butter in a glass bowl and placed it into the microwave to melt a bit more.

"No."

She had expected him to say that but hadn't expected him to look sad when he did. If someone had taken money like that from her, she wasn't sure she'd be sad not to see them again. Of course, she didn't know who her father was. Candi had never told her. Maybe she'd feel differently if she did.

"I'm sorry he never showed up again," she said. It felt like the right thing to say, even if it didn't make a difference.

"Thanks. What about you?"

"Me?"

"Did your dad make you learn to box?" He bumped his shoulder gently against hers, and she thought she might faint. She inhaled sharply, accidentally inhaling the searing heat from the oven as she opened the door.

Suddenly, his arm was around her, his hand patting her on her back. "You okay?"

Scarlett nodded, closing her eyes and breathing him in as she breathed slowly to steady herself. "I'm fine, thank you. I inhaled the oven heat."

Tristen's fingers lingered on her back until she moved away to check the bread. It was turning golden brown and smelled like heaven, which would of course be a bakery where calories didn't count.

"Smells great," Tristen said, his voice hoarse. Scarlett turned her head and found his chin only inches from her lips.

She knew she shouldn't lean in, shouldn't encourage anything between them. What would it make her to kiss Tristen only days after Cory had been at her house?

"Scarlett, are you ready?"

Scarlett jerked her hand so quickly a loaf of bread flipped. Tristen grabbed at it but dropped it immediately, shaking his hand.

"What happened?" Ben stood staring at them with narrowed eyes.

"You scared me," Scarlett said through clenched teeth. She carefully pulled the other loaves from the oven and turned it off. "Are you okay?"

Tristen nodded on his way to the sink. He hit the faucet and held his hand under it.

"Wanna go for ice cream, Ben?" he asked, his voice strained. "I might need some directly on my fingers."

Eighteen

AFTER THE WEDNESDAY MARKET, Scarlett stood in the middle of the street, staring at Candi's house. Or actually, Brody's house. Whoever the owner was, the house was much nicer than the trailers she'd lived in while growing up. It had rosebushes and hedges around the foundation and a walk lined with tiny, purple flowers that led to a cute porch with two chairs on it. Scarlet doubted her mom and Brody ever sat in those chairs.

She'd hoped Tristen would stop by the stand that morning, which was a stupid hope, since he was running the boxing camp and he had said nothing about coming by. When they'd gone for ice cream, things had been awkward at first; she had never been out with Ben and a guy that sent so many flutters down her spine before. He and Tristen had goofed off most of the time while she daydreamed about having a family and licked her melting mint chocolate chip cone.

"Ready to go?" Tristen had asked when she'd polished off her cone. He had held out his hand, and she had just looked at it.

"Sure," was all she had said. Then, without notice, his hand took hers and helped her up.

She couldn't ever remember someone helping her up before. It would have been another opportune moment for Tristen to kiss her, but Ben was right there, practicing his hooks or whatever they were called.

She had almost invited Tristen for dinner, but he'd said, "I have to get back to the gym." So she and Ben had gotten out of his car and gone home alone.

She had dreamt about him being in her apartment, smiling and sipping coffee, which she stupidly thought was a sign. While at the market she'd tried to come up with an excuse to go to the gym, but she'd sold out of all her sandwiches and lost her nerve. And then, as she was packing up, Candi had called asking her to stop by the house.

And here she was.

There was a small voice in her head, laughing at her inability to grow up and tell Candi no. No matter how many times she psyched herself up to defy her mother, she reverted to being thirteen again and reliant on Candi to give her a roof over her head. She told the voice she was obeying because she wasn't sure what Candi was up to yet. It had something to do with Ben, and she'd be wrong not to find out.

But the voice kept laughing.

A car sped by, the driver shouting expletives to remind her she was in the way. Scarlett quickly shut the truck's door and moved into the sidewalk where she paused.

The next car to pass by pulled into the driveway, and a young woman in green joggers and a white vest got out. Scarlett had never seen someone wear joggers as though they were work clothes, but the woman pulled it off well. She had long brown hair and giant sunglasses and looked too pretty to be a social worker.

"Hello! You're not Candi, are you?" the woman asked. Scarlett almost choked.

"No, I'm Scarlett."

"Of course, the aunt. I'm Jenn. I didn't know you were coming, but it's fine," Jenn said quickly when Scarlett opened her mouth to interrupt. "This is a friendly guardianship procedure. Everyone seems happy to allow the other to understand what's going on." She flipped through some papers. "I have an appointment to speak with the grandma, Candi. She's your mother?"

"Yes," Scarlett said. Clearly there had been conversations that she'd been left out of. "Will you be speaking with me today? I'm the one who has guardianship now."

"Well," Jenn said, shifting through some of her papers. "Actually, legally you have notarized care of Ben, but you don't actually have legal guardianship. Eric, Ben's father, is requesting custody and the grandma, Candi, has also mentioned she would like custody."

Scarlett's heart raced at that piece of news. "But the biological parent usually gets custody, right?"

Jenn nodded slowly. "Usually. But there are some cases in which we work something else out. Why?"

"Rhoda, Ben's mom, entrusted him to *me*." The pressure in her chest was back. Once again it was hard to get a deep breath.

"Are you wanting to contest custody against the father?"

Scarlett swallowed hard. "What does that mean?"

"That you would like to be considered for getting custody of Ben."

Scarlett coughed. "What would happen if Rhoda came back?"

"The mother always has the right to petition custody again," Jenn said, heading up the sidewalk. "Come on, let's talk about this in the house, why don't we? I want us all to meet each other and see where Ben will live. Did Ben come?"

"No, he's at a summer camp. And his dad is picking him up later."

"Are there agreed-to terms about how often he can visit his dad?"

Scarlett snorted. As though she could keep him from Eric. Barring Eric hitting him, she would never keep Ben from seeing his dad. "No. Everything is amicable. Eric used to have a job where he traveled a lot, which made it difficult for him to have Ben full-time, so Ben lived with me. But Eric always came between jobs to see Ben. Sometimes it was only for an afternoon, but he always made time. And now with his new girlfriend—Eric's, I mean, not Ben's girlfriend. Ben doesn't have a girlfriend. I mean, Eric now has a place for Ben to spend the night and spend more time with him and Brandy. The girlfriend."

"And Ben likes staying there?"

"Ben loves his father." Scarlett was sure she was making her situation worse. Her first instinct was to make Eric look like a good dad. She didn't want anyone thinking he wasn't. But then she couldn't help worrying that the more she talked up Eric, the less chance they would decide to give her Ben. Everything had gotten scrambled in her mind when Jenn mentioned Candi. Truth be told, if the choices came down between Eric and Candi, Scarlet would do anything to make sure Ben didn't go to her mother.

"Where the hell is Ben?" Candi called from her porch. "You were supposed to bring him with you. This don't have as much to do with you as it does with him. Do you see what I'm up against?" The last question was directed at Jenn, whose smile wavered slightly.

"We're having a friendly conversation," Jenn said. Her voice was chirpy. Scarlett couldn't tell if it was genuine or an act; what she did know was that she'd never seen anyone happy to see Candi. "This is a friendly, family affair. We're here to collect some information so the judge can make the best decision for Ben."

"Is she putting her hat in the ring?" Candi asked. Her arms were crossed, fingers gripping each forearm.

Scarlett wet her lips and tried to stay calm, but her calves were shaking and her palms were sweating.

"Let's go inside," Jenn said.

"I'd rather only you bend me go inside," Candi said. "I'd like to present my case without any outside influence."

Jenn glanced at Scarlett.

Scarlett swallowed her frustration and plastered a smile on her face. "That's fine. I can wait outside."

"If you wish," Jenn told her. She pulled out a business card. "Or you can call me, and we can set up another time to speak."

The front door closed behind them, blocking the rest of the conversation.

Scarlett got back into her car and started driving nowhere in particular. At least in the beginning. She was too angry to think as she crawled past Candi's new neighborhood and turned right. Before she knew it, she was headed towards the trailer park she'd grown up in.

Everyone wants to live in a trailer park these days.

Candi was right; it was nicer, with paved streets and flowers lining the windows of a few trailers. Most were double-wides now, though when Scarlett had been a kid they were almost all single.

Things had certainly changed in the past years. Even the reputation of living in a trailer had changed. When she was a girl, living in this area had marked you as the one with parents who were drug addicts or alcoholics or both. Parents who couldn't seem to quite get anywhere in life. Single moms like Candi, who had several children with different men—men who never came back to claim their children.

Scarlett parked her car outside the trailer park and walked in. Fifteen years ago, a stranger walking into the park would have had everyone stopping what they were doing to look, warn with their eyes that they were seen. But today a woman smiled at her from her tiny porch and a little boy waved. Scarlett kept walking. She couldn't seem to leave.

Five streets in and to the right, she stopped mid-step. Instead of the rundown single wide, there stood a double wide that was as big as a small house with a porch in the back and a garden at the side. The street wasn't in the best shape, but there wasn't trash everywhere. And at the very end of it was a small park with swings and a slide built of colorful plastic right next to the walnut tree she used to climb.

Despite the inviting visual, Scarlett's skin crawled. The street might look nice now, but it held ghosts of abuse, loneliness and humiliation.

She shook away her memories and marched forward. Ghosts couldn't hurt her, and the past had already happened. What she needed to do now was gather her resolve to keep Ben from living with Candi.

Because there was a reason Rhoda had given Ben to her even though they hadn't seen each other in years. Scarlett hadn't even known Rhoda had a kid until she showed up one day at Devon's place and demanded to see Scarlett.

The memory made Scarlett smile. She had been trying to find a way to move out, and somehow Rhoda knew. Growing up, Rhoda had always known everything. Scarlett used to think she was a witch.

"Hey, there, baby sister," Rhoda had said. She stood cross-legged, leaning against the rotting railing. She wore black jeans and a black leather jacket with metal zippers along the pockets. Cool as always. "I've been looking for you. Why you living here?"

"It's a roof," Scarlett had said. Then nineteen, she'd been working at a local diner and trying to finish high school. Devon and his girlfriend had moved into a trailer the year before and were willing to let her sleep on the couch if she paid rent. But she'd recently been let go from the diner, and with no job on the horizon, she wasn't sure she'd be allowed to stay there much longer.

"I got a place for you," Rhoda said. "Leave this shitty one behind."

"A place with you?" Scarlett had asked. An embarrassing amount of hope rose within her at the thought of living with Rhoda. Her sister had always been the mountain in her life. Scarlett would have done anything to live with Rhoda the rest of her life. When she was with Rhoda, nothing bad ever happened. Rhoda kept Candi's boyfriends from creeping into their bedroom. Rhoda made sure they were fed. No one messed with Rhoda.

And when she'd left, everything had gone to hell.

"Not with me," Rhoda told her, throwing her arm around Scarlett's shoulders. "But I need you to take care of my baby boy."

"Your what?"

"My kid, sis." Inside the sleek, black car that Scarlett had never seen before in her life was a little boy about five years old. He smiled at her, and she smiled back. "This is Ben."

"You have a kid?"

"Get in."

Scarlett obeyed and Rhoda floored it, the tires squealing down the road.

"His dad is working out in the oil fields, and I got a job—" Rhoda paused. "Doesn't matter. I have a job to do that pays well, and I gotta go. Ben here knows he's gonna stay with you for a little bit, right, Ben?"

"Right." Ben seemed excited. Scarlett was not.

"How am I—" she tried to ask, but Rhoda hushed her.

"Let's go."

A screen door slammed somewhere down the road, startling her out of her memories.

"Can I help you with something?" someone shouted.

Scarlett realized she was still standing in the middle of the street. She turned to find an old man waving at her. "No, thank you. I was just leaving."

"Looked like you were lost in your thoughts," he said, wobbling down the street with his cane. "Happens to me sometimes, too. You live here?"

Scarlett shook her head. "No. I used to."

"Ah."

"Have a nice day," she said quickly, not liking the way the man looked at her now. Maybe it was more her imagination, but maybe it wasn't.

She walked quickly to her truck. Once safe, Scarlett inhaled deeply to settle her breath. She refused to break down sobbing like she had when Rhoda showed her the apartment that she now lived in. Two bedrooms, one bath. A kitchen and a small back patio. All for her and Ben, as long as she took care of Ben.

But now she was going to lose him and the apartment.

The idea of returning to a place like the trailer park brought up a well of anxiety that made her hands shake. It was best not to think about it. To push it all away and hope for the best. Hope that Rhoda came and rescued her again. Before it was too late.

Nineteen

Tristen looked up from his phone as Owen entered the gym. Jared had the group of boys under control, so he'd snuck away for a break from the mayhem. He couldn't wait to get to Camp Soul and see Scarlett. This morning he'd planned to go see her at the market, but Ivy had needed him to open the gym, and things had been so busy he wasn't able to get away.

Which was probably better. He didn't need to come off so strong.

"Mornin'," Owen greeted him.

"Morning. Why you so fancy?" Owen's hair was slicked back, his beard trimmed, and for possibly the second time in Tristen's life, he wasn't wearing track pants.

Owen flicked the collar of his blue Oxford shirt and smiled.

Tristen moaned as a tease. "Where you guys going?"

"To church."

Tristen choked on the coffee he was drinking, but before he could make a comment his phone rang.

"Hello, Mr. Levisay. This is Marjorie, Elijah's assistant. He asked me to see if you were free to talk to him."

"Hi, Marjorie," Tristen said, turning away from Owen for some privacy. "I can talk now."

"Alright," she said. "Let me see if he's free to speak with you now."

"Thanks," Tristen said, trying to sound upbeat, though the hold music was already playing. It continued to play for another two minutes before Elijah picked up.

"Tristen. Glad we could talk today. Have you heard?"

"What?" Tristen asked, not liking the sound of Elijah's voice. It was usually deep and serious, unless he had a glass of whiskey in him. That was when he could get funny. But today there was a gravity to his tone that Tristen didn't like.

"You should have a call from the laboratory."

Tristen groaned. "I had a call this morning from some New York number. I didn't pick up."

"Don't blame you, but that was probably them."

"What's up, Elijah? Sounds like you think I'm going to lose or something."

Elijah sighed heavily into the phone. He was about to say something bad. Tristen could sense it.

"Listen, Tristen. We aren't done fighting this, but we're gonna have to convince Talon to take on his responsibility in the matter. That's the only way out."

"What do you mean?"

"You two are identical twins, right?"

"Yeah. That's how he was able to convince Lamia he was me, obviously."

"And what do identical twins share as far as biology?"

Tristen frowned. His head was starting to hurt. "Can you just tell me, Elijah?"

"DNA, Tristen. You guys came from the same egg and sperm until you two split and became two people. The process we use for paternity testing isn't high-tech enough to know if one identical twin is the father or if it's the other identical twin. My kindergarten lawyer informed me today that the test will come back inconclusive, which will give the judge enough to say that since there is a high likelihood that you're the father, you can start paying for child support."

"Shit." Tristen looked around, glad that Rob wasn't around to hear him. "Even though the likelihood could also be my brother?"

"You're the one she's taking to court, not your brother. The money from February came from your account, not your brother's. Of course, like I said before, we could bring in the accusation that the kid is Talon's, and we could sue Talon, but that would be an entirely different lawsuit, and the judge does not have to consider that when making his verdict. And this judge doesn't like leaving things hanging while other lawsuits go through. He'll tell you that he could always bring her back into court if you get a favorable judgement in suing your brother."

Tristen had to work hard to keep calm. He hadn't felt this angry since Talon had left the band. In less than a year, his brother had managed to ruin his life twice. If the judgement came down in Lamia's favor, for the next seventeen years a woman he hadn't knocked up would receive part of his paycheck. And Talon, who lived in Portugal, wouldn't pay a dime.

It was all so infuriatingly complicated.

"I don't want to sue Talon. It would…" Tristen trailed off, letting the sentence hang in the air. It would ruin any relationship between them, that's what it would do.

"I know, man. I know. I mean, we could still hold out hope that Lamia will screw this all up somehow. Or you could convince Talon to come clean."

"Yeah, sure," Tristen said. "Even if I get a hold of him, which I haven't been able to do for weeks now, he'll say no. And I can't even sue him—not that I would, but I can't cause he doesn't even live in the US anymore. This sucks." The pounding in his head was getting louder. His eyes were twitching, and his mouth was dry. "What're we gonna do?"

"I don't know, kid."

That was not what he wanted to hear.

"I'll keep looking, and you keep your chin up. And stop taking calls from Lamia. You'll get frustrated and say something stupid." With that, Elijah hung up.

Tristen stared at the phone as though it might have an answer for him.

"That your lawyer?"

Owen's voice startled Tristen. He'd forgotten he was standing there, listening to the entire conversation.

"Yes. He had some bad news—" He couldn't finish his sentence. Too many emotions were coming out of him all at once.

"About the DNA test?"

Tristen took in a deep breath, covering his need to do so with a cough. "The judge ordered it, but one of the guys who works for Elijah found something out." He choked on his own words.

"I overheard the conversation," Owen said, his mouth set in a grim line. "I wouldn't have thought of it either, the DNA being the same. To be frank, I wouldn't have guessed your brother would let it get this so far. Have you talked to him?"

"I can't get a hold of him. And now the judge is about to order me to pay for his kid. And he isn't doing anything about it. He's abandoning him to live with that crazy woman. I mean, if I were Talon, I'd take responsibility so that kid had some stability in his life. The last time Lamia called me, it sounded like she was on drugs."

Owen grunted a reply. "I guess your brother thinks it's better this way. I mean, he's busy running around the world, playing in concerts. Plus, he lives in Portugal. That would be quite the trip for the kid to make, wouldn't it?"

Tristen rolled his eyes. Everyone was always covering for Talon, making excuses for his brother when there were none.

"What's wrong?" Ivy asked as she came down the stairs from the office. She was wearing a long, beige skirt and a blue Oxford.

"You guys dress the same on purpose?" Tristen asked.

Ivy ignored him, but she did smile at Owen and touch the collar of his shirt in a way he'd never seen Ivy touch anything. As though she was in love.

Tristen breathed in slowly. "Your son is driving me crazy."

"He's your brother, you know," Ivy reminded him. "But come on, it's been months since he left. Shouldn't you be a little happy for him?"

"Happy for him how?"

"Art of Rendering sold half a million and got that award, or whatever you get."

"Half a million?" Tristen asked, unable to keep his voice neutral. He couldn't believe it. Art of Rendering had only become more popular. They'd come out with an album in March and had even made their way onto the pop and country radio channels as well as the rock channels. Some fans had been annoyed about the experimental songs, but obviously it had ended up working out well.

But that wasn't something he cared about now.

"I'm not talking about his career. I'm talking about this situation with Lamia, which is far from under control. He won't take responsibility for it. It's his son, and he's walking away and leaving me to pick up the pieces."

Ivy placed her slim hand on her hip and stared hard at Tristen. "Your brother..." she said slowly. "Had to make a choice, so he did. And he made the best one that he could at the time. He chose to be with his wife and his daughter. What else do you want him to do?"

Tristen returned her stare, unfazed. He wasn't eight anymore, but Ivy didn't seem to have received the message.

"My brother," he hissed, stepping forward, "could have made some other choices. Like wearing a condom, or keeping his damn pants on while separated from his wife. Or you know what? If he wanted to go around screwing crazy women, he could at least have used his own damn name!"

Ivy didn't look at all pleased. She shook her head the tiniest bit, then turned around and marched away, hands in fists at her sides.

"That wasn't nice. She thinks you were talking about her. And you two. And you know, me and Luke."

Tristen turned to Owen. Everything about this day and everyone in it was suddenly very annoying. "You know what, Owen? Not everything is about Ivy. I was talking about Talon and the things he could have done, but sure, I guess I can see the parallels. So perhaps we could say that the apple doesn't fall far from the tree, does it?"

Tristen expected Owen to get angry, but instead of yelling he stepped back and spoke quieter than before. "You're right. I get it. Maybe Ivy and I could have made better decisions. And maybe this anger you have isn't only about your brother."

Tristen tried to make a rebuttal, but he couldn't articulate more than a snort.

"At any rate, your brother made a decision. And now there's a kid out there who needs a dad."

"Are you actually saying that I have a responsibility to take that kid as my own?" Tristen asked.

"All I'm saying is that there were times I wanted to know if I was your dad, and there were times I was glad I could pretend Luke was. I'm not a perfect guy and I know I haven't been a great father, but every kid needs a father figure, don't you think?"

There had been so many times when Luke was an ass, a shitty father who seemed more concerned about himself than anything else. But then it was Luke who'd gotten Tristen and Talon construction jobs, taught them how to box, and change a tire, and grill a burger. And not to cry. And to take care of the women first.

In his strange, violent way, Luke was a father figure. Even if he hadn't been a great one.

And then there was Owen. He claimed he was always looking out for them from the sidelines. Then he got involved during the underground boxing years. And, in the past few months, it was Owen who had walked Tristen through everything. Two imperfect men who had influence Tristen's life. For better or worse but influenced all the same.

But Tristen wasn't Luke or Owen. He knew for certain Lamia's kid wasn't his and he wasn't about to volunteer to take it.

"It's Talon's kid. Why don't you call him and tell him that?"

Owen shook his head. "I'm not saying you should take on your brother's stuff. All I'm saying is… well, I don't know what I'm saying. You do what's right for you, Tristen."

"I'm trying to do what's right for me, Owen. I got a gig at O'Donnell's, and Lin is coming in to record his next album, and I'm trying to write something up for my own album. Plus, I work here and help out at the camp. How would I do all of that while watching a kid that isn't even mine?"

"You're right, Tristen," Owen said. He tapped the counter. "Of course you're right. I'll see you around. Gotta get your mom to that support group she goes to."

"Thought you were going to church?"

Owen grimaced. "They hold it in the basement of the Baptist church."

Twenty

THURSDAY AFTERNOON, TRISTEN FOUND himself in a small cabin room surrounded by five twelve-year-old boys, each holding a cheap guitar and asking when he would teach them cool songs. It was his third class of the day, and he was over it. When Rob had called him in on a favor, he hadn't thought to ask specific questions. He'd said yes thinking it gave him the perfect excuse to see Scarlett again. At this rate, seeing Scarlett later was the only thing keeping him going.

"Not like that, Dave. Move your fingers like this," he said, adjusting the kid's hold.

"How are things in here?" Rob called from the front door. He entered, grinning from ear to ear at the kids. "How do you like your teacher?"

"We like him," a kid said, concentrating so hard on getting his finger placements correct that he didn't notice his tongue sticking out. "But we still aren't playing cool songs."

Tristen looked at Rob and shook his head.

Rob chuckled. "I'm sure you'll get there. Class time is over. We're outside, ready to play some games. Can you boys set the guitars back against the wall and come outside?"

The boys scrambled down, their shouts of joy deafening in contrast to their playing.

Tristen looked around the room as the door closed behind Rob. He hadn't known he'd have to straighten up the classroom, too. As he set the guitars in their proper place, his phone rang.

"Hello, Tristen Levisay. We have things to talk about." Lamia.

"As I said, I'm not sure we're supposed to be talk to each other on the phone. Our lawyers are figuring this out."

There was mumbling on the other end of the phone. He wasn't sure if Lamia thought she was hiding the other voice, or if she didn't care that he could hear it. Either way, he waited. He could have hung up. He should have hung up. But he was curious. And she'd probably call back.

"Can you put your camera on?" Lamia asked.

"No. I'm at work."

"Your son wants to see you," Lamia said, her voice insistent and low.

That might have worked if he was the kid's real father.

"I don't want to turn on my camera, Lamia."

"Hold on a minute. Before you go, let me say that you had a really good idea with this DNA thing. I'm glad we're doing it. And when the judge gets you on the hook to pay child support and my legal fees, I'm gonna go dancing," she said. "Dancing on your grave."

She knew. Someone had told her about the DNA. He had no more chips to play. He was screwed.

"I'm not the father, Lamia, and I think you know it."

Lamia made a noise like she didn't believe him. A baby cried out in the background. "I'll tag you. You should watch it."

"What? Watch what?"

"You'll see."

Then she hung up, which was what he should have done the minute he heard her voice on the other end of the phone. He was still staring at the phone when it pinged about someone going live. And he couldn't help it. He clicked.

"That's right, ya'll. Just got off the phone with him. Hmm-mmm. Wait till he gets the news he has to pay for this child. You know what I'm talking about, StarRay. You know. Yes, SlimMama, I will make him pay. Let's talk about men and their inability to take responsibility. I mean, look at this man who hasn't ever even held his son. Not once. Doesn't care to do it. He doesn't even have a real job now."

Lamia was close to the phone, her skin beautifully smooth, her eyes outlined perfectly in black, her full lips smeared with pink and moving slowly as she spoke. She was a beautiful woman, yet everything about her repulsed him. Tristen couldn't believe his brother had been attracted to her enough to start a relationship with her while being separated from his wife, Sandra. And when Talon had returned to Sandra, he'd left Lamia pregnant.

But his brother's biggest moral failing, in his opinion, was that he'd told Lamia his name was Tristen Levisay. Talon had twin-swapped for a fling. Sex. Something they had never talked about—because it should have gone unspoken that it wasn't necessary. It wasn't done. And the why of him doing it? Tristen could only assume it was in case Talon had ever got back together with Sandra. He'd thought it was bad enough when Talon left the band without warning; that betrayal had hit him hard. But this got him so angry every time he thought of it, he wasn't sure he'd ever be able to forgive his brother.

"Damn, Talon." Waves of anger swelled up in his chest until his whole body was hot as Lamia continued on and on about how terrible men were.

"How was I supposed to know that my rockstar boyfriend would end up practically homeless? I mean, the guy is living with his mother again. Isn't that pathetic?"

Overcome with fury, Tristen tapped out a quick response defending himself but then reconsidered. Lamia was talking to her audience, people who probably weren't up for listening to anything he had to say in his defense. Which meant that they wouldn't believe anything he said.

He shook his head and deleted the response but still couldn't get his finger to swipe away from the video.

"Oh, it's going to be a great day when I'm vindicated," Lamia said, her entire face filling the screen before the phone went black and informed Tristen that the live was over.

"Damn. Crazy bitch," Tristen muttered under his breath as he locked up the cabin. A group of kids walking past sidestepped him, their eyes wide.

"Everything alright?" Rob asked, coming out of nowhere. Tristen took a deep breath to keep himself from jumping out of his skin.

"Yeah. Sorry. Family issue."

"Okay," Rob said. Tristen looked up from his phone to find Rob still standing in place. He wasn't smiling.

"Is something wrong?"

Rob cleared his throat, glancing away before looking at Tristen again. "We have a policy not to swear around the kids."

"Right. Sorry. I'll try to keep it in check."

Rob didn't seem satisfied with that answer. "It isn't about trying, Tristen. We don't use certain words, and we don't behave in, well, certain ways. We also don't talk about politics or sex. There's a reason for the policy."

Tristen wished he could turn around and walk away, but Rob was his friend. On the other hand, he was making him feel bad about words. It all seemed very stupid. "Okay, Rob. I get it."

"But?"

"You and I turned out fine, and we heard worse things in our lives."

Rob smiled, but it didn't quite reach his eyes. "We turned out okay, sure. But imagine if the adults in our lives had put up boundaries about what we were exposed to and instead allowed us to be little children playing? What if the adults in our lives had let us be innocent? I want the kids to know what it feels like to have adults put them and their innocence first. Even if it's just for five days."

Every answer Tristen thought of seemed petty.

"Makes sense," he said, clearing his throat. "I get it."

Rob grinned and patted him on the back. "Thanks, Tristen. You heading into the studio? Need anything from me for it?"

"No," Tristen said. He smiled and waited for Rob to leave before he ducked back inside the cabin. A European number had called him twice in the last few minutes and he was pretty certain he knew who it was.

"You finally decided to call me back."

"We need to talk, Talon."

"Yes, we do. You need to stop sending me emails about this, Tris. I don't want a paper trail. Sandra is due in less than a month. Stop trying to ruin everything."

Tristen ground his teeth. "I'm not ruining anything," he gritted out. "We need to talk."

"I paid her a few thousand to leave me alone."

"She's coming after me for child support, Talon," Tristen hissed.

"Well, maybe it's your kid." Talon laughed. Living in Portugal had obviously ruined his ability to be funny.

"You know perfectly well it's not my kid. And so does Lamia. She's annoying, but she isn't stupid."

"Someone getting a crush on Lamia?" Talon asked. Tristen would have punched him for that comment if he were standing here. "Fine, not funny. Listen, she and I had an agreement that I would pay her once and she'd lay off."

"Well, it looks like she's changed her mind. She's taking me to court. Elijah is helping me fight it, but it'd be easier if you would testify or something."

Talon was quiet for a moment. "You didn't have to get Elijah involved or the courts. But now that you did, it's your problem."

"My problem? Your mistress wants me to pay for a kid that isn't mine. I'm not the guy who knocked her up."

Talon snorted. "Yeah, I know. You're the brother who rescues everyone so he can rub it in my face."

The accusation left Tristen without a response. He lowered his voice and tried a different tactic. "I've tried to get a hold of you several times. You never called back."

"I was on tour, Tristen."

"Fine," Tristen said, trying to breathe steady. "Lamia asked for the DNA test—"

"Oh, man. You really screwed yourself." Talon laughed so loudly Tristen had to hold the phone away from his ear. "The DNA test won't show a damn thing."

Tristen squeezed his eyes shut. "Exactly. It won't prove anything." He couldn't believe Talon had known this might happen.

"Look, I can try to pay her a little more and see if she'll stop, but I can't keep doing this. I'm over here waiting for my daughter to be born. I can't keep paying Lamia."

Tristen hoped his brother realized what he had said the second the words left his mouth. He gave him a second to take it back, but Talon didn't say any more.

It suddenly occurred to him that if he were smarter, he would have recorded this conversation to take to court. But he had no idea how to even do that, and it was too late now.

"You should have thought about that before you knocked her up," he said, trying hard to keep his voice smooth, to not show how angry he was. "Using my name without my permission. Figure this out, Talon. Call the crazy bitch and get this figured out."

"I can't call her," Talon said. He sounded angry. As though Tristen had insulted him. "I can't have her know my number or where I live. She'd call my house."

"That isn't my problem," Tristen said.

But the line went dead before he could rant further.

"Stupid idiot." Tristen choked on the words he really wanted to say before hurling his phone at the wall. A guitar fell and crashed to the floor, splintering into pieces.

Twenty-One

"Scarlett," a voice called out behind her.

Standing in the Camp Soul parking lot with Eric, Scarlett turned to find Tristen waving at her as he jogged through the parking lot. She pasted on a smile.

"Is that your new boyfriend?" Eric asked, jerking his chin towards Tristen. He had called that morning after Scarlett told him about Candi being home. He wanted Ben at his house in case the guardian ad litem called him for an interview. Scarlett couldn't see that happening without him being told ahead of time, but she hadn't argued. She could use some days alone. The day before had drained her more than she would have thought possible. When she was younger, she'd assumed that the older she got the less her mother would affect her, but it didn't seem to be working. Sometimes it seemed like she affected her even more.

"That's my boxing teacher," Ben told Eric, his tone exasperated. "And I think he teaches sound here. I don't know. He's here a lot, aren't you, Tristen?"

Tristen was grinning, his forehead shining with new sweat from his jog. "What's that, Ben?"

"I said you're here a lot," Ben told him. He rolled his eyes and pointed at Eric. "My dad thought you were Scarlett's boyfriend."

"Maybe someday, Ben," Tristen said, winking at Ben. "I'm Tristen."

Scarlett wondered if they could tell how much she was blushing. Thankfully, she was already flushed from the heat. The men shook hands while she grabbed Ben's bag and sleeping bag from her truck. At least it was working. She made a mental note to send Jared a thank you note. Somehow, he had managed to get the bill down to four hundred dollars.

"Have a good night tonight, Ben." She looked at Eric while Ben climbed into the car. "Don't answer any calls from Candi if they come in."

Eric nodded, then got into his car and drove off.

"Everything okay?" Tristen asked as Scarlett watched it go. "You look like you're stressed."

"I had a rough day," Scarlett told him. She hoped she looked a little better than she felt, but doubted it. "Some family stuff. What are you up to?"

"Came to see if you needed a ride."

Scarlett patted the side of her truck and grinned. "Jared brought the truck to my apartment on Tuesday night. How are your fingers? You haven't whined about them since we got ice cream."

Tristen wiggled them. "Almost like new. And I didn't whine." He sighed when she raised her eyebrows. "Okay, maybe a little. At any rate, it was a reasonable excuse to get out of folding towels at the gym."

"Well, I'm glad I could help get you out of work, even if it was painful."

Tristen shifted closer. "You've been busy. I haven't seen you around."

He smelled of fresh clothes with a hint of cologne. Part of her wanted to snuggle up to him; press her head against his chest, wrap her arms around him and squeeze hard. She imagined he would feel like stability, a rock in the middle of her life's walls cracking.

"I've been here, at least today and Tuesday. Yesterday I was at the Wednesday market and then had some things to do. Rob and Dariana have been really understanding."

Tristen pushed aside the chunk of her hair that had blown across her face. "Good," he said. "I mean, it's not good you're having a hard time. I was beginning to think that you were avoiding me."

Scarlett watched him, reveling in his fingers lingering against the side of her face. She wanted to close her eyes, nestle against his hand.

"I'm not avoiding you," she said. "So far, you've taken me to my new favorite restaurant and to the best ice cream in the county. I wouldn't avoid a friend like that."

He laughed, but dropped his hand when he did. She glanced at it, feeling its absence from the side of her face intensely.

"I'm playing a live set over at O'Donnell's tonight and I was wondering if you'd want to come and, well, listen. Or if you sing, we could do a duet."

"No way! I do not sing on stage."

"What about listening with other people?"

Scarlett squirmed. She was tired, but going out might be good for her. "Tonight? All the way at O'Donnell's?"

"I could pick you up and take you, if you want. Or we could get some dinner now and then go."

"Oh, no. If I'm going to go out, I'm changing first. I'm not showing up with the happy hour crew in my baking clothing. I have flour all over myself."

"I think you look great," Tristen said. "But I get it. My ex never went anywhere without trying on at least six outfits."

Scarlett didn't like him talking about an ex. "Well, I don't have six different outfits that would work for a night out, but I'll probably try on at least two."

"You'll come then?"

"It sounds fun, so yes, I'll be there."

Scarlett ran into the apartment, stripping off her clothes before the door was shut and locked. Her energy had skyrocketed during the drive home. Tristen wanted her at the bar to listen to him play. She would be the girl in the audience who knew the musician, who'd been invited specifically by the musician.

It felt like a movie.

Her phone rang just as she decided to leave her hair down.

"Scarlett?"

"Cory, hi."

"What're you doing?"

"Uh, nothing. What's up?"

"Okay. We still on for later?"

"Tonight?" She had forgotten they made plans. Getting some good sex might help end the week better. "I'm going out, but I'll be home later."

"With Nasreen?"

"Maybe. Or maybe by myself."

"By yourself?"

Scarlett winced. "Or you could come." She made a face at herself in the mirror. "See some live music or something."

"Can't. I got a work thing."

Scarlett almost sighed in relief but caught herself in time.

"But I'll come by around eleven."

"That's late, Cory."

"You don't want me over?" he said, lowering his voice to the husky one he used when kissing her neck. It usually sent butterflies through her stomach, but tonight it did nothing.

"Not tonight," she said. "It's too late and I have to work tomorrow."

Cory sighed loudly into the phone. "Guess that's what I get for encouraging you to get a job. But fine, I'll see you Sunday? Will Ben be with Eric?"

"I don't know, Cory."

"Sounds like you want me to get off the phone."

"I need to get showered. I smell like bread."

"Fine."

After the line went dead, Scarlett couldn't unclench her jaws. Cory was a great part-time lover, but he wasn't her boyfriend, and she refused to feel bad about not wanting him over that late at night. She inhaled under the hot shower. He hadn't invited her to his work thing. Or to anything really. He never took her out.

But Tristen invited her places. Even to see him play.

Scarlett froze as she stepped out of the shower. If Cory hadn't called, she could have brought Tristen home with her only to find Cory waiting for her. That would have been embarrassing.

No, that would make you a whore. Candi's voice was loud in her head, as if she stood in the bathroom with her.

Scarlett brushed the criticism aside. It wasn't like she was exclusively dating either one of them. Not that she wouldn't become exclusive for a man, if he wanted her. But Cory had never wanted her exclusively. And while she dreamed of Tristen wanting her, she knew he was probably being nice.

And men slept with several women at the same time all the time.

She stepped back and took a hard look at herself in the mirror. Despite feeling pretty the way Tristen looked at her, she was still the chubby girl with over-sized boobs and full lips that had invited more than a few lewd comments since she was twelve. She hadn't been exclusive with a man since George, and he had warned her that she wasn't the kind of woman men married.

Candi used to say the same thing.

Scarlett tied on the wrap-around black dress she had found in a thrift store months before which accentuated her boobs and made her feel sexy. Then she pulled her hair to one side. Putting on earrings, she looked at herself again.

It was still the same Scarlett.

Except with a slightly more determined look in her eye. And why not? There were women on social media who traveled and went out alone all the time. So why shouldn't she?

She pulled out her phone and looked up O'Donnell's. It would take her less than twenty minutes to get there. Not having any money for a ride share meant she'd have to drive, which meant she'd need to eat something before she went.

She marched to the kitchen and heated leftover pizza. She was going out. At least for a few hours. And there was no stopping her.

⟝

"Beer," Scarlett told the bartender with gauges in his earlobes and three piercings in his right nostril. He barely registered her presence, but handed over the cold beer. Scarlett paid and opted to stay at the bar for a little while to pretend like she was waiting for someone to show up. Sitting alone in a dress suddenly seemed more pathetic than fun as groups of co-workers and couples entered the bar. "What time does the music start?"

The bartended glanced at her and pointed to a sign behind him before moving to the next customer.

"Scarlett."

She turned to find Tristen standing in jeans and a black T-shirt with a guitar slung across his torso. He looked good enough to eat.

Scarlett swallowed. As kind as Tristen was, she was not his type. She was much too pudgy and slutty for someone like him.

"Beer and water?" the bartender asked. Scarlett couldn't help chuckling.

"Please," Tristen said. He looked at Scarlett. "You laughing at me? Did I have something on my face?"

"No," Scarlett said, taking a gulp of beer to clear her throat. "No, sorry. That guy didn't say a word until now. Not even when I asked when the music started. All he did was point to the poster."

"Andy is a man of limited words. Aren't you, Andy?" Tristen asked when Andy came back with his drinks.

"Don't speak if I don't have to," Andy said with a shrug before sauntering off.

"You don't have to pay?" Scarlett asked.

"Perk of being a performer."

"Maybe I should learn guitar," she teased, more comfortable now that she wasn't standing at the bar alone. "Getting the star treatment would be nice every now and then."

Tristen snorted. "I wouldn't say it's star treatment. And you don't want to be a musician. It's a thankless job, and the number of times you have to start over are endless."

"Maybe you should write a song about it," Scarlett said. "A country song."

Tristen threw his head back and laughed. "I think it would work, actually."

Scarlett grinned. She liked making him laugh.

"Wanna get some Indian food after the show?"

Scarlett scrambled to form words that weren't her screaming 'Yes!'

"Listen, we'll talk more at intermission, okay?" Tristen said, giving her arm a squeeze. "Andy, get this woman another beer on me. Once you get your beer, go over there to that table. Are you alone?"

Scarlett's bubble burst. She squirmed. "Yes. I couldn't find anyone to come with me."

"Even better," Tristen said.

"Really?" she asked, thrilled he was pleased.

"Absolutely. The best table in the house is little. If you get your beer and come with me, I'll show you where it is."

Twenty-Two

Tristen strummed his guitar strings while he allowed himself to sneak another peak at Scarlett.

As though feeling his eyes on her, she turned her head, locking eyes with him. He always chose one person to perform to at every concert. Tonight he would sing directly for Scarlett.

"Good evening, everyone," he said. "I'm Tristen Levisay. No, I'm not the Levisay playing with AOR."

Chuckles rippled through the crowd. Probably the Thursday night regulars who had heard the spiel several times at that point.

"I'm the more handsome twin," he went on.

It was the same joke he said every week, but it always landed well, especially when he turned his face so they could see his profile. A whistle went up in the crowd, along with some female shouting.

"Thank you, darlings," he said, using his deepest voice. "I always love to hear from a fan."

He kept strumming. When he'd started at O'Donnell's he had feared the excitement of playing for a crowd wouldn't be there, but that worry had been baseless. In fact, when he didn't have the stress of running it as a business and trying to make money, when he could just play for the fun of it, he was more excited.

When The Seethers found a small amount of success, Tristen had found himself starting to compare the crowd size each time they played, as though a small amount of money made meant their crowds should double and triple. But it had never happened.

The only time he'd seen large crowds was with the small tour they'd done opening for AOR—which ended in AOR taking Talon on as their lead singer and finishing The Seethers.

Starting from zero on his own, he just tried to take in the moment and enjoy playing for a crowd, big or small. The stuff he played at O'Donnell's wasn't the music he dreamed of playing, but it still made him feel alive. When Aimee, his sister, and he used to play and sing together, the hours had passed so quickly in a state of such peaceful euphoria that Tristen remembered thinking it was equivalent to being high.

No, it was better than being high. No downward effect. No hangover. No mental spiral or trouble sleeping.

And no overdosing.

Tristen strummed louder as some in the crowd realized he was playing a new rendition of *Walking on Sunshine*. At the chorus, half the crowd joined in.

"Welcome to Friday night, everyone," he said as he strummed out the last notes. "If you have a request, please bring it up. I get real excited when someone brings up a Britney Spears song. Just FYI."

A group of women in the back corner hollered and giggled. One started singing *Oops!...I Did It Again.*

"Well, if you want to sing, come on up here," Tristen said, using the lowest tone he could muster. The women giggled more but declined to join him. "Fine, fine. I'll perform all alone. Guess that's what they pay me for. We'll continue with a little song from a not very well-known artist—"

"Sing Art of Rendering," someone shouted.

"We could do that," Tristen said, ignoring the spike in his heart rate. "But so you don't all get on social media with a lie, like I said before, I'm not the Levisay that sings with them. That's my brother, Talon."

A smattering of groans rose from the newbies who had wandered in.

"You guys always make me feel so loved," he joked. The groans turned to laughter. "All right, let's play some music."

His fingers strummed and flicked, the beat starting low and then rising as it grew faster. The women in the back were the first ones to recognize the song as one that had recently gone viral: an indie folk group from Iceland who had managed to get their song played millions of times by using a short clip. He had never seen the value of social media until Lin showed him how many downloads it received.

"Say you'll stay right here with me." The crowd joined him in the bridge, the most used clip in all the videos online. He still froze at the very idea of recording himself and posting it online, but he was warming to it a little more every day. *"Cause right here I'll remain."*

Almost everyone in the bar clapped at the end. Another indication of social media magic. The bar was about two-thirds full by now, with another group of young professionals in polo shirts and khakis entering.

"Talon!" one of the new customers yelled, getting some giggles in reply.

"I'm Tristen." He vowed that was the last time he would say anything about it. "But since you're a fan, let's sing an Art of Rendering song, yeah?"

The one woman with the new group giggled and elbowed the loudmouth in the ribs. Tristen turned away and focused more on the women in the back. They would probably end up being his loyal listeners that evening.

"There was a time, when we were young, you still thought life was fun. Then everything stopped."

More than half the crowd joined in with him on the last three words. Art of Rendering always cut the music for a beat right then, emphasizing the 'stop,' so he did as well, but he was too impressed not to say something. "Nice, nice. Let's keep going. *Isn't it just like life to fade away just like that?"*

The lyrics weren't poetry, but they spoke a simple truth that the crowd obviously liked.

The idiots in polos grew noisier despite some customers throwing them dirty looks. Instead of trying to speak over the noise, Tristen continued his set, trying to figure out a song the loudmouth didn't know. It turned out he knew Johnny Cash, but when Tristen started a Joni Mitchell remake, the guy lost interest. Finally.

"Alright, then. This boy's gotta take a break. I'll be back in about fifteen," Tristen announced.

A smattering of clapping responded as he turned off the mic and stepped down from the stage. The stereo in the bar picked up right away, blasting into some classic rock from the eighties that had people immediately bobbing their heads.

"You're good," a woman said, leaning in close to him as he put his guitar back into its case. She smelled of cheap beer.

"Thanks."

"And hot," said another from behind him. Tristen ignored that statement.

"Excuse me," he said, before walking towards Scarlett.

"Got some groupies already, huh?" Scarlett asked. She was beautiful with her pink cheeks and dark brown curls swept to the side, her dress hugging her body perfectly.

Tristen looked back at the women and shrugged. "You want another beer?"

Scarlett squirmed, tugging on her dress to cover her cleavage. Tristen's eyes dipped down involuntarily before he yanked them back up. It had been too long since he'd been with a woman.

"I wouldn't mind, but there aren't any waiters. I was afraid I'd miss your set if I got up."

Her words fed his ego; he couldn't help standing a little taller at her wanting to hear him sing. It had been a long time since someone came to listen to him. "Come on. If someone takes the table, I'll give you a seat next to me."

"Heck no," Scarlett squealed. "I'm not going on stage."

"Why not?" Tristen teased, pulling her gently to her feet. "Everyone can sing. I mean, it's not like I have the voice of Frank Sinatra. I try to not let it crack in the middle of the song, and I don't attempt Mariah Carey."

Scarlett laughed as they made their way to the bar, which was crowded.

"Two," Tristen shouted over to Adam. His shaved head bobbed up and down in response.

"Scarlett."

Tristen and Scarlett turned to find Cory, that client of Jared's who'd been at the market the other day, looking angry. He'd walked in with the loudmouth crowd.

"Hi, Cory," Scarlett said, barely audible above the buzz of the crowd.

"It's weird you decided to come here," Cory said. "So close to where I work."

Scarlett looked at the door as though it held a map. He was acting like a jealous former boyfriend. Operative word 'former'. Tristen hoped Scarlett hadn't lied about not seeing anyone.

"How'd you know I'd be here?" Cory asked.

"I didn't," Scarlett said. "I didn't realize this was close to your work. I guess I didn't put two and two together."

"Yeah, that would be math," Cory muttered. Scarlett's cheeks turned pink. Tristen had the impulse to clock the guy, but with his boxing background he couldn't just go around punching people and not expect to get thrown into jail.

"You guys missed most of the set," he said, moving so he partially blocked Scarlett. "You gonna stay for the second half?"

"Yeah, maybe," Cory said. He turned to Scarlett. "Is he bothering you?"

Scarlett burst out laughing, which Tristen felt was somehow an insult to him. "No, he's a friend. Or rather, a co-worker. He's helping Rob at the camp. Besides, he invited me."

Cory pulled away, his chest puffing slightly, his shoulders rolling back. "Invited you, huh?"

"Cory, we found a table." Three more men in polos showed up, each holding a beer or harder liquor, each grinning stupidly at Tristen and Scarlett. "Who's this?"

"That's the singer," the red-head said.

"This is my friend, Scarlett. We were friends in high school," Cory said, indicating Scarlett with his beer.

"Scarlett?" one guy squealed, but the moment he said it Cory slapped him on the back. The man closed his mouth into a smile.

"Thanks a lot, boys. A girl goes to use the lady's room, and suddenly all her dates are gone."

This woman was dressed in heels and a slim skirt suit. Her hair was a thick mane of flowing curls; her skin appeared flawless, with bright red lips that curved into a beautiful smile.

Scarlett seemed to perk up slightly at the sight of her. Cory shifted uncomfortably.

"Rebecca," yelled the redhead, unnecessarily loud. "We would never abandon you. We're celebrating, aren't we? This is Tristen, the singer, and Scarlett."

Rebecca laughed, clinking her glass of wine against the man's bottle of beer. Then she turned to Tristen. "Well, hello there, singer. Hi, Scarlett. Nice to see you again."

"Thanks," Scarlett said. "Nice to see you. I hope we can talk soon about catering to your office."

"I told Scarlett that you put her card into the rotation pile and that the office would call when it was her turn," Cory said quickly.

"That is how it works at our office," Rebecca said, smiling between Cory and Scarlett. "Daddy thought it was the fairest way to support local companies."

Cory gave a slight, almost imperceptible nod. He was gazing at Rebecca in a strange way.

Rebecca cocked her head to the side, as though waiting for Scarlett to say something. She gave off an air of viciousness that Tristen didn't like. His leg jerked instinctively to block Scarlett from Rebecca, but he stayed where he was.

"I'm having a party on Saturday to celebrate my engagement. I mean, not this Saturday. That would be crazy," Rebecca said with a laugh.

"So next Saturday? Or further out?" Scarlett asked politely.

"Next." Rebecca pushed her hair back over her shoulder and took a sip. "Maybe we could talk about you catering that?"

Cory's hand jerked, spilling his beer on the red-head and earning him some unfriendly remarks. Rebecca's eyes flickered towards them.

"I'd love to, but you don't have a caterer already?" Scarlett asked.

Rebecca laughed again. It sounded like a noise she made just to fill in the air-time. "Well, I just thought of it on a whim this morning. If you don't want to do it, I'm sure I can find someone else willing to."

"No," Scarlett exclaimed, moving her whole body to get back into Rebecca's view. "I'd love the opportunity to cater for your engagement party. You have my card. Call me and we'll talk through what you want."

Tristen flinched inwardly. Something was wrong. He didn't know who these people were, but they gave him the feeling Scarlett was being played, like she was the butt of a joke.

"I gotta get back on stage," he said, wanting to get as far away as possible.

He saw Scarlett's eyes for the first time move between Rebecca and Cory. Her smile weakened, but only slightly.

"Music is back, everyone. Anyone have a request, besides Art of Rendering?" Tristen asked the crowd, receiving a barrage of pop and rap songs the crowd clearly thought would be hilarious if he could sing them—a white guy with a blond beard and ponytail from Kentucky.

"Carol Burnett," someone shouted. The suggestion broke the tension wound up inside Tristen as he burst into laughter.

"I'm a musician, not a red-headed comedian from the sixties. But the sixties is a start," he said, starting the intro to 'Top of the

Bay'. Then he rolled into some Motown and the Rolling Stones before coming back to contemporary music again with Mumford and Sons and Lady Gaga.

He watched for Scarlett as he sang, but she seemed to have disappeared.

His last song was his own version of 'Jolene'. No matter what age the crowd was, they always seemed to know the words. And ending on a song everyone knew seemed to bring in more tips.

"That's all, folks," Tristen said, setting his guitar immediately into the case. Sometimes he was willing to play some encores, but not tonight. He needed to find out what had happened to Scarlett. "Have a great night."

Twenty-Three

TRISTEN SQUEEZED HIS WAY through the crowd, apologizing constantly until he made it out the door. The night was hot and humid with a hint of rain in the air. He looked up and down the deserted street, then jogged to the parking lot in the back.

"Scarlett," he called out to the only silhouette underneath the dim parking light. The silhouette turned. "Scarlett, wait. Are you leaving?"

He jogged closer, taking it as a good sign that she was staying still.

"I had to step out and call Rob," she said.

"Rob?"

"Yeah, that woman in there—"

"Rebecca?"

Scarlett nodded excitedly. "I thought maybe she was being polite, but when I came back from the bathroom, she cornered me and said she was serious about hiring me for her engagement party. She said a brunch at first, but I can't deliver on Saturday morning, so she changed it to a tea. Which was so nice of her. I mean, I would have figured something out if I had to. But, anyway, I had to call Rob to see if he would mind me being in the kitchen more. I'll need the ovens." Scarlett beamed at him. "She's so rude, though."

Tristen laughed—out of relief that she wasn't leaving the show; relief she was getting a job. And because he couldn't help thinking the same about Rebecca. Something about the way she looked at Scarlett put him on edge.

Scarlett shrugged, her smile fading. "Rude or not, she hired me to make desserts for her engagement party. I need these kinds of jobs. You understand, being a musician and all. It's hard to get a business off the ground."

Tristen said, stepping closer, "Working for rude people is still work. I'm happy for you, Scarlett. You scared me though."

"How?"

"Thought you'd left me behind to eat Indian food on my own."

Scarlett looked behind her. "I was thinking I should be getting home. I've been up since five in the morning, and tomorrow I'm working at camp. After that I'll have to start figuring stuff out for this engagement tea." She paused. "Sorry, I'm babbling, aren't I?" She pulled her fingers through her hair as she laughed.

"That's okay," Tristen said, his eyes trailing where her fingers had combed back her hair. "I'll walk you to your car."

"You don't have to," she said quickly. "I mean, you probably have fans in there who want to talk to you."

"I'd rather be with you, Scarlett."

Even under the poor lighting, he could see her lips part into a smile. It was better than a thousand people clapping for him.

"Did you figure anything else out about Ben?" He wasn't sure if he should ask, but he wanted Scarlett to know he cared to hear about her problems.

"Uh, no," she said, turning so they could walk side by side. "I mean, I'm not sure what to do. Nasreen thinks I should contact the guardian ad litem and see if they want to interview me, sort of get my hat into the ring. I've tried to call Rhoda on the last number she gave me, but it's disconnected. I don't want to mess anything up about the custody 'cause I know Rhoda doesn't want custody taken away from her. But then I also don't want Candi to get custody. I don't know what to do, honestly."

Tristen put his guitar on the ground near her truck. "That sounds complicated."

Scarlett turned to look up at him. She brushed something away from his forehead, and it took all his strength not to grab her wrists and kiss her hard.

"Your situation is complicated, too, isn't it?"

"No reason to talk about that now," Tristen said. "If you don't mind me asking, where is Rhoda?"

Scarlett leaned against the back of the truck. "I don't know. She never tells me where she's going. But if I had to guess, I'd say she's working some illicit job."

"Whaddaya mean?"

"You haven't met her yet, but if you had, you'd know. She has a slightly scary, mysterious air about her. She always knows stuff about people. And she deals in cash for the most part. Like, wads of it."

"Huh." Having grown up the way he had, Tristen could imagine a number of jobs Rhoda could be doing. None of them good for Scarlett to be involved in.

A group of people talking loudly on their way to a car interrupted them. Tristen glanced up, recognizing some of the polos. He grabbed Scarlett's hand and returned his attention to her as the car sped off.

"Are you going to fight for guardianship?"

"Are you?" Scarlett asked, turning to him. "The child that woman says is yours. That you said you'll have to pay child support for."

"I'm the parent, so it'd be custody," Tristen said. He choked when he realized what he'd said. "I mean, I'm not really the parent but I'd be declared the parent. At any rate, I hadn't planned on suing for custody. I'm fighting against being forced to pay right now."

Scarlett nodded. "I don't know what I should do either," she said, pushing herself off the truck. "I better go. Thanks for helping me, Tristen."

"Anytime," he said, but neither of them moved. Another streetlight turned on, sending streams of highlights into her hair. His throat suddenly went dry. "Hey."

When she swayed as though she might leave, he cupped her face with both of his hands and pressed his lips to hers.

She froze in place. For a moment he wondered if she didn't want him kissing her, but then she stepped forward, pressing her hips to his and opening her full lips. He didn't hesitate. His lips pressed hard, devouring hers completely.

In two steps he had her against the side of the truck. Her hands gripped his hair as he pressed his hips harder into hers, his tongue exploring her mouth.

"Scarlett," he whispered into her ear as he kissed her neck.

"What the hell is going on here?" a voice demanded behind him.

Tristen let go of Scarlett and whipped around. Cory stood alone under the lights, his face red with anger.

"Come here, Scarlett," he demanded.

Scarlett shifted behind Tristen, but he put his hand out to stop her.

"Is he your boyfriend?" he asked her over his shoulder. She shook her head. "Then you don't have to go anywhere."

"Scarlett," Cory said in a warning tone. "Come here."

Tristen tilted his head, his eyes on Cory. He'd seen him during his boxing lessons with Jared. It would be fun to set him straight.

"She's not doing anything you tell her to do, Cory," he said. "She isn't your girlfriend."

"She yours?" Cory asked. He stopped walking forward and threw his hands in the air. "Okay. I get it. She's giving you some on the side, isn't she? Damn, Scarlett. How much time do you have on your hands? Or should I say, knees?"

Tristen clenched his fists but didn't take the bait. "I'll give you one warning," he said. "The next time you're rude, I'll shut you up."

Cory chuckled.

"Just go, Cory," Scarlett said through gritted teeth.

"Yes, Cory, leave." Tristen stepped closer.

"She has a certain talent for all the things, doesn't she, Tristen? You know I was here first, right? I taught her the things she's using on you now. Are you paying her? Scarlett, you should at least get some cash, since he only wants a fast screw."

Before Tristen could rationalize his actions, his fist was crunching into Cory's jaw. The man flew through the air and landed hard on the gravel drive. If it had been up to him Tristen would have continued, but Scarlett pulled on his left arm, waking him to rational thought. He could not pummel Cory for his words. He could go to jail for it.

"Go home," he said through a clenched jaw. "Go home now."

Cory scrambled to his feet, gripping his bleeding nose and muttering obscenities. Tristen stood firm, watching him go until he was in his car and driving out of the parking lot.

"I'm sorry," he said, turning to Scarlett. "I probably shouldn't have punched him."

Scarlett threw her arms around his neck. "No one has ever defended me like that," she whispered, her lips so close her breath warmed his face.

He wanted to pick her up and take her home. Make love to her all night and whisper promises that he would punch every man on earth if it would make her feel safe—but instead Tristen stepped away. Compared to many men, he wasn't the smartest, but he knew when a woman had been mistreated all her life. And he knew if he tried to sleep with her now, he'd be no better than Cory.

"All women deserve to be defended," he said quietly. "Especially you, Scarlett."

Then he took a deep breath, smiled at her as she waved at him out her truck window, and watched her drive away. She deserved to be wooed, and he was determined to give her everything she deserved.

Twenty-Four

THE NEXT MORNING, SCARLETT could barely contain herself. Waiting until after two in the afternoon to see Tristen was the most painful thing she'd done in a long time. Each minute was agony; the clock moved so slowly she was beginning to think there was a conspiracy against her. At one point she asked Mrs. Beatty what time it was, only to have the older woman look at her like she was insane and point to the same clock that had been taunting her all day.

But now, finally, the kitchen was clean, and Maria and Mrs. Beatty had gone outside to enjoy the Friday afternoon. Since the campers had left that day at noon, with no student concert that afternoon, everyone was starting their weekends early, leaving Scarlett to bake in peace—if her brain would let her.

"Scarlett, I'm here," Ben yelled from outside the kitchen. He burst through the doors, his backpack bumping against his backside with each stride. "I went to guitar class."

"I know. Rob told me he was going to let you," she answered.

"What?" Ben yelled, turning as Tristen walked in.

Scarlett nearly dropped the cinnamon bun she was twisting together. Somehow Tristen had gotten more handsome since the night before. And she felt dumpier. She rolled her shoulders back and hoped she was standing at a flattering angle, even though she knew it was no use.

She wondered if he thought she was less cute in the full sunlight without the black dress and without the alcohol in his beer.

"You took me in as a charity case?" Ben demanded.

Tristen stopped mid-stride, glancing at Scarlett with panic in his eyes. "No. I didn't. I thought that the kids whose parents, or guardians, work here got access to all classes," he said.

Ben whipped his head around to glare at Scarlett. "Is that true?"

"As far as I know," Scarlett lied. She busied herself with putting a sheet of already risen buns into the oven to keep from looking directly at Ben. Maria's kids were too young to take guitar classes. "Besides, why would Rob let you in if you weren't allowed? You think he doesn't have any control over his camp?"

Ben glared at her, but when she managed to keep a straight face, he finally relaxed. "I'm bored. I wanna go home."

"Okay. We'll leave soon. You have time for a quick dip in the pool, if you want. I have to put these into the freezer and then pull the buns that are in the oven out. Once they're cool, we'll go."

"Can I have money for a drink from the vending machine?" Ben asked, his eyes narrowed. Scarlett could tell he was trying to keep his cool.

"In my purse," Scarlett told him. She normally said no, so this positive answer got the reaction she was hoping for. Ben's eyes lit up. He scurried to her purse and pulled out a dollar, yelling his thanks as he ran out the door. Scarlett couldn't help chuckling.

"He doesn't usually get to buy drinks," she explained to Tristen. "Sorry about him being a bit sensitive about the class. He's suddenly very aware of money and whether he has as much as the other kids."

"It's okay," Tristen said, giving her a wink and sending a cascade of shivers down her arms. "I was like that too when I was a kid."

Scarlett mulled over the question she had practiced a million times in her head, wondering if she had the guts to ask it. If he said no, it would devastate her more than he probably understood. But if he said yes, they might be on their way to an actual relationship.

It was almost too much to hope for, but she'd kick herself if she didn't say it. Scarlett took a deep breath and looked up at Tristen.

"Want to come over for dinner?" she asked, the words stumbling out quickly. "I don't have Indian food, but I could use the company. And I'm sure Ben would like it."

"Like what?" Ben asked. "I forgot to grab my swimsuit. What would I like?"

Scarlett swallowed. She had hoped to get an answer out of Tristen without Ben around. Now he might say yes to not hurt Ben's feelings. "I thought it would be nice to invite Tristen over for dinner."

"Yes," Ben shouted. "And you can help me set up the boxing bag."

"Boxing bag?" Scarlett asked.

Tristen looked sheepish. "First, if I'm still invited after I explain the boxing bag, I would love to come over for dinner. I'm not much of a cook, so anything outside of scrambled eggs and toast would be heaven."

Scarlett twisted her mouth in feigned disappointment. "That's what we eat every Friday night, though—breakfast for dinner."

Tristen turned as red as Ben's sports drink. "I didn't mean it like that."

"She's kidding," Ben said, punching Tristen on the bicep. "Camila is probably bringing tacos."

"I like tacos," Tristen said, his face returning to its natural color.

"We haven't determined that you're still invited," Scarlett said, crossing her arms over her boobs. "What's this about a boxing bag?"

"Right. So, we're revamping the gym and have some extra boxing bags."

"So?"

Tristen cleared his throat, glancing at Ben, who was beaming. "I said I would give one to Ben. If you're okay with it. He says he lives on the first level, so the neighbors below wouldn't be a problem."

"We could put it on the patio," Ben announced.

Scarlett threw her hands up. "Fine. I don't care. I'm not setting it up, though. You two are."

"And Zander," Ben said.

"Fine. And Zander."

"Does that mean he's still invited to dinner?" Ben asked. His lips were bright red from the drink, his eyes hopeful.

"Yes, he's still invited," Scarlett told him. As though she would un-invite him.

"Looks like I'm getting the punching bag. I'll meet you at your apartment later?"

"Can I come with you?" Ben asked. "I'd rather do that than go swim. And that way I can let you in if Scarlett isn't there. Okay, Scarlett?"

"Sounds like a plan," she said.

The sliding porch door opened; a cacophony of chattering filled the room.

"Time to wash up, boys," Camila called out. "Shoes off and hands washed. I brought the leftover enchiladas from the catering job I had today. We have plenty."

"I don't want enchiladas," Miguel whined, but no one paid attention to him. He complained about every food but pizza. The boys shuffled past in their bare feet towards the bathroom, Tristen included, until Camila stopped him with a palm on his chest.

"Isn't your brother the guy who sings for Art of Rendering?"

Tristen's eyes flickered over Camila, probably taking in her long, fake eyelashes and Olivia Rodrigo look. "He is. Are you a fan?"

Camila laughed, shaking her phone. "No. I did some background on you. Can't be too careful when a guy starts dating my friend."

"You remember Camila, don't you, Tristen?" Scarlett said, pointing at Camila. "You can wash your hands in the kitchen if you want. The boys take forever."

Camila let go of Tristen's chest. Scarlett glared at her, but Camila winked.

"These for eating?" Tristen asked, pointing at the basket of small sausages wrapped in croissant bread.

"Yes," Scarlett said. "Would you like a beer?"

"Sure." Tristen took a pig-in-a-blanket and popped the whole thing in his mouth.

"You aren't on social media a lot," Camila said. She lifted her phone to prove her point. "I thought a musician would be there more, trying to get fans or whatever."

Tristen paused, then continued chewing. Scarlett sipped her beer.

"I'm trying. Guess I'm not the social media type, unlike most of the rest of our generation. But you can see some of my uploads."

"They aren't very good," Camila told him. "You should wear a mic that goes directly to the phone. Or have someone record you while you're playing with a real camera. With the mic connected to it. Listen, hear how bad the recording is?"

Scarlett couldn't tell if Tristen was embarrassed or not. He seemed to pay attention as Camila scrolled through other videos, but Scarlett couldn't sit still. She hated Camila pointing out something Tristen did wrong without really knowing him.

"Camila is our social media addict," she explained. "I mean, expert."

Camila rolled her eyes but kept her smile. "I'll help you, if you want. I told Scarlett the same, but she won't get on social media."

"We found clips of your band," Nasreen piped up from the couch. She'd been quiet since she showed up.

Tristen stopped chewing. Now he *was* blushing, and Scarlett wished she had never invited him to a Friday night with her friends. "The Seethers," he said. "We broke up."

"What video is it?" Scarlett asked.

"A video of the end, I suspect," Nasreen said, tapping and scrolling until she found what she was looking for. Tristen leaned in, his cheeks flushing a deeper red.

"That was our last concert, right after Talon left. We were definitely not prepared for the changes his ditching us caused."

Nasreen raised an eyebrow. Scarlett tried to call her off, but she wasn't paying attention. Nothing stopped Nasreen when she was on a mission. "Your ex-girlfriend likes to tag you a lot."

"Meegan?"

"This one," Camila said, obviously in on the ambush. She held up her phone, showing a picture of a Kim Kardashian look-alike.

Tristen's mouth pulled down, his face filling with more disappointment than Miguel eating his cucumber. "That isn't my ex-girlfriend. That's Lamia."

Scarlett grabbed the phone. "The crazy lady?"

Tristen nodded.

"Well, no wonder your brother slept with her. She's beautiful."

Tristen scrunched his nose at the comment. "She has issues."

Camila laughed. "Sounds like she could be my cousin."

"Why does she say you're her kid's dad?" Nasreen asked.

Scarlett tried to send Tristen an apologetic look, but he kept his eyes on Nasreen. She should have known her friends would try to protect her, but it was a little embarrassing.

"My twin used my name and knocked her up. That's him, there." Tristen pointed to a man who looked exactly like him but without the beard.

"Looks like you to me."

"That's because we're identical twins," Tristen said, pulling up his left sleeve. "But look. No falcon tattoo."

Scarlett's heart skipped a beat at the tattoos he had crawling up his muscled arms. She inhaled slowly, afraid she'd start drooling any second.

Nasreen had to acquiesce. But only the battle. "So that baby isn't yours? She seems to think it is."

"Not my baby. But I can't seem to convince anyone of it."

"Why doesn't your brother take responsibility for his actions?" Camila asked.

Tristen glanced again at the photo and seemed to grimace. Scarlett thought the woman was beautiful, but then she wasn't pursuing her for child support. "Talon probably didn't plan on this woman getting pregnant, but she did."

"And now she's suing you for child support?"

"Yep."

"Where's your brother?" Camila asked.

"He's in Portugal. With his wife and daughter."

"Damn," Nasreen said. Camila whistled.

"Exactly," Tristen said. "And he's not answering my emails or phone calls."

"What about a DNA test?" Scarlett asked.

Nasreen shook her head. "Won't work if they're identical."

"Exactly what I found out," Tristen said, his voice tinged with anger. "I'm assuming I'll be declared the father and told to pay up."

The boys ran back into the living room like a hurricane, putting an end to any adult conversation.

"We're hungry," Ben announced. The rest of the boys echoed the sentiment.

"To the table," Nasreen ordered. "No one gets food without sitting at the table."

The following minutes were full of serving children and making sure Miguel didn't get the wrong hot sauce, but a loud knock at the door put an end to the frenzy.

Nasreen opened the door, her gasp hard to miss.

"What's wrong, Nasreen?" a familiar voice asked.

Scarlett almost dropped her glass of wine as her mother, Candi, stepped in.

Twenty-Five

"Well, what a welcome. Why are you all staring at me like that?"

Candi stood in the doorway in her usual jean jacket and jeans, her legs straight and long. Her black-dyed hair was piled on the top of her head with a folded blue bandana holding back the fly-aways right past her forehead.

The boys turned back to eating.

"Hi, Mom," Scarlett said. "You look good. Tan."

"And you look a mess." Her cackle hadn't changed; it sent the same shiver down Scarlett's spine. She never knew if her mom was teasing or being serious. Candi always claimed to be teasing. Scarlett always assumed she was serious.

"What's going on in here, little lady?" boomed a voice from behind Candi. Candi rolled her eyes and moved aside.

Scarlett smiled as Brody, her mom's boyfriend, came into view. He was the only nice boyfriend Candi had ever had. "Brody. Nice to see you."

Brody walked in dressed as though he was still on the beach with a floral oversized shirt and Bermuda shorts.

"Ben. Come say hi to your grandma. Where're your manners?" Candi barked the words, startling Miguel, who seemed to think shoving chips into his mouth as fast as possible was his best line of defense.

Ben stepped forward but didn't move to hug her.

Candi smirked, patting him hard on the back. "What is this? Don't know how to hug? That's okay. We'll teach you."

"Scarlett, hand us a beer, would you?" Brody said.

"Why are you both so tan?" Camilla asked. Brody grinned at her, but Candi was the one who answered.

"Caribbean, Camilla. Brody bought a house down there." Candi inspected the apartment. Her lips curled into a sneer. "This place looks the same. Like a dump after being in Brody's Caribbean place."

Scarlett looked around, avoiding eye contact with Tristen. "Yeah, I'm sure it does."

"Why don't you try to make it look like a home? If not for you, at least for Ben?"

Nasreen's cool, firm hand placed a beer into Scarlett's hand, unfolding her fingers from their clenched position. "Candi, tell us about your vacation. I've never been to the Caribbean."

"Well, you should," Candi said. "Lots of your people there. Of African descent, you know?"

Nasreen looked at Candi with a stiff smile. Her father was from Zimbabwe, but Nasreen hated when people talked like she wasn't American enough. "I was born here. That's literally as American as anyone else," she would usually say.

"I believe they consider themselves Caribbean, Candi, not African."

Candi didn't pay attention. She had caught sight of Tristen; her eyes bugged out of her head.

"Who is this hunk of a man?" she demanded, punctuating each word. "Scarlett! Do you have a boyfriend? Wait. No. He's yours, isn't he, Nasreen? That makes more sense."

Nasreen shook her head, walking towards Candi with her pink-painted finger wagging, but Candi plowed forward to touch Tristen on the bicep, leaving Nasreen behind.

"My, my. You are built. Brody! Look at this man. Why don't you look like this?"

"That's my boxing teacher," Ben said. "He's a boxer."

"Well, if he's your boxing teacher then he's probably a boxer, Ben," Candi snapped. She turned back to Tristen, shaking her head as though he might commiserate with her on how dumb her grandkid was.

Tristen stood as still as a statue.

"I used to look like that, too, Candi. Before everything started sinking downwards. Just like you, darlin'," Brody said.

Scarlett braced herself for the possible torrent of swearing from Candi after a comment like that. Before it could come, Tristen snapped into motion. "I'm Tristen Levisay. Nice to meet you, ma'am."

Candi took his hand, the fury slowly leaving her face until awe replaced it. "You're from Art of Rendering!" She glowed at the realization. "How did you meet Nasreen?"

"You're thinking of my twin brother, Talon. I work at Top Gym."

Candi dropped his arm. "Aren't you a lawyer, Nasreen? You gonna settle for a gym worker?"

"He's not my boyfriend, Candi," Nasreen said through clenched jaws.

Candi turned her narrowed eyes back to Tristen. "You tappin' my daughter?"

"Mom, stop."

Candi laughed, her hand landing on Tristen's bicep again. Her fingers ran up and down it. "I'm kidding, Scar. Shit. You're all so serious. You gotta get to the Caribbean a little and relax."

Scarlett needed something to do with her hands before she tried to strangle her mom, so she picked up a plastic container and dumped out some sourdough. It hit the counter with a slurping sound.

"What's that?" Candi asked, pointing.

"Sourdough dough."

"You still making bread as heavy as you and trying to sell it? Damn, girl." She broke into cackles that no one else joined in with. Scarlett pulled the dough towards her, then turned it clockwise, breathing slowly.

"Scarlett makes delicious bread, Candi. Practice has made perfect. She's killing it at the farmer's markets," Nasreen said in the voice that always got the boys' attention. They looked up with wide eyes from their enchiladas.

"You still bothering with the markets instead of trying to get up higher in the bank? What you gonna do about a retirement?"

"I'm saving for my retirement, Mom." She glanced at Nasreen, who knew it was a lie. Saving was the dream, not the reality.

"Scarlett works at Camp Soul," Ben offered through a mouthful of food.

Scarlett braced herself as Candi's lips curled up into a snarl.

"Of all the stupid things, Scarlett. You got fired from the bank, didn't you?" Candi laughed. "Oh, God, of course you did."

"The branch closed, Mom. Over a year ago. They didn't have enough positions for everyone when they merged it with the other branch in Pelton. I was one of the unlucky ones."

Candi snorted. "They knew what they were doing, not bringing you along. Bet they merged so they could let you go."

"Grandma, you wanna eat dinner with us?" Ben asked. His eyes shifted between Candi and Scarlett, back and forth.

"No, no," Candi said. "We only came over to give you all the good news."

"What's that?" Scarlett asked.

"Things went well with the Jenny lady and we've officially started the process for guardianship. After seeing how you're bringin' Ben up, I think it's my turn to get him."

Scarlett froze. "This isn't musical chairs, Mom. We aren't passing Ben around."

Candi sauntered closer to Scarlett. She pinched a piece of dough off and popped it into her mouth. "*You* aren't doing anything, and I'm not playing."

Scarlett stood her ground, pushing the dough to the side and keeping her eyes on her mom.

"We're all trying to do what's best for Ben, Scarlet. Clearly Eric isn't gonna work out as a full-custody father. He's a loser."

Ben's face turned red at the comment, his hands balling at his sides. Tristen knelt and whispered something in his ear which seemed to calm him a little.

"Candi, you don't need to talk like that in front of the boy," Brody said. Candi bared her teeth at him; he shrank back with a shrug.

"I'm sorry it's hard to hear the truth for some people," Candi said. She turned back to Scarlett, her eyes gleaming. "I think that you're ready to give up this whole experiment, aren't you? I mean, Rhoda said it would only be a year, and it's been five. Brody and I've decided to take Ben off your hands. At least I know what I'm doing. I raised two kids."

Scarlett tried to ignore the stares on her, her embarrassment that Tristen was witnessing the situation, and Ben's misery, and instead focused on answering Candi. She had to answer, otherwise her mother would assume everything she said was true.

"I never said that," she managed to say through clenched teeth, but her voice was quiet. She cleared her throat and tried again. "I never once complained about having Ben with me. We're doing well together. I don't see the point of changing his environment now."

Candi snorted. She twisted left to right but kept her focus on Scarlett. "You're clearly not up to the task. You can't even create a home. You have no experience. You barely have a job."

"I think it's time you go, Candi," Camila declared, but nothing ever stopped Candi. Scarlett knew it; she'd seen it all her life.

Her mother marched forward, index finger wagging. "I'll tell you something, Scarlett. You don't appreciate me and what I did for you all your life. I made the hard decisions that you weren't willing to make. For example, you should be grateful I didn't let you become a mom at seventeen. That sure was the right choice, since you've barely kept a job since and wouldn't even be able to afford this place if Rhoda wasn't paying for it."

Scarlett pressed her lips together as shame flowed over her body in waves of heat. She couldn't look at Nasreen, who was moving around to the side of her, and she refused to look in Tristen's direction. She wished she had never invited him.

"Time to go!" Nasreen practically yelled, her booming voice sending everyone into motion. Scarlett stayed still. "I think it's unfair of you, Candi, and I think you don't know at all what you're talking about. But tonight isn't the time to discuss it. Despite what you think you know, Scarlett has a job to wake up to tomorrow."

Suddenly, Candi laughed out loud. When she was growing up, Scarlett had always thought her mother would make a great witch—especially on Halloween. There was an eeriness to Candi's laugh, as though to tell all those around her that she had nothing to lose and was willing to show it.

"Okay, I'm going. Come on, Brody. No one wants to have this hard conversation. Course, this is exactly why Ben should live with us, where hard conversations happen. And the environment is more stable."

"You think that's what Rhoda wants?" Scarlett asked. The short sentence left her breathless.

"I don't give a rat's ass what Rhoda wants," Candi said, leveling her gaze again on Scarlett. "I brought up the two of you on my own, and I'm not gonna let you ruin him. I let you have your chance. You blew it, as usual. But Ben is not an experiment. He's a boy who need discipline and stability. And we're the right folks to give it to him."

If Scarlett's hurricane of emotions hadn't left her frozen, she might have laughed. But she said nothing as Candi marched out the door, shrouded in her own self-importance.

The rest of them left soon afterward, leaving Scarlett to pick up the pieces Candi's storm had ripped up and left behind.

Twenty-Six

Scarlett looked at Ben, who sat stunned at the table.

"Ben, I will make sure you don't go to her," she said. She didn't know how she would do that, but the words brought Ben to a stop.

"How?" he asked quietly, his back still turned to her.

Scarlett scrambled for words. "Listen. Eric is your dad, and the judges want kids to be with their biological parents. There's no reason for you to go to Candi when Eric wants you. Candi won't get you. She's like fifth in line."

"What about Mom?"

Scarlett hadn't expected that line of questioning. "What about her?"

Ben turned. Scarlett wanted to run to him and wrap her arms around him, but she crept closer slowly and kept her arms at her sides. When he'd first come to her as a five-year-old, he'd hated hugs and would fight her each time. They had learned to respect each other's boundaries, though now Scarlett wasn't sure if perhaps they had gone too far. But she sensed that if she moved too quickly, Ben would run away.

"Does she want me?"

"She loves you," Scarlett said.

"Then where is she?"

"I don't know," Scarlett finally admitted. She reached out, but he flinched away.

"I want to sleep over at Zander's house."

"Tonight?" She didn't want to tell him no, but Nasreen didn't allow last-minute sleepovers. "Maybe tomorrow, okay?"

Ben shrugged, then brought his wide brown eyes up to meet hers. "I'm going to bed."

"Okay." Scarlett watched him walk down the short hallway to the bathroom. "Goodnight, Ben. I'll see you in the morning."

"Yeah," was all he said before he shut himself into the bathroom.

Scarlett released her clenched jaw and breathed in slowly. Her phone vibrated somewhere against a hard surface.

I'm outside still. Want to talk?

She looked out the sliding patio door but saw nothing in the dark. Her first instinct was to answer that she was fine, but the truth was, she wasn't. It would be nice to talk.

Before she could think herself out of it, she pushed the patio door open and walked outside.

"Hey."

Scarlett jumped.

"Sorry," Tristen said, jumping over the low fence. "Didn't mean to scare you. You okay?"

Scarlett nodded, a lump forming in her throat. The world blurred through her tears, and she realized coming outside had been a mistake. Now Tristen would see her cry, maybe lose control, and he would find out she was an unemployed, fat loser.

"Hey, it's okay," Tristen murmured. He wrapped his arms around her shoulders and pulled her closer.

Scarlett stiffened, refusing to melt into him. Candi's jab from her teenage years echoed in her head: *Men only want one thing from big-breasted women.*

She did allow herself to rest her forehead on his shoulder. That was safe enough. He smelled of aftershave and detergent, the smell growing stronger as her tears fell faster. It took her a moment to get under control again, and by the time she lifted her head Tristen's shoulder was soaked.

"I'm sorry you had to witness that," she sniffled. To not abuse his kindness and not give him the wrong idea, she pulled out of his arms and plopped down into one of the second patio chairs. Tristen followed suit, elbows on his knees.

"You don't have to apologize for other people's behavior."

His words spoke more to her than a hug could. She thought about them for a minute, leaving him to sit in silence next to her.

"Still," she said into the darkness. "I invited you over to dinner, not to experience my mother. And for that, I'm sorry."

"I'm a big boy, Scarlett," Tristen said. "I can handle crazy mothers. Mine has had her moments in life." He breathed out hard, probably bombarded by memories as Scarlett was at that moment.

"I used to wish she would die," Scarlett murmured, the darkness giving her a boldness she didn't usually have. She glanced at Tristen, but his features were hidden in the shadows. "I guess that's terrible to say."

"From what I witnessed tonight, I don't really blame you. Not that I want people to die," he said quickly. "But growing up with parents who probably shouldn't have been parents puts a lot of pressure on us kids. My mother dabbled in drugs and alcohol all her life, and even though I can now understand that she was probably also struggling with the aftermath of trauma and depression, my understanding as an adult doesn't erase the hurt she caused when I was a kid."

"Hmm. Can I tell you something?" Scarlett asked. She didn't wait for him to answer. "I'm not sure I like her, much less love her. And I'm not sure I can ever forgive her."

Tristen was quiet. Too quiet, reminding Scarlett why she didn't tell people her real thoughts. Ever.

"Tell me the stories, Scarlett."

His voice and his words shocked her. Scarlett scoffed. "No. No one wants to hear that." Because no one would believe a mother could do the things Candi had done.

His strong, warm hand covered hers. "It helps to talk about them. And I want to listen. Start with one story. Any of them."

"You won't believe me," she whispered, staring at the dark outline of his hand still over hers. Her heart raced as she considered allowing herself to speak.

"I will." His hands squeezed hers gently, and Scarlett thought she might dissolve into tears, but she knew she was going to tell him. As though fate had written it down somewhere and she could only obey, open her mouth and say two words.

"April seventeenth."

Tristen waited, then asked, "What about it?"

"I was a sophomore in high school. Well, obviously. I never went to college." He didn't chuckle, so Scarlett moved on. "I guess I should start in September of that school year. I came home one day to that lovely trailer home where Candi and I lived, to find it empty. No note, no explanation. Nothing. Hardly any food, even. Not that I really cared. I was sixteen and was almost relieved to be by myself. I slept alone for a week before her boyfriend, the one at the time, showed up. He told me Candi ran away with a new man. He also claimed Candi told him he could have me as a consolation prize."

"*What?*" Tristen sounded the same as he had the night he'd punched Cory. His indignation sent a shiver up her spine.

"Those were the kinds of men Candi dated," Scarlett said slowly, visions of her childhood lighting up her memories. "Anyway, he was gross, so I left. I wasn't about to sleep with him." She paused. It probably wasn't the time to tell him Drew hadn't been the first man to sneak into her room. After her thirteenth birthday, Candi had sent Lee to 'make a woman' out of her. Candi had shouted those words to make sure Scarlett heard.

But that was a story for a different day.

"Anyway, I was homeless. I showered at the school and sometimes slept there. The janitor caught me a few times, but he didn't turn me in. Instead, he started leaving the back door propped open so I could get in. I'm not sure why, but I lived in constant fear that the school would find out. I thought they'd send me to foster care if they knew. Rhoda always told me how horrible the foster care system was, so I thought it would be worse than being homeless."

"What did you eat?"

Scarlett thought for a moment. "I was on the food program at school, so I had breakfast and lunch there. I skipped dinner at first, but then I started stealing from Walmart. That's how Mr. Warren caught me stealing chicken. He was my literature teacher. After catching me trying to shove some chicken nuggets into my coat, he brought me back to his house. I thought he was gonna expect me to do stuff, but at that point I was so tired, I almost didn't care."

A low growl emitted from Tristen's throat, but he didn't say anything.

"Anyway, Mr. Warren was a complete gentleman. He lived with his wife and their son, who was severely handicapped. They fed me and when they found out I was homeless, they let me move into the apartment above their garage. I stayed there until February, when Candi suddenly showed up again. At my school."

Scarlett remembered it had been an unusually cold day, and she had worn two sweaters to school, even though they made her look fat and dumpy. The girls in her class had no problem telling her so. Mrs. Warren had gotten her some clothes from the second-hand store in town, but they couldn't afford to give her too much on his salary and with the treatment and medication their son required. Scarlett hadn't cared; she was grateful for the room they had over their garage. She'd gotten the deepest sleep of her life while living there.

"Did she have an explanation for you?" Tristen asked, prompting Scarlett to return to the present.

"No, she just told me I was expected home that night."

"Did you go?"

"Heck no," Scarlett said. "I figured Candi would be happier that way, but she doesn't give up easily. When I didn't show all week,

I was called to the school psychologist's office and found my mom there in tears. Fake tears, of course, but the school psychologist either didn't notice or didn't care. When she stepped out for more tissues, my mom told me that if I didn't come home, she would formally accuse Mr. Warren of sleeping with me."

She hadn't even gotten to the part about April 17, but remembering everything about that year was starting to exhaust her. She could call it a night. She didn't have to tell him.

But then Tristen squeezed her hand. And Scarlett saw no reason to stop.

The truth might push him away, which was just as well. If, on the off-chance, he was attracted to her, it was best he knew how broken she was. That way, he could step away before he broke her heart.

"I went home that day. First thing Candi told me was I would have to pay rent by sleeping with the owner, Jonathon."

Tristen swore under his breath.

"Yeah, I don't know where Candi found these men. Thankfully, Brody is a normal human. But I complied because I knew that Candi would get Mr. Warren fired otherwise. My mom doesn't like to be defied."

"I sensed that," Tristen murmured. "What happened then?"

"April seventeenth," Scarlett said, the date turning her mouth to sawdust. "Candi picked me up from school and drove me to a clinic. I remember clearly everything about that ride, the way she jerked the car into park and what she said."

"What did she say?"

"'Beautiful day to get rid of stuff we don't need, you know?'" Scarlett quoted. The words brought back a torrent of emotions. "Then she said, 'We don't need to be paying no more for anything growing in there,' and she jabbed her finger into my belly."

Candi had also suggested she ask the doctor to suck out some of the fat from Scarlett's stomach as well, but she didn't mention that part to Tristen.

"I hadn't even realized I was pregnant, but Candi had. She told me she'd be back in two hours. I watched her drive off and, like a robot, went inside. Looking back, that's what gets me the most. That I always did what she told me to do. Like I had no thoughts of my own."

Tristen squeezed her hand again, but didn't say anything. He probably thought she was weak. He probably regretted asking her to talk, but now she couldn't stop.

"They were expecting me. They led me into a room, where a nurse gave me an exam and then handed me some pills and a glass of water. She watched me swallow the pills, then gave me a bottle and the instructions on when to take the next ones and the difference between them. I was supposed to leave after that, but it had been less than an hour, so I stayed in the waiting room, pretending I didn't feel well. When Candi didn't show up, I pretended I saw her, slipped out the door and started walking home."

Scarlett took her hand out from under Tristen's and automatically pressed it to her lower belly. She remembered the cramps as though they had happened this very day. "Halfway home, the cramping started. I was passing the school when I started bleeding. Thankfully, there was some sport event, so I went inside and snuck into the girls' locker room. I curled up in a spot between lockers that's a little dark and everyone avoids, and got through the pain."

Two hands pressing against her cheeks jerked Scarlett out of her memories. She was surprised to find Tristen kneeling on the ground, his hands cupping her entire face.

"I'm sorry," he said, so earnestly that she believed him. "I'm sorry you had to go through that."

She shrugged and tried to look away, but he held her face too firmly. "It isn't your fault."

"No, it isn't. But I want you to know that I'm sorry."

Scarlett nodded, closing her eyes as his lips pressed gently into her forehead.

"I'm very tired all of a sudden," she whispered.

"I'll let you get to bed," Tristen said. He pulled her to her feet as he stood.

When he started over the fence, she had to bite her lip to keep herself from asking him to come to bed with her and help her forget the memories again.

"Scarlett," he whispered, almost invisible in the darkness.

"Yes?"

"I'll see you tomorrow."

Scarlett stood still, listening to his car engine start and then fade before she finally went to bed.

Twenty-Seven

Sunday afternoon, Scarlett was parking her truck after cleaning houses for Camila's cousin when Nasreen met her in the parking lot.

"How you doing?" Nasreen asked, her eyes searching Scarlett's. She was leaning into the driver's window of the truck, blocking Scarlett from exiting.

Scarlett didn't want to the answer the question for fear she would cry, so she nodded.

"How was Isa today? Same as always?" Nasreen asked, moving to let her out.

"If you mean to ask if she was a control freak, the answer is yes. But she pays well and in cash, so I went along with it. Worked my ass off today and yesterday with her and managed to make three hundred. I'm tired as hell, though."

"Not too tired to celebrate, though, are you? The boys are having pizza so I thought we could hang out, the two of us." She waved a bottle of champagne in the air.

Scarlett nodded eagerly. "I'll take a glass or two of that. My place?"

"Yes. Let's leave the boys to their mayhem." Nasreen winked, her grin so wide Scarlett could see all her teeth. They ran up the sidewalk to Scarlett's building, giggling like schoolgirls.

"Have you heard from Candi?" Nasreen asked as Scarlett unlocked her apartment and cranked up the air.

"Only a text telling me to bring Ben the next time Jenn, the guardian ad litem, is at her house again. And to tell me I should lose weight." Scarlett knew she should probably call Jenn herself and maybe set up an appointment, but she kept putting it off. A sense of dread came over her whenever she thought of calling. She wasn't even sure what to say to her.

"She's such a bitch," Nasreen muttered. "Sorry, I know she's your mother, but you don't deserve that treatment."

Scarlett shrugged, not wanting to talk about Candi. "She's been like that her whole life." She pulled down glasses and rolled back her shoulders. "Let's drink. What are we celebrating?"

"I finished packing," Nasreen said. "That's reason enough. But also, because I figured out school for Zander and got all the classes that work well for my schedule. It's all coming together, and I need to celebrate."

Scarlett sipped the sweet, bubbly wine and forced herself to focus on being happy for Nasreen instead of sorry for herself for losing a friend. "And I forgot to tell you that I got a catering job. An engagement tea this Saturday."

"Look at you," Nasreen exclaimed, kissing her stemless wine glass to Scarlett's. "Good for you. How'd you get that gig?"

"It's Cory's boss. She came by my stand once and then I ran into her the night I went to see Tristen play, and she kinda hired me on the spot. I guess maybe it takes time for people to know I'm an option."

"Little by little, right?" Nasreen said. "That's all we can do."

"To both of us finding success," Scarlett said. They clicked glasses again.

"Speaking of success, what about that man, Tristen?"

"Do you like him?" Scarlett asked, daring to watch Nasreen's face.

Nasreen's red lips parted into a wide smile. "I do like him. And I haven't found anything on him except for charges that were dropped."

"What charges?"

"For fighting illegally," Nasreen said. She topped off their glasses, which were already almost empty. "But they were dropped."

"I guess there's hardly a guy around these parts that hasn't been arrested for something," Scarlett said with a grunt. "But also, he told me a little about that. No surprise there."

"Have you seen each other since the other night?"

Scarlett sighed. "No. He came back on Friday to see if I was okay."

Nasreen turned her entire body to face her. "Tell me everything."

Scarlett recounted the evening quickly. Thankfully, Nasreen already knew her stories, so she didn't have to explain anything else. By the end, Nasreen looked impressed.

"He's a nice guy, Scarlett."

"Yeah, he is."

Nasreen pursed her lips at Scarlett's sigh. "What? What's wrong with him?"

"Nothing's wrong with him. I can't believe I told him all that. I'm a little embarrassed."

"Did he call you this weekend or ghost you?"

"He called, but I missed it. I was busy cleaning. Then he texted."

"Did you answer?" Nasreen asked, putting her face close to Scarlett's. Scarlett pulled away.

"I answered. Geez, Nasreen."

"All I'm saying is that I can see you—"

"See me what? Messing it up?"

Nasreen shook her head. "Getting cold feet."

That was hard to argue with, since it was true. Scarlett was getting cold feet.

"He wanted to hang out this weekend, but I couldn't. Now I'm kinda afraid he thinks I'm avoiding him."

"Are you?"

"I had to make some cash." She hadn't meant to whine, but she sounded like a teenager.

Nasreen nodded, looking away. "I know."

"You know? You know what?"

"I heard a rumor, Scarlett," Nasreen said, her voice serious. "That you're in trouble with Johnny."

Scarlett stood up. The intimacy of sitting on the couch like this was getting to be too much. She wanted to be in the kitchen, rolling dough between her fingers so she could avoid eye contact.

"What have you heard?" She kept her voice neutral to give her more time to think of a better response.

"Word around the apartments is that Johnny paid you a visit. Said you owed six months of rent. Tiffany isn't too happy about that. Says it's unfair that you got away with not paying for six months without getting kicked out."

"Well, you can tell Tiffany to mind her own business."

"So it isn't true?" Nasreen asked.

Scarlet paced the small living room. She had been thinking about the money and at the same time ignoring the implications of not being able to pay. But with Nasreen asking questions, the deadline and the consequences were suddenly coming into focus. She might be homeless soon. Again. With Ben.

"Scarlett?"

"It's true," Scarlett said. The admission caused a sharp pain in her stomach. She didn't want to be homeless, and she certainly didn't want Ben to experience that. Her breathing started coming faster. She needed to get a hold of herself before she started hyperventilating.

"What happened?" Nasreen asked quietly. "How'd you get so far behind?"

"Johnny came around, I don't know, over a week ago? He told me I owed six months and gave me a fourteen-day notice. I asked him why he hadn't said anything for six months. Six months! I mean, who can pay that?" Tears sprang up in her eyes, but Scarlett blinked them away.

"What did he say?"

"Said it wasn't his responsibility to tell me anything. Rhoda's been paying so I never even checked. Like ever. Johnny has never come around before or anything. No warning, Nasreen. I knew nothing until last week."

Nasreen nodded, her face thoughtful.

"I have to pay three thousand by the end of the month, which I won't have. I mean, I might. Like barely. Especially since I got that catering job. I cancelled everything I can think of, but having to pay cash for that transmission hurt." Scarlett sank heavily onto the couch again. "I might have to borrow some from Cory."

"Don't take money from Cory," Nasreen said, her eyebrows raised.

"He's a friend, Nasreen. And sometimes he lends me money."

They sipped again in silence.

"And what about the next month's rent?"

"I'm hoping I can get a hold of Rhoda by then. I've been sending her messages on the last number I had for her, but she isn't answering."

"It doesn't look like you can rely on Rhoda, Scarlett."

"What do you want me to do, Nas?" Scarlett asked, her nerves barely under control. "What do you want me to do? I don't know what to do."

"Well, that was the first notice, right? So you have two more weeks after that. Pay him what you got, and then maybe we can find some financial assistance for you."

Scarlett sucked in air and released it slowly. She didn't want to cry. She didn't want to have this conversation with Nasreen. "Yeah, I guess I could go file for financial assistance, Nas, but I don't get an extra two weeks. My rent is on a monthly. And I don't have a copy of the contract."

The ticking of the clock was the only sound in the apartment. Scarlett stood still, breathing in and out slowly.

"Breathe, girl, you got this," Nasreen crooned, her hand rubbing circles along Scarlett's shoulders. "You got this. And you got plenty to give Ben."

Her fingers and voice worked magic on Scarlett. Slowly, her body cooled down, her heart stopped racing and her breathing settled. But nothing could stop the tears.

"You got love and goodness. You've managed to take care of him for over five years. He's healthy and happy."

Scarlett snorted, rocking back on her butt until she was sitting. Nasreen handed her the box of tissues, but it was too late. She'd already wiped her face with her T-shirt.

Nasreen sighed. "I think it's time you stop thinking of Ben as Rhoda's kid, Scarlett. Like you're some kind of babysitter."

"But I don't. I mean, he is Rhoda's kid. I can't stop that. But I'm not his babysitter."

"So you're ready to ask for custody?" Nasreen asked. "Like an aunt?"

"I don't know."

Nasreen set down her glass and picked up her purse. She patted Scarlett's shoulder on the way out.

Every ounce of energy left Scarlett's body. She stared at the door until Ben burst in to grab his sleeping bag. Then she dropped off almost all the money she had at Johnny's door and drank herself to sleep.

Twenty-Eight

Tristen stood outside the small studio at Camp Soul, waiting for Lin to show up. Although most of the kids were at dinner, Tristen thought it would be best to take Lin in a straight beeline to the studio, since the original idea of him coming on the weekend hadn't worked out.

"I'm too busy having brunch," had been Lin's excuse. "In LA."

"Monday it is then, Lin," Tristen had said. There wasn't anything else he could say.

Thankfully, Rob was okay with it. But Tristen wasn't about to allow Lin, who usually had colorful ways to describe things, to wander through a kids camp unsupervised. Especially not after Rob's lecture the week before.

A man in black slacks and a crisp white shirt, his face mostly covered with mirrored sunglasses, appeared on the road into camp. It was so clearly Lin that Tristen almost started laughing.

"What is this place, man? So cute," Lin shouted as he came up the main road of Camp Soul.

"Your new recording studio," Tristen said, pulling him in for a quick hug. "What's up, man?"

"What's up with you, man? You looking good," Lin exclaimed. He squeezed Tristen's bicep. "So strong. Look at me, I lost ten pounds, you see it? I started dating this girl, her name is Emi. Oh, so beautiful. So slim and beautiful, you know? She loves exercise, she has her own YouTube channel. I'll show you, I'll show you. Here, look."

"She's beautiful," Tristen agreed, leading the way in as Lin held up his phone with Emi's photo lighting up the screen. "Did she come with you?"

"Oh, wow. This place is tiny. Phew. Like in Asia," Lin said, taking off his jacket and seeming to take an interest in inspecting the studio. He tapped the microphone, lifted the one chair, touched the headphones. "Okay. If you say this is done, then okay. But no, Emi didn't come with me. I mean, not here. She's in New York City. I'll go see her soon. Can't go too long without some loving, you know?"

He winked so hard it hurt Tristen's head.

"Well, that's too bad. I would've liked to meet the woman who can control you, Lin."

Lin chuckled. "Sure. One day. But now we have to work. And Emi would distract me. Which song should I warm up with?"

Tristen handed him the headphones and hit the switch to play Lin's first hit. It had a nice warm-up range, not too high or too low. Lin let loose, singing with all his heart the song that he claimed had got him more attention at his cousin's wedding than his cousin.

"He deserved it," he'd said every time they spoke over the phone since April.

From there, Lin warmed up with his exercises before they started with the first song on the list. Almost from the first recording, the song was perfect.

"You been practicing?" Tristen asked through the microphone.

Lin winked. "Every day. You know, I want to get this done quickly. Your work takes longer than my work."

Tristen was glad he was wearing a hat to shadow his face because he was almost certain he was blushing. It had taken him a long time to get the songs ready because he hadn't done the work like he should have. "Okay, let's run it two more times. Then it'll be time to go over to the chapel."

"Chapel? Are you making me religious? Good thing Emi isn't here, or you would make me marry her, no?"

"No, Lin," Tristen said, laughing. He shut down his mic and rolled his fingers. Lin gave him the thumbs up. It was better not to respond to everything Lin said, otherwise recording took double or triple the amount of time. He'd learned that the hard way a few months back.

"Tristen?" Rob whispered from the door, his head poking through.

"Yeah?"

"Dang, that guy has a voice."

"Yes, he does. But he also has a mouth. You okay with us moving to the chapel?"

"That's what I came to tell you. They're done fixing the leak. It's all yours."

"Thanks," Tristen whispered back as Lin hit the last note. "That was perfect, Lin. Let's head over to the chapel. I have everything set up over there for us to record *Come, One and All* and *My Way*."

"I love singing *My Way*," Lin declared as he marched into the sound booth. "Phew, it's a little hot in there. If I really had it my way, I would make a whole album singing Frank Sinatra. He was the man, you know? Probably mafia, too, so I hear."

"I didn't know," Tristen said as he gathered their things. "Come on, let's get this show on the road."

"But I don't understand the part about a chapel. This is a temple, no? And where is the statue of Jesus? Isn't there supposed to be a statue that you worship?"

Tristen was glad he was up in the sound booth and not the one Lin was asking. Rob, because he was a better person, was answering every question Lin had methodically and with more patience than Tristen thought humanly possible.

"Okay, okay," Lin said, which was his signal that he was done with the conversation. He waved up to Tristen. "I'm done, yes? That is, what? Three songs done today? I will drink my lemon water and be back tomorrow and Monday for three more. Then I go to New York to rest. Well, not rest physically, if you know what I mean."

He pumped his hips back and forth, laughing. Rob didn't seem very amused, but the five thousand Lin had offered as payment to use the facilities to record his music kept him quiet.

"You have girlfriend, Rob?"

"I'm married," Rob told him.

"Ah, then you get exercise all the time. Good for you. Is she hot? Of course she is. You're a handsome man."

"I'm coming down, Lin," Tristen said, jogging to the end of the balcony.

"Okay, okay. Wait, who is this? This is your wife?" Lin asked. Tristen heard the question but not Rob's answer. Coming to a screeching halt at seeing Scarlett and Lin by the entrance had probably made him look like an ass.

"She's very pretty, huh?" Lin asked when he saw Tristen.

"Lin, this is Scarlett," Tristen said. "Yes, she is pretty."

"Thank you," Scarlett said, her face turning red. "It was nice to meet you, Lin."

"Oh, I see, I see. We will talk again soon, Scarlett," Lin said. He grabbed her hand and kissed it before she could walk out the door. "You are making my friend Tristen blush. We will speak very soon. Tristen, get to know this girl, she'd be a perfect girlfriend for you. Natural. And nice. Not like that last one."

Tristen glanced at Scarlett, trying to look at her as though she hadn't poured out an extremely sad and exhausting story of her childhood on Friday night after her terrible mother's behavior. He had to admit, at least to himself, that the story had scared him away a little. But it had also intensified his desire to be near her, to protect her. To cover her in his arms and be the man that kept her from harm's way.

It was a new feeling to him.

Ivy had her flaws, but Tristen suddenly had an entirely different view on how bad a mother she was.

"Okay, Tristen, stop drooling over this lovely woman. We have business to discuss."

Tristen returned to the conversation at hand, hoping Lin hadn't offended Scarlett while he was stuck in his thoughts.

"I'll text you later," he said, trying to say 'sorry' with his eyes, though Scarlett looked as though she might burst into laughter.

"Bye," she called back as she left the building.

"She'd be good for you, man," Lin said, slapping Tristen hard on the back. "But oh, wait—" He patted his jacket pockets, then his pant pockets. "If I don't give this to you, my accountant will be furious. That bank number you gave to Watsu doesn't work. Or maybe it's closed? I don't know. I wasn't listening. My accountant is a very boring man."

"I closed it. It was a joint account with my brother," Tristen said, not wanting to go into detail. Thankfully, Lin wasn't interested in getting more information.

"Okay, okay, this is for you. A check of the residuals. Or royalties? Again, I don't know. I didn't listen. But here is your name, see?"

Tristen did see. His name was next to a figure he hadn't seen on a check addressed to him in a very long time. Twenty thousand dollars.

"That can't be right," he said. "You paid me for recording you. Why would you pay me this much?"

"Because we have a royalty agreement. Or whatever it's called. And because when I said my songs hit the charts in Asia, I wasn't kidding." Lin looked at the check. "I think this is all from my song being used for a dance."

"A dance?"

"A dance all the kids love to do. Betty Rose made up the dance."

"Wait a minute, what song did they use?"

Lin started to giggle.

"That extra song at the end about telling a girl you loved her with a cocktail napkin?"

Lin laughed harder. He had always thought the word 'cocktail' was very funny. "Yes, yes. That song."

Tristen couldn't believe it.

"Which is why we must record that song 'Hopping to You' when I get back."

"Seriously? It's such a stupid song."

"Hey, man. We aren't talking about beautiful, artistic songs. We're talking business. And the kids want things to dance to. It's about the money, man. You want some money? You want your own studio?"

Tristen shifted in his chair. "You're right, Lin. You're right. I guess I have to shift how I think of music."

Lin held out the check. "Get yourself something nice."

"After I pay for a kid that isn't mine," Tristen told him. "The problem with this check is the child support. I wonder how much they'll make me pay."

Lin sucked air in through his teeth. "I don't like to think about it. You need a lawyer? I can get you a lawyer. They take all your money, too, but maybe it would be worth it."

"No, I got one. Thanks, though."

"No problem, no problem. I see you this weekend, okay? Go take that woman out for dinner. A nice dinner. Try to dress up a little and woo her Lin-style."

Tristen couldn't help chuckling. "Get out of here."

Lin did a little wiggle, then left, leaving Tristen alone to stare at the check in his hands. Even after a few minutes of staring, he still couldn't believe it. And he still didn't know what to do with it.

"Hello?"

"Hey, Elijah. It's Tristen."

"I know. Your name comes up on the screen."

"Your words are polite, but your tone says all I need to know," Tristen retorted.

"That you're a dumbass?" Elijah asked. "Well, good. I'm glad I don't have to spell it out for you."

"Any news on the judgement?"

"We expect it in about twenty minutes. But I don't have much hope for you."

"Me either. And I have another problem."

"Which is?"

Tristen waved the check in the light overhead. "I got handed a check for twenty thousand from Lin, my client. What do I do with it?"

"Deposit it," Elijah said. The sound of papers rustling came through the phone.

"But…" Tristen hesitated. "There isn't any other way to do it? So that Lamia doesn't know I have the money?"

The paper rustling stopped.

"Are you asking me, your lawyer, if there's a way for you to hide the fact that you earned money? Like, what? Open an account in the Bahamas? Are you seriously asking me to advise you on how to illegally keep your money from the eyes of the court?"

Tristen swallowed. "Sorry, Elijah. Okay, I'll deposit it."

Elijah sighed through the phone. "Listen, this isn't fair. I get it. But life has thrown this your way and there's not a whole lot you can do about it. Look, the more you make, the more the judge might tell you to pay. You can wait to deposit it until tomorrow or the next day, if you want. But it won't stop Lamia from taking you back to court someday as your income grows. It is what it is, man. Especially if you don't want to implicate your brother."

"Got it. Okay. I'll wait until tomorrow."

"Still might not do any good," Elijah said. "Only warning you. A kid is a kid, and they gotta be cared for."

"Yeah. Sure. I got it. Thanks, Elijah."

Tristen sat back down, the check near his elbow, as he edited Lin's songs. Before he finished with the first one, the news he'd been dreading came through in an email and text at the same time.

He'd been declared the probable father.

Tristen held his head in his hands, exhaustion filling every pore of his body. He'd known it would come, and yet he had been foolish enough to hold on to a sliver of hope. That Talon would put a stop to it. That Lamia would admit she knew it wasn't him. That the DNA test would miraculously come back with a solid decision.

He'd hoped, and like every time he dreamed and hoped, it had come crashing to the ground.

Of course, he still had the check from Lin, which meant there was a hope still worth holding on to. Tristen dragged his head up and cursed being an adult. If he were a kid again, he would allow himself to mope for longer than five minutes. But being an adult meant being grateful for the good things even when bad things happened.

He couldn't remember where he'd heard that from, but at any rate, it sounded correct. He'd better be grateful for that check, since it was part of his ticket out of Kentucky. And he knew he should be grateful for Lin, since he was bringing him another opportunity.

As though hearing his thoughts, a text from Lin came in. *You know Seraphina? She says she knows you. She says to call her. She wants to talk about you producing a song for her. I told her you were the best.*

The text ended with a smiley emoji, a party emoji, the peace sign emoji and an eggplant emoji. Tristen laughed to himself, his gratitude for Lin growing ten-fold.

Twenty-Nine

THE PEACE INSIDE THE camp chapel contrasted heavily with the constant music around the camp. There were only a few kids this week, but they were the most serious Scarlett had seen yet. They didn't stop playing their instruments even to eat. With the kids so focused on their music, she had managed to come and go quickly from work, barely talking to anyone but Mrs. Beatty. Top of her mind was the engagement tea she needed to prepare for, then figuring out a way to pay Johnny the next installment and buy groceries. Thankfully, Tristen was also busy and, so far, hadn't complained about not seeing her. Which was nice, but also scary. It wasn't that Scarlett didn't want to see him; she just needed some time to work. And make sure he forgot about Friday night.

She was starting to miss him, while he was probably realizing he was better off without her.

Scarlett pulled out a flimsy plastic bag full of grapes, her stomach growling angrily. She hadn't eaten lunch yet. She had barely eaten anything the last few days; her stomach was too tied up in knots.

She popped a grape into her mouth and rolled it between her teeth, trying to convince herself that Nasreen's upcoming move didn't signal the end to their friendship. That she wouldn't move on to a better life and leave Scarlett behind.

The grape burst, its sweet juice pouring onto her tongue. She loved the moment when the skin of the grape was taut and yet still holding strong. A little more pressure had to be applied before it exploded.

Scarlett felt like that. Like maybe one more thing and she would explode. But maybe that had already happened. Maybe she'd exploded Friday night, overwhelming Tristen, scaring him away from her. It was possible he wasn't busy and didn't want to see her.

She had too much on her plate to add a new relationship to it anyway. She should be grateful if he didn't want to be with her. She inhaled slowly.

"Oh, hey. I didn't know anyone was in here."

Scarlett twisted around to find Dariana sinking into a chair. Her sigh sounded like she felt the same as Scarlett.

"Tired?"

"Pregnant," Dariana said. She blinked, and her eyes widened. "Ugh, I wasn't supposed to tell you that. Rob wants to keep it under wraps until the twelfth week or so."

"Well, congrats anyway. I won't tell anyone," Scarlett said, offering her the bag of grapes. Dariana took one and nibbled on it like a mouse. "Is that really a thing? Keeping the news of the baby until the second trimester?"

Dariana shrugged. "I don't know. My sister had trouble staying pregnant, so I think Rob is a little jittery about what could happen. It's hard, obviously, not to say anything. Especially when I feel like I could throw up every second of the day."

"Were you planning on getting pregnant now? I mean, it seems like a bad time to be in your first trimester, what with all the work you have."

"We threw all precaution to the wind over a year ago, so there wasn't too much planning for it. I'm not sure what would be better, honestly."

"I hear the second trimester is the best," Scarlett offered.

"I've heard that, too," Dariana said, reaching for another grape. "Have you ever been pregnant?"

Scarlett paused, glad she had two grapes in her mouth to swallow. She wondered if Dariana would judge her if she told the truth.

"Yes," she finally said. "But I didn't have the baby."

"Oh?"

"My mom made me get an abortion." Scarlett swallowed her dread and looked up at Dariana, expecting her to be horrified. Instead, she looked concerned. "Maybe that isn't fair. I didn't really fight her about it. I mean, I guess I could have walked out of the clinic or moved out sooner, or whatever."

"You didn't feel supported," Dariana offered.

Scarlett shook her head. "Definitely not. I was surprised to find out my sister had a baby when she showed up with Ben. As much of a hard-ass feminist as Rhoda is, she judged me for the abortion."

"People won't always agree with what you do in life," Dariana said. "My parents didn't agree with me marrying Rob. My sister thinks we're dumb to take on this place and for renovating that ancient farmhouse we live in. They all thought I was dumb to go to college, too. My sister loves to point out that attending college did nothing to help me in my career, since I'm not working in marketing, but at a summer camp."

Scarlett ate another grape to keep herself from saying she agreed with Dariana's sister about college. It was too expensive.

"They probably won't approve of us having this baby either. My mother once said she wouldn't have kids if she could go back in time."

"Sounds like your mom and my mom might be kindred spirits. Mean for the fun of it."

"Like they have no filter," Dariana said, chuckling. "I don't want to be like her with my kids. But I'm scared I will be sometimes. Do you ever find yourself acting like your mother with Ben?"

Scarlett chewed slowly, trying to think of a time she'd acted like Candi. "Well, when my temper blows, I feel like I'm acting like her. But I've worked hard to bite my tongue when I'm tired or mad. I think sometimes he knows my silence also means I'm annoyed or upset, though. What I mean is, Ben knows I'm mad whether I yell or stay silent. But there's something about him not being mine that makes my situation a little different. Sometimes I feel like I'm the placeholder for him in some way, which keeps me from making certain decisions I might make if it were my kid."

"What do you mean?"

"I mean, for the most part, Ben's a really good kid," Scarlett said, pushing herself off the floor and into a chair. "I'm lucky that way. But I rarely discipline him more than sending him to his room because I don't feel like I have the authority for more. He's my sister's kid, you know? I try to think about what she'd approve of and then go from there."

"You're right," Dariana said. "You're lucky he's a good kid."

They sat in silence for a moment. Dariana closed her eyes and leaned back in the chair. Scarlett watched her from the corner of her eyes, awed by how pretty she was, even looking as exhausted as she did.

"Ugh, I better not fall asleep," Dariana said. "Tell me how you're doing with the job and the markets and all that. I bet you're killing it. Your baked goods are so amazing."

"Thank you. I'm trying," Scarlett said. "I'm really grateful for this job, I have to say."

Dariana waved her hand. "We're grateful to have you here. That's that."

"I have a small catering job on Saturday," Scarlett ventured. "Would it be okay if I stay a bit later towards the end of the week to bake what I need?"

"Of course. You need us to watch Ben? He could come out here and help Rob with some stuff on Saturday."

"No, that's okay. He'll be at his dad's house. They have the guardian ad litem coming in the morning."

Dariana's eyes shot open. "Are you losing Ben? Or are you asking for permanence?"

She must have seen Scarlett's surprise, because she rushed on. "Rob had to go through that. His mom kept demanding him back every time she got sober, and it became too much for his grandpa. He hired a guardian ad litem and eventually got full custody of Rob."

"What does 'eventually' mean? How long did it take?"

"Two years."

Scarlett almost choked on her grapes. She left the bag for Dariana, no longer hungry. "Who did Rob live with during those two years?"

"On and off with his mom. She kept leaving him with Grandpa and then coming back. But it ended well."

"Geez," Scarlett muttered. "I don't know what will happen. Rhoda left Ben with me about five years ago and all of a sudden, Candi says she wants custody. And his dad, Eric, too."

"What about you?"

Scarlett shook her head. "I don't know where I land."

"Do you want custody?"

"I want what's best for Ben."

"What is that?" Dariana asked, finishing off the last of the grapes.

"Him being with my mom is not the best, but I can't say being with his dad is a bad thing. I mean, Eric's his dad."

"What does Ben want?"

"Does it matter?"

Dariana raised her eyebrows.

"I mean, does the judge ever consider what the kid wants? Rhoda was in foster care for a few years. I guess I was too, but I don't remember, and she was placed back with Candi once the judge decided Candi had cleaned up enough. Rhoda loved her first foster-parents, the ones that held her during transition. But then her next foster-parents were horrible, according to her. She wouldn't give me details. Then she went back to Candi and so did I. The good thing was that we were back together, Rhoda told me, otherwise she wasn't sure who she preferred."

"Do you have an interview set up with the ad litem?" Dariana asked. She pulled her long hair back into a ponytail and watched Scarlett with her dark blue eyes.

"Should I?"

"Why not? If this thing takes two years, you don't want them placing him in foster care, do you?"

"Is that possible?" Scarlett asked, her heart racing.

"I don't know," Dariana said. When she shook her head, the long ponytail shivered across her shoulders. "But I would think the best way to avoid Ben being placed somewhere else would be to get in front of the guardian ad litem and prove to them that Ben is doing well with you."

She stood; Scarlett joined her. She was finished in the kitchen, and she couldn't hide out all day.

Ben shouted to her when she emerged from the chapel, shading her eyes from the Kentucky sun. "Eric here yet?"

His hair dripped water onto his shoulders, his skinny legs poking out like sticks under his shorts. He looked exactly like Rhoda at fifteen when she'd chopped her hair short.

"Not that I know of, but you can call him with my phone if you want," Scarlett said. Before Ben could find the contact list, they found Eric standing at the door to the cafeteria, talking to Tristen.

"Hey, buddy," Eric said, returning Ben's hug with his own. Scarlett watched, suddenly doubting her plan to call Jenn for her own meeting. Ben never ran to hug her. And sometimes she forgot to hug him. "Ready to go?"

Ben replied with a yelp and a jump in the air. "I'm gonna get my stuff," he said, before barreling into the cafeteria.

"We have the meeting tomorrow with Ben's guardian ad litem, Scar."

Scarlett smiled weakly. "I know."

Eric nodded. "Thanks for keeping him from Candi's house for her meeting. I didn't open the email about it until after it happened. I didn't think anyone would contest my say in this."

Scarlett knew he was trying, but opening emails seemed like the minimum he should be doing. "No problem."

"You haven't heard from Rhoda, have you? I didn't expect Candi to show up in this, but I kinda thought it would get Rhoda's attention. Maybe bring her back here."

"No, I haven't. Not sure how Rhoda would hear about this, since she doesn't live here."

Eric shrugged, unable to keep eye contact with her. "Rhoda seems to hear about things even if she doesn't live here."

"Well, I haven't heard from her."

Finally, Eric glanced at her. "Okay. Well, I want you to know I appreciate what you've done the last five years taking care of Ben. Whatever happens, you know?"

Scarlett nodded, unsure what she could say in response. 'Thank you' didn't seem appropriate. "How's Brandi feel about all of this?"

Eric shifted his weight. Scarlett wondered if there was trouble between them, but Ben burst through the door, ending their conversation.

"See you later," she said. She reached out to kiss him on the head, but he moved suddenly, and she ended up kissing air.

"You okay?"

"Shit, Tristen, you scared me. Were you standing there the whole time?"

"I was inside the cafeteria. I didn't want to interrupt." He stepped closer. Now it was Scarlett who couldn't keep eye contact. She wasn't feeling up for pity. "You okay?"

"Fine," she lied.

"I feel like I haven't seen you."

"You've been busy," Scarlett said. When his hand took hers, she almost cried with relief. Maybe he'd forgotten everything she'd said on Friday.

"Want to catch dinner tomorrow?" he asked. He stepped so close her stomach spun like it was on a rollercoaster. He was wearing a cologne she wasn't familiar with; it smelled clean and manly. Scarlett looked up as he grazed his thumb against her cheek. "We haven't gotten to talk very much all week."

His voice was husky. She shivered.

"What would you like to talk about?" she asked. She felt the warm pressure of his hand on her hips, but kept her attention on his eyes.

"Maybe about the weather," he murmured, his voice cracking.

She glanced at his lips and immediately they were pressed against hers, hungrily demanding she open them to him.

She complied. Every night since he had kissed her in the parking lot, she went to sleep dreaming about pressing up against his chest, pulling his hips against her own, tumbling directly into bed. Starting a new relationship might be too much with everything going, but if Candi had taught her anything, it was that sex didn't mean a relationship. It was just for the moment.

"My place is empty," she said as his lips moved to her neck.

Suddenly, he stopped and pulled back enough to look at her.

"I have to go see my mom tonight," he said, brushing her too-long bangs out of her face. "I'll take you out tomorrow, but I want to tell you something first."

Scarlett swallowed. Her lips tingled from rubbing against his short beard.

"I don't want sex from you."

Scarlett stared at him.

Tristen shifted and cleared his throat. "I want to woo you."

"What the hell does that mean?"

"No sex," he repeated.

"Until when?" she asked. Tristen looked away, and her heart sank. This was a new way to be told she wasn't desirable. "I should go."

She turned to leave, but she was stopped by his hands cupping her face, his lips pressing against hers.

"Until you're in love with me," Tristen murmured against her mouth.

Thirty

Owen and Ivy were sitting at the small, round table in the galley kitchen when Tristen walked into the house. It was Wednesday night; the night Owen had been trying to make into a family night ever since Tristen moved back to town.

"Nice to see you, Tristen," Owen called out as he walked in. "Pull up a chair. Your cousin Bobbi is gonna be here soon."

"Bobbi's coming?" Tristen asked, pouring himself coffee before he sat down. The booze in the house had dwindled down to almost nonexistent. "Must be serious."

Ivy fidgeted with her mug and smiled at Tristen when she caught his eye, but strangely said nothing.

"Hello," Bobbi shouted, knocking at the same time that she lumbered into the house. "Okay, I'm here. What's the big event?"

Ivy and Owen exchanged looks.

"Which one first?" Owen asked.

"I'll go first," Ivy said.

She looked between Tristen and Bobbi, always one for added suspense. They waited, Tristen slurping his coffee and Bobbi crossing her arms. They both knew not to ruin Ivy's show.

"Owen and I are going to Portugal. I got my passport today." She squealed as she produced the little blue book. "Isn't it cute? I can't wait to start putting stamps into this thing."

"I'm real glad for you, Ivy. You used to talk about seeing places, and now you're finally doing it." Bobbi slapped the table with a grin.

"Owen, are you sure you're allowed to travel internationally? You don't have a warrant out for your arrest somewhere in the world, do you?" Tristen asked.

"Ha, ha," Ivy said, pouting out her bottom lip. "That isn't funny, Tristen."

She smoothed back Owen's hair and kissed his forehead. His skin turned cherry-red.

"It's kinda funny," he said, winking at Tristen. "But I got my passport, too, so I must be an upstanding citizen."

"I hear they eat a lot of fish," Tristen said to his mother. He couldn't help himself, even if he knew it was immature to be so jealous.

"Don't ruin this for me," Ivy said, wagging her finger at him. "I'm sure I'll find something to eat that isn't fish. Wait, what language do they speak?"

Bobbi huffed. "Portuguese."

"Well, sorry. Not everyone can be as smart as you, Bobbi." Ivy stuck her tongue out at her cousin. "Anyway, that isn't the whole news."

"You're doing the whole European tour?" Tristen asked drily. He willed his jealousy to fade as he poured himself more coffee.

"No," Owen said, clearing his throat loudly. They all waited in silence.

"I can't stand it," Ivy exclaimed. "We decided to get married in Portugal."

"Well, I'll be," Bobbi said, her eyes shiny.

"Congrats," Tristen said. He was a little relieved they weren't expecting a whole ordeal of a wedding.

"Thank you," Ivy said, admiring her ring. "We're getting married on the beach. The travel agency is doing everything. We thought about a ceremony here with friends and family but figured everyone had better things to do than see us old folks say our vows."

Bobbi rolled her eyes. "When are you two leaving?"

"Baby is due any day now, so Talon said we could come anytime from the end of August onward. He's helping us find a hotel and all that. First we'll see the baby, and then we'll travel around."

"You're gonna see Talon while you're there?" Tristen asked.

"That's how this whole thing started," Ivy told him. "I wanted to go see the baby and then Owen said he would come, and then he said, 'why don't we get married?' and I said, 'okay,' and then—"

Tristen waved his hands, stopping her short. "Okay. I'm happy for you. Take a lot of pictures while you're there."

Ivy's face softened. He hadn't noticed how tense she was until her shoulders relaxed and lowered a few inches. "Thank you, Tristen. I appreciate it. I haven't told Talon yet, but I hope he's as supportive as you." She paused and searched his face. "You sure you aren't upset?"

"About you and this guy getting married? Heck no. I hope you two are happy together. I'm really happy for you," he told her. "But when you're there, can you please tell Talon he's an asshole?"

Bobbi heaved a sigh.

"I was declared the probable father of his son."

Owen grunted. "What're you gonna do?"

"Well, since I can't drag him outside and beat the shit out of him, I'm gonna comply with the courts. Last thing I want is to be sent to jail because of my brother."

"Good thing you got family here," Bobbi said.

"What do you mean?"

"To help watch the baby," she explained.

"What?"

"The baby you're paying for," Bobbi said, enunciating every word like she used to when he was young and would ask stupid questions.

"I don't have him. I'm paying for him."

The other three exchanged looks around the table.

"What?"

Bobbi shrugged her large, rounded shoulders. "Guess they probably thought what I thought. That you'd have at least partial custody of the kid."

"Only seems fair," Owen said. "You're paying for him, after all."

"Fair?" Tristen sputtered. "I don't want custody of the kid. He isn't mine. I don't have time to take care of Talon's kid."

"We know," Ivy said. She grabbed his hand and held it. Tristen would have pulled away, but he didn't want to look like more of a jerk. "We figured you'd want to have some sort of an influence in his life if you're paying for it."

"I can't sue for partial custody when I'm still looking for a studio in Cincinnati. I have too much going on."

"You're still moving?" Ivy stopped stroking his hand, her voice squeaking.

"I've always planned to move, Ivy."

"We know Pelton wasn't where you wanted to be a few months ago, but your circumstances have changed," Owen said.

"Besides, I'm moving in with Owen after Portugal."

"Okay. I don't know what that has to do with me."

"We're signing the house over to you," Ivy told him. Her voice was quiet, but steady. "For one dollar. There's the paperwork there. We thought it was only fair you should have it."

Tristen breathed in slowly. That news was unexpected.

"What am I supposed to do with it?" he asked.

"Whatever you want. Keep it or sell it."

"Or rent it," Bobbi suggested. "My Danny makes good money being a landlord. Gotta be tough, though."

Tristen looked at each one of them. "It's not that I'm not fine here, but... I don't know. I never wanted to live here all my life. I'm finishing up Lin's second album. Plus, I got paid some royalties off the first. Because of the work I did on his and on Meegan's—"

"Who's Meegan?" Bobbi asked.

"Ex-girlfriend," Owen said.

"Yes, thank you, Owen." Tristen breathed in slowly. "Anyway, I need space to work with Lin and hopefully more people. It's nice that Rob's letting me use his tiny studio, but I can't be bringing clients all the way out here. It isn't convenient."

"If they like you that much, won't they come wherever you are?" Ivy asked.

Every once in a while, she could make very valid points. That was one he hadn't considered. "I don't know."

Bobbi finished off her coffee with a satisfied sigh, slapped the table, and pushed herself up. "Well, that's me done. I'm real happy for you, Ivy. I'll watch over the house for you if this guy doesn't move in. As for you, Tristen, you know we'll love you either way. Just remember, I'm not your mama but I sure as hell half-raised you. And I think you're the better for it."

Tristen couldn't argue with that. Bobbi had saved him from a number of scrapes and always allowed him and Talon to wait out Luke's fury at her house. She gripped his chin as she used to when he was a boy and kissed him loudly on the cheeks.

"Actually, I'd say I did the hard part," she added, cackling at her joke. Tristen glanced at Ivy, expecting her to be angry or indignant, but instead the two of them exchanged winks and smiles.

"You and Bobbi sure are getting along," Tristen said when the door closed behind his second cousin.

"Therapy'll do that for you," Ivy said. "Helped me figure out what was worth fighting about and what wasn't. Apparently, there really isn't much worth it." She looked out the window, where Bobbi was probably ambling towards her house. "She's the only one who's ever really stuck around, no matter how I treated her. And I sure treated her badly sometimes. Worst thing about therapy is making you confront that stuff. Makes me embarrassed to remember, honestly." Ivy grabbed Owen's hand. "Had to apologize to her and everything, and the greatest thing is, she forgave me. Without hesitation. She's a better person than me, isn't she, babe?"

Owen wasn't stupid enough to answer, so Ivy looked at Tristen.

"I will not argue or agree," he said, laughing.

"At any rate," Owen said, waving his sausage fingers. "You have some decisions to make. And even if we don't agree or don't understand, whatever you decide, we will support you."

It was hard to miss the look he gave to Ivy, challenging her to disagree with him, but she nodded. "Exactly. We'll support you either way."

Thirty-One

Friday morning, the only thing that got Scarlett out of bed and into work was her date with Tristen that night. She could use a break and good food. The way he made her comfortable, the way he listened, the way he kissed… Scarlett sighed to herself as she thought about it.

The only thing that could break her spell was seeing three missed calls from Rebecca when she finished drying her hair. Scarlett took a deep breath and hit call back.

"Hello? Who's this?"

It was a strange way for a woman to answer her phone, but Scarlett ignored that. "This is Scarlett. You called me this morning? I have three missed calls."

"Oh, the baker. Yes. Of course I called you. I would think that we would have a meeting scheduled. The tea is tomorrow, and we haven't finalized the menu."

That was a surprise, since Rebecca had sent her a long list earlier in the week. She pulled up the email on her phone, settling onto a stool for the call. It was worth being late to work for Rebecca. She couldn't lose this job.

"I have right here that you want mini gluten-free brownies, strawberry tartlets, mini croissants and mini lemon bars."

"Gluten-free lemon bars. And mini muffins. With no eggs. Does any of this stuff have dairy?"

"I can substitute the butter in the recipes to make them dairy-free. Would you like that?"

"Of course I would. I don't eat dairy, and I don't need upset stomachs at my engagement tea. There will be silver trays for you to arrange things on. I don't need you to bring whatever you usually use. And did you receive the email with the instructions on which door to enter through?"

"Yes," Scarlett said, scrolling through it. There was a map showing her the old servant entrance to the kitchen. Big, red letters told her not to use the front door.

"Mrs. Carr will show you where everything is. And what else did I need to tell you?"

Scarlett waited. Rebecca didn't seem like she would take kindly to being interrupted.

"Oh, yes. A black dress. Please, no pants. This is a tea. I'll have Mrs. Carr fetch a white apron for you."

"You want me to wear a black dress?"

"A plain black dress. The longer the better. Do you have one?"

Scarlett thought of the black knit dress she had from H&M. It wasn't fancy, but it probably was roughly what Rebecca was thinking. "I have one. It's past my knees."

"Perfect. I don't want you in one of those weird French Halloween costumes. The last lady I had cater for my birthday thought that's what I meant. Which is why I didn't hire her for this tea. Also, the payment. Once you're done, I'll send you the money through the app I'm sending you now. It's the only one I trust. I won't pay any other way, so don't ask. And I certainly won't be paying in cash. Everyone has to pay their taxes, even bakers."

"Agreed," Scarlett told her. Apps usually required a several-day holding time before payout.

"You're a very agreeable person, Scarlett. Probably too agreeable. I mean, it's great for me and for customer service, but being agreeable doesn't take you far. Not in business, anyway."

"Oh—"

"But I'm not here to coach you. I'm at work. I'll see you on Saturday. And, please, next time I call, pick up. I might have some things to tell you before the tea."

"Yes, see you Saturday," Scarlett said, just before Rebecca hung up. She put away her notebook and shook her head. If she was ever going to make money, she would be dealing with the rich people of Kentucky; they were the ones willing to pay three dollars per mini brownie, after all. But if all the rich people were like Rebecca, Scarlett wasn't sure she'd keep her sanity.

She ran out the door, texting Dariana as she went. As soon as she got into her truck, her phone rang.

"I'm really sorry I'm late," Scarlett began, watching for cars on the highway before she pulled out.

"It's me, baby sis. What're you late for?"

"Rhoda!" Scarlett nearly dropped her coffee thermos. She set it carefully in the cup holder and gripped the steering wheel hard. "Where are you calling from?"

"Here and there," Rhoda said. Her usual response.

"Are you coming home? Eric said you might be coming home."

There was silence. Scarlett checked to see if they had gotten disconnected. But then Rhoda spoke.

"I'm heading to Candi's place now. And what's-his-name."

"Brody? He's an okay guy, Rhoda."

Rhoda hummed her disagreement.

"You've heard what's going on around here? I tried to call you. Sent a few messages to that old phone number I had for you, but nothing went through."

"I change up my phone every few months. And besides, I've been a little out of commission the last few months."

"Were you sick?"

"Nah, in jail," Rhoda responded. "But the charges got dropped. No worries. Was kinda fun, actually."

Scarlett shivered with fear. She hated the idea of jail. "What jail? And how could it be fun?"

Rhoda chuckled. "Like being in high school again. Queen of the playground is the name of the game, basically. Anyway, sorry about the phone. Had to toss that one."

"I'm glad you're okay," Scarlett said, knowing her sister would scoff at the sentiment. "You know what's going on with Ben?"

Silence again.

"What I hear is that you're trying to rid yourself of Ben," Rhoda said at last, coolly.

Scarlett swallowed hard. When Rhoda became icy, everyone ran. She sipped her coffee to keep from panicking and ended up almost choking. "That isn't true. A few weeks ago, Eric came home and said he wanted Ben. Then Candi appeared, said the same thing."

Rhoda sniffed into the phone. "Another birdie told me you're working at a religious summer camp."

"I needed a job, Rhoda."

"I thought when I set you up with the apartment, paying for it and everything, that you'd find a way to make something of yourself. Thought you'd be somebody by now."

Scarlett swallowed. This day might go down as the worst in her life.

"I'm trying, Rhoda. I gotta pay Johnny back some months' rent. He didn't tell me you weren't paying him until a few weeks ago. If he had told me, then I could've been paying it."

"If you could've been paying it, you should be able to pay it now."

"Well, there's life to pay for, Rhoda. I was baking for a realtor, but she fired me when her husband came on to me, and then I had to fix the truck and—"

"Damn, Scarlett. Stop." Rhoda blew out hard. "I have to say, I never thought I'd be paying your part of the rent for this long. Maybe me going to jail was for the best. Light a little fire under you. I was paying for my own apartment by your age. And then I started paying for your apartment."

Scarlett opened her mouth to reply but shut it again. Rhoda had always been more resourceful than her, smarter than her, harder-working than her. She didn't know why Rhoda was surprised that she hadn't made it farther than she had. Scarlett wasn't.

"I'm sorry." She swallowed hard to keep her tears at bay.

"We'll figure that out later," Rhoda said. "Ben is more important."

"Right. Of course."

"Damn it," Rhoda said. The sound of her fist hitting something came through the receiver. "I knew Candi would be pissed when her payments stopped coming in, but I never thought she'd tried to take Ben."

"Wait, you think she's doing it for revenge? Would Candi do that? I mean, she's not a good person, but I can't see her using Ben to get back at you."

Rhoda chuckled. Scarlett had missed her sister's laugh. It always sounded like that of a cartoon princess. With her dark moods, aggressive nature and black clothing, most people thought the laugh didn't suit Rhoda, but Scarlett did. It reminded her of when Rhoda wasn't a teenager yet and would push her on the swing.

"And what about Eric? He's a jackass, too. Can't believe I ever thought I was in love with him. He's so spineless, but man, he knows how to make a woman swoon. I sent him money all these years to make sure he had the means to visit Ben when he could, give him presents or take him out for dinner, and now look. I get no thanks at all. I bet the lady guardian litem or whatever it's called never even asked how Eric how he got the money."

"You've been paying Eric off?"

"Paying him off?" Rhoda sounded offended. "I've been keeping him afloat. Ben needs a dad, don't you think? Would've been nice to have a dad when we were kids. I didn't want Ben to grow up without one, and I wasn't sure when you'd find yourself a man. You still foolin' around with that Cory?"

"No." Scarlett wondered if that counted as a lie or not. "I started dating someone else. Someone you don't know."

"Good for you, Scar. He's got a job, right?"

"Of course." Scarlett almost told Rhoda she wouldn't date a loser, but she caught herself in time.

"Good. I gotta go. Gotta figure out what we're doing here."

"What're you planning on doing? I think Eric wants to have full custody of Ben, and I wasn't sure if you would want me to have him full-time, even though I would love to have him. But I didn't want to take him from you. I mean, you're his mother."

Rhoda made a noise between a grunt and snort, but Scarlett kept talking.

"If Eric doesn't have enough money, maybe that's what we could tell Jenn, the guardian ad litem. I mean, if you're okay with Ben being with me, of course. I don't want to take over for you. You are his mom."

"You said that."

"I just meant—"

"I got what you mean," Rhoda said. "But here's the thing: I can't have people asking how I earn my money. It wouldn't pass any inspection. I'm gonna need you to not tell Jenn anything."

Scarlett nodded to her window shield. "Okay. I won't say anything."

"Good."

"But what's the plan?"

"I'll tell you when the time's right. I'll see you soon, Scarlett."

Thirty-Two

"This is good," Lin shouted, his head bobbing to the beat streaming through his headphones.

Tristen nodded his agreement as Lin's voice rose and fell in their ears. It was Friday afternoon, and they were in the tiny recording studio, listening to the six songs they had recorded in a matter of three days. Despite singing each several times, Lin's voice had held up.

Tristen pressed pause and marked the time where he needed to tweak some outside noise, then hit play again. Lin waited patiently now that he finally understood what Tristen was doing. At first, he'd asked for specifics every time.

"Done," he declared. "Oh, I think I moved myself to tears with that last song. The women all over the world will be crying for Lin to sing to them."

"And what will Emi do about that?"

Lin wiggled his eyebrows. "She will have to make sure to keep me a happy man, you know? Because I have so many other choices in this world. So, so many. How are your choices going out here in this place? Have you hooked up with that cute girl yet? She's a little chubbier than you, but I was going to tell you not to be a jerk about that. Chubby girls have big boobs, you know? And they are very cuddly."

"You're such an ass, Lin," Tristen said, laughing at his friend. The man had no filter and yet the more Tristen hung out with him, the more he liked him.

"No, no," Lin said. "I'm not being an ass. I'm saying for you not to be an ass."

"I think she's beautiful," Tristen said. "We've hung out a few times, and the more I'm with her, the more I want to wrap my arms around her and make sure nothing bad ever happens to her again."

"Oh, yes. You tall, manly men can say those things to women. I pretend to be a manly man. But really, if anyone robs us at gunpoint, I will push Emi in front." Lin's contagious laugh filled the tiny studio.

"How does she put up with you, man?" Tristen asked, shaking his head.

"I don't know. Must be love." Lin stood up and stretched loudly. "I should go. I have an early flight. Should I come back this weekend? How many more songs do we need to finish?"

"This is six here that I have to finish up, and we have the other three. So maybe we record two of the four you have lined up."

"Only two more? And then we have another album?"

"Yep."

Lin yelped. "This is why I like you, Tristen. This is why I work with you. Look at us. We are releasing two albums in one year. This is amazing. And it will shoot to the chart like the last one." He shook his hips and pretended to pull the air towards him.

"What are you doing?" Tristen asked.

"The dance that will go to my song. You like it?" he asked, finishing it all off with a shake of his head. "I hired a choreographer."

"Is that how these things go viral?" Tristen asked, laughing as Lin stretched his legs. "I thought it was organic."

"Nothing is organic, my friend. We help things along, you know?" Lin gave him a slow wink. "I better go before I miss my plane. Have you talked to Seraphina?"

"I thought she was going to call me."

"Always call first. A rule my father taught me since I was this big," Lin said, holding his hand at his hips. "I sent you her contact info, remember?"

"Will do," Tristen said, as they shook hands. "I'll see you soon?"

"And soon you will come to Singapore, yeah? With that cute girl."

"Sure, Lin. Sounds good."

Tristen stretched and looked around the tiny studio at Camp Soul, aching for a drink of whiskey. Instead, the small fridge only had sports drinks and water.

He opted for water as he played back his last round of edits, trying his best to put the whole day out of his mind. He hadn't even had time to process the fact that Ivy was betraying him by going to see Talon. The idea didn't sit well with him. While he didn't want Ivy to disown Talon, he knew that she wasn't ever going to bring up the fact that he was an ass because she didn't want to risk being told she couldn't see the baby.

His phone vibrated with a text from Scarlett.

Might need to cancel tonight. Gotta finish up some things for the tea.

Tristen sent a tearful emoji back, disappointed he wouldn't see her. But he didn't want to pressure her if she was that busy. *Do what you need to do. I'm ready when you are.*

"Tristen? You in here?" Rob's voice came from the front of the studio.

Tristen saved his files and opened the door to the office space. "In here. I was editing some songs."

"I heard the music and wanted to make sure it was you and not some random kid sneaking back in over the weekend," Rob joked. "You don't look so good. You sick?"

"Nah. Not sick. Just got some crazy news and I'm not sure what to do with it."

"Wanna talk over a bourbon?"

Tristen pulled back in surprise. "You drink?"

"Sometimes," Rob said, laughing. "I mean, not around the kids. But I don't believe it'll send you to hell or anything."

"That's interesting," Tristen murmured, closing down his computer. "Then yes, I'll take you up on it. I wouldn't mind having someone else's opinion on this whole situation."

"Sounds serious," Rob said, clapping him on the back. "Come on. Dariana is waiting for me. We'll sit on the porch and listen to your woes."

Both Dariana and Rob were quiet for a long time after Tristen finished the story about Talon and Lamia and the baby. Dariana opened her mouth, then shut it again. She looked at Rob, and Tristen started to laugh.

"I'm sorry," Dariana stuttered. "It sounds a whole lot like some Hallmark movie. I mean, I thought my family was a bit off their rockers, but I wouldn't expect my brother to do something like that."

"I think you'd have to be identical twins for this whole scheme to work," Rob pointed out.

Tristen laughed harder, cutting the tension in the air. "It does sound like fiction, doesn't it? I guess I'm over the surprise of it all and I've moved on to the anger."

"Oh, well," Dariana said. "I'd be angry, too."

"Have you tried talking to this Lamia woman?" Rob asked.

Tristen's laughter turned into a grunt. "I've talked to her. Several times."

"And she doesn't believe you?"

"I don't know if she doesn't believe me or if she doesn't care."

"It's possible she needs proof, right?" Dariana asked.

"Dariana likes to believe the best in people," Rob said, patting his wife's knees. She swatted at him but shrugged at Tristen.

"I mean, think about her position. She's a single mom and needs financial support. And I think we would all agree that a man should be held responsible for taking care of his kid. Too many of them leave the woman behind and pretend nothing happened."

"Agreed," Rob said, kissing her on the cheek.

"Sure, I agree with that. But I didn't knock her up, and I'm being asked to pay for the kid. How would you like to be told you had to pay for a stranger's kid?"

"But he isn't a stranger," Dariana pointed out. "He's your nephew."

Tristen shook his head. It was the injustice of it, not that the kid was related to him by blood. The kid wasn't *his*. "Would you want to be forced to pay for your nephew and watch your brother do nothing?"

"No," Dariana said. "I wouldn't. But from the judge's point of view, it's his job to make sure the child is taken care of. And since the DNA is inconclusive, there isn't much else he can do."

Tristen's nerves tingled. He looked out over the back field so Dariana couldn't see how angry he was. "Let's also consider that Lamia is not a victim here. She got involved with a married man. Whether or not he told her, that's the game we all play now. She jumped into bed with him, and they either didn't use protection against pregnancy or something went wrong. It's partially her fault, and I don't see how I should have to pay for her choice to sleep with an asshole." Tristen tried to prevent his voice from crescendoing. "We can't forget that if Talon and I weren't identical twins, the father would be obvious and Lamia would be stuck trying to force my brother to pay from Portugal. It wouldn't change the circumstances or consequences to their decisions and actions, but it would leave me out of it."

He tried to calm his heart from beating out of his chest. The situation was not only unfair, but it was also unhealthy for him.

"I see your point," Dariana said quietly. "But I can't help thinking about the little boy in the middle of all this."

Tristen rolled his neck to loosen it up. "I think of him, too. In the end, kids are always at the mercy of adults and their bad decisions, aren't they?"

"We're so vulnerable as children, and if we aren't blessed with the parents who are really trying their best to put us first, we get screwed," Rob said. "The good thing is that there are parents out there who are trying. And there are adults like us who live through some stuff and come out stronger on the other end."

"But there are a lot more who keep the cycle going," Dariana commented.

"True," Rob said. "But we can only control our own actions, can't we? We can make sure to go to therapy if needed, have children when we're ready, provide for them, put their needs first when they're little, learn to discipline without abusing." He shrugged.

Dariana smiled, her face glowing with pride at her husband. Tristen finished off his bourbon. He was glad they had a strong marriage, but they weren't helping him at all.

"You leaving?" Rob asked as Tristen shifted in his chair.

"I should let you two have dinner," he said, though he didn't really want to go home to his empty house. All he would probably do was drink a few more and brood over his situation.

"What are you going to do?" Dariana asked.

"I'm going to pay," Tristen said firmly. "Because I'm not going to jail over my brother. And as far as asking for partial custody of the kid, I don't think I'm ready for that. I might be too angry."

Dariana tilted her head and seemed to be fighting a smile. "I meant, what are you going to do for dinner," she said. "Because you could stay with us. We were going to grill some hamburgers."

"Oh."

"I hadn't thought about you asking for partial custody. I guess if they declare you responsible, technically you should have access to the child, right?" Rob asked, pouring more bourbon into Tristen's glass. "It's only fair."

"Right. Fair," Tristen repeated. "Owen and my mom have hinted in no uncertain terms that I should be the bigger person and be part of the kid's life."

"Everyone needs a father figure," Rob said. His nodding rubbed Tristen the wrong way, but not enough to leave.

"Just think," Dariana said. "You could influence a child for the better. Show him there's more to life than cheating and being selfish. You could teach him all the things you know. And how great would that feel at the end of your life? To know that you helped raise a functional adult?"

Tristen held his bourbon a few seconds longer before swallowing. Looking towards the end of his life was not something he liked to do. He leaned back in the porch chair and listened to the crickets starting to sing, trying to envision himself as an old man. What his regrets might be, what his proudest moments might be.

And there was no denying it. He couldn't imagine himself being proud of deliberately rejecting contact with a child who would need a father figure. Especially after listening to Lamia over the phone.

"I think I'll stay for dinner," he said. "If I'm still invited."

Thirty-Three

Scarlett pushed the door to the old Kentucky mansion open with her hips, her hands full of tubs of brownies and gluten-free muffins, smiling like an idiot as she did. There wasn't anything anyone could do to sour her mood. Not the crabby man at the market first thing, not Patty reducing her prices, nothing. Not even a reply from Jenn saying she couldn't give Scarlett a meeting until Sunday afternoon.

For the first time in her life, she was with a man who wanted to know her, who wanted to *woo* her, whatever that meant. Tristen had sent her good luck that morning through a text and asked to see her afterwards for coffee. Cory never did stuff like that.

"Hello there." Rebecca stood in the middle of the kitchen, staring at Scarlett.

Scarlett gripped the tubs tighter to keep from dropping them. "Good morning, Rebecca," she said, her voice so cheery she almost didn't recognize it. "You're absolutely gorgeous in that dress."

Rebecca simpered a smile and turned slowly around. Scarlett almost laughed at the idea that she needed a full view of the outfit. She managed to cough as cover.

"Thank you, thank you. There was a problem with the delivery but thankfully it made it here in time. I mean, I have two other dresses on stand-by, but this is the one I wanted to wear today." Rebecca paused.

"Oh, yes. It's definitely the right one," Scarlett rushed to say. She busied her hands with lining up the silver trays that had been left out for her to fill.

"My guests will start arriving in thirty minutes. I wanted to say hello and ask if you have everything."

Scarlett looked around the enormous kitchen and nodded. "I have everything. Mrs. Carr showed me where to put the trays out on the table."

"I'll need those out soon," Rebecca interrupted. "I don't want you going back and forth once the guests arrive. You aren't dressed properly?"

"I have the black dress with me," Scarlett said quickly. "It's right there."

Rebecca sighed at the plain black dress hanging in the corner. "I want you to take the empty trays back into the kitchen once we start playing games. Other than that, I expect you to be invisible."

Scarlett nodded. Not even that comment was going to bring her down. She was a worker, not a guest.

"Wonderful," Rebecca said. She gave Scarlett another glance over before slipping back through the swinging door.

Inside the small bathroom off the kitchen, Scarlett wiped herself down with a towel she'd brought in case she was sweating and put on her simple black cotton dress. Then she put up her hair into a tight bun and finished arranging the miniature brownies, scones, muffins, and quiches as quickly as she could. The giant windows throughout the house gave her a glimpse at the large, old Kentucky horse farm—what many people thought of when thinking about Kentucky. From the looks of it, the land had been parceled out for a new development in the back, while leaving a large lawn for Rebecca's family estate.

The doorbell rang, startling Scarlett. She scrambled back to the kitchen, grabbed the last two trays and finished setting up in the dining room as echoes of screeching and air kisses trailed in from the entryway.

"You're so gorgeous."

"He's the luckiest man in the world, isn't he?"

"He better know he has the prettiest bride."

"I can't believe you're getting married before me."

Scarlett made a face at her tray of brownies, then rolled her shoulders back and chastised herself quietly for being jealous. Things were going well with Tristen. And if Tristen didn't work out, she still had Cory.

The table was arranged with giant bouquets of flowers, Scarlett's pastries, trays of cheeses, berries, and tea in fine China teapots. It was possibly the most beautiful setting Scarlett had ever seen. She couldn't imagine what the wedding would look like if this was the engagement party. Quickly, she snapped a few pictures, then slipped back into the kitchen as what sounded like a large group of people came down the hallway.

For the next hour, she sipped coffee and scrolled social media. The dining room buzzed with excitement through the door. Scarlett checked her watch and thought about her coffee date with Tristen. A rush of energy zipped up her legs and pooled in her lower belly as she relived his kisses from the day before.

The swinging door slammed open and shut. Scarlett scrambled to her feet, her nerves popping.

"Are you the waitress?" The woman stood near the door, holding the skirt of her long, flowery dress close to her as though simply entering the kitchen might dirty her hands.

"I'm the caterer."

"Whatever," the woman said, waving her fingers. "Would you mind cleaning up a little? Rebecca said she asked you to, but you haven't come."

"Sorry," Scarlett said, making sure her hair was still up, though it was so tight her head was starting to hurt.

"Don't apologize. Ugh." The woman stepped back. "Just do your job. And quietly. They're starting the speeches."

She rolled her shoulders back and walked regally through the swinging door without another word. Scarlett caught the door before it could hit her in the face, but held back a moment to not follow too close behind. The group of women in flowy dresses had moved from the dining room to a smaller room off to the side with large windows and floor-to-ceiling plants.

"Thank you all for coming," Scarlett heard Rebecca say as she quietly moved around the dining room, shifting what was left onto a few trays. "Now that we've had our tea, the champagne is going around. Everyone take a glass. Even you, Georgia."

There was a smattering of giggles.

"Before we start playing some games, the groom has made an appearance."

Applause burst from the other room, along with a few cat-calls and whistles.

"Settle down, ladies," Rebecca said. "He's taken. And poor baby, he got into a fight the other day. He was defending a woman's honor outside our office building and got punched in the nose for his trouble, isn't that awful? Some people don't deserve good men, do they?"

Scarlett shook her head at the story. She hoped the groom would heal before their wedding.

"Thank you, ladies," said a man's voice. "Thank you. I would defend any of your honor any day."

Scarlett froze.

"Excuse me."

Scarlett started at the voice so close to her shoulder. It was Mrs. Carr, the house manager—whatever that was. "Yes?"

"Are you ready to take those trays in? If you grab one and I grab the other, we can do so quickly. Ms. Rebecca wanted the ladies to be able to snack as they played the games."

"Of course," Scarlett said, trying to settle her nerves. She picked up the heavier tray, then waited for Mrs. Carr to pick up the other and start marching to the other room. Scarlett tried to emulate the older woman by rolling her shoulders back and keeping her chin up slightly higher than needed.

"When I met Rebecca, I knew immediately I wanted to marry her," the male voice continued.

Scarlett almost dropped the tray. Mrs. Carr made bug eyes at her, jerking her chin towards a small, circular table near the front of the room. Scarlett pressed forward, keeping her eyes on the tray, concentrating hard.

"Oh, Cory. You're such a flirt."

"It's true, though."

The tray safe on the buffet behind the couches and chairs, Scarlett stepped back. She couldn't resist; she looked up to find Cory and Rebecca kissing passionately on the lips. The women at the party howled their approval.

"I can't wait to make you officially Mrs. Cory Stalwinsky," Cory said.

Scarlett stared until he looked up and spotted her. His face drained of all color except for the blue and green bruise under his eye.

A rush of anger and hurt filled Scarlett, but before she could do anything, Mrs. Carr grabbed her by the wrist and jerked her head in the direction of the kitchen. The older woman returned to her chin-lifted, straight-backed walk, and Scarlett followed suit.

"Please close the doors as you leave," Rebecca said loudly. Scarlett turned to find Rebecca smiling smugly, her hand entwined in Cory's. "Thank you, Scarlett. That's all we need from you now."

Scarlett closed the doors and left the house as quickly as she could.

Thirty-Four

Scarlett kept herself together as she gathered her things and left Rebecca's estate. At this point she no longer cared if she was supposed to stay or go. She needed a good cry, and she refused to do it in Rebecca's kitchen.

But when she was finally in her truck and able to cry, Eric texted to ask if she could pick Ben up. Scarlett would have preferred to be alone, but she didn't dare say no.

"Are you and Cory together?" Ben asked when they were halfway home.

"No, Ben. Why would you ask that?"

"Eric said something about it."

Scarlett gritted her teeth. "Well, he's wrong. Eric doesn't know everything. I'm not with Cory."

"Good."

Scarlett grunted. "How was your time with him?"

"Fine. A lady, Jenn, came over to talk to me and then to Eric and Brandy. Brandy had a hard time 'cause she was puking like two minutes before the lady came. That baby sure is giving her a hard time, and she ain't even born yet."

"Is it a girl?" Scarlett asked. She'd always thought of the baby she hadn't had as a girl. Another ache filled her chest. If she wasn't careful she'd start crying.

"Yeah, that's what Brady says. I don't know how she knows though. That picture is so fuzzy I can't hardly tell where the butt and where the head is."

"And did you like Jenn? Was she nice? What did she ask you?"

Ben sighed at her questions. "Yes, she was nice. I don't know if she was the guardian or the litem, though. Eric said both were gonna come, but only Jenn showed up."

"It's called a guardian ad litem, Ben. The 'i' is long. And it's one person. I think it's Latin or Greek or something."

"What's it mean?"

"Guardian ad litem? No idea. But her job is to be your ally and make a report so the judge can decide who you should live with. I think."

"Sure hope it ain't Grandma," Ben muttered.

"Don't say 'ain't,' Ben. And I hope it isn't your grandma, too."

"Is it gonna be you?"

Scarlett avoided looking at him for fear he might see the truth in her face. "I don't know, Ben. Jenn is supposed to come by Tuesday and talk with me."

"Why can't you and Eric share guardianship?" he asked when Scarlett put the truck into park.

"He's your dad, Ben. If he requests you, there isn't much I can do. I bet he'll let me see you, though."

"So, you don't want to be my mom anymore?"

Scarlett turned to face him. "Rhoda's your mom, Ben."

Ben grunted and opened the door.

"Ben," she called. He froze but didn't turn. "I love you, you know."

He nodded, but he was looking somewhere else. "Are you dating Tristen?"

The change in topic startled Scarlett. "Why do you ask that?"

"'Cause he's standing over there watching our house like a stalker."

Scarlett followed Ben's pointer finger until she saw Tristen leaning against his car, his face mostly covered by large sunglasses. She'd completely forgotten about their coffee date.

"Hey, Ben," Tristen called when he saw them.

Scarlett checked her face while the other two talked. Their voices were too low to be heard, but she could hear Ben laughing as she yanked open the back of her truck.

"I'm gonna go see Zander," Ben announced, jogging past her. He slowed down slightly, his face flushed. "He says to tell you that you look really pretty."

Scarlett looked down. She was still wearing the black dress.

"Did he relay my message?" Tristen asked. He stopped directly behind her, reaching around to stroke her hand. Scarlett swallowed but was unable to stop the excitement zipping through her body at his scent and warmth.

"Yes, he did," she said, turning her face to find Tristen's inches from hers. "I'm sorry about coffee. Eric called me to pick up Ben and I just forgot."

"What's wrong?" he asked, his fingers leaving her hand to stroke her cheeks. "You look upset."

"Stress, I guess." Scarlett moved to grab a box, forcing Tristen to move as well.

"How was the tea?"

"Oh, it was fine." Scarlett hefted an empty box, almost toppling over from the force she used.

"Scarlett, what happened? You seem really upset."

"I got—" She paused. "I got blindsided."

"Did someone treat you badly?"

"People always treat me badly," she murmured, surprised at herself when she heard it.

"What do you mean? Why would someone treat you badly?"

She turned to face him, to see if his question was serious. "Everyone around here knows who I am and where I've come from. You don't know better."

The muscles in his face tensed. "It doesn't matter where you come from, you don't need to accept people treating you badly."

She couldn't help but snort. It was no use to pretend anymore. She was too tired, and the truth would come out eventually. It would be better if Tristen figured out who she was sooner rather than later. Scarlett looked at him, her heart sinking. She could so easily fall in love with him if she allowed herself to.

And then what? Being dumped or betrayed by Tristen would hurt so much more than Cory doing it.

She stepped forward, determined to show him the truth. "Look at me, Tristen. I'm twenty-four with no college education, no prospects, about to be evicted because I have no money, and even my sister thinks I'm a loser. The people who hire me treat me like I'm less than a servant, and my childhood friend thinks he can use and dump me as he wishes."

"Who? What happened today?" He tried to grab her hand, but she pulled away. "You were so excited for today."

"I was, but then—" Scarlett swallowed back the tears welling up in her eyes against her wishes. "Well, I found out she's engaged to Cory. And I'm pretty sure she hired me to show me."

Tristen pulled back while she stacked two boxes on top of each other, then lifted them before facing him. He stood still, staring at her.

"What?" she asked.

"You said you weren't dating Cory."

"I'm not."

"Was he your boyfriend?" he asked. "At some point? Are you still in love with him?"

"Hell no," Scarlett said, trying to push past him. "Tristen, move."

"Why're you upset he's marrying someone else, then? What is he to you?"

"He's my friend. And he didn't tell me."

"You said he wasn't an ex-boyfriend."

"He's not."

"I don't like lying, Scarlett."

"I'm not lying," Scarlett shot back, trying to keep her emotions in check.

Suddenly Tristen's face changed, and Scarlett knew everything was over. "But he was and is, what, a lover?"

Scarlett tried hard to fight it, but she felt her cheeks warming. "He's my oldest friend. Except a friend would tell me if they were engaged. Rebecca did this to hurt my feelings."

"If he's your friend, why aren't you happy for him? Don't you want him to be happy?"

"You don't know Cory. He isn't marrying her for love, he's doing it for money. And power. Her daddy is the owner of the company he works for. I know Cory."

Tristen opened his mouth, then shut it.

"This marriage isn't going to last," Scarlett said, unable to stop herself.

He folded his arms across his chest. "You don't want it to last?"

"I don't even care," she retorted. "They can do or not do whatever they want. I don't care at all."

"Huh."

Scarlett snapped her mouth shut. The day was full of mistakes. She couldn't put her finger on what she was feeling and why. Was she in love with Cory? It didn't feel like love, but him marrying Rebecca felt like a betrayal.

"I want to go inside, Tristen. It's been a long day and I have a lot going on." She pushed past him and this time he let her through, but he didn't follow. "Are you coming in?"

"Do you want me to?"

Scarlett set the boxes down and folded her sore arms across her chest. "Do whatever you want, Tristen. I don't want to make you feel like you have to. I'm not some sad woman. I can handle drinking my beer alone."

She didn't even believe her own lie, but she dared him to contradict her.

"I wanted to take you out because I'm leaving for Cincinnati tomorrow. I gotta be in court to hear my verdict on Monday and tomorrow I'm meeting with my lawyer. I won't see you for a few days."

"Oh." Scarlett nodded, trying to act like it didn't matter if he was gone for a few days right when she needed him the most.

"This is a lot, isn't it? Me figuring out child support and dealing with Lamia while working on my business. And you're dealing with stuff with Ben and your mom and everything."

Throwing bricks at her would have hurt less. But luckily, years of pretending she was fine helped her look at him without tears and even give him a half smile.

"I get it. It's a lot. I'm bone-tired tonight and tomorrow I think I have a meeting with the guardian ad litem."

"See? There's a lot going on. You won't even miss me."

"Right," Scarlett said. She kept her tone as aloof as possible. "Be safe, Tristen."

Tristen hesitated. His right foot came up almost as though he might step forward, before he changed his mind and set it back down. "Tell Ben I'll be back for the last week of camp."

"Yeah, I'll tell him," Scarlett said over her shoulder, unsure how long she'd be able to keep her tears back.

She walked to her apartment without looking back, listening to Tristen drive away. Inside, she put the boxes away, then got in the shower to cry again, reliving the conversation over and over in her head. No matter how terrible it made her feel, she couldn't help but think she'd done the right thing.

She stared at her mascara-streaked face in the mirror. Pathetic, that was what described her and her ridiculous hope that a man like Tristen would stick around. Would give her a chance.

But she had hoped, and she had dreamed. About a house with him in it. About babies. About security. About love.

It was instinctual, all that dreaming, even though she had known this part was coming. He'd never said those three words after all. Instead he'd snapped her heart in two and left her discarded on the parking lot.

Scarlett picked up her toothbrush and rolled back her shoulders. The end had been inevitable. She had seen it coming, and yet she'd still dreamed about a whole different ending. And that was on her.

Thirty-Five

Finally composed, Scarlett cranked up the air conditioning and grabbed two beers, ready to let the alcohol soothe her spirits. Not too much. Just enough to take the edge off.

When the apartment door opened, she didn't bother standing, assuming it was Ben or Nasreen.

"Double-fisting it tonight? Does my engagement upset you that much?"

Scarlett stood up so fast she spilled half a beer down her front. Cory threw his head back and laughed, his body stumbling slightly.

"Cory."

He cocked his eyebrow and marched towards her. Scarlett tensed her back and separated her feet to give her a better stance. Cory had never been violent with her, but she didn't like the sneer on his face.

"You can't walk in without knocking, Cory."

"Don't tell me what to do, Scarlett. Your boxer friend isn't here. I watched him leave. Just like everyone leaves you."

He smiled, relaxing his shoulders. Scarlett didn't relax hers. "Screw you, Cory."

"Isn't it true, though, Scarlett? Even Rhoda." Cory watched her, his eyes narrowing the more he spoke. "Everyone ends up leaving you. Moving away or firing you. Everyone, except for me. Maybe that's because I know you. I know who you are and what you've done. And I accept it."

He took the full beer out of her hand and drank half of it in one gulp, still watching her. Scarlett put distance between them. She sat on the bar stool and picked up her phone. She wasn't sure who she would call if Cory got rough, but if things got too out of hand, she could at least call the cops.

"It's interesting, Scarlett," he went on, settling on the arm of the couch.

"What is?"

"That Tristen left. I heard what he said at the end—that this is all too much. Which it is. That's why no one wants a long-term relationship with you. There's always so much going on with you and Ben and your family. Ugh, it's too much. But I'm still your friend, so I'm sorry he hurt your feelings. I mean, I could have told you that was going to happen, but you wouldn't have listened to me anyway." Cory smiled. "I hope he at least said you were a great lay."

"Shut up, Cory." She wanted to yell, to wipe the smug look off Cory's face. "We weren't breaking up. We were only talking." She stopped, hoping her lie was believable.

He finished the beer and tossed the can to the floor. "How many times did he manage to sleep with you?"

Scarlett made the mistake of looking away.

"It's true, then? That he tricked you into thinking he wanted you when he didn't even want to sleep with you?"

"What are you talking about?" Anger constricted her throat, choking the strength of her voice.

Cory smiled, seemingly enjoying himself. "He said something about wanting to date you properly, or some such nonsense. Crap men say when they find themselves in a corner and want to distance themselves. It's the opposite of saying you want to marry them so you can sleep with them."

"Is that what you're doing with Rebecca?" Scarlett shot back, enjoying the way his eyes flashed at her being able to turn the conversation.

"No. I'm marrying Rebecca because I love her."

"You're marrying Rebecca because you like her money and you think she'll take you places, Cory."

He shrugged, looking much like the preteen Scarlett had once been in love with. "What's wrong with that? At least I go after women in my league. At least I've changed my league enough so they'll fall for me."

"Good for you, Cory," Scarlett said. Her whole body was starting to lose energy. "I hope you're happy with Rebecca. Now, get out."

"Why? Nothing has to change. That's why I came by tonight. To make sure you understood that. And I know you don't actually want me to stay away. Otherwise, you would have begged Tristen to stay."

"He had to go to Cincinnati—" Scarlett choked on her words, not wanting to tell Cory about the trial. "For work."

"Damn, Scarlett. I knew you weren't bright, but if you think he wasn't just using it as an excuse you're stupid."

"He has work," Scarlett repeated, immediately wishing she could slap herself. She should be kicking Cory out, not explaining Tristen to him.

"Scarlett."

"Leave, Cory."

"I don't think you want me to leave," Cory told her.

In two strides he had her in a vice grip by the back of her neck. For the first time in her life she was frightened of him, even though he was smiling.

"I think you know you're not good enough for him. And you know what? You're right."

He pressed his lips so hard to hers that she tasted blood.

"Wanna know why I don't ever suggest I marry you, Scarlett? Wanna know why I don't even spend the night when we screw?"

His fingers dug into her scalp, pulling the small hairs at the nape of her head. When she whimpered involuntarily, Cory snickered, but he let go.

"I'll tell you, because I think you need to understand it, Scarlett. Everyone in this world needs to understand their place in it, don't you think? Otherwise, they wander outside of their space, and get frustrated. And no one likes to be frustrated, do they?"

Scarlett shook her head. Behind Cory, Ben stood on the cement patio looking in through the glass doors with wide, frightened eyes. When she jerked her chin up, he turned and ran, disappearing before Cory looked. She hoped he was going to find Nasreen.

"That's your problem, Scarlett," Cory continued. "You keep trying to leave your space."

"What's my space?" she asked, embarrassed at how small her voice sounded.

"Your space," Cory said, with a grin, "is to get on your knees for men willing to pay a few minutes of their time with you. That's always been your space. Now, maybe it's partly Candi's fault, putting you in certain situations throughout your life, but whether it's nature or nurture, it's still your place. Maybe if you hadn't become such a slut in high school, you could've have created a different path for yourself. Rhoda did. But you chose to be weak. And weak people do the bidding of stronger people. Hence you being stuck with that nephew of yours for so long. It's the reason why George broke up with you and that Jamie guy didn't stick around."

Scarlett gagged. "As though I wanted Jamie around."

"As though you could do better," Cory said, clicking his tongue. He swiped her beer off the counter and slammed it back. "I'm hitching my ride to a rich woman, Scarlett, but we can continue if you can stay in your place."

She stood up as he came closer. When he tried to reach for her, she picked up the stool and threw it at him. It missed.

"Get out," she yelled. "I don't want to see you again."

"You should be grateful," Cory sneered. "At least I'm willing to screw you. You're not bad at what you're good for, despite being, well…" He waved his hand over her body, and immediately her blood ran cold. "It's not like you're sexy, you know?"

A loud knock at the door interrupted her slew of expletives. Scarlett backed into it and turned the knob without taking her eyes off Cory. She expected Ben and Nasreen to be at the door, but when Cory's grin got bigger, a shiver of fear ran through her.

"Hello, Johnny. Is it payment night?"

Scarlett spun away from the open door, frozen in her surprise as the two men exchanged chuckles and high fives.

"How you been, Cory?" Johnny asked, stepping into the apartment.

"Fine. Got engaged."

"Congratulations," Johnny said. He opened the fridge door and tossed Cory a beer as though it was his to give, then opened one up for himself. "You got visitors, Scarlett."

The sliding door opened, and Nasreen glided in.

"What's going on in here?" she asked, her voice cold.

"Nasreen," Cory said, nodding slightly. Scarlett knew he didn't like her, but she had never seen the look on his face before. Almost like he was afraid of her.

"Cory. Wanna tell me what's going on?" Nasreen asked, positioning her body between Scarlett and the men. "Johnny, how about you go first."

"Ain't got nothing to do with you, Nasreen. You're all caught up on payments. But Scarlett here owes me a good chunk of money."

"I heard a rumor about that," Cory said, laughing.

"I gave you part of the payment already, Johnny. And I got more of it here," Scarlett said, her hands trembling as she took out the envelope. "It's only seven hundred, but I have another payment coming from a thing I did today."

Cory snorted into his beer.

"Look, Scarlett," Johnny said. "I've learned that I'm not a very patient man. I found someone to rent this place come the first of the month. I know you ain't gonna have the money in time, so let's part ways amicably."

"You can't throw her out in a week's time," Nasreen said. "She'll get counsel."

Johnny's lips twisted. "Ah, yes. The lady who thinks she's a lawyer. Well, Nasreen, I might not be going to law school, but I know the law. There's no contract between Scarlett and me. Nothing signed even between Rhoda and me. There's no evidence that Scarlett has the right to this place at all. It was a gentleman's agreement. And since I'm not running a charity, there's very little you can do."

"Well, I might be able to help," Cory said. His voice was soft and kind; the glint in his eyes told Scarlett he was going to act anything but. "I'll pay you for things we usually do together. You know, the stuff you give over for free, like a slut."

Scarlett threw herself towards him, but Nasreen pulled her back. Cory and Johnny both burst into laughter.

"I told her I could work out a payment plan, too," Johnny said, still chuckling. "What do you say, Scarlett? You wanna stay here?"

"Screw you," Scarlett hissed.

Johnny shrugged. "Okay. You got a week."

His laughter echoed down the hallway.

"You, too," Scarlett told Cory, but he moved much slower. She and Nasreen watched him finish his beer, place the can next to the sink, then walk slowly towards them.

"Offer stands," Cory said. "Some women aren't meant be much more than a man's bitch, Scarlett. Tristen knew. It's why he left."

"I never, ever want to see you again," Scarlett said, her breath wheezing from her lungs. "Don't ever speak to me again."

Cory's face twitched, but he said nothing else before turning on his heel and walking out the door.

"I'm so sorry, Scarlett."

Nasreen wrapped her arms around Scarlett's neck, but she didn't want human contact. She wanted to be alone.

"Can Ben sleep at your house tonight?" she whispered.

"Sure, hon. You wanna come over, too?"

"No," Scarlett said, her voice barely audible. "I want to be alone."

Thirty-Six

"You listening to me?" Elijah glared out over his glasses, his big brown eyes locking on Tristen's when he looked up from the paper he'd been staring at.

It was Sunday evening already. They'd been going over the paperwork, filling out forms and gathering all the information Elijah thought they might need for the case the next day, but Tristen couldn't focus. He couldn't stop thinking about Scarlett and how they had left things. He admitted as much to Elijah.

"A girl? You're ignoring me because of a girl?" Elijah asked. He stood up and went to the liquor cart for the second time that evening.

"She's more than a girl," Tristen said.

"Ah, a new woman."

"Maybe." Tristen picked up his phone, then set it down again. "If I could figure out if I left things bad or not."

"Seriously, call her already so you can focus on what's ahead. I'll go check on the wife." Elijah shook his finger at Tristen, piercing him with his gaze. "But be ready by the time I come back."

Tristen picked up his phone again. He'd called her twice since they'd last spoken, but she hadn't answered. Trying to stay focused on only one thing was becoming more and more difficult. Everything kept mixing together. When she'd stomped off the day before, he'd been too mad to go after her. All evening he had fumed about her keeping the fact that she had obviously been involved with Cory from him. It seemed to him that only a woman who was still in love with a man would be that upset if he was engaged. But Scarlett had said she wasn't in love with him.

He paused. He couldn't remember if she had actually said those words or not. He'd thought of their last conversation so many times that he no longer knew if what he remembered was what had happened.

An image of Cory intruded on his thoughts. The guy was so smug, so overly confident. He rarely listened to Jared during his boxing class and always thought he had something more important to say than anyone else.

But Cory's attitude wasn't the problem. The problem was that Tristen should have known there was something going on the night he'd punched Cory in the O'Donnell's parking lot. A friend wouldn't act like Cory had, but a boyfriend would. Or an ex-boyfriend.

Tristen shook his head. As long as Cory was an ex-boyfriend, it shouldn't matter. He had ex-girlfriends. He couldn't expect Scarlett not to have them.

But there had been something in Scarlett's demeanor that told him Cory was more than an ex-boyfriend; he was the man she had hoped would come around for her. Which meant she felt for Cory what Tristen was starting to feel for Scarlett.

Which made him a fool. Again.

Tristen erased the lame greeting of 'hi' he had typed to her. After all that reasoning, he still couldn't shake the feeling that he had done something wrong.

He paced up and down the room, willing his brain to come up with the right message to send. Not too personal, not too impersonal. He didn't want to come off as desperate if she was into Cory. He also didn't want to come across as cold in case he was reading everything wrong. And it was urgent he sent it as soon as possible. Elijah had warned him that he was to leave his phone behind when they entered the courtroom.

"No distractions and no keeping your face in the phone. I want you to look responsible and focused. Plus, judges hate it."

Tristen closed his eyes, erased his thoughts, and started his text again.

Hope you didn't think I meant I didn't want to try the relationship when I said it was a lot. I didn't mean that at all. I like you, Scarlett. And I figure if we can maneuver through this, we can get through anything. I should have said that last night. It was what I was trying to say in words, but as you have witnessed, I'm not good in the moment. I hope you also want to give us a try. I think we could be good together.

Tristen sank his teeth into his bottom lip and tried to think if there was a better way of saying everything he wanted her to know.

I have my court thing tomorrow and I won't have my phone, but can we talk when I get back? Of course, if you don't want to see me or be with me, I understand.

The last sentence screamed at him from the screen. It was a lie. If she had feelings for Cory, Tristen wasn't sure how he would handle it.

He deleted it.

"You done now? Let's go," Elijah said, strolling back into the room.

Tristen nodded, then hit send right before Elijah took his phone out of his hand.

"Elijah, seriously. I said I'm ready."

"Good. Now, time to focus and work and then go to bed. I'll give you your phone after court tomorrow."

"You'll be there, right?" Tristen asked, filling his whiskey glass with water.

Elijah nodded. "I'll be there. You know this is in the chambers, right?"

"I figured," Tristen assured him, though he had been imagining a full courtroom show with jury and everything. "Do you think Lamia will be there?"

"I hope she'll be there. We want her reactions to things, since she sometimes can't keep her mouth shut, you know?"

"Sure—you want her to sabotage herself."

Elijah grinned. "People do what they want. I can't control them. And if she can't control herself, well, that will benefit us." He pointed his half-empty whiskey glass at Tristen. "You stay quiet and do as I tell you to do."

Tristen wasn't as confident, but he nodded.

"Alright. Look over this and tell me if it's what you want."

Tristen looked over the piece of paper, his eyes homing in on one word: Elliot.

The boy in the middle of the whole issue was named Elliot.

"My client objects to the proposition made by Mr. Levisay. He hasn't shown any interest in the child in the past year. Why the interest now?"

Elijah didn't bother to look at the other lawyer. Cool and collected, he kept his attention on the judge who was sitting at the large, antique-looking desk, flipping through the papers. Tristen sat in his chair, quietly sweating through his shirt. His life was about to drastically change.

"The relationship between Ms. Hofferman and my client has been rocky this past year—"

"Yeah, he claimed he wasn't the father," the other lawyer said, scoffing. He threw a disgusted look at Tristen.

Elijah waited a beat before continuing. "The relationship has been rocky, and there was never established evidence that Mr. Levisay was the father. Now that the courts have decided on the matter, he would like to exert his rights. After all, if he is going to pay child support, he should have a right to see and be part of Elliot's life. Isn't that the point?"

Tristen could see on the judge's face that Elijah had hit the correct nerve.

"Being a father is more than paying money, is it not?" Elijah went on, tapping his finger against the stack of papers he held. His gold ring glistened in the sunlight, blinding Tristen, but he refused to flinch. Instead, he ignored it like he was ignoring the sweat rolling down his back and the itch he had to adjust his tie. Elijah had told him to stay still, and he was determined to obey. "Being a father is about being part of the child's life. Nurturing the child. Mr. Levisay wants to begin that process."

"But partial custody? How is that going to work when the child doesn't even know him?"

"That's why we've requested a guardian ad litem to be with the child and Mr. Levisay for some visits. We ask that custody be determined by the judge."

"I don't see any problem with a child and his father getting to know each other. I grant the father, Mr. Levisay, access to the child. Have you found a guardian ad litem, or are you requesting the courts find one for you?"

"We have the paperwork here, your honor. We've spoken to them over the phone and found Mrs. Steinke to be satisfactory. She is licensed through Kentucky and Ohio and lives close by. She is also available on these dates, your honor." Elijah handed papers to both the judge and Lamia's lawyer.

"We will be contesting this decision, your honor, and filing paperwork requesting that Mr. Levisay not have access to the child."

"On what grounds?" The judge glared at the man over his glasses.

Lamia's lawyer looked as though he was going to shrug, but then rolled back his shoulders.

"We will submit the paperwork as soon as possible," he finally said.

Elijah winked at Tristen.

"Until I see that paperwork, the visitation request is allowed to move forward. The guardian at litem will be in touch with Ms. Hofferman. If she doesn't cooperate, she will be in contempt of court, and I will review the child support verdict."

"Yes, your honor," the lawyer mumbled. He gathered his things and hurried out the door.

Elijah gathered his things as well but stayed back long enough to shake the judge's hand before marching Tristen out of the chambers.

"That's what you wanted, right?" he asked, pulling Tristen's phone out of his briefcase and handing it over.

Tristen breathed in and nodded. "I think so. I mean, it's a big deal. At least, it feels like a big deal. But I think it's the right thing to do."

Elijah grinned. "I agree. It's the right thing to do. Come on, let's get breakfast." He slapped Tristen on the back and hurried faster down the hall. "I even got time for a Bloody Mary."

Tristen took another breath and checked his notifications, scrolling through until he reached the day before. There was nothing from Scarlett.

"You coming?"

Shoving aside his disappointment, he jogged to catch up. "Yep. Coming."

Thirty-Seven

By mid-afternoon on Monday, Elijah had left Tristen—slightly drunk from several bloody Marys—on his own to check out a few warehouses he'd been looking at to turn into a music studio. In the middle of him stepping over what looked like feces in one particularly run-down building, Seraphina called.

"Hello, there, Mr. Tristen. I've been wanting to talk to you."

Tristen concentrated on the floor as he made his way to the exit. "Sorry about that, Seraphina. Things have been a bit busy."

The owner of the warehouse cut him off, impatience showing on his face. "You interested in this place or not?"

"Sorry, man. It's a bit much. I don't have the money to invest—"

"Yeah, yeah." The man was already half-way to the door, muttering about Tristen wasting his time.

"What was that about?" Seraphina asked.

"I'm in Cincinnati, looking at some places to build a studio. Most look like something from the apocalypse."

"Why you looking at places in Cincinnati? I thought you were settling down in Kentucky."

"Kentucky?" Tristen shook his head at no one, trying to reach the door without needing a Tetanus shot. "No, I'm moving back to Cincinnati as soon as I can."

"Huh, okay. Anyway, I called 'cause a friend of mine asked me for help finding a producer for his album and I thought of you."

Tristen's heart sank a little. "A friend of yours?"

"My friend is a jazz musician looking to do some collaborations. Talent doesn't always take you very far in this industry, you know?"

Tristen didn't bother to respond. They both know there was more talent in the world than even the number of songs on the music apps.

"I'm going to give him vocals on a song and help him promote it. Anyway, last week Lin sent me one of the songs y'all recorded so Luther could hear it and he's ecstatic."

"He did what?" Tristen braced himself. He hadn't gotten to editing all of Lin's songs yet, and he didn't trust Lin to know which was which.

"Calm down, Tristen. The song is good, and Luther wants to meet you. He's been trying to do everything himself, and I told him that it was time he invested in a real producer. Someone like you."

"Sure," Tristen said, licking his lips. He wondered how much a jazz musician could possibly invest in himself. "I understand."

"Wait a second. You said you're in Cincinnati now?"

"Yeah." He walked across the parking lot and got into his car.

"Then why don't you come by right now and we can talk in person? Luther stopped by. You two can talk things out. You got more samples you can show him?"

He never left home without his computer and backup drive. "I got some stuff."

"Good. I'm down on thirteenth avenue. Michelle will send you the address."

"Got it." Tristen sent a message to cancel his next empty warehouse visit and put the car into gear.

"This is good. You're good at this, Tristen. Real good. I'm starting to think I want to do a project with you myself. Davis'll be jealous, but you got some ears on you. And I like your funky beat. It's like that one guy, Austin or something. He isn't like the other rappers, you know? He moves to a different groove? He even used banjos on that one song, which I like a lot."

Tristen wasn't sure who Seraphina was talking about but nodded along to save face.

"That's what I was thinking," Luther said. "When you were busy, Tristen and I worked on this one beat here for the song you're singing for me—check this out."

Tristen held his breath as Luther played the rhythm they had manipulated together. Seraphina closed her eyes, head moving to the beat, mouthing the words when it was her time to sing. He wasn't sure if she would think he'd overstepped his bounds, but he hadn't been able to help himself earlier when he and Luther had put it together. To him, this track sounded better like this, but musicians were jealous people and they didn't always like others messing with their parts.

"*Yes*," Seraphina hissed as the track ended. She opened her eyes and turned to Tristen. "Yes. That's what I'm saying. This is what was missing. The other track was good, but this took it to a higher level, you know. Remember how we were saying it could be higher, Luther?"

"Yes, I do. Now listen to it when I put the trumpet in over here and then the violins over here," Luther said, the computer's blue light shining on his face. "Right here, Tristen?"

Tristen leaned in to move the track before pressing play.

"Listen, Seraphina. Do you hear that?" Luther paused, his hand held out as the trumpets faded in. "The way they're almost so quiet you can't hear them, but you can if you listen and then… *there*. You hear that? They sneak up on you. It's genius." He shook his head, his body still moving to the beat after the track ended.

Tristen smiled, trying to contain his own excitement. He couldn't remember the last time he'd felt so proud, so elated. Not even going on stage lately got him this feeling. The compliment from another hard-working musician held more weight for him than he'd thought it would.

"Tristen, honey, I think you were made for this."

The compliment dissolved his elation. "Made for what?" he asked, keeping his hands busy until the discomfort passed. "All I did was move a track a few seconds over. You would have figured that out."

Seraphina shook her head. "No, I wouldn't have. I got too much work to do all the time. Maybe Luther would have, but probably not, 'cause he's also doing ten jobs at once. This is why musicians used to work together—and the smart ones still do."

Tristen grunted in agreement. "I'm trying to write up my own album, and I can tell you that working with a band is much easier."

"You thinking of going solo?" Seraphina asked.

"Yes, eventually. I mean, that's what you do, right? Keep going. Isn't that what you told me a few months ago?"

"When's the last time you wrote a song?"

"Couple of weeks ago I got slightly drunk and wrote one." He grimaced. "Half a song. It's coming along."

"You still play live music?"

"Yeah."

"You play your music or covers?"

Tristen suspected where she might be going. "I play a lot of covers. Gotta give the people what they want."

Luther raised his eyebrows at him but didn't say anything. Tristen had half expected him to jump to his defense. It seemed impossible that Luther never had to play covers when he was hired for live music.

Seraphina's long eyelashes seemed to flicker at him, her lips pressed hard into a line that said she couldn't believe him.

"I wrote some songs for *The Seethers*, so I play some of those. But there are a few that don't really work with a guitar and nothing else."

"How many have you written since the band dissolved?"

Tristen let his silence speak for him.

Seraphina hummed her disapproval. "You gotta live and breathe music, Tristen. There are too many out there who can play a guitar and sing a song. If you're a musician, you hear songs in every story of your life."

"Maybe," he said, rushing to defend himself before she could contradict him. "But playing at a bar requires keeping the drinkers happy."

Seraphina took a swig of her water bottle, her finger shaking at him. "What I said doesn't mean you ain't good. You're very good. You hear things differently, and you aren't afraid to change stuff up. You might not be in this world to be on stage. You might be here to come alongside the rest of us and help our songs become better than they are raw. Help us not make a fool of ourselves. Bring out the beauty in our songs to a whole new level, right, Luther?"

"Amen, sister. This tiny bit right here already makes this song everything. I can't wait to see what we can come up with together for the rest of the album."

Tristen swallowed hard. It wasn't the first time someone had told him he should stay in the background, editing or producing while the musicians got the glory and the big money. From the time he had decided to leave Pelton, he'd worked towards being a musician, not a producer. Producing and editing had always been for extra cash.

But then, there was no reason it couldn't change into his full-time job. After all, he was the one who'd been looking for a studio a few hours before. And the excitement he'd felt as he laid down the track with Luther earlier hadn't come to him lately while playing live. Still, that could be the stress of the past year. How else could he explain his jealousy when he saw his brother on stage with Art of Rendering?

"We can talk about my lack of a music career later. Does this mean you're hiring me?" he asked, finally looking up from his sound board.

Luther laughed. He pretended to play the trumpet in the air. "That is exactly what that means, Tristen Levisay. Seraphina has a contract ready for us. She's all business like that."

"I'm *professional* like that," Seraphina corrected him, giving them both a look that said they should be as well.

"Only thing is, I gotta find us a studio here—"

"What about where you're recording Lin? Why can't we come out there?"

"In Kentucky?" He thought about the small studio at Camp Soul. It was so obviously a kid's camp that he blushed at the very idea of Seraphina going there. Maybe he could record Luther there, but not Seraphina. She was a top artist with several connections in the industry. Forcing her to record at a kid's camp could kill his producer side hustle.

"I don't have a solid set-up there. Lin needed something done fast, so I put something together a bit hodge-podge. But I'm looking at a place in Nashville or Cincinnati—"

"When?"

"Soon," Tristen assured her, eyeing Luther, who also seemed alarmed at the timeline. "I can start with Luther, though."

Seraphina stood with her hands on her ample hips. "Tristen, I gotta record the vocals now. I'm doing Luther a solid, but now's the time."

Luther nodded. It was two against one, though it shouldn't have been a surprise to Tristen. Everyone always needed everything done yesterday in the music industry.

"This fall I got a new album coming out and then a tour," Seraphina went on. "If you can't record me now, then I might have to look elsewhere."

Tristen did a double-take. "No need for that. I can record you. I'll find a place, maybe in Nashville, and we can meet there."

"Nashville? You telling me I gotta fly to Nashville when right now you're an hour from me by car?"

He sighed. "Listen, Seraphina, you won't like the studio where I'm recording Lin. It's small, and it's inside a kid's camp."

Luther and Seraphina looked at each other, then at Tristen. "A camp?" she asked. "You're recording Lin in the woods?"

"No," Tristen said, chuckling at the image. "It's at a music camp. Like a summer camp."

"Well, now, I gotta come see it. Do they teach singing and everything?"

"Uh, yeah. I guess. A friend of mine runs it."

"You teach there?"

"I'm recording some of the kids. There were a couple of them last week that were very talented. They play violins and that kind of thing."

"Pshaw." Seraphina's glossy pink nails fluttered in the air. "That's downright amazing. So why are you saying you don't want me there to record? 'Cause the place I record here is full. I thought you'd be able to at least record my vocals where you are. And to be honest, I don't think Luther here cares how big the studio is. All he wants is a good album."

The plan was both ideal and horrendous.

"I'll send you the directions," Tristen said reluctantly. "But you gotta understand that it isn't glamorous."

Seraphina was quiet for a few seconds. The sound of her nails tapping and her direct stare started to make Tristen squirm like a five-year-old after six hours in school.

"What?"

"I wanna know why you would rather record me in Nashville."

He shook his head. "You'll see when you come to the middle of Kentucky, Seraphina. It's not music town. There's nothing elegant about it."

"But it's cheaper than Nashville, isn't it?"

"That's not it! It's not—practical. I mean, I can set up maybe two people in there. But not more."

"Fine, maybe this camp place isn't perfect, but it'll do for now. And setting up a bigger studio in Middle-of-Nowhere, Kentucky would be cheaper than trying to rent something in Nashville."

Tristen glanced at Luther. He was busy agreeing with Seraphina.

"I don't know," Tristen said. "No one comes to Pelton, Kentucky to record their album. Everyone's in Nashville."

"Everyone?"

"Or Atlanta."

Seraphina made a disapproving sound. "Atlanta has too many distractions. Can't tell you how many people there can't stop drinking and partying. They don't do anything. It's like LA. Can't finish nothing in that place."

"But there's nothing in Kentucky, Seraphina. I mean, there are more empty factories and buildings than there are people."

"I've recorded in broken-down warehouses and studios with peeling paint. I'm not above recording in a dive. You gotta make sure the sound is good and the song is edited well. That's what Luther here will be paying you for. That's what anyone would be paying you for. And you don't need to go to Nashville for that. Besides, the competition there is brutal. Out in Kentucky, you'll be working with the people you want to work with. Gives you exclusivity."

"Okay." Tristen wasn't sure why everyone was conspiring to convince him to stay in Kentucky lately, but it was starting to grate on his nerves.

"You don't need to go to Nashville or anywhere else. What you need to do is become an expert at what you do so that people come to you. And the more they come to you, the bigger and more comfortable you can make your studio. Hell, you could paint it maroon if you like. Although I won't come if you paint it maroon. Can't stand that color. Makes me gag."

She chuckled at her own joke. Luther joined her.

"You really think people would come to wherever I set myself up?"

"More or less," she told him. "I mean, you're close enough now to an airport like Cincinnati. I'm not sure Nashville is any more convenient. Anyway, for this project, when can you fit me in?"

"What days do you have free?" Tristen asked, relieved to drop the studio question. "I'll go along with your schedule."

"I should be there this week. Luther, what do you think? You want to be there with me, or do you want me to lay down the vocals when I can?"

"I'll try to be there when you can, baby," Luther said. He must be a very old friend. Tristen couldn't imagine anyone new calling Seraphina 'baby.'

"What about Thursday? Is that when the kids are there?"

"Kids are there all week. You can come in the evening, though."

"I kinda wanna see these kids. They give a concert of some kind?"

Tristen's mind raced, suddenly realizing that Seraphina's appearance at the camp could be a game-changer for Rob and Dariana. "I gotta check with Rob, but I think they're having a mini concert on Friday this week."

"Okay, Friday it is then. You tell them that Seraphina is coming to see them. And afterwards we can record. Shouldn't take long. I better look for a hotel."

"You'll find a nice one in Lexington," Tristen said.

"Maybe I'll stay at your house," she retorted.

"Always invited, Seraphina." He zipped up his bag and slung it onto his shoulder.

"We'll see then. Tell me what Rob says and I'll be there Friday."

Leaving the studio, Tristen felt somewhere between cloud nine and wanting to vomit. In the last few hours, he'd secured a contract to record a twelve-track album with Luther and might have made the marketing decision of the year for Rob. Plus, Seraphina liked the work he had done on the song she was singing for Luther's album so much that she'd implied she might work with him on a project too, which could turn into a full album, if he was lucky. Things were looking so good, but he had to figure out the studio situation. Seraphina had a point about the location, but he didn't want to stay in Kentucky. He had never even considered staying there.

Tristen checked his phone. No notification from Scarlett. If she was done with him, he wasn't sure he *could* stay in Kentucky. Running into her would be inevitable, after all.

There were a few messages from Ivy; one from Jared asking where the black jumping ropes were; and one from Ben reminding him about the going-away party this week, which he couldn't go to if Scarlett didn't want him there.

He tapped on Scarlett's name and his heart skipped a beat, turning his skin cold.

He hadn't sent his message.

"Shit," he muttered to no one. The text he had so carefully typed out was still waiting to be sent out. "*Shit.*"

He considered sending it now, but decided against it. It would be better to show up and explain himself in person. He could be at Scarlett's house by eight in the evening.

As he got into the car, his phone lit up. A voice message from Lamia.

"Hey, asshole. You want visitation rights with your son? The son you wanted nothing to do with for over a year? I'll give you visitation rights, and I bet you'll be sorry. You won't be able to handle one day. Be on the watch, darling. 'Cause he's coming your way."

Thirty-Eight

All day Sunday, Scarlett stayed in bed.

On Monday morning she called in sick. Then again on Tuesday. She didn't eat, didn't sleep, and let her cell phone run out of battery without bothering to plug it in.

By Wednesday, the day of the guardian ad litem visit, she was so exhausted she skipped the market, forfeiting the money she'd paid for her spot. At seven in the morning, despite being awake, she decided to stay in bed again, staring at the ceiling. She listened as Ben got ready for his almost last day of boxing camp. He'd stayed the weekend with Nasreen then gone to Eric's house Monday night, but had come back Tuesday after camp claiming he needed more clothes and time in his own bed. Scarlett was convinced he was checking up on her, but she didn't care. Of all the horrible things that had happened the weekend before, the worst was realizing that Ben had heard everything from their patio. Everything. She could hardly look at him, knowing she was probably the last person he wanted to live with.

"Scarlett, you awake?" he asked from outside her bedroom door. "You gotta take me to boxing camp. Dad says he can't."

Scarlett groaned. Of course he couldn't. She had managed to avoid Cory by not going to the market, but the way her life went, she was certain she wouldn't be able to avoid Tristen if she went near Top Gym.

With an effort that felt like she was benching three hundred pounds, she crawled out of bed and opened her door. Ben stood in the doorway, holding out a glass of orange juice.

"I thought you could use some vitamins," he said.

For a moment Scarlett considered telling him to go away. If he were Rhoda or Candi or even Nasreen, she would have. But he wasn't them; he was Ben. A kid. And whether or not he saw her differently now after hearing those awful things Johnny and Cory had said Saturday night, she didn't want to be cruel to him.

"I'm awake," she croaked, going to sit back down.

"I think you should come into camp and talk to Tristen," Ben said, his eyes wide and serious.

Scarlett almost choked on her juice. "Tristen? Why?"

"'Cause you like him," Ben said, spreading his hands across the bedspread. "I thought when you liked someone you called them and asked them on dates and stuff."

"I don't think he likes me like that, Ben."

"Yeah, he does."

Scarlett squinted at him.

"He does," Ben exclaimed. "I know he does."

She didn't have the heart to tell him that Tristen hadn't texted her all weekend. "Well, why don't we eat some breakfast and take you to camp?"

"I am out of bed," Ben said. "I've been out of bed."

"Right," Scarlett told him. "But who's gonna make breakfast? You or me?"

"I'll make toast, and I can make eggs. I remember how."

"Perfect. And coffee."

Ben made a face. "Fine, I'll make coffee. You go take a shower, 'cause you smell."

Scarlett lunged as though to spank him on the butt, but he jumped away, taunting her.

"Don't be rude to your aunt," she muttered.

"Not rude," he taunted. "Just honest."

"I'm the only one here who can drive, mister," she called as she shut the bathroom door. "So watch it."

After a quick shower, she met Ben in the kitchen, where coffee was percolating in the machine and a pan heated up on the stove. A knock sounded at the door as Ben cracked open an egg, and they both froze.

"Who is it?" Ben asked.

"I don't know."

The person knocked again before Scarlett could reach the door.

"It's a little early, isn't it?" she grumbled as she yanked the door open.

Rhoda stood in the hallway, puffing on a vape. She grinned at Scarlett, smoke surrounding her face. Her eyes were hidden behind large sunglasses, and as usual she was dressed in tight black jeans, a tank top and a leather vest.

"Rhoda." Scarlett stared at her sister.

"Morning to you, too, sis." Rhoda laughed, her usual jovial, confident self, and walked into the apartment. "Where's my Ben?"

Ben threw his arms around his mom with such force that she almost fell over. Scarlett watched, wishing she was Ben. Wishing Rhoda would wrap her strength and confidence around Scarlett's shoulders so she could believe that everything would eventually be okay again.

"I missed you," Ben said, his voice muffled.

"I missed you too, bud." Rhoda cradled his chin in her hand and giggled in wonder, like a real mama. Her hand seemed slightly twisted, as though her fingers had been broken and not healed properly, but Ben didn't seem to notice.

"I can't believe you're here." He threw his arms around Rhoda again. "Wanna see me box?"

"Box? Are you a boxer now?"

Ben puffed out his chest. "Course. I go to boxing camp that Dad got me into, and Tristen set up a bag for me on the porch. A heavy one, too. Like the professionals."

"Who's Tristen?" Rhoda asked.

"Scarlett's boyfriend," Ben said as he ran to flip the eggs.

"No," Scarlett said. "He's not."

Ben looked up and flushed red. "Sorry, she says he isn't her boyfriend. But he should be."

"Interesting," Rhoda replied, her eyes on her sister. "What are we having for breakfast?"

"Eggs and toast. Coffee is already made over there. Want some?"

"I'll take some coffee, but I only want toast. Eggs don't sit well with me."

"When did you get back in town?" Scarlett asked as they sat at the table.

"Told you I'd see you soon." Rhoda smiled. "I heard Cory is marrying some rich chick. Made himself a match that he deserves."

"You know Cory?" Ben asked, setting full plates in front of Scarlett and him before serving two cups of coffee. "He's an asshole."

"Ben, language!" Scarlett said, but Rhoda was laughing.

"I always thought that about him, but Scarlett here was his friend, so I tried to be kind."

"They ain't friends anymore," Ben told her, his mouth full of eggs.

Scarlett wasn't ready for the change in subject. She could feel Rhoda's eyes on her, but she kept watching Ben.

"It's a good decision, not being friends with Cory anymore," Rhoda said. The way she said 'friends' made it clear she knew exactly what kind of friends Scarlett and Cory had been. "I hear his fiancée is jealous and like her daddy—bossy, bitchy and arrogant. You don't want to get mixed up with them."

Scarlett squirmed. She wondered if her sister thought the same about her. "What have you been up to, Rhoda?"

Rhoda's eyes flashed. "This is good toast, Ben."

"Thanks, Mom. I could make you another, if you want."

"You know what I want? I want to see you box on that heavy bag out there. Do you have time before camp starts?"

"If I go fast," Ben said, already halfway to his bedroom. In less than two minutes he was tightening his gloves with his teeth and heading out to the patio. "Be sure to watch, Mom."

"You got it," Rhoda said, turning her chair to keep her eyes on him.

Soon an inconsistent rhythm of muted pounding seeped through the sliding door.

"You're lucky not to have Cory anymore."

"What do you know about Cory?"

Rhoda kept her eyes on Ben, making Scarlett feel like they were in some sting operation, talking while pretending not to talk. "I know you've always been on and off again with that guy, and I'm glad to hear that he's moving on. You're better than him, Scarlett."

Scarlett picked up the breakfast dishes instead of answering. "How long you staying in town?"

"As long as I need to be. Gotta clear some things up. You go dark for six months and everything goes to shit."

"I guess a lot of people rely on you, Rhoda."

Her sister snorted. "A lot of lazy people rely on my wad of cash."

"Where do you get the cash?" It was the first time Scarlett had asked in years. Rhoda had never told her.

"You know the drill, sis. I can't tell you. Don't want you involved."

"Fine," Scarlett told her. She refilled their coffee mugs, unable to stop herself from noticing the gold bracelets around Rhoda's wrists, the gold earrings lined up her ears and the expensive-looking watch. Not to mention the black leather jacket in pristine condition. "What's going to happen? With the guardian ad litem and Candi and Eric?"

"That's what I'm gonna find out," Rhoda said. The rhythm against the boxing bag was slowing dramatically. They only had a few more seconds before Ben would come inside.

"You can't let Candi have him."

"I don't have much sway this time, Scarlett. Johnny's kicking you out of the apartment I set up for you, and you haven't found a new place. And after this summer you don't even have a job lined up."

Scarlett closed her eyes as she rinsed the plates. "I was hoping to clear things with Johnny. I didn't expect him not to care that I have over half the payment for him."

"That's how guys like Johnny are, Scarlett. You gotta started wising up. You're too old to be going around this life like you got no idea how things work. I was already making a name for myself by your age. You need to do the same. It's the only way to survive."

Scarlett wondered if she could do the kind of work Rhoda did, but immediately answered her own question. Whatever it was, they were too opposite for it to be the right thing for her. Everything Cory had said the other day was starting to make sense, and she hated him for that. "I gotta take Ben to camp."

"Did you see?" Ben shouted as he came back inside. Rhoda answered him with a double high-five.

"Let's go, Ben. Teeth brushed." Scarlett turned to Rhoda. "You coming with us?"

Rhoda slipped her sunglasses back onto her nose and gave a nod. "Wouldn't miss it."

Thirty-Nine

After dropping Ben at Top Gym, without going inside, Scarlett took Rhoda back to the apartment, where she hopped into an Audi and drove off, saying she'd call later. Scarlett wasn't going to hold her breath. Half the time Rhoda said that, she disappeared. This time she had reason to stick around, but Scarlett didn't hold out any hope. While Rhoda seemed to genuinely love Ben, she never stayed. She wasn't the type of woman who lived up to anyone's hopes or expectations.

Scarlett sighed and dropped to the couch. She should go into work to bake once the meeting with Jenn was over. She needed to make things for the camp and for Nasreen's going-away party. Why Nasreen had to jet off before the weekend, Scarlett didn't know. Thinking about it irritated her.

Not that it would have mattered, since Scarlett apparently had to move as well.

Rhoda's words came back to mind, angering her. *You haven't found a new place.* Rhoda had no idea what it was like to work and take care of Ben. She hadn't had time to look for a place. It wasn't fair for Rhoda to lecture her about it. She was the one who hadn't bothered to mention the payment stopping in the first place.

Her thoughts were interrupted by a knock on the door. She glanced around the apartment, suddenly remembering all the scrubbing she had planned to do. The living room was free of leftover dishes and dirty socks, but the floors hadn't been vacuumed in a while and she knew the bathroom was in disarray. It was too late now.

Besides, even a shiny new apartment probably wouldn't help her keep Ben against Eric.

Jenn stood in the doorway, smiling, her black hair framing her sweet face. "Scarlett?"

"Yes," Scarlett answered. Jenn was charming, unlike most of the social workers Scarlett had met in her life. Her eyes were bright instead of dull and her smile genuine.

"I'm not sure if you remember me. I'm Jenn. Can I come in?"

"Of course," Scarlett said, stepping away from the door. Her memory flashed to when she had been maybe seven. A woman wearing a flowing skirt had walked in through the front door, the sun shining behind her. The first thing she'd done was lean all the way down to Scarlett's nose-level. She remembered mostly the gold, overly large glasses the woman had worn.

She shook the memory away and focused on Jenn. "Would you like something to drink?"

"Some water would be nice," Jenn said. With her smooth skin and peppy, youthful mannerisms, it was possible they were the same age. And yet Scarlett already mistook herself for middle-aged half the time she looked in the mirror. "Have you been living here long?"

Scarlett looked around, hearing Candi's voice in her head. *This isn't a home.* Not that Candi knew what a home was. "About five years. Going on six. I know we don't have a lot of stuff, but I try to keep a minimal lifestyle."

She'd learned the phrase on social media. It sounded better than admitting she didn't have the money for stuff.

"That's fine. No need for more stuff, right?" Jenn made a note on her paper. "Ben goes to the local school?"

"Yes."

She continued to answer each question, resisting the urge to over-explain her answers each time. Who Ben's friends were, what activities he did, how he got along with his teachers, what grades he was getting, if he seemed happy, what Scarlett's job was, how many hours she worked, was she happy.

"I think that's about all I need. If you don't mind, could I see Ben's room?"

"Sure," Scarlett said as they stood up. Thankfully Ben had picked up his dirty clothes, made his bed and organized his shelves the day before. The basket of clean laundry tucked against the wall was still full, but at least it was clean.

"You've done a really good job raising him until now, Scarlett. It must have been difficult to step into that role so young," Jenn said. Somehow it didn't sound patronizing.

Her tone encouraged Scarlett to tell her how hard it had been, but then she remembered Jenn was not her friend.

"I was happy to help my sister," she finally said. "I love having Ben."

Jenn beamed at her and nodded. "That's all I needed to hear."

"What happens now?"

Jenn looked at her phone. "Well, there's a discussion between the biological parents going on right now."

"What about the grandmother?"

"Candi? She pulled out a day ago. Said she changed her mind. I wasn't really surprised," Jenn told her. Her eyes widened. "Sorry, I shouldn't have said that."

Scarlett almost cried with relief. "How long will this all take? Who makes the final decision?"

"To be honest with you, Scarlett, most kids go to their biological parents. And the fact that you're in an unstable living situation isn't necessarily helping."

"Why is it unstable?" she asked, pushing past the lump in her throat.

"You have no contract here. And the manager says that you've been asked to leave in a week."

"I have another place to live."

"I'm glad. But at any rate, I'm not the judge. I don't make the decision. The parents are meeting tomorrow about what to do and if an agreement is reached, I'm sure you'll be told." Jenn looked up from her phone. Her smile had turned into one of pity. "I'll make sure you know. Okay?"

"Yeah, okay," Scarlett managed to say as Jenn opened the door and let herself out. "Thank you."

"Are you okay?" Dariana asked.

Scarlett looked up, startled. She'd been alone in the kitchen for the past three hours preparing bread. She had no idea how many turns she'd given the ball of dough in her hands.

She smiled to pretend she was okay. "I'm fine. How are you feeling? The baby still giving you trouble?"

"Not so much today," Dariana said. She looked healthier, with a little color in her cheeks.

"Want a brownie?" Scarlett asked, taunting her with a perfect chocolate square on a small plate.

"You're so mean," Dariana said, laughing. But she took the plate and bit the corner off. "If this baby comes out at ten pounds it'll be your fault."

Scarlett laughed, which felt good. She hadn't laughed in a few days. "I promise not to feed you any more brownies until after the baby is born."

"Don't you dare," Dariana said, moaning with relish at her next bite. "Seriously, these are so good."

Scarlett picked up another ball of dough out of a shaping basket and started dragging it towards her, turning it ninety degrees each time.

"Scarlett, do you have a job to go to after this summer?"

Scarlett paused, shaping the dough. Rhoda's accusation that morning came back to her. *Your situation is unstable,* Jenn had said.

And she wasn't wrong. The truth was that she hadn't thought of looking for a job. She lived each day from one hour to the next, half the time forgetting that she should think about the future.

She swallowed hard. Thinking about the future was too stressful. Maybe that was what differentiated her from Rhoda.

"No," she said simply.

"Have you heard of a place called Sourdough Mama?"

Scarlett shook her head, leaving the dough off to the side and pulling another towards her.

"She's on social media. She started baking bread and posting about it online. When people started asking if they could buy it, she started selling it. Don't me how you sell bread online, but she made quite a company out of it."

"Huh." Scarlett had seen women like that. The differences between her and them was their beautiful kitchens with good lighting, whatever camera or phone they used for the videos and pictures, their time and knowledge on posting, their ability to not look or act like a fool, their usually slim and pretty appearance... She could go on, but Dariana interrupted her thoughts.

"She lives close to here, and her business has grown so much that she's opening a kitchen in Beakersville to fulfill all her orders. She put out this whole message last night on social media," Dariana said, falling quiet.

"And?" Scarlett asked. Dariana's cheeks were turning bright pink and she was looking at the floor.

"I reached out and asked about the position. And then I sent in your resume with a recommendation letter from me," she said quickly.

Scarlett blinked. She dragged the dough towards her again, then blinked again.

"Are you mad?" Dariana asked.

"No. I'm not mad." She was so pathetic that Dariana felt she needed an advocate. Scarlett swallowed her embarrassment. At least she wouldn't have to suffer the rejection. Dariana would probably just not tell her. Scarlett hoped they could move on and not talk about it anymore.

Dariana clapped her hands with a sigh. "Good! I'm so glad you aren't mad, because she wants you to go in for an interview."

"An interview?"

"Yes. And listen to this, the interview is literally making a loaf of sourdough. So it's gonna take you, well, whatever it takes you to do that."

Scarlett turned to look Dariana in the eyes. "Seriously? Making a loaf is the interview?"

"Yes. It sounds more like a competition because she's doing them in groups. I mean, I guess that's good since you won't be alone, but also still scary." Dariana's eyes rolled back into her head as she groaned. "I shouldn't say that. You're great at this whole baking thing. I'd be terrified because I can't tell a cup from a tablespoon. But anyway, the interview or audition or whatever she wants to call it is on Friday afternoon. Well, there's one on Saturday as well, but I told her you usually sold your own stuff at the market on Saturdays, which she seemed really excited about."

Everything slowly sank into Scarlett's brain.

"You're mad, aren't you? I didn't really have the right to do that, I'm sorry. And you probably have your own ideas and thoughts for a job. Rob says I get too involved in other people's lives, and he's right. I guess I feel bad we can't keep you on throughout the year, but that doesn't mean I should take over your life. I'll call her."

"Wait." Scarlett grabbed Dariana's phone from her hand. "Don't you dare call her. Thank you for thinking of me and caring about me. I—I appreciate it."

Dariana's worry wrinkles relaxed as she broke into a smile. "Oh, I'm so glad you see it like that. Because I was worried you'd be mad once Rob told me I shouldn't have meddled. But I want the world to taste and see how good you are at all this." She waved her hands at the balls of dough.

Scarlett's chest expanded until laughter bubbled out of her. After the stress of the weekend, losing Cory and possibly Tristen, she couldn't think of a nicer thing someone could have done for her. The fact that Dariana had thought of her, had worried about her future during the weekend—Scarlett couldn't fathom it. Someone wanted something good to happen to her, someone thought she could bring value to another person.

It wasn't long before her laughter turned into tears.

"Don't cry, Scarlett." Dariana threw her arms around Scarlett. "I'm pregnant and emotional. I'll cry if you do."

Scarlett pulled away, wiping her eyes quickly. "Okay, then tell me more details. Like what time I need to be there, what should I wear, all that."

"For that I'll need my phone," Dariana said. "And I forgot it. Wait a second, I'll be right back."

Scarlett scored the balls of dough as Dariana left the kitchen. When her own phone rang, she expected it to be Dariana from somewhere in the camp. Instead, it was Jenn. Scarlett wiped her hands on her apron and answered.

"I wanted to let you know that there's no need for anything more from you. The parents have come to a resolution."

"A resolution? Like they decide what happens?"

"It's the type of situation everyone prefers, honestly," Jenn said. Scarlett could hear the blinker on her car.

"But—"

"The parents ultimately can make the decision if there's no history of neglect or abuse. And in Ben's case, thank goodness, there's none of that. The two parents have decided what is best and how they will split time with Ben. The resolution will be sent formally to the judge tomorrow morning, but as Ben's caretaker for the last five years, I thought you should be aware of it. I'll come by when you're free to go over everything with you. I will have some papers for you to sign."

"Okay." Scarlett wished she was home so she could throw herself into bed and cry. "I understand. Thank you."

"I found it," Dariana called out from the other side of the kitchen.

Scarlett plastered a smile onto her face and pushed away the bad news. She'd deal with all the bad stuff later.

Forty

Scarlett's truck rumbled up the road to Brody's house, where Candi had lived the last few years. Rhoda's Audi sat in a driveway that was in dire need of a weedwhacker.

Before she could reach the house, the front door opened. Rhoda stood dressed in her usual black, despite the oppressive humidity, staring at Scarlett and looking either surprised or pleased. Scarlett couldn't tell which. Candi was right behind Rhoda, holding the screen door in tiny cut-off jean shorts and a tube top. She looked furious.

"Well, well, look who decided to show up," she drawled. Vape smoke surrounded her black hair, piled on top of her head. She narrowed her eyes at Scarlett and glared hard, as though she might be able to strike her with laser beams. "This ungrateful bitch never visits. Not unless she wants something."

"Hi, Mom." Scarlett stood still, sweat beading down her spine. She glanced at the front door, willing Candi to go inside, but she stayed where she was.

Rhoda lowered her sunglasses onto her nose and smiled at Scarlett. "Hey, sis. It's nice to see you again. You didn't have to come here. I was going to come by and see you before we left."

"Where are you going?"

"Here and there. Gotta head south for a little bit. I was gonna come by and maybe try to talk Johnny down from the ledge he's on." Rhoda smiled. "I have a few tricks up my sleeve. We'll see if he bites. I don't want my little sister to get kicked out."

For the first time, her help felt out of place. Scarlett tried to look past the sunglasses to her sister's eyes, but all she could see was her own reflection and Rhoda's cool smile. She swallowed, willing away the discomfort crawling on her skin, but it refused.

"Hello? Scarlett. Why are you staring?"

Something had shifted. As though Rhoda had taken Scarlett off the 'sister' list and put her on the same list as Candi. "There's nothing to talk to Johnny about, Rhoda. He already rented the place. I'll be fine. I already have something lined up."

Rhoda's mouth twitched into a half-smile. She didn't believe her, and Scarlett couldn't blame her. She was lying.

"Well, I put some money into your account. You know, a kind of thank you for taking care of Ben all these years. You did a good job, Scar."

Scarlett realized her sister expected a polite 'thank you' and for her to be on her way. Rhoda expected her to just take the money, like everyone else did.

Candi squinted past the sunlight, her lip curled in disgust. "You leave here, Scarlett. No one has no use for you no more."

Scarlett ignored her mother and gathered her courage, even as she felt the front of her shirt absorbing the sweat that had pooled between her breasts.

"I want Ben, Rhoda," she said quickly. "He's better off with me."

Candi screeched with laughter, slamming her fist against the door frame. "Damn, you can be funny sometimes, Scarlett."

"Why?" Rhoda said, ignoring their mom.

"He's safe with me, Rhoda, living a good kid life. Traveling around with you, seeing whatever you do, won't be good for him."

Rhoda crossed her arms and raised her eyebrows. Scarlett's hands trembled, but she shoved them in her back pockets and went on. "You disappear for months at a time."

"I don't actually disappear," Rhoda said, her sarcasm producing a laugh from Candi. "You don't see me, but I am around."

Scarlett stepped forward. "What do you do, Rhoda? Since you don't work for some secret government agency because, well…" She paused; the list of reasons Rhoda wouldn't be working for the government didn't need to be spoken aloud. "The only things I can think of are drug-smuggling, drug-selling, people-smuggling or people-selling. Or weapons, maybe. Whatever it is, I know it's not a good life for Ben." She paused, then gestured to Rhoda's hand. "Did you break that in a fight? Or in jail? Was it punishment for something?"

Rhoda lifted her chin, her lips now curling into a snarl. But when she spoke, her voice was very quiet. "You have quite the imagination, Scar. Maybe you should lay off the television."

"He deserves better. Ben needs friends, and he needs school."

"But his only friend moved away," Candi taunted. "Nasreen couldn't stand being around you, so she left. Probably thought you were a bad influence on her kid, what with your reputation and all."

"Shut up, Candi," Scarlett snapped. She took a step forward. So did Candi.

Between them, Rhoda started laughing. "Damn. Baby sis found her voice. Shit, took you long enough." She waved her poorly healed hand in the air. "Should we let the two of you duke it out?"

"Fine by me. This girl needs an ass-whooping," Candi growled.

Rage bubbled under Scarlett's sweating skin and for the first time in a long time, she didn't push it away. When Candi took another step forward, Scarlett marched past Rhoda, stopping inches from her mother's face.

"This has nothing to do with you, Mom. You know nothing about Ben or about me. You can barely stand being around him, just like you can't stand being around me."

"Well, that last part is correct," Candi shot back. "But I know how to raise a child and you don't."

"You only wanted to get Rhoda's attention for more money," Scarlett hissed, refusing to lower her gaze. She would lose everything in the next few days, and she no longer cared to keep her mouth in check. She didn't care if Candi flew off the handle. It would feel good to have an excuse to punch something.

She whipped around, her index finger in Rhoda's face before Candi could figure out a response. Rhoda's eyes darkened, but Scarlett didn't care.

"*I* know how to take care of him. Not you. Not Eric. I know whether he eats three meals a day, I know where he is at all times, I take him for check-ups and to the dentist, I know who his friends are at school, why he likes basketball, who his favorite teachers are, what he wants to be when he grows up and that he can't understand why anyone would want to be a lawyer. I've held him while he was puking and run hot water for him when he was coughing and made him laugh when he was sad."

"I'm his mother," Rhoda said, her voice flippant. She flicked her hand towards the house.

"If you could keep a man, you could have a kid of your own," Candi taunted.

"I've seen you sit around crying the past few days about Cory," Rhoda added.

"And Ben's been fine. Even when I'm upset about something, I'm providing a life for him. Which is more than you or Candi would do."

"Which is why she was told to bow out. Some people do as they're told for the benefit of others."

Candi huffed her indignation, then marched away, muttering about her ungrateful little brats. The screen door slammed again; something that sounded like a dish or glass smashed against the floor soon after.

"She never changes," Rhoda said, shaking her head.

"But you did."

Rhoda's eyes twitched. She opened her mouth then closed it again, her throat constricting as she swallowed. "So have you, Scarlett. You've grown some balls. I hope you can keep them."

"I don't need to be like you and Candi," Scarlett snapped back. "I want Ben. He's the reason I keep living, though I probably don't do a very good job at it. And he's the reason I'm here now. I want custody."

Rhoda sighed, expression back under her control.

Scarlett started to panic. When Rhoda lost interest, nothing held her in place. "Rhoda, listen to me."

"Why? You aren't his mother. I'm his mother."

"You left him, Rhoda."

"For his own good, Scarlett."

Scarlett tried to lick her lips, but her mouth was dry. "Giving birth to him doesn't make you his mother. Candi never should've been taken care of us."

Rhoda shrugged. "People try their best."

"Do they? Did she?" Scarlett demanded, pointing at the house. "You left him with me because it was best for him. So, what's changed?"

"He's older," Rhoda said, her voice even, but her eyes flickered.

"I love him, Rhoda. I'll give him a childhood. Remember when all we wanted was a childhood?"

Rhoda crossed her arms and stared hard at Scarlett. "We don't always get what we want, and, at least for me, not having a childhood has come in handy. It's the only way I've been able to become what I am; one of the most feared women in my niche. It allows me to buy off Candi and pay Eric to do as I say." She looked Scarlett up and down, her smile hardening to a straight line. "And you."

"And me what?"

"You do as I say. I pay your rent, send you some crumbs every once in a while, and you stay in the same position as before, like a dog waiting for his owner to come home."

The sun still glared in her eyes, but Scarlett's body went as cold as if it had been put out. Hearing Candi say something like that was normal, but Rhoda had never been cruel to her before. At least never to her face.

"I told you back then I'd be back for him someday. If you thought you got him permanently, that's your fault," Rhoda continued. She turned on her heel and started to walk away.

"A mother does what's right for her child. You're being selfish, Rhoda. You got your pride hurt and now you're taking him away." Scarlett could feel a panic attack coming on. She wanted to scratch Rhoda's eyes out, but managed to stay still.

"I have the right to take him anywhere I want."

"Having the right doesn't make you right. You're wrong about this."

Rhoda looked over her shoulder, the beady eyes of her snake tattoo now staring directly at Scarlett. "You're saying I'm not good enough?"

She was whispering. Something Scarlett hadn't heard from her sister ever.

"I'm not saying you're not good enough," she said, scrambling to find the words. "You're still his birth mother, but I could be his day-to-day mother. Maybe I haven't become anything compared to you, Rhoda, but I've made sure he is safe. I've made sure the crap we dealt with growing up stops with us."

"I'll ask Ben," Rhoda said, her vulnerability gone.

"No," Scarlett said. A few days ago she would have acquiesced to that comment, but she had changed her mind. "He's eleven, Rhoda. He's a child and he shouldn't have to choose. We're the adults. We know what's best for him. You know what's best for him."

She stopped short of repeating herself again. If she hadn't convinced Rhoda by now, there would be no convincing her ever.

Rhoda took a few steps towards the house, and Scarlett's heart sank. But then her sister stopped again, and her shoulders fell from their usual squared-off stance. Rhoda turned around slowly, her cheeks wet under the giant sunglasses.

"That's what I wanted to hear, little sis."

"What?" Scarlett tried to keep herself from being too hopeful; she had no idea what Rhoda was saying.

"I wanted to know that you'd fight for him. Because despite me not being with him day-to-day, as you say, I'd die for him."

"I'd die for him, too, Rhoda."

Her sister nodded, but then she walked into the house and shut the door.

Forty-One

"You back in town?"

Tristen yawned into the phone before answering. He'd gotten back to his house after midnight, and it wasn't even seven in the morning yet.

"Yes, I'm in town. And yes, I'll be at the gym at eight-thirty."

"I'm not calling to check up on you," Ivy said. "I want to show you something. Owen and I both want to show you something. Can you meet us in about twenty minutes? You'd have to leave now."

"Yeah, sure. I'll leave now. Just gotta brush my teeth."

"Hurry up," Ivy said. Her voice sounded excited.

Tristen looked at the phone when she hung up, but it only answered with an address popping into his messages a second later. "5768 West Pollard Road. What the hell is that?"

He hurried through brushing his teeth and jumped into his car before he clicked on the address, the link opening to a small town called Beakersville between Lexington and Pelton. Tristen drove there, passing horse farms and small main streets until he pulled into what looked like a semi-abandoned edge of Beakersville near its old train station. Some of the area had been reclaimed, with a few restaurants, bars, coffee shops and a bookstore. As cute as they were, the other buildings were still abandoned. At the far-left end stood Owen and Ivy, in front of a metal building.

Owen's arm was around Ivy's shoulders; he was kissing her temple when Tristen walked up. He wanted to complain about how gross they were, but the truth was, they were cute. Even he could see that. And Ivy was clearly happy.

"New gym opening?" he asked, pointing at the abandoned building that looked like an old shed.

"Gym?" Ivy asked.

"I figured you brought me here to check out Top Gym expanding. Looks like it would be a good place for another gym. Maybe a bit small."

Ivy and Owen exchanged looks. Tristen had come up with the answer on his way over and couldn't help feeling proud of himself for figuring it out.

"That's not why you're here," Owen said.

Tristen's pride deflated. "Oh. Then why?"

Ivy's grin widened as she pulled out a key and opened the large door. Upon closer inspection, the building looked like an old horse-training barn.

"What was this place?" he asked. It had clearly gone through some changes. The inside of it wasn't raw building bone as he had assumed it would be. The walls were all wood, stained dark walnut, and the floors were tile. Lights hung from the tall ceilings, but sunlight also streamed in through skylights along the roof as well. There was a semi reception area with a large desk and two hallways.

"This is your new studio," Owen said. "Come on."

"My what?"

Ivy pulled him down the first hallway, her smile almost breaking her face, it was so wide. "Your new studio. Owen used to use this place for his import and export business. This back here was a storage area that we were thinking you could use for bands to record in. Look."

The room she was talking about must have been twenty by fifteen feet. The ceilings weren't as high, a little less than ten feet, and to the left the wall had a large plexiglass window that looked into an office.

"See? Over there you could put the sound stuff or whatever you call it, and then you could see them in here. I mean, maybe it would be better if it was turned. Like this you'll see them from the side, but it's workable, right?"

Tristen was stunned. "Yeah, it's workable."

"Needs a little work," Owen said, looking around. "We'll have to panel it with those sound boards. I've been doing some research. And you'll have to invest in the equipment, but I bet between the two of us we can get it done in a few weeks."

"And that isn't all. Come here," Ivy said, tugging Tristen's arm.

Across the hall were two doors. Ivy opened each to allow Tristen to peek in. They were smaller rooms, both empty.

"Here you could have a smaller version. Owen was reading about how you don't want too big a space when recording one or two people, so he was thinking you could put a plexiglass window between the two rooms here and have another recording studio."

"This is amazing," Tristen stammered. "I don't know what to say."

Owen smiled. "We aren't done. Come."

They rounded the reception area again and walked down the next hall.

"There are five rooms here of various sizes. We weren't sure if you would want that many studios, but we were thinking you could also rent them out to music teachers. You know, have a one-stop place where people could learn to play and sing, et cetera. I don't know. It was just a thought."

"It was a good thoght," Tristen murmured. He turned to face Owen and Ivy. "How much?"

"A good price," Owen said.

"How much?"

"We know you've been through a rough patch, and that a lot of what's happened hasn't really been fair."

Tristen stiffened, even though it was what he'd wanted Ivy to say for a long time. Something about her saying it made him feel a bit like a child.

"I'm divesting of a few things," Owen said. "Including some of the buildings I own—this being one of them. You can either buy it straight out, or you can rent-to-own it. I'm willing to sell it for the loan I have out on it, about twenty-five thousand. We can look over your finances. I mean, if you want the place. We'll give you the family rate," Owen said with a wink.

"Looks like you could make money on this place," Tristen pointed out. "The area seems a bit up-and-coming."

Owen shrugged as he looked around. It might have been the first time Tristen had seen him with nothing to say.

"I told Owen it would make a good studio." Ivy's excitement was clear in her eyes. "Wouldn't it?"

"It actually would," Tristen said. He looked around, allowing his imagination to fill the reception area with musicians and the studios with bands and singers. And him the owner. "I don't know what to say."

"Say yes," Ivy said. She bounced up and down on her toes.

"You went to a lot of work to convince me to stay."

Ivy giggled, still bouncing. "I know. Is it working?"

"Possibly."

Owen and Ivy gave each other high-fives.

"You don't get all the credit. I met with Seraphina when I was in Cincinnati, and she also told me to stay. Said people would come to me. In fact, she's coming to Kentucky to record at the camp this Friday."

"Seraphina is? I can't believe I won't be here," Ivy moaned. "My one chance to meet Seraphina, and I'm going to Portugal!"

"You could stay here," Owen suggested. Ivy stuck her tongue at him like she was eight years old.

"You aren't getting rid of me that easily," she said, grabbing his hand. "Okay, time to get to work. Poor Jared is all by himself.

Let's go. You and Owen can figure out this whole building and payment thing tomorrow."

The boxing camp hours sped by. Tristen found himself enjoying the day, despite being anxious to return to Camp Soul and speak to Scarlett. By the time he'd left Seraphina and Luther yesterday, he had driven directly home, not thinking to send her a text until he got home. And then it had been too late. He'd then had every intention of sending one this morning, but seeing the building and the news that he would be the owner had distracted him so much, he'd forgotten.

Some boyfriend he was.

"Heading out?" Jared asked.

Tristen was going through his paperwork as quickly as possible so he could leave when the boys were ready. "Gonna take the boys to Camp Soul."

Jared's eyebrows shot up. "The boys? They already left. Rob picked up Alex for a doctor's appointment, and Ben already left. He said he was going to say goodbye to his best friend who is moving today."

"Shit. Nasreen's party. I forgot. I guess I better head over to Scarlett's then."

"You talk to her lately?" Jared asked.

"I saw her last Saturday."

"She find out about Cory?"

Tristen looked up from filing the camp paperwork and nodded. "Yeah. She was pretty upset. Maybe someone should have told her before she accepted that job to cater the engagement party."

"I would have, but Cory didn't tell anyone until after that engagement brunch and the newspaper announcement," Jared said. "You seem mad."

Tristen sighed. "What is Cory to her?"

Jared shook his head as he picked up a basket of clean towels from behind the counter. "They've been friends since they were kids. And honestly, he's always stuck up for her throughout the years. Not always publicly. I was friends with his brother, so I saw them a lot. Caught him pretending not to be Scarlett's friend in public sometimes, which I told him was a shit thing to do, but you know, he never abandoned her."

"You saying they've been secret lovers since they were kids?"

Jared chuckled. "Don't look like that, Tristen. All I know is that they've been on and off friends, like pretty tight, since they were maybe eleven. Him not telling her he was serious about this relationship, even if they were never involved, was probably surprising."

"You're saying I had no right to be upset with her."

Jared shrugged. "Proof you like her. But nothing kills a relationship faster than out-of-control jealousy."

Panic spread through Tristen. Suddenly he needed to see Scarlett.

"I'm crap with relationships, so I'm not saying anything. I'm only telling you who Cory was to Scarlett. That's what you asked, right?"

"Right," Tristen answered. His phone rang. "I'm going to go now. Looks like I need to talk to Scarlett."

He stepped outside before answering the unknown number.

"Hello, Tristen."

Tristen closed his eyes for a moment as he reached his car. "Lamia. What do you want?"

"If we're going to share a child together, we better start talking to each other, don't you think?"

It might have been the first time Lamia had made any sense.

"I think we shouldn't talk unless the guardian ad litem is involved. At least at the beginning."

"We don't need that. I've changed my mind."

"About what?"

"About sharing custody. You said you wanted to meet your kid, right?"

"Yes."

"Well, here's your chance."

"What are you talking about?" Tristen asked.

"I'm on my way to your house now—the one you lived with your mom at—with Elliot. I've started dating a guy and he invited me to go to Barbados, which I wouldn't normally do, but since you want to be a dad, I can."

Tristen got into his car and turned the engine. "What do you mean? Why are you going to my house?"

"So you can meet Elliot."

"There's an appointment for me to meet Elliot with the guardian ad litem on Saturday afternoon."

"Yeah," Lamia said, dragging out the syllables. "You're gonna want to cancel that."

"Why?" She was starting to scare him. "What are you going to do, Lamia? Don't hurt Elliot."

"I'm not going to hurt him," Lamia said, sounding offended. "I'm dropping him off with you. Partial custody parenting."

"Dropping him off?"

"I need to catch a plane, so I don't have much time. I'm leaving you two days' worth of diapers, but you'll need to buy more afterwards. I'm not buying them. And I'm leaving the stroller and the car seat, which I expect back. You'll need to buy your own. I'll be back in ten days."

"Lamia, wait."

But she didn't wait. She hung up. Tristen tried calling her back, but the call went straight to voicemail. He was a few streets away, but suddenly the distance stretched out before him. All he could think about were worst-case scenarios.

His entire body was shaking with anxiety when he pulled up to the curb at Ivy's house, the car jolting into park. In the front yard was a giant black stroller, a duffle bag, and a car seat that looked as big as a rocket, but no baby and no Lamia. Tristen scrambled out as Bobbi lumbered into view.

"What's going on?" she demanded. "Some lady squealed into the driveway—you can see the tire marks there—started throwing stuff out of her car, and then squealed away. I swear she left a baby here."

A sound came from the stroller. They both rounded the sidewalk and looked at the same time.

"Mary and Joseph, that's a baby."

"He's bigger than I thought he'd be." Tristen peered closer at the blond boy.

The big brown eyes widened and focused closer on Tristen's face before exploding into laughter.

"He thinks I'm funny," Tristen said, a strange feeling of pride coming over him. "Hey, Elliot."

The baby burst into tears.

"Hey, now, that's okay," Bobbi said, using a tone Tristen had never heard from her before. "Wanna come to Aunty Bobbi?"

The boy's bottom lip protruded out so far Tristen could see his gums, but the wailing stopped as she picked him up.

"I'm Bobbi. Can you say Bobbi?" Bobbi poked gently at his mouth, making the kid laugh. "How old is he?"

Tristen shrugged. "I think she had him in April."

"Let's get some milk," Bobbi said, marching towards her house.

"Where the hell we gonna get baby milk?" Tristen asked.

Bobbi didn't bother looking over her shoulder at him. She kept walking to her house.

"Wait, can I come?" Tristen asked, jogging to catch up. He stuck out his fingers, and Elliot immediately wrapped his hand around them.

His heart skipped. He had the sensation of the world stopping and throwing him into a time funnel before spitting him back out into that exact second. The warmth from Elliot's tiny hand spread from his fingers to his chest.

"Are you crying?" Bobbi demanded, hand on her hip as she held her front door open.

"No," Tristen said, sniffing. Elliot squealed, letting go of Tristen's finger. "Can I hold him?"

"He's your kid," Bobbi said with a shrug.

For the first time, Tristen didn't want to argue. For the first time, he wanted Elliot to be his.

The boy's face was inches from his. They both looked into each other's eyes.

"Bah," Elliot exclaimed, clapping Tristen's face with two chubby hands.

Tristen startled at the touch. "Bah," he said back, receiving a grin from Elliot.

"Dad or not, he likes you," Bobbi said. "And that's already saying something. Now, keep him happy while I run to the store for formula."

Forty-Two

Scarlett saw Tristen's car pull into the large apartment complex parking lot as she reached for a beer. Her heart froze and her throat went dry.

"Is that who I think it is?" Camila murmured, sidling up to Scarlett as the boys continued to show off their boxing skills.

"Yes." Scarlett breathed out.

"What do you think he wants?" Camila asked, focused on Tristen's car.

Scarlett turned away. Her heart raced with the possibilities. He could be here to yell at her. Or embarrass her.

Or apologize to her.

She winced. "I'm going to find out."

She marched past Camila and into the dark apartment building hallway. Tristen was leaning into the back seat of his car when she finally reached him. Probably to grab another boxing bag for Ben, or something equally stupid.

"Tristen," Scarlett called. "What are you doing here?"

Tristen backed out carefully, clearly struggling with something, then stood holding a baby in his arms. A blond, brown-eyed baby sucking on a pacifier and looking at her with big, curious eyes.

"What is that?"

"I came to—" Tristen stopped. The baby smacked him in the face as though to wake him up. "To say goodbye to Nasreen. And talk to you."

"To me?"

"Grab my phone, will you?"

Scarlett reached into the front seat for his phone. It was balanced on a diaper bag.

"Look at my messages," Tristen said.

"Your messages?"

"Yeah, the ones to you. I want to apologize, but first I want you to see something."

Scarlett tapped the messages app, then her name.

"Will you send that message?" Tristen asked, jutting his chin towards the phone. "I wrote it out on Sunday and was stupid enough not to send it."

Scarlett rolled her eyes but hit send anyway. "You know, you could have typed that up a few minutes ago and I wouldn't know. It's not like it has a time stamp on it. But you know what does have a time stamp?"

Tristen shifted the wide-eyed baby to the other arm, waiting for her answer.

"A sent message," Scarlett said as her phone beeped.

Tristen chuckled. He caught the baby's hand before it smacked him again. "True. But I thought it was a cute way to start my apology." He grinned.

The baby looked at him, then back to Scarlett, his pacifier falling from his mouth to the ground.

"Damn. How do parents do this?" Tristen asked, squatting awkwardly to pick it up.

Scarlett took it from him as the baby reached for it. "You gotta wait, little man," she said. "And I believe parents buy these little ribbon things that hook onto the baby's shirt, so the pacifier doesn't hit the ground."

Tristen groaned. The baby sneezed.

"Okay, seriously, you have to admit that was cute," Tristen said. "But baby aside, and I'll explain him in a minute—" He grabbed Scarlett's hand with his free one. "I couldn't sleep after I saw you on Saturday, but then I had to work with Elijah on

Sunday and had court on Monday. And things kept coming up. And I tried to call you, but you never answered."

He took a breath. Scarlett shifted her eyes from the baby back to him. "Sorry about that. I let it run out of battery and I've... I don't know."

The baby reached out and touched her hair as Tristen stepped closer. "I wanted to tell you that I'm sorry, Scarlett."

"For what?" she asked, swinging the baby's hand back and forth.

"Scarlett."

She swallowed hard and challenged herself to look up.

"I'm sorry. For what I said. I know it probably sounded like maybe I didn't want to date you, but that isn't further from the truth. I want to date you. I was jealous, and I acted stupid. I really like you."

"I'm sure I should apologize, too. I should have told you about Cory. I shouldn't have been so upset about him."

Tristen dipped his head to meet her eye level. "You don't have to tell me anything until you're ready. And you had the right to be upset, even if I don't understand it. I'm sorry I upset you when you were already struggling, 'cause I don't want to be that guy."

"What guy?"

"The guy that upsets you. Hurts you." Tristen grabbed her hand with his free one. "I want to be the guy who protects you."

Scarlett took a deep breath. She had come outside ready to tell him off and instead had received the sexiest apology ever. It took her a few seconds to orient herself.

"Protect me as what?" she asked.

Tristen's eyebrows furrowed in confusion. "What do you mean?"

"Like as your girlfriend?" Scarlett asked, her heart skipping a beat at putting it into words. "Exclusively?"

There was a second of silence that made her start to feel doubtful, but then he stepped closer to her and whispered, "Yes. As my girlfriend."

He cupped the right side of her face and pressed his lips to hers. "That's exactly what I want. We commit to each other. Exclusively. I think I'm falling in love with you, Scarlett."

Scarlett wondered if she might die from someone being so nice to her. His words were more than she had ever hoped for from a man. She leaned into his kiss, pressing her lips harder against his. Right here with him was where she wanted to be, forever.

Or until the baby squealed and pulled her hair.

"Hey, man, that's no way to treat a lady," Tristen said. Another squeal answered him.

"Using a baby to apologize is a strange choice, Tristen," Scarlett said, taking him in her arms when he reached for her. "What's his name?"

"Elliot."

"And he's yours? I mean, this is Lamia's baby, right?"

Tristen nodded, his throat constricting. "He's not mine, except the courts say he is. I decided to ask for custody rights, which is why I had to go to Cincinnati. On Saturday I came to tell you because I wanted you to know, but then I screwed it up."

Scarlett laughed nervously. "It's safe to say we both screwed up Saturday, and that we'll both screw up again."

Tristen gave her a half-smile, then motioned to the baby. "You inspired me, you know. To ask for custody."

That fact that she had inspired anything in anyone surprised Scarlett. "Me?"

"Of course. I watched you and Ben," Tristen said, nodding toward her patio. "You showed me that I can love Elliot as my own. It doesn't matter that he is technically Talon's. And then, to be honest, I figured I should be a part of his life, since I'm paying for it."

Scarlett wanted to jump into his arms and make out with him in the hallway, but instead she grabbed his hand and pulled to him to the front door.

"I'm glad you decided that," she told him. "I love babies."

Tristen nuzzled his face into her neck as they walked through the apartment building door. "Want me to give you a baby?"

She laughed, her whole body singing from his touch. "Down, Tristen. There are people in my apartment right now, so more babies will have to wait. Besides, I thought you wanted to woo me?"

Tristen twirled her around until she was locked in his arms, Elliot between them. "I do." His gaze pierced her. "But do you know why?"

Scarlett shook her head.

"Because you deserve to know you're worth it. I don't know everything about you or your past, Scarlett. I hope one day to know it better, but I can see something similar in you that I used to see in Ivy, my mother."

"Which is?"

"That no one ever told you were worthy. Worthy of being respected and treated well. Worthy of waiting for until the time's right for you. Worthy of being loved. I want to be the man who changes that."

Tears sprang into her eyes. She shook her head to make them go away, but Tristen had seen them already. He bent forward and kissed her gently on the cheek. "Shall we go say goodbye?"

"Yes," Scarlett said. She wiped the tears from her eyes, unable to keep her smile subdued as they walked into her apartment.

"Tristen," Ben shouted from the patio. He and Zander were both sweating and breathing hard. "Come outside."

"Hello, Tristen," Nasreen said, not needing to yell. She looked from him to Elliot and back to Tristen. "Where have you been?"

Scarlett knew her friend was trying to protect her, but Nasreen was leaving. It was time she believed in Scarlett to make the right decisions.

"He was in court fighting for the right to see his son," she said. "And now that he's back, we've determined he's my boyfriend."

Nasreen's eyebrows lowered as a smile spread across her face. Camila squealed from the kitchen.

"Scarlett has a boyfriend," she shouted. "*Madre mía!* And a handsome one. And let me see this baby. *Ay, díos, que guapo es, por favor.*"

"She speaks in Spanish when she's really excited," Scarlett told Tristen, who looked a bit stunned. "Go ahead and see the boys outside. Camila will keep Elliot happy."

"Elliot is your name?" Camila cooed, taking the baby from Scarlett without bothering to ask permission.

The front door opened again, catching everyone's attention. Nothing could have tanked Scarlett's happiness more effectively than seeing her mother standing in the doorway, muttering to herself.

"Scarlett," Candi said as she walked through. "My darling girl. Just the person I wanted to see."

Her voice was dripping with sarcasm. Scarlett stiffened. Tristen, who already had a hand on the sliding patio door, stepped forward.

"You managing to keep this guy around?" Candi turned her attention to Tristen, her hips swinging in a circular motion. "I taught her what she needs to do to keep a man, you know. In case you ever want to taste the source."

Scarlett's face burned, and her heart sank.

"Mom," she snapped, then swallowed, her words vanishing within seconds. Candi turned to her, moving slowly, like a cat on the prowl. Behind her, Tristen started moving forward, but she stopped him.

"Why are you here, Candi?" Nasreen asked, also positioning herself to stand between Candi and Scarlett.

Candi stopped where she was, her shoulders relaxing slightly as she looked at Nasreen. "Came to see you, honey. A little birdie said you were leaving. Don't blame you. This town is a dump."

She smiled. Scarlet could tell something had gotten her riled up and she blamed Scarlett for it, whatever it was. This was exactly like when she'd been a kid. Candi would come home and take her frustration out on her.

Tristen stood directly behind her now. She could feel his chest moving against her back as he breathed. Scarlett put her hand behind her, against his hip, to stop him.

Candi clicked her tongue, her smirk irritating Scarlett the most. "What's gotten into everyone? Scarlett, give me beer. It's the least you can do."

"I think you should leave," Tristen said.

Candi bounced her head to mock him, her mouth turning down. She looked like the puppets on a show Scarlett used to watch as a kid.

"I think you should mind your own business. This ain't even your place. It ain't Scarlett here's place either. She got herself kicked out, didn't you?" Candi started to laugh as she helped herself to a beer from the counter. "You didn't know that? Bet you don't know the half of what you got yourself into with this one. Did you know she used to bribe my boyfriends to sleep with her? From the time she was twelve, too. She got them big titties and started throwing them in men's faces. I had to take her for an abortion three times when she was a teenager. She even slept with her teacher."

Scarlett inhaled quietly, reminding herself that it wasn't worth fighting with Candi. Especially about all her lies. She hoped Tristen didn't believe her.

"What're we having for dinner during this party?" Candi asked.

"You aren't staying," Nasreen said quietly.

"Nasreen," Scarlett said calmly. Usually, she would have been relieved for Nasreen to speak up to Candi for her, but this time it felt out of place. If she was going to advocate for herself more, she needed to stand up to Candi. "It's okay."

"Yeah, Nasreen. It's okay. I'm the one who birthed this girl, and I got business with her. I want an explanation on where she gets off thinking she's better than me. Hmm? 'Cause I know you, Scarlett. I know you ain't any better than me."

"I don't know what you mean, Mom."

"Rhoda came by a few days ago, and we had a chat. I don't know what lies you told her, but all of a sudden she doesn't want me near Ben. Goes to show how ungrateful both my children are. They don't even know the half of what it takes to care for a child, but fine. I told her fine. That's why I bowed out."

Candi gave a physical bow to emphasize her words, her smile still cruel when she lifted her head.

"I know, Mom. Rhoda told me. But I didn't have anything to do with that."

Candi narrowed her eyes. "You know, when you're homeless again, Scarlett, you could always come live with me. I know you think you're so much better, but at least I got myself a place to live. I've never been homeless."

"Thanks, Candi," Scarlett said, her throat surprisingly relaxed. "But I won't be living with you again. This is the last time we'll see each other on purpose, since you won't be told where I live. You are not invited to come by ever again. And if you refuse to follow my wishes, I will take out a restraining order on you. Now," she concluded, holding up her phone, "I'm calling Brody. He can come get you if you refuse to leave."

"Who the hell do you—"

Scarlett put her hand up, taking one step closer to her mother but keeping her eyes wide and on her the entire time. "This is my place, even if only for the next few days, and you are not invited. Leave. Now."

Forty-Three

WHEN THE DOOR CLOSED behind Candi, Scarlett turned around to face the crowd in her apartment.

"I think it's time to party a bit, don't you all?" she asked.

Ben and Zander blinked at her.

"I agree," Nasreen said. "Listen, life brings changes and we gotta roll with those changes. Ben, you're gonna come visit us, aren't you?"

"Can I?" For the first time in days, Ben's face wasn't filled with worry. "Can I, Scarlett?"

Scarlett almost retorted that she wasn't even sure where they were going to live in the next few days, but she bit her tongue. Tonight, they both needed reassurances.

"Of course," she assured him. "We'll go up there and paint the town red."

Ben looked confused.

"Paint it red?" Zander asked.

Camila giggled, and Elliot joined her. "The point is that we will all go. Now, it's time for karaoke. I want to sing my favorite song with Tristen."

"No," Nasreen groaned.

"It's cultural, Nasreen," Camila said, her eyes wide as she pretended to lecture. "Are you not willing to participate in my culture?"

"Go on," Nasreen said, shaking her head. "Scarlett and I will stay in the kitchen, as far away as possible."

Elliot moved to Nasreen's arms as Scarlett joined her in the kitchen for a glass of wine. The karaoke machine came on with a shriek before connecting to the television.

"You ready?" Camila asked as *Como la Flor* started playing. Camila moved her hips and hands to the beat in her best Selena imitation, belting into the microphone at the exact time. Tristen stood, at a loss.

"You got this," Nasreen called from the kitchen, before chuckling quietly to Scarlett and Elliot. "This baby is cute. Aren't you, baby?"

Scarlett was unable to stop tears welling up in her eyes as she watched her friend. "I'm going to miss you, Nasreen. I'm going to miss you a lot."

"Don't you dare cry," Nasreen said to Elliot, though the words were for Scarlett. "You can cry tonight in bed and tomorrow after we leave. Will you see us off tomorrow?"

She finally looked at Scarlett, her eyes red-rimmed.

"Wouldn't miss it," Scarlett said. "Ben's already set five alarms, even though you aren't leaving until nine. It isn't that far, though. Why can't you stay until the weekend?"

"I told you, I'm dropping stuff off at my mom's and headed to Chicago to see my dad before we start school."

Scarlett's shoulders slumped. "I know. I was hoping something had changed."

"You gonna be okay, Scarlett? I can't help being a little worried about you. Where are you going to go?"

Scarlett waved away the comment as she sipped her wine. "I'm sure Rhoda will fix it. I think that's why I haven't been worried about it, you know? I mean, I've been a little worried, but not a ton. Because Rhoda always gets what she wants, and I don't see Johnny going against her. As much as he's an ass to me, I think he's scared of her."

"He seemed pretty serious the other night."

"Because he's not scared of me. And he's a jerk. But the more I thought of it, the more I think he's bluffing."

Nasreen raised an eyebrow, but Scarlett was glad she didn't say anything else. If Nasreen pried anymore she would end up telling the truth, which was that she would be homeless in a few days' time, no question.

Camila belted the last few notes, striking a Selena pose that took up the entire living room, garnering eye-rolls from her son.

"Okay, now we sing something I know," Tristen said with a laugh. "How about Shakira? Or Tupelo?"

"No."

"Gloria Esteban?" he suggested, arms folded, eyes challenging.

"Oh, you're on!" Camila said, searching through the machine.

"You gotta keep an eye on that girl," Nasreen said, nodding towards Camila.

Scarlett smiled. "We'll keep an eye on each other."

"What about work?" Nasreen asked, giving Elliot another cracker when he showed her his empty hands. "Can you stay working at the camp? Do you need a loan?"

"I forgot to tell you," Scarlett said, her gloom replaced by excitement in a second. "Have you heard of Sourdough Mama? That's her social media handle. I think her real name is Brittany, actually."

"You know I'm never on social media. But I'm assuming she makes sourdough bread?"

Scarlett grabbed Nasreen's hands, hardly able to contain her excitement. "No. I mean, yes. She makes sourdough, but lots of people do. That's not the exciting part." Nasreen's forehead wrinkled. "Ugh. Okay, I'll start again. Dariana follows her on social media and saw that she's local. She lives in Beakersville. And she's opening a bakery there. She sells bread online, which is weird to me, but also cool. But she's grown out of her kitchen and wanted to open something locally. And listen to this, she needs workers but has specific qualifications for them." Scarlett held up her hand. "They must be local. Obviously. They have to know how to make sourdough. They have to use social media. And they have to participate in this baking audition that's happening this weekend."

"How could you not tell me this?" Nasreen said, her smile back. "You're gonna win it, for sure. How many people around here know how to bake sourdough bread?"

"A few," Scarlett said, thinking of the three others that showed up at the market. "But I think you're right. I think I'm going to get it."

"Yes, you are!" Nasreen yelled it so loudly and proudly that the karaoke singers stopped.

"What?" Camila said through the microphone. "What's going on? Are you having more fun than us? Because that isn't allowed."

Scarlett laughed. Nasreen's excitement had rubbed off onto her skin, which was already humming with nervous tension. She told Camila and Tristen the news about her interview, receiving a round of applause at the end.

"Did you say Beakersville?" Tristen asked.

"Yes—I know, I know. I hadn't heard of it either, but I swear it will be up-and-coming very soon. And it isn't too far from here, so the drive in will be fine." Scarlett chuckled. "Look at me, already assuming I'm hired."

Nasreen wrapped her free arm around Scarlett's shoulders and gave her a squeeze. "And I was telling her she would be, when you rudely interrupted."

"Well, excuse us for wanting to hear the news," Camila said, whipping around to face Tristen. "Congrats, Scarlett." This she said into the microphone. "This one is for you."

She put on Foo Fighters, and Tristen's face lit up so much Scarlett almost burst out laughing.

"Let's go, boys," he yelled. "Give me your best air guitar." Ben, Zander and Miguel complied immediately as Tristen sang.

For the first time, Scarlett got to see him as a rock star. He jumped and strummed his air guitar and strained his voice to sound like Dave Grohl. She could tell he was in his element, and the boys were loving it—even Elliot, who clapped his hands off-beat.

When the music ended the four boys, including Tristen, fell into a sweaty heap on the floor.

"Being a band member is hard," Zander muttered.

"We didn't usually jump around as much," Tristen said, his chest heaving.

Elliot squealed. Scarlett picked him up and plopped him on top of Tristen.

"He likes music," she said, sitting next to Tristen. Elliot smacked Tristen's chest, then lay down. "Maybe he's tired."

"I should probably take him home," Tristen told her, rubbing his fingers lightly across Elliot's back. "Do you mind?"

"That you have to leave?" Scarlett asked. "No. I know you have responsibilities."

"And we're good, right? Can I see you tomorrow?"

Scarlett looked down. Whenever she looked into his eyes, the rest of the world disappeared. "Yes, I'll let you take Ben and me to that Thai restaurant."

Tristen laughed, the sudden movement disturbing Elliot, who burst into tears.

"You made the baby cry," Zander accused.

Ben looked at Elliot with a mixture of curiosity and horror as Tristen jumped up from the floor and started to gather baby things. Camila became a human swing for Elliot, who went between crying and sucking on a pacifier.

"I'll call you tomorrow." Tristen glanced at Elliot. "Or maybe tonight if things go south."

Scarlett laughed. "You can do this. Call me if you need me. Are you going to your place?"

"No," Tristen said. "Heading to my aunt's house. She lives across from my mom, who's leaving for Europe tomorrow. She and her boyfriend are getting married in Portugal."

Scarlett couldn't help being impressed. "I'd like to see Portugal one day. Although I never thought of it before."

Tristen chuckled. He brushed her hair back before kissing her softly on the lips. "I'll take you there someday," he said. "I would like to see it myself."

"Bye, Tristen." Camila and Nasreen stood with their arms crossed, watching them.

"Bye, ladies," Tristen called out. Scarlett watched him walk down the hallway before she finally closed the door.

"Come over here, lover girl," Camila called out. "We're gonna have a slumber party. I'm gonna get drunk. And we're all gonna cry."

As she watched Nasreen and Zander climb into their car, Scarlett realized she had never said goodbye before. Cory wouldn't show up for weeks or months at a time, even when they were kids. And Candi had never told her anything, much less when she was leaving for long stretches of time. The closest she had come to a sad goodbye was when Rhoda had left the first time. But since Scarlett hadn't expected her to be gone very long, it hadn't felt sad so much as confusing.

Watching Nasreen settle herself in the car was the worst she had felt in her entire life. Her chest was heavy with grief, and tears were once again threatening to come.

"Scarlett?" Ben looked at her with puffy eyes, from trying to keep himself from crying.

"Hey," she murmured, pulling him to her side.

Nasreen and Zander rolled down their windows, the car shifting into drive. Scarlett realized then that they had to rip the band-aid off. To let Nasreen and Zander go.

And there was no good way to do it.

"Text me when you get there," she said. Nasreen pressed her lips together and nodded. "And send me a picture of Chicago. I've never been there."

"It's cold there," Zander said. "But only in the winter. I'll send you a picture of the silver bean."

"The bean?" Scarlett asked.

"It's a giant silver bean in the city," Ben told her. "Zander showed me last night."

"We better head out," Nasreen said. She held her hand out the window. Scarlett grabbed it and squeezed. "Love you."

"Love you too."

"Tell Camila she's crazy and I love her as well," Nasreen said, letting go.

Scarlett and Ben stepped away as the car slowly moved through the parking lot, pulling the small trailer behind. They watched the car disappear down the road before they gave a collective sigh.

"Ready for boxing camp?"

"Yeah," Ben mumbled. "It won't be the same, you know. Living here without Zander."

"I know," Scarlett said, squeezing him tightly. She still didn't know how to tell him he would be leaving with Rhoda soon. "But we got each other, right?"

Ben nodded, then pulled away. "I'll be ready in five minutes."

Scarlett waited outside, staring at the empty parking spot that would soon be filled by whoever would live in apartment 305.

Forty-Four

WHILE SHE WAS WAITING for Ben to come out, a car rolled up next to Scarlett, pulling her out of her thoughts.

"Rhoda?"

"Hey there, sis. What's going on? Why you so puffy?"

"Nasreen left today," Scarlett said, touching her eyes involuntarily.

Ben ran outside, stopping dead in his tracks when he saw Rhoda. He walked the last few steps, looking between them as he approached.

"Hi, Mom. I'm going to camp now."

Scarlett could have sworn he was saying it more like a question. More like, *you aren't here to take me now, are you?* She swallowed hard. She wasn't sure she could say goodbye to Ben on the same day.

Rhoda stepped out of her car, forcing Scarlett to back up. "It's time for me to go, Ben."

"Am I going with you?" he asked in a small voice.

Scarlett looked at Rhoda, unable to breathe.

"Your aunt here came to yell at me the other day when you were at Eric's house."

Ben looked at Scarlett, his eyes wide, but he didn't say anything.

"I didn't yell at you, Rhoda," Scarlett started, but Rhoda interrupted.

"What? I can't hear you, sis. Could have sworn you said you didn't yell at me. But if it wasn't yelling, what was it?"

"I was telling you…" Scarlett trailed off. She glanced at Ben and wondered if he'd be angry with her for trying to keep him from his mom. "I went to tell you why Ben should stay with me. Why it would be better if I had custody of him."

Rhoda leaned into the open window of her car and pulled out a folder. "Here it is."

"Here is what?" Scarlett asked, opening the folder. It was full of notarized papers.

"Papers that give you authority over Ben. Officially," Rhoda said. Scarlett could have sworn she detected a struggle in her sister's voice.

"You're giving me away?" Ben asked.

Rhoda hesitated. She pinched her lips together.

"Mom?"

Rhoda slowly squatted until she was eye-level with Ben. "I will never give you up. Never. But I shouldn't take you with me, you know? I was in a dangerous situation a few weeks ago and honestly, if that happened again, I'd be worried about you."

"Did you almost die?"

Rhoda scoffed. "Hell, no. I mean, heck no. I won't ever die. I'm too good at what I do. But if I had been worried, I might have slipped up and gotten hurt. So I need you to stay with Scarlett. These papers let her be your day-to-day mom, okay?"

"What about Dad? I thought he wanted me to live with him?"

Tears sprang into Scarlett's eyes again at the hurt she heard in Ben's voice.

"Those papers say Eric gets you every other weekend and every other holiday, and for a month in the summer."

"A month," Ben repeated, happiness finally back in his voice. "That's enough time to go camping."

"Exactly, dude," Rhoda said. "I even wrote in there that he has to take you camping. He'll want to, anyway. Girl babies cry a lot, and he'll need a break." She laughed at her own joke, and Ben joined her. "You gonna be okay, Ben? Someone I respect once told me that it wasn't fair to make kids make adult decisions, so I made the decision without asking you."

Scarlett's heart skipped a beat. She looked at Rhoda, but her sister was still staring at Ben.

"I'm okay," he said with a nod. "When are you coming back?"

"Here." Rhoda handed him a phone.

"A phone? For me?" Ben had been asking for a phone for two years.

"I think you're big enough for a phone. There's a number in there you can reach me at."

Scarlett peeked at the screen and smiled. Above the number, the contact name was *Your Cool Mama.* She laughed, relief and joy bursting through her.

"Look, Scarlett." Ben held up the phone.

"It's better than my phone," Scarlett told him, pushing her bottom lip out in a pretend pout.

"I gotta go, dude," Rhoda said, enveloping Ben into a hug. "Why don't you head to the truck while I say goodbye to Scarlett? And I'll see you between Thanksgiving and Christmas."

"Promise?" Ben asked.

"Promise."

Scarlett and Rhoda watched him skip to the truck, his phone already in front of his face.

"I better go, sis," Rhoda said.

"Thank you, Rhoda."

"I can't give him up."

"I know. But I think he's better living with me."

Rhoda nodded, looking towards Ben. "One more thing. I couldn't convince Johnny to let you stay."

Scarlett froze. She'd expected it, and yet she couldn't believe it.

"Here. It's what I would have given the dumbass if he wasn't so stubborn. I could have pushed it, but I figured you'd be better off leaving here."

Scarlett looked at the apartment building, then back at Rhoda. "When do I have to be out?"

"One week."

At least it wasn't one day. Scarlett wondered what Rhoda had to threaten to make Johnny give her an entire week.

"Take the money, Scarlett. It's for the apartment and for Ben's care and everything. I'll try to be more consistent."

Scarlett shook her head.

"It's only fair that I pay for my son, Scarlett. Take it."

Scarlett took the envelope, then found herself enveloped in Rhoda's arms for one quick hug before her sister pulled away.

"I'll see you around, sis." Rhoda slipped back into her car, the engine revving as she rolled the window down. "You take care of yourself. And Ben."

"Of course," Scarlett said. "But Rhoda?"

Rhoda stopped. "Yeah?"

"I'll miss you."

Rhoda gave her a small smile, nodded, then drove away.

A few hours later, as Scarlett finished mixing yet another batch of muffins for the camp, her phone rang. Tristen's number.

"Hi," she said, wiping her hand with a tea towel.

"Hey," Tristen breathed.

His voice sent shivers down her spine. She couldn't believe that 'hey' was for her.

"I got your text. Sorry I didn't call before. Boxing camp and the gym have been a bit crazy, since it's my mom's last day here before she leaves. And then this little monster refused to let me put him down. I don't know what I'm supposed to do with a baby at a gym, but anyway. Your text said Rhoda came by and said Ben could stay?"

"Yes. She signed all the guardianship papers and left him with me." Scarlett filled Tristen in on the details as she went around the kitchen, putting things away and filling up the industrial dishwasher.

"Is Ben happy?"

"I believe so. I think he's a little disappointed about Eric, but it's not like he won't see his dad. He'll get access to Ben at my discretion, but I talked to him last night and he admitted he couldn't handle full custody." Scarlett heaved a sigh to stave off her anger at the man before setting the phone down to put away the large box of flour, putting Tristen on speakerphone again. "The bad news is that Rhoda couldn't convince Johnny to let me stay in the apartment."

"Good."

"Homelessness is not fun, Tristen." Scarlett hoped her voice sounded light and teasing, because the words spoken out loud made her want to panic.

"You should find a different place to stay. I don't like that guy."

She thought of the last time she'd seen Johnny and nodded. "I don't like him either, but I have to find a place to stay by the end of next week."

"That's something we could talk about tonight. Are we still on for going out? I'd really like to see you."

"Of course. I want to see you, too. And Ben would probably kill me if I changed my mind."

"Perfect. Come to the address I'm sending you by six."

Scarlett had hoped he'd come pick her up, but it made more sense for her to drive her truck, since she already had it at the camp.

"We'll be there," she said.

"Why are we at a house?" Ben asked as he unbuckled his seatbelt.

"Dunno, Ben," Scarlett said, looking around for Tristen.

"Up here," Tristen called from the front porch of a yellow box house. Holding Elliot, he motioned for them to come up the five steps.

They hurried up, Ben entering first, Scarlett receiving a soft kiss on the lips before being allowed through the door. Inside, the small living room was decorated sparsely but with good taste. And it smelled like fresh Pad Thai.

"I got us take-out dinner," Tristen explained.

"Is this your house?" Ben asked, peeking down the short hallway.

Tristen caught Scarlett's line of sight and winked. Ben looked as confused as she felt. "Okay, yes. The answer is sort of. I grew up in this house."

Scarlett looked at Elliot, who was now sitting on a blanket on the floor, and could easily imagine twin Tristens crawling around there as well.

"It's cute," she said.

"It's small for a family of five. It only has one bathroom, but it has three bedrooms. And a back porch."

"Nice." Scarlett wasn't sure what else to say. The house was nice. Tidy. Clean. She was starving. "Should I set the table?"

They gathered around the small table in the kitchen, Elliot in what looked like a brand-new highchair.

"I thought we were going out to eat," Ben said.

"Ben, don't be ungrateful," Scarlett murmured, though she, too, was disappointed. Tristen was still grinning.

"He isn't being rude," he said. "We were going to go out. I just wanted you guys to see your new home. If you want it, that is. I promise I'll be a really nice landlord."

Scarlett dropped her fork as she looked around the kitchen and part of the living room. It was like seeing a whole new house.

"You're going to rent this place to me?" she asked. Or maybe they were going to move in together. That seemed fast, but she wouldn't argue.

"Where would you live?" Ben asked, shoveling the long noodles of his Pad Thai into his mouth.

"Where I live now. I have a lease on that place for almost a year still. And my mom is giving me this house because she's getting married and moving in with Owen. That's her new husband. Since I helped her keep it a few months ago, she thought I should have this house." He looked at Scarlett. "That's a story for another day. And I'm rambling. Anyway, I've been wanting to offer it to you for the last week or so, but wasn't sure how to approach the subject. And then everything got so busy. When I stopped by today to say goodbye for my mom, I was informed the paperwork on the house was done, so I thought today was as good as any. Plus, you're leaving your place in a week, right?"

He took a breath, and for the first time Scarlett saw the small droplets of sweat forming on his forehead. He'd hardly eaten anything, but kept moving the noodles around his plate. And he was no longer looking directly at her, but busying himself with Elliot.

"I don't know what to say, Tristen," she said, reaching across the round table for his hand. She only reached his pinkie, but when she touched it, he finally looked at her. "Except thank you."

"Ew. Are you going to kiss or something?" Ben asked. He was mid-bite, with noodles hanging out of his mouth.

"Someday, Ben, you'll want to kiss, too." Tristen winked at Scarlett, but they dug into their noodles instead of kissing.

Scarlett could barely eat anything; she couldn't believe she had a house to stay in. Part of her didn't believe it could be true, while the other part screamed for joy.

"You okay, Scarlett?" Tristen asked. She looked up to find him looking at her, searching her face.

"Yeah," she finally said. "I am."

An hour later, she and Tristen picked up the kitchen while Ben entertained Elliot. Tristen snuck up behind her and wrapped his arms around her. She melted into him until his heart pulsed against her back, his cologne surrounding her.

"You aren't offended, are you?" His deep murmur vibrated from her ear down to her toes, making her shiver. "With the offer of the house?"

Scarlett sniffed, trying to stop the tears from welling up. They refused to obey.

"Are you crying?"

She nodded. She closed her eyes and took a deep breath before facing him again to speak the words of truth she wanted him to know.

"I'm not offended," she whispered. "I'm grateful. And—" She searched for the right way to describe what she felt. "And maybe overwhelmed. Aside from Rhoda and my high school teacher, no one has helped me like this before. I've definitely never had a boyfriend who wanted to make sure I was safe."

She closed her eyes to breathe again, fighting against collapsing into a puddle of relief and happiness. Tristen kissed the tears away from her cheeks, but pulled away before kissing her lips.

"Scarlett," he whispered, kissing her lips lightly. "I'm no savior. I'm too imperfect for that. But I do want you to know that I want you to be safe. And happy." He pulled her forehead gently to his, his thumb rubbing circles at the base of her head. "I think I'm falling in love with you."

It wasn't the first time he'd said it, but it still made her smile like an idiot. "I think I'm falling in love with you, too, Tristen Levisay."

Forty-Five

"Is this where the audition is? Or where you'll work if you get the job?"

Tristen and Scarlett were sitting in his car in a large parking lot in Beakersville.

Scarlett checked the address again. Her hands had been shaking so badly all morning that she'd had to call Tristen to bring her to the audition. Even comprehending words was taking longer than usual for her.

"I think the audition is inside her new bakery."

Tristen turned in the driver's seat, his mouth open. "Here?" he asked.

"I know it looks old, but they're renovating all the buildings. I've seen the pictures of the bakery online and it's so cute inside. Tristen, seriously, why are you looking at me like that?"

He pointed to the left. "Do you see that building over there?"

"Yes."

"I'm buying it from Owen. When he comes back from Europe, he's going to help me turn it into a studio."

Scarlett's mouth dropped open as she put meaning to his words. "Wait, so if I get this job we'll be working across the street from each other?"

"Is that too much?" Tristen asked. "Like it would jinx this?"

Scarlett laughed. With the nerves she had there were only two choices—laugh or burst into tears again. And she'd cried too much that week already. She threw her arms around him and buried her face in his neck. She couldn't believe how quickly her life had changed since last Saturday.

"I don't think so at all," she said, her voice hoarse. "I think it's fate."

"Kismet," Tristen said.

"Kiss me," Scarlett teased, before pressing her lips to his mouth hard. "I have to go."

Tristen groaned and tried to grab hold of her, but she had already anticipated his move and was too far away.

"Good luck," he said before she closed the door. Scarlett grinned, feeling slightly wobbly on her feet.

The chapel was humming with life and excitement. All the kids were sitting in the first few rows, nervously bouncing their legs or trying their hardest not to play their instruments and failing. Parents and other family members were filtering in, their own anticipation for the concert growing within the energy of the sanctuary.

Seraphina was harder to corral than Lin when it came to her star status. After years in the business, she did whatever she wanted to do. When she had shown up that day, instead of walking to the studio as Tristen had tried to direct her, she'd marched through camp greeting everyone she saw with a giant smile and loud 'Hello.' Even though Dariana had known Seraphina was coming and spent three days being nervous about meeting her, she'd still stopped dead in her tracks and almost fainted at the sight of her.

"She actually came," she had whispered as Seraphina walked into each camp cabin, greeting the kids and listening to them play or sing—even singing with some of them. It took Tristen an hour before he could drag her into the studio and start recording.

When she was done laying down several versions of her track, Seraphina had decided to explore the camp. And somehow, she'd decided to sing with the kids that evening at their concert. She didn't bother asking if she could, just announced that she would. Rob didn't dare say no.

Which was why Tristen found himself at the sound booth. Rob wanted him to supervise the kids running the show.

"There's the signal," Tristen told his group of sound operators. "Rob's coming on now."

"Welcome, parents, friends and family, to Camp Soul's first ever summer concert," Rob said, walking out in black pants and a crisp white shirt.

Tristen sat at the back of the booth, checking the schedule and dropping hints to the three kids while keeping an ear on Rob's speech.

Then the lights went down, and the first group of kids filed onto stage to play their songs.

At Tristen's nod, the older kid, Derek, pushed the button up enough to pick up all the instruments. And the concert started.

The worst part of being sound crew was that the kids had heard all the songs several times already in practice, which risked complacency. Tristen kept them on their toes by having them check things he already knew were fine. Better to keep them busy than have them fall asleep.

He sighed when the curtain went up again for the second half.

"Now?" Kevin asked as the first song of the second half ended. Tristen nodded. "Now."

"That's the last note," Kevin told the backstage crew. "Seraphina's up."

Seraphina didn't need anyone to tell her; she was already walking on stage. Tristen could tell by the collective gasps and squeals of delight from the audience.

"Hello, Camp Soul!" she yelled out, as though she were at her own concert surrounded by thousands of people. Her energy was so contagious, even the grandparents in the crowd shouted back and clapped. "I'm Seraphina. I came by today to see how amazing your kids were and I gotta say, they are so talented!"

That got another resounding round of applause. At this rate, the concert was going to take all night. Tristen checked his watch. He didn't know why Scarlett was taking so long. She had texted she was done with the audition an hour ago. More at this point.

"Now, we've only had a few hours, but your kids are so professional already that they were able to work with me to put together an extra few songs for you. Is anyone interested in hearing them?"

More applause. Tristen checked his phone. Kevin told the backstage crew to turn on the microphones of the singers who were about to be introduced. Garbled whispering ensued on the other end.

"Give it up for Tonya, Shaun, and Keyon for the first song," Seraphina shouted to the crowd as they clapped.

"Tristen." The whisper was fierce and came from outside the sound booth.

He leaned back in his chair and saw Scarlett beaming at him in the darkness. She motioned for him to join her.

"Here we go. We're going to sing *Rollin' On the River*. If you know it, sing along with us," Seraphina said from stage as the instruments started up.

"How'd it go?" Tristen asked.

Scarlett's smile told him everything before she said it.

"I got the job," she squealed in a low whisper before throwing herself at him. Tristen was ready, pulling her in close as the notes from the song became faster and faster. "I can't believe I got it, but I signed the papers and everything."

"I knew you'd get it."

"Well, I had enough doubt for the both of us."

"Was it hard?" Tristen asked, pulling her towards the booth so he could keep an eye on the kids. If they hadn't been there, he would have pulled her into the shadows to make out. Which Rob probably wouldn't have liked.

Scarlett shook her head. She was still so close to him that her hair rubbed against his chest, lighting him up from the inside. "Once I started, I got into the zone. I realized I'd done it thousands of times before and that even if I didn't get the job, I could do it thousands of times afterwards. And from that point on, it was easy. The hours flew by."

"I'm so proud of you, Scarlett," he whispered in her ear as the first song ended.

The crowd was going wild below them as Seraphina moved into one of her own songs, with the band and singers joining her.

"She's so talented," Scarlett said, still nuzzled up against him. He squeezed her tighter around the waist, feeling the depth of her against him, and breathed in her scent. The way she fit in his arms gave him a sense of completion he had never felt with any other woman before.

"Yes, she is. Not only as a singer, but also with the marketing and all that. I might produce an entire project with her soon."

Scarlett smiled at him over her shoulder. "You must be better at this producer stuff than you let on."

Tristen watched as Seraphina belted out the last notes of the song, Scarlett's words hitting him. Perhaps it was time he admitted he wasn't a novice, that he had something to offer other musicians. Even the ones he found extremely talented. Just the thought shifted something within him.

"We're excited to bring you our last song of the night," a small voice from stage said. It was the girl named Devone, and she was smiling brightly into the audience as her voice boomed over them. "We're gonna sing something called a mash-up. For all you out there who don't know what that is, it's two songs put together."

That was the cue for the brass to come in. Tristen smiled. The kids had done a great job at this mash-up. The parents were going to love it.

In came the wind instruments, making the first song sound slightly distorted as it morphed into the intro for the second song. Scarlett leaned in as the rest of the audience did, probably trying to figure out what songs they were.

Seraphina stepped forward and smiled. Right when the audience was about to sing Rihanna's 'We Found Love', she started singing Whitney Houston's 'I Wanna Dance With Somebody'.

A shout rose from the audience. Then a whistle and applause.

It was Devone's turn. Tristen was almost certain she sounded exactly as Rihanna must have at her age.

"They're cute," Scarlett said. Her eyes were sparkling, her smile wide, as she moved her shoulders to the beat.

"They are." Tristen twirled her to face him. "I had them mash this up just for you," he whispered.

She jerked her chin up from his chest in surprise. "Really?"

He chuckled. "No, but I can't help thinking it's saying exactly what I was thinking."

Scarlett giggled as he twirled her around. "That you wanna dance with someone?" she asked.

"No. Well, that, too," Tristen said, pulling her in. "That the two of us found love in a hopeless place."

Scarlett didn't have time to agree or disagree before he cupped her face and kissed her.

Did you enjoy *Bended Love?* Please leave a review on Google Play here.

Want the recipes from Bended Love?

Get the recipes from Bended Love and bake along with Scarlett. Find them here: katcaldwell.com/bended-love-recipes

About Kat Caldwell

Kat is a novelist and short story writer. She writes everyday and can't seem to stick to a genre, having dabbled in historical fiction, contemporary family drama and romance, as well as speculative fiction. Kat is the creator of the Pencils&Lipstick podcast, a podcast for writers with author interviews, craft and insight into the publishing world. She is also an accredited book coach. In between conducting interviews for her podcast and writing, you can find Kat traveling the world, reading, or volunteering with her church—always with a cup of cold brew close by.

You can find out more about Kat on her website https://katcaldwell.com and follow her on Instagram @author_katcaldwell on Facebook @katcaldwellauthor and on TikTok at @katcaldwell.author.

Follow her on BookBub @katcaldwell_author to see what she's reading.

Read Tristen's Story

When Talon ditches their band, Tristen is left with no choice but to go home, where he never wanted to return.
Can he find a way back to his dream of playing music?

www.ingramcontent.com/pod-product-compliance
Lightning Source LLC
Chambersburg PA
CBHW061113310726
48974CB00002B/510